Praise for Michelle Shocklee

"'That is our mission, dear. To *see* people for who they are beneath the pain. Beneath the sin. To see them as God sees them: a beautiful creation, with plans and purposes only he knows.' This is my favorite quote from *Count the Night by Stars*, a moving historical fiction that explores darkness as well as the beauty that can emerge from it when the right person takes on the purpose of seeing people for who they are beneath the pain."

T. I. LOWE, author of *Under the Magnolias*

"In her latest compelling novel, Michelle Shocklee brings to light the long history and hidden forces of human trafficking as well as our country's treatment of immigrants, the poor, and those we view as different from ourselves. *Count the Nights by Stars* is a timely reminder that caring for our neighbor is a privilege that requires our time, patience, and resources, as well as the courage to step outside our comfort zones, freeing our hearts to leap in faith."

CATHY GOHLKE, Christy Award–winning author of *Night Bird Calling*

"Shocklee's masterful descriptions thoroughly transport the reader to this unique time and place while bringing to light an issue both historically troubling and heartbreakingly current. *Count the Nights by Stars* is a beautifully written reminder of our need to see—and be seen—by both God and others."

JENNIFER L. WRIGHT, author of *If It Rains*

"Experience Tennessee's Centennial Exposition, presented by Michelle Shocklee as a sensuous feast in *Count the Nights by Stars*, then look deeper as two women, one in the late nineteenth century, the other in the 1960s, uncover the lavish celebration's dark, disturbing secret. The story's main setting, the Maxwell House Hotel, is a vivid character itself in its splendid heyday and decline, but it's the heroines who call it home, Audrey and Priscilla, who give this story its true shine, as each seeks to forge a life of purpose, integrity, and love, despite the obstacles she faces. With a mystery that unfolds with irresistible suspense, I predict late nights of page-turning for fans of Michelle Shocklee's books and new readers alike."

LORI BENTON, Christy Award–winning author of *Mountain Laurel* and *Shiloh*

"Shocklee beautifully unveils Frankie's past while developing Lorena's awareness of inequality. Though set years ago, this title resonates today, and many struggle with the same issues and questions of racial reconciliation. With its haunting message of forgiveness, this is a must-buy for any Christian or historical fiction collection."

LIBRARY JOURNAL on *Under the Tulip Tree*

"Shocklee elevates the redemptive power of remorse and the grace of forgiveness in this moving saga."

PUBLISHERS WEEKLY on *Under the Tulip Tree*

"*Under the Tulip Tree* . . . is an inspiring story of incredible courage in horrific circumstances, of faith, forgiveness, redemption, love, and friendship."

CHRISTIAN NOVEL REVIEW

"Get ready to fall in love with characters who step from the pages of history straight into your heart. With exceptional skill, Michelle Shocklee weaves a tale of betrayal and redemption that will long reside in the reader's memory. I cannot recommend [*Under the Tulip Tree*] highly enough!"

TAMERA ALEXANDER, *USA Today* bestselling author of *With This Pledge* and *A Note Yet Unsung*

"Michelle Shocklee's latest novel, *Under the Tulip Tree*, takes readers into the heartache of the broken Leland family during and after the Great Depression. The story of Rena Leland captured me from the first page, and I loved reading about her journey as one of the writers for Roosevelt's Federal Writers' Project. *Under the Tulip Tree* moves seamlessly between two time periods, beautifully capturing the relationship between Rena and a former slave woman whose powerful story begins to heal the entire Leland family."

MELANIE DOBSON, award-winning author of *The Curator's Daughter* and *The Winter Rose*

"As a fictional account of one of FDR's slave narratives, *Under the Tulip Tree* gives testimony to not only the social injustices of a country fueled by slavery, but the wounds that would last well beyond the field hospitals of war. In some ways, Rena and Frankie's conversation is one that

America should have with itself: one that faces the pain head-on and brings a true spirit of repentance. Then, and only then, will we see healing begin."

ALLISON PITTMAN, author of *The Seamstress*

"*Under the Tulip Tree* is a brilliant and authentic look at the power of story to break through the complicated entanglement of racial tension. Brave, authentic, and moving, Michelle Shocklee takes readers on an adventure of historical significance that is sure to leave them with hope. A grace-filled and beautiful reminder that every story—and every person—matters."

HEIDI CHIAVAROLI, Carol Award–winning author of *Freedom's Ring* and *The Tea Chest*

"*Under the Tulip Tree* left an indelible stamp on my heart. A story of pain, forgiveness, and restoration—Frankie and Rena's story will forever remain a testament to the power of love . . . and God's peace in the midst of heartache."

TARA JOHNSON, author of *All Through the Night* and *Where Dandelions Bloom*

Count the Nights by Stars

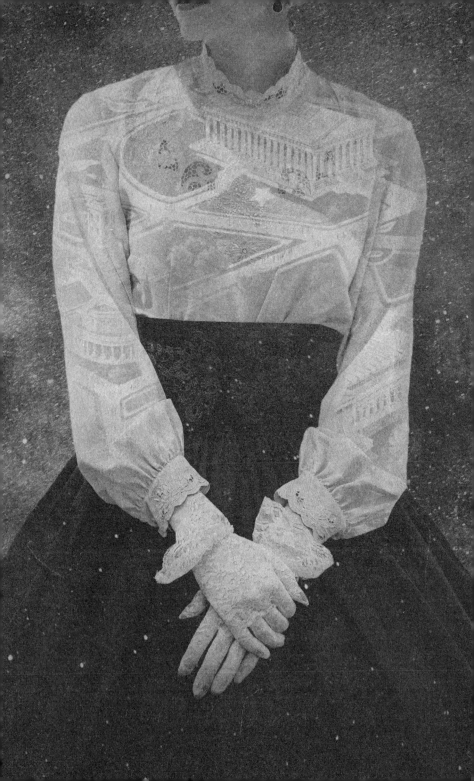

Count
the
Nights
by
Stars

A NOVEL

MICHELLE SHOCKLEE

Tyndale House Publishers
Carol Stream, Illinois

Visit Tyndale online at tyndale.com.

Visit Michelle Shocklee's website at michelleshocklee.com.

Tyndale and Tyndale's quill logo are registered trademarks of Tyndale House Ministries.

Count the Nights by Stars

Designed by Libby Dykstra

Edited by Erin E. Smith

Published in association with the literary agency of The Steve Laube Agency.

Unless otherwise indicated, all Scripture quotations are taken from the *Holy Bible*, King James Version.

Proverbs 31:8-9 in the epigraph and Genesis 16:13 in chapter 26 are taken from the *Holy Bible*, New Living Translation, copyright © 1996, 2004, 2015 by Tyndale House Foundation. Used by permission of Tyndale House Publishers, Carol Stream, Illinois 60188. All rights reserved.

Count the Nights by Stars is a work of fiction. Where real people, events, establishments, organizations, or locales appear, they are used fictitiously. All other elements of the novel are drawn from the author's imagination.

For information about special discounts for bulk purchases, please contact Tyndale House Publishers at csresponse@tyndale.com, or call 1-855-277-9400.

Library of Congress Cataloging-in-Publication Data

A catalog record for this book is available from the Library of Congress.

ISBN 978-1-4964-6109-4 (HC)
ISBN 978-1-4964-5993-0 (SC)

Printed in the United States of America

28	27	26	25	24	23	22
7	6	5	4	3	2	1

For my sister, Kim
Sisters by birth,
Sisters in Christ

Speak up for those who cannot speak for themselves;

ensure justice for those being crushed.

Yes, speak up for the poor and helpless,

and see that they get justice.

PROVERBS 31:8-9

Prologue

May 29, 1897

My darling,

No one could accuse Luca Moretti of being a coward.

I thought you brash and arrogant that day I saw you in the lobby of the Maxwell House Hotel. You stood taller than all the other men in their tailored suits, not caring that the elbows of your coat were worn or that one of the brass buttons was missing. Instead, you kept your shoulders back and your gaze steady, even when the men treated you as though they bettered you somehow. I'd never seen that kind of boldness before, and it intrigued me.

I know now you weren't brash or arrogant. You simply demanded to be seen as an equal in a world that said you weren't.

What if we all stood up for ourselves as you did?

What if I found even a hint of that kind of courage somewhere deep inside me?

They would have to listen, wouldn't they?

Peaches

Chapter One

NASHVILLE, TENNESSEE
DECEMBER 9, 1961

Elvis Presley's soulful voice echoed in the deserted lobby of the Maxwell House Hotel, bouncing off marble floors and wood paneling, both in need of a good cleaning.

"Are you lonesome tonight? Do you miss me tonight? Are you sorry we drifted apart?"

If the radio weren't so far away—at least six long steps—I'd tell Elvis to mind his own business and switch off the music. Silence was a better companion than the melancholy mood his words brought.

But I didn't rouse. I remained where I'd been the past hour, slumped behind the guest services desk at the far end of the cavernous entrance hall, bored out of my mind.

Such was the exciting life of the daughter of a hotel manager.

A puff of frustration passed over my lips.

Dad shouldn't expect me to work the front desk on a Saturday. Just last week he'd promised to hire someone to

1

replace Bea Anderson now that she was a giddy newlywed, beginning a grand and exciting life with her new husband in Texas. Bea's whisper of *"It'll be you next"* when she hugged me goodbye still rang false. She and I both knew I hadn't had a date in over a year. Not since Mama's unexpected passing and Dad's near breakdown.

An issue of *Life* magazine, discarded by a guest, lay on the desk. With little enthusiasm, I picked it up. A picture of actress Sophia Loren stared back at me. No disrespect to Ms. Loren, but I had no interest in reading about the "tiger-eyed temptress." Hollywood and all its glamour seemed a million miles away from Nashville and the dull existence I endured these days.

With a groan, I tossed the magazine aside and stared out a tall window at the far end of the lobby. The front entrance to the Noel Hotel across Fourth Avenue filled the view, and downtown Nashville hummed with midafternoon activity. Automobiles, buses, and streetcars zipped past. Saturday shoppers jammed the sidewalks, heading to various department stores and shops. Life carried on outside the brick walls of the hotel, but for me, time seemed to stand still.

I planted my chin on the palm of my hand and stared at nothing in particular, my mind going where it often went these days.

Mama.

It's strange how one person's life could be so completely interconnected to another's without them actually being aware of it. Mama and I hadn't been like most mothers and daughters I knew. Her world had revolved not around me but around my brother, Emmett. The two were inseparable, or at least that's how it always seemed to me, an outsider looking in at their giggles, secrets, and shared joys. I didn't think Mama intentionally left me out. There simply wasn't room for me in her all-consuming devotion to Emmett and his care. Even now, a year after her sudden death, Emmett talked to her as if she sat right next to him. Dad said Emmett's seventeen-year-old mind was actually that of a five-year-old child, and he couldn't process the full meaning and permanence of death. Maybe he never would, making me wonder if that was actually a better way to live rather than suffering under the heavy mantle of grief and guilt I carried every day.

I heaved a sigh and picked up the novel I'd laid down an hour ago. Maybe reading would get my mind off the sad state of my life. *To Kill a Mockingbird* was all the rage, but I'd had a difficult time becoming immersed in the story. I brought it with me today, determined to get past chapter five and see if Boo Radley really does come out of his house.

I'd just turned the first page of chapter six when the front door to the hotel opened, the afternoon sun causing such a terrific glare on the brass and glass, I couldn't make out the returning guest. Certain whomever it was would bypass me and head for the elevators, I continued reading. With the Maxwell House now a residential hotel rather than the center of Nashville's social and political life as it had once been, help from the front desk clerk was required only when a guest had a clogged commode or saw a mouse dart down the hallway.

Footsteps echoed in the foyer at the same time the telephone on the desk jangled. I reached for the receiver, the most exertion I'd expended since lunchtime.

"This is Audrey Whitfield. How may I help you?"

A female chuckled on the other end of the line. "Audrey, this is Lucille."

Lucille Clark, the hotel switchboard operator. "Sorry. I thought you were one of the guests."

"Get ready." Her voice lowered.

"For what?"

"He's making a beeline right for you," she whispered; then the line went dead.

I glanced to Lucille's small office, located not far from the hotel's main entrance. I couldn't see her, but I could now see to whom she referred. A young man, suitcase in hand, walked slowly across the vast expanse of black-and-white marble toward the desk, his gaze not on me but on the second-floor mezzanine above us. Even with the hotel long past her glory days, I had to admit it was still breathtaking upon one's first visit. Salons and an elegant main lobby, mahogany cabinetry, gilded mirrors, and sparkling chandeliers all harkened back to days when belles in stylish hoopskirts peered down upon men dressed in their finery, preparing for a ball or the hotel's famous Christmas Day dinner.

With the stranger still a few steps from the desk, Patsy Cline began to belt out her latest hit on the radio, her sultry voice echoing through the lobby. I lunged for the knob and flicked her off before she completely fell to pieces in front of our new guest.

The stranger arrived at the desk.

I understood Lucille's brief message.

He was a dreamboat. Smartly dressed in a bright-white Ivy style tennis sweater-vest, crisp long-sleeved shirt, and slacks, he looked like he'd just stepped off the pages of Spiegel's catalog.

"Hello. May I help you?" I forced myself to speak with the same voice I always used, whether the guest was old Mr. Hanover and his dachshund, Copper, or Mrs. Ruth, who'd lived on the fifth floor since her husband passed away ten years ago.

"Hello. I'm Jason Sumner. I have a reservation."

I blinked. Then frowned. A new reservation? Why hadn't Dad mentioned it?

4

"Of course, Mr. Sumner." I acted as though his smiling presence on the opposite side of the long, polished desk hadn't caught me completely off guard. "If you'll give me a moment, I'll get you checked in."

I hurried down the narrow hallway behind the front desk to the manager's office. Dad had left the hotel after lunch to see the county tax assessor and haggle over some discrepancy. He wouldn't be back for ages, so I had to shuffle through the scatter of papers until I located what I sought. An invoice filled out in Dad's scrawling hand, dated three days prior, with Mr. Sumner's name and a surprising reservation for the next fourteen days. Even with Christmas just a few weeks away, we didn't get too many new guests. People much preferred the Hermitage Hotel on Sixth if they wanted to experience luxury and a bit of Nashville history during their stay.

I snatched up the paper and stalked back toward the front desk.

As manager of the hotel, Dad had every right to accept new reservations, but it would be rather helpful if he made me aware of them. Had he informed the maid to freshen one of the guest rooms for Mr. Sumner's arrival? Doubtful.

So many things had changed in the last fourteen months, with Dad's business acumen and passion for his job being among them. It didn't help that the hotel had been sold in the midst of our time of mourning. The new owner, Mr. Edwin, seemed like a nice man and allowed Dad to take some time off, but a few weeks ago he told Dad he planned to make major changes in the New Year. To modernize and breathe new life back into the hotel, he'd said. What exactly that meant, we didn't know, but I could tell Dad was concerned.

How would the changes affect the many long-term residents? How would they affect our family?

I turned the corner and plastered a smile on my face. "I have your reservation here, Mr. Sumner."

A lopsided grin tipped his mouth. "Good. I thought there might be a problem. I've always wanted to stay at the Maxwell House."

"There's no problem. I just needed to locate the paper-work." I set about entering his name and address into the guest book, noting he lived in Charleston, South Carolina. I was rather curious about his extended stay in Nashville, especially so close to the holidays, but one of the first rules of hotel service Dad drilled into me as a teenager working the desk for the first time was *do not ask questions*. Let the guest share whatever they were inclined to share about their personal life and leave it at that.

With all the information recorded, I glanced up. "Would you like to pay by the day or weekly?"

"Weekly." He pulled out his wallet and laid down the neces-sary bills to cover seven days. "I'm here on business," he added.

I nodded, sorely tempted to break Dad's hard-and-fast rule and ask about his work, but the telephone buzzed again. I glanced toward Lucille's office, where she stood in the doorway and motioned for me to take the call.

"Please excuse me for a moment."

He nodded and focused his attention once again to the sec-ond floor above us, studying the intricately carved balusters that circled the wide opening and flowed down the marble staircase.

I made a grab for the telephone and turned my back. "This is Audrey," I said, my lips tight. "I'm with a guest."

"I know. I'm sorry to interrupt." The teasing tone Lucille had used earlier was gone. "Mrs. Ruth just called. Emmett is hysteri-cal. He says there's something wrong with Miss Priscilla."

A chill of alarm swept through me. Miss Priscilla Nichols, our resident recluse. I'd always been a little intimidated by the old spinster's oddness on the rare occasions I accompanied Dad to her suite. But Emmett, who never met a stranger, was one of the few people she willingly interacted with. I didn't know her exact age or health situation, but it didn't bode well if my brother was upset.

"Thank you. I'll take care of it."

I replaced the handset on its hook and met the curious gaze of our new guest. "My apologies. Let me get the key to your room."

I unlocked a cabinet on the wall behind me that held the room keys, each with an oval metal tag bearing the name of the hotel, a room number, and a *Postage paid* inscription. As in the days of the hotel's renown, if a guest mistakenly took the key home, they could simply deposit it in a mailbox and the post office would return it to the hotel. While we'd had our share of lost keys over the years, we'd had very few returned by mail.

Dad had reserved a room on the fifth floor for Mr. Sumner, but with all the commotion going on up there with Emmett and Miss Nichols, I thought it best to put him on the third floor instead.

He reached for the brass key. "Thank you, Miss . . . ?"

Heat flooded my face at the interest sparking in his blue eyes. "Whitfield. Audrey Whitfield."

"It's a pleasure to meet you." He extended his hand.

I'd shaken my share of hands before, but was it my imagination that mine seemed to fit inside his rather perfectly?

"My father is the hotel manager," I blurted, more as an explanation of why I worked in an old hotel that had lost its charm than information he required for his stay.

He smiled good-naturedly. "Good to know."

Just as he bent to retrieve his suitcase, the elevator doors opened a short distance away. Emmett burst out, followed by elderly Ruth Simmons attempting to keep up.

"Audrey, Audrey." Emmett's wail echoed off the recessed ceiling of the second-floor mezzanine as he raced toward me. "Miss Priscilla won't wake up. Hurry, hurry, Audrey."

I shot a quick glance to Mr. Sumner, hoping he'd be the one to hurry and vacate the lobby before Emmett's hysteria was on full display. But the young man didn't move. His face bore a look of concern as he watched Emmett draw near.

I had no choice but to address my brother when he arrived on the opposite side of the desk. His fleshy face was mottled, with evidence of tears clinging to thick lashes, and my heart softened.

"It's okay, Emmett." I tried to soothe him the way Mama had always been able to do. "I'll check on Miss Nichols. I'm sure everything is fine. You go on to the apartment and wait for me there."

I stole a look at Mrs. Ruth, expecting her to wink or give some indication that all was well, but she shook her head and appeared as distressed as my brother.

Lucille joined the group, her headset still in place with a loose cord dangling down her back. "I'll watch the desk."

"Come with me, Emmett, dear." Mrs. Ruth gently took my brother by the arm. "You can show me the new comic book your father brought home yesterday."

Normally thrilled to show anyone the latest addition to his growing collection, Emmett shook his head. His woeful eyes sought mine.

"Mama wouldn't wake up either, Audrey," he whispered, his voice panicked. Tears sprang to his eyes, and I realized in that moment that Dad was wrong. Emmett understood more about death than we thought.

"You go with Mrs. Ruth to the apartment. I'll be there soon."

A wobbly smile touched his eyes. "I love you, Audrey."

"I love you, too."

I watched the odd twosome make their way down the hall toward the back of the hotel and our apartment. How I wished Dad were here. He'd know what to do. But I didn't expect him back for several hours. Too long to wait.

I turned to find Lucille's and Mr. Sumner's serious gazes on me.

"Do you think . . . ?" Lucille's eyes widened as her question trailed.

A shiver raced through me at the very thought. "I don't know. I guess I'll go find out."

I traded places with Lucille and headed for the elevator. Footsteps sounded behind me as I pushed the call button. The doors slid open.

"Miss Whitfield, I wonder if your father is available?"

I turned to find Mr. Sumner a few steps away, the look of concern on his face having deepened into a genuine frown.

"I don't believe a young woman should . . . well . . . you know. Be alone, in case . . ." He didn't finish his sentence either.

The elevator doors started to close, so I leaped inside the car. Surprisingly, Mr. Sumner did too. Although dread filled every inch of my being at the prospect of finding the worst scenario in Miss Nichols's room, I didn't like his insinuation that I couldn't see to the matter on my own because I was a woman.

"I appreciate your concern, Mr. Sumner, but I'm fully capable of handling this situation." My bravado rang false in my ears, but hopefully it fooled him.

His brief nod indicated he wasn't convinced, but he remained silent while the elevator chime rang at each floor as we inched ever higher.

9

Finally the car stopped and the doors opened into the gloom of the fifth-floor hallway. Although the hotel boasted well over two hundred windows, the hallways did not benefit from the natural light.

Miss Nichols had occupied room 504 for more than twenty years. As far as I knew, she'd never had even one visitor and kept entirely to herself. Mrs. Ruth once told me that Miss Nichols—Priscilla, as she'd called her—wasn't odd. The woman simply desired privacy.

When we reached the door bearing the correct brass numbers, it stood slightly ajar. As annoyed as I'd been to find Mr. Sumner in the elevator with me moments ago, I suddenly felt grateful for the presence of a living, breathing person next to me, stranger and all.

I inched the door open.

The light scent of rose perfume greeted us, a reminder that Miss Nichols always wore the old-fashioned fragrance. Peering into the darkened room, I noted the thick drapes on the windows were closed against bright afternoon sunshine. Muted light from a single lamp on the bedside table, however, revealed what I'd feared we would find.

Miss Nichols lay in her eternal rest, just as Emmett said.

Mr. Sumner moved forward, but my feet stayed rooted to the carpet in the hallway. Was this how Dad felt when he'd found that Mama had slipped into heaven while she slept? I'd been away at school, but I would never forget the pain in his voice when he called to give me the most heartbreaking news of my life.

Mr. Sumner checked for a pulse, then leaned down to listen for a beat. Just when I expected him to say what I already knew to be true, he spun to face me.

"She's still breathing, but barely. We need to call an ambulance."

Air whooshed from my lungs. I'd thought for sure . . .

I hurried forward, grabbed the telephone handset, and dialed 0.

"Lucille, we need an ambulance. Hurry! And please try to track down Dad. He went to the tax office to meet with a Mr. James."

Ending the call, I peeked at Miss Nichols's pale face. With her translucent eyelids closed and bluish lips unmoving, I could detect no sign of life. But if Mr. Sumner said she was alive, I'd take his word for it.

He checked her pulse again, nodded, then looked at me. "We should notify her family."

"I don't think she has any," I whispered.

Concern filled his expression. "None?" When I shook my head, he frowned. "That's really sad."

The compassion in his voice touched something inside me, and tears filled my eyes.

I didn't know Miss Nichols well. She spent her days, weeks, years alone in her room. On the rare occasions when she left the hotel, Lucille and I giggled over jokes about her outdated clothes, long gray hair, and funny appearance. Jokes that felt shameful now.

While we waited for the ambulance, I glanced around the room. Miss Nichols had lived in this tiny space almost as long as I'd been alive. Every so often, Dad offered her one of the larger suites at the same monthly rate, but she declined every time.

Now I felt like I'd traveled back in time. Old-fashioned furnishings filled every available space. Bookshelves spilled over with dozens and dozens of worn volumes, and the walls were covered with framed posters of the Tennessee Centennial

Exposition. I recalled studying about the expo in my high school history class, but I couldn't remember the exact year it took place. Sometime in the late 1890s, if I had to guess.

Sirens soon echoed in the street below. I looked out the window to see two police cars and an ambulance pull up to the curb in front of the Fourth Street entrance to the hotel. Dad was right behind them and ran inside.

When I heard the elevator chime in the hallway a few minutes later, I hurried to meet him.

"I'm sorry, honey." He took me in his arms. "I should have been here."

Just being in his fatherly embrace bolstered my strength. I sniffled and stepped out of his arms. "It just reminded me of Mama. I'm okay now."

We moved aside as two white-clad ambulance attendants rushed down the hallway, pushing a gurney on wheels, with police officers trailing behind. They disappeared into Miss Nichols's room, and I heard Jason Sumner's voice, explaining what we'd found.

"Where's Emmett? Lucille said he found Priscilla unconscious."

"Mrs. Ruth took him to the apartment."

Dad glanced into the room. "I need to stay here. Would you please see to your brother? I imagine he's very confused."

After giving Dad one more hug, I made my way to the apartment. Mrs. Ruth sat on the couch with Emmett reading his new comic book aloud when I walked in. He jumped to his feet and hurried over.

"Is Miss Priscilla awake?"

His eager innocence hit my heart. I hated to tell him the truth, but lying, even to protect him, wasn't something Mama would ever tolerate.

"No." I reached for his hand. "But we hope she will be soon. She needs to go to the hospital so the doctors can help her."

His shoulders fell and his eyes filled. "I'll miss her."

Although he outweighed me by many pounds, I took him in my arms, this brother of mine, suddenly wishing I could keep the world and all its pain and sadness at bay. Was this how Mama felt, raising a young man who would always be a little boy?

"I know you will, but everything is going to be okay."

Those words of assurance had often been on Mama's lips, no matter what was going on. She firmly believed God was in control despite how things might look or how we might feel. Her faith carried her through many hard times, right up until the moment she left this earth for her heavenly home.

Today, my brother needed me to be the strong one. The one who believed it would all be okay.

But somewhere deep inside, I knew I didn't.

I didn't believe that at all.

Chapter Two

"Good gracious, Priscilla. Look at the crowd. It's enormous."

I barely heard Mother's exclamation over the train's hissing brakes as we slowed to a quaking stop after long hours of travel from Chattanooga. The din outside our car as we pulled into the congested station was terrific, and the conductor, determined to be heard despite the commotion, practically yelled to alert us to the obvious: we'd arrived at our destination, Nashville, Tennessee.

Mother's words, however, didn't begin to describe the vast numbers of people filling every crevice of the platform and terminal building. Hundreds of passengers spilled forth from train cars on multiple lines of track, all here for the same reason—to attend the Tennessee Centennial Exposition, set to open in two days in celebration of the state's one hundredth birthday.

I shaded my eyes from late-afternoon sunshine and couldn't help but gape at the scene out the window. I'd never seen so many people in one place. How would we ever find Papa in the pulsating crowd? He'd traveled with the president of the railroad and other executives earlier in the week, making sure their exhibit on the expo grounds was ready for the millions of visitors expected to pour through the gates over the next six months.

The handful of passengers in our private car—wives, children, and friends of railroad executives—began to gather their belongings and disembark, their excited voices added to those outside.

"Priscilla, take care with your handbag. I thought carrying our jewels with us was the wiser decision, but now I'm not so certain." Mother yelped when a young man rapped on the window and shouted something unintelligible, laughing when she shooed him away. "Look at them. Surely your father could have arranged for us to arrive in an area that wasn't so *public*."

I chuckled. Mother's snobbishness showed like a torn petticoat. "Just because Papa is an investor in the Nashville, Chattanooga, and St. Louis doesn't mean we should receive special treatment. We're no more important than any of those people out there." I indicated the throng of humanity on the other side of the ash-coated glass. "They're here to celebrate the state's birthday, same as we are."

Mother gave me one of her long-suffering sighs. The kind I'd heard all my twenty-five years as the only daughter of Cora and Eldridge Nichols. The kind that told me I'd disappointed her yet again.

"You know as well as I that your father and grandfather have been instrumental in building this railroad. You need to take more pride in your heritage. Your father is still wounded by the fact you didn't want to accompany us to Nashville. Why, you would have missed seeing the result of all his hard efforts in making the Railway Exhibit one of the finest in the park."

I knew it was best to remain silent when Mother was in the mood for a lecture. While I truly was sorry to have hurt my father's feelings, I'd had no desire to travel to Nashville for what I could only predict would be a spectacle of gigantic proportions, if all the hoopla about the exposition could be believed.

A giant seesaw? A replica of the Parthenon? Two hundred acres of amusements and attractions?

Mercy sakes.

Anticipation for the state's birthday celebration—which was in actuality one year too late for the true anniversary of Tennessee's statehood—had reached a fever pitch in the final months leading up to the May 1 opening. It was all anyone, especially my family, could talk about. I couldn't count the number of times Papa and his business partners rode up and down the tracks, crisscrossing Tennessee in a special railroad car decorated with banners and painted with giant letters that read *Exposition*. The car attracted so much attention along its scheduled route, people came from miles around to gawk and cheer as Papa and the others waved and gave speeches touting the exposition's exhibits and attractions.

Yet I had no desire to participate in the glorified affair. Tennessee might be celebrating one hundred years of statehood, but its female residents were still denied the right to vote in the election of officials who would govern said state. Women's suffrage continued as a struggle of great importance across the nation. The deprivation of the rights of nearly half of Tennessee's citizens wasn't something to celebrate, in my estimation.

"There's your father now."

Mother's voice drew me from my thoughts. It would do no good to repeat the argument I'd tried in vain to win the past weeks. My presence on this train spoke loud and clear to whom the victory had gone.

Papa wove his way through the crowd and entered our car. The other women had already disembarked with their children, leaving us the last passengers aboard.

"I'm sorry I'm late." He took a handkerchief from the breast pocket of his jacket and mopped his brow. "You will not believe it, but nearly sixty trains are expected to arrive by the end of the day. The crowd is larger today than it has been all week."

Mother harrumphed and adjusted her hat. "Exactly why we should have come ahead with you. You know how I detest being jostled."

While Papa smoothed Mother's ruffled feathers, I gathered my things, ready to disembark and stretch my legs. Despite my ongoing grumblings about the expo and making the journey to Nashville, now that we'd arrived, a hint of anticipation pecked at me, almost daring me to enjoy myself these next four weeks we were scheduled to remain in the city.

"You'll be pleased to know Kenton accompanied me."

Papa flashed a satisfied smile my way. "He's securing a place for the carriage near the front of the station."

With both my parents looking on, I forced a smile. "How nice of him."

I trailed them down the train car's steep steps to the station platform, the bud of excitement from moments ago in danger of shriveling. It was my turn to emit a frustrated sigh.

Kenton Thornley, the man my father hoped would soon be his son-in-law, might be the one person in the crowd I'd rather not see.

While I waited for Mother to straighten her skirts, I peered over the mass of travelers, looking for the familiar blond-haired man I'd known since childhood. Kenton's family and mine had long been friends, with our fathers both involved in the railroad industry. Granted, the Thornleys' pedigree was far more impressive than ours, but both sets of parents thought it a famous idea to turn the friendship and business collaboration into familial ties with the union of their offspring. Kenton was a willing participant despite not even an ounce of attraction between us, but I had yet to give an answer to his proposal. A modern woman didn't need a husband in order to make a difference in the world, did she? And certainly not a husband who held no affection for her in his heart. But if I turned him down, would another opportunity for marriage and family come? Spinsterhood wasn't something I sought, as some women in the suffrage movement did.

Upon leaving the safety of the railroad car, we felt the immediate crush of humanity. Papa kept a firm grasp on our hands and tugged us forward amid shouts, whistles, and laughter. Coal smoke and hot steam from the locomotives saturated the air, making it impossible to fill one's lungs completely. We were out of breath when Papa rounded the terminal and located Kenton and the carriage.

"Ah, here you are." Kenton greeted Mother with a light kiss on the cheek.

"Kenton, you can't know how welcome it is to see your handsome face, is it not, Priscilla? The racket from the crowd is dreadful. Do take us to the hotel, posthaste."

Mother didn't wait to be helped into the open carriage, a sure sign of her flustered composure. Kenton hurried after her while Papa spoke to the porters loading our trunks and cases onto the back of the vehicle. I thought to retrieve my smaller bag from the trolley so it wouldn't be crushed beneath the heavier items and moved in that direction.

"May I assist you, *signorina*?"

I turned to find a tall man behind me. Had his accent not revealed his Italian heritage, his dark eyes and the midnight-colored hair poking from his cap most assuredly would have.

"No need." Kenton arrived before I could answer and took possession of my elbow without my permission. "You keep to the horses, Moretti. A gentleman will see to the ladies."

Mortified by Kenton's rudeness, I removed my arm from his grip. "A gentleman would have better manners." The stranger—our driver, apparently—fought a grin rather than shame at being put down so harshly. "I appreciate your offer, sir, but Mr. Thornley will assist me."

The man inclined his head, but when his gaze met mine again, a flash of something—admiration, perhaps?—sent an unexpected tremor through me.

"Priscilla, you'll be glad you changed your mind and made the trip west," Papa said once I settled in across from him and Mother, his face flushed and beaming with excitement. "The expo grounds more than exceed our expectations. Isn't that right, Kenton?"

Kenton, who sat next to me, and Papa regaled us with the wonderful preparations for Tennessee's birthday celebration as we slowly made our way through congested streets. My ears, however, caught the occasional voice of our driver as he spoke to the horse in Italian. For some odd reason, it made me smile, knowing the big animal understood the foreign words.

"See there, Priscilla." Papa claimed my attention when he patted my knee. "That smile on your face is exactly why I insisted you come with us. I daresay you young people will have a marvelous time exploring the park in the coming weeks."

Mother laughed, evidently over the agitation brought on by the crowd at the station. "And what of us, Eldridge? Are we not to have a marvelous time simply because we're past our youth?"

Papa grasped her hand and kissed her gloved knuckles. "You're as beautiful as the day I married you thirty-two years ago, my dear. Nevertheless, our sightseeing will be done at a much slower pace, I imagine."

They continued their lively conversation until the carriage came to a stop in what appeared to be the heart of Nashville. Buggies, horsemen, and pedestrians crammed the streets and sidewalks, reminiscent of the crush at the train depot. I hoped Mother wouldn't issue another complaint, for there was little Papa could do to alleviate the problem.

I craned my neck and gaped at it all. Admittedly, I'd been curious to see the famed Maxwell House Hotel for myself. Papa'd bragged on it for years, claiming it the finest hotel he'd ever stayed in during his travels, including those in New York City and Boston. Known for its elegant men's and women's salons, the Maxwell House was always Papa's first choice for accommodations when visiting Nashville.

The first things I noticed were the massive columns, welcoming guests at the Cherry Street entrance. Eight of them, reaching to the second story, held up a narrow, Southern-style portico. Five floors of arched windows ran from end to end of the great hotel, all with a view of the city below. If a person hadn't heard tell of the vast and elegant rooms within the enormous building, they would need only view it from the street to guess at what lay inside this behemoth.

"If you ladies prefer, the driver can take us around the corner to the entrance on Church Street that leads directly to the women's salons. You may find it more to your sensibilities than the men's quarter entrance."

Papa moved to claim the driver's attention, but Mother stilled his hand. "There's no need for that, Eldridge. Priscilla and I aren't so delicate that we can't use this entrance. We're here and ready to be in our rooms. Besides, look there. I see several women of means accompanying their escorts into the hotel."

The driver opened the carriage door a moment later. With a quick glance at Papa, who gave an affirmative nod, he held out his hand to Mother. *"Signora."*

Mother gathered her skirts, climbed out, and remarked

on the grandeur of the hotel to no one in particular. Kenton exited next since it would have been awkward for me to climb over him. I let Papa go ahead of me, leaving me last to grasp the driver's hand as he assisted me to the sidewalk.

"Thank you." I smoothed my skirts, more for something to do than for care of the wrinkles embedded in the fabric from the long day of travel.

"*Signorina.*" His lips turned up at the corners. "It is an honor to assist such a beautiful woman."

The practiced compliment might bring a flush to other women's cheeks, but flattering words were lost on me. As the only daughter of Eldridge Nichols, I'd heard my fair share of pretty, meaningless words from would-be suitors since before I'd come of age.

"Sir, my outward appearance should have no bearing on whether you feel honored to assist me or not. It is your job, plain and simple."

I expected a hint of contrition at my rebuke. Instead, a dimple appeared on each side of his face as his grin deepened.

"You are correct, *signorina*. However, my dear *mamma*—God rest her soul—taught me that a man should take every opportunity to tell a woman of her beauty. Every woman, she said, is a unique creation of our Maker and should be reminded of this."

Before I could respond, he bowed, then retreated behind the carriage.

"Priscilla, why are you dallying? Come."

Mother's call from the hotel entrance forced me to move forward, yet I couldn't help but turn and take one last look behind me. The driver helped the hotel porter unload our luggage but paused when he saw me watching, doffed his hat, then resumed his work.

As I followed my parents into the famous hotel, I had an odd feeling I'd missed something in my brief exchange with the man.

Something of significance.

Chapter Three

I stood in front of the closed door to room 504 for a solid minute before I gathered the courage to turn the knob.

Three days had passed since Miss Nichols suffered a stroke. Dad had gone to the hospital each day, but the news wasn't good. She couldn't speak, and her right arm and leg appeared paralyzed. The doctor on duty told Dad it was highly unlikely Miss Nichols would ever return to the hotel. She would need full-time care from now on.

After the ambulance took her to the hospital, Dad had alerted her attorney, a snooty Mr. Richards, and he'd arrived the next day to survey the belongings in her room. Her will, he'd said as he viewed the old-fashioned items with obvious disdain, made no mention of how to dispose of the hodgepodge of personal belongings. With her dire prognosis, he planned to hire someone to simply dispose of it all. When Dad protested, asserting there might be sentimental items Miss Nichols would want saved or given to friends once she settled in a nursing home, the man shrugged, told Dad it was now his problem, and left.

The familiar rose scent greeted me when I pushed open the door. It felt strange being in her room alone. I'd never been here without the elderly woman seated at her small desk or in the worn floral armchair by the window. Dad gave me the task of sorting through personal belongings; then he'd help decide what to do with the larger furnishings. We'd performed this same heartbreaking duty less than a year ago, going through Mama's things, and I think repeating it so soon was more than Dad could manage. I would've preferred to pass it on as well, but there wasn't anyone else.

First thing, I pulled back the thick drapes and pushed open a window despite a bit of chill in the December air. Downtown Nashville hummed with activity below me, with noisy city buses, honking cars, and bundled shoppers rushing about in search of the perfect gifts for their loved ones. Christmas decorations in the windows of the Noel Hotel across the street reminded me I had yet to decorate the lobby of the Maxwell.

Sunshine peeked over the tall building and warmed my face, a promise of familiarity and routine within the bright rays. "Morning always comes," Mama used to say, especially after a difficult night with Emmett. She'd give a weary smile and remind us a new day was full of blessings waiting to be discovered.

I inhaled a deep breath of cool air, then turned to face the challenge in front of me.

Was there a blessing lurking in this jumble of outdated belongings?

A glance around the crowded room told me I'd seriously underestimated the number of cardboard boxes I'd need. With the freedom to move about rather than waiting stiffly by the door as I'd done on those rare occasions when I accompanied Dad to check on Miss Nichols, I saw things I'd never noticed before. Curio cabinets filled with collectibles. An armoire stuffed to capacity with clothing, hats, and shoes. A dresser and vanity crammed with everything from socks and scarves to jewelry and money. Books and more books jammed shelves and sat in piles on the floor. There were even boxes of who knows what shoved under the bed, collecting dust.

I blew out a breath.

It was going to take all day, maybe all week, to sort and pack everything.

Dad always praised my organizational skills, so I sat down on the chair by the window and came up with a plan. I'd start with valuables and breakables, then move on to books and miscellaneous items. Clothing and personal belongings would be last.

With the small radio in the corner tuned to WMAK, a station that broadcast from right here in the Maxwell, I got to work.

I'd completely lost track of time when a knock sounded on the open door. Even with the occasional nosy resident stopping by to inquire about my task, I hadn't felt comfortable being here with the door closed.

Expecting to see old Mr. Hanover or Mrs. Ruth, I was surprised to find Jason Sumner in the doorway. His stiff white button-down shirt and dark tie told me he'd just come from one of his business appointments or was on his way to one. In all the commotion with Miss Nichols, I still hadn't discovered why this handsome young man was in town, staying at the Maxwell. I'd only seen him a few times since the morning he arrived and then only in passing.

"Hi." A sheepish smile played on his lips. "Lucille said you were up here."

I remained where I sat cross-legged on the floor, surrounded by boxes and stacks of old newspapers Dad brought up to use for packing. I was sure I looked ridiculous, with a scarf tied around my hair and one of Emmett's old T-shirts hanging off my shoulder.

"Hi."

A few silent moments ticked off the clock on the bedside table before he stepped into the room. He glanced around; then his gaze came back to me.

"Your dad said Miss Nichols lived here for more than twenty years." His voice held wonder but no judgment.

I nodded. "It's kind of sad. As far as we know, she doesn't have any family. I'm not sure what we'll do with all of this."

He gave me a thoughtful look. "There are charities that accept donations of clothing and furniture. I'd be happy to get the names of several for you and your dad to look over."

"That's a good idea. Thanks for the offer." Curiosity wouldn't let the conversation end. Why would he know about charities in Nashville? "What is it that you do exactly?"

He shoved his hands into his slacks pockets. "I'm in my last year of law school. I hope to work on civil rights cases once I pass the bar exam."

His answer wasn't at all what I'd expected. "Really? Wow."

He chuckled. "Yeah. My dad's a lawyer, but he's always worked for big corporations. I'm more interested in helping people who might not get a fair shake."

"Why are you in Nashville?" I asked, Miss Nichols's collection of unusual salt- and pepper shakers completely forgotten, along with Dad's rule about probing the lives of our guests.

"I wanted to talk to some of the people involved in the lunch counter sit-ins that took place last year. I've already spoken to the students in Greensboro who started the whole thing. Did you know more than three thousand demonstrators were arrested before lunch counters were finally desegregated? A lot of those people weren't treated fairly in court." He gave a slight shrug. "I'd like to do something about that in the future, if I can."

I found myself speechless.

I thought back to the early part of last year. On the day before Valentine's Day, groups of African American students walked into Woolworth's, Kress, and McClellan's, made purchases, and then proceeded to take seats at the all-white lunch counters. When they were refused service and told to leave, the students respectfully held their ground. The stores closed the counters after two hours and the students left, but that was only the beginning. People, both black and white, demonstrated at lunch counters around the city, demanding they be desegregated—a decision that wouldn't come until May 10.

"That's really . . . admirable."

He gave me a curious look. "Were you here when the sit-ins took place?"

"I was at school in Chattanooga." With a hint of shame, I shrugged. "Some of my friends participated in the sit-ins there, but . . ."

I let my confession trail.

I'd been afraid to join them, pure and simple. Although the sit-in participants were nonviolent and followed rules like "be on best behavior" and "no profanity or loud talking," people who opposed desegregation caused trouble that eventually involved violence and the police.

"That's okay. Not everyone is called to be a frontline soldier."

I met his gaze. "A soldier? You make it sound as though it's a war."

He nodded. "In a way, it is. People fighting for rights that should have been theirs all along. Many of the Freedom Riders from May were beaten and the buses set on fire while authorities looked the other way. All because the riders want the freedom to travel on desegregated buses. Black Americans have been fighting for their rights since the days of slavery. Linking arms with them, as Dr. Martin Luther King calls it, is the right thing to do."

I hadn't thought of it like that.

"Well, I better let you get back to work." He turned toward the open door but faced me before exiting. "I'm free tomorrow, if you need any help."

A warm flutter in my tummy made me fidget under his intense gaze. "Sure. That'd be great."

He flashed a satisfied smile before he disappeared into the hallway.

I went back to my work, but our brief conversation wasn't far from my thoughts. Jason Sumner was certainly an interesting young man.

After a lunch of ham sandwiches and potato salad with Emmett and Dad, I finished packing the many knickknacks, tea-cups, and anything I thought might hold value, then turned to the shelf of books. Miss Nichols, it seemed, was quite well-read. Classics like Shakespeare, Alcott, Dickens, and Stowe occupied space on the crowded shelves. There were books of poetry, history, and curiously, several novels in Italian. I put them in a box, taking care not to let it get too heavy. Neither Dad nor I needed a sore back.

When the room began to grow gloomy, with December's late-autumn sunshine fading fast, I decided to pack one last box and call it a day. Mrs. Ruth had volunteered to stay with Emmett after lunch while Dad conducted interviews for a new assistant manager, but I needed to start dinner soon.

I reached for the next item on the shelf—a large square album of sorts, its blue leather cover beautifully embellished but worn and tattered around the edges. I was about to toss it into the box when something fell out. When I reached for it, I discovered an old, yellowed postcard. A picture of Nashville's famous Parthenon graced the front, but what caught my attention were the other buildings pictured near it, including one shaped like an Egyptian pyramid.

I'd been to the Parthenon dozens of times. Those buildings did not exist.

I flipped the card over.

Neat handwriting filled the back side, but I also found tiny printed type that informed me the picture was taken during the Tennessee Centennial Exposition of 1897.

I glanced up to the framed posters covering the walls. I hadn't paid them much attention throughout the day, but now I scanned them and found one that looked very much like the postcard.

Curious, I read the handwritten note.

My darling Luca,

I walked to the Parthenon today. It was nearly dusk, and I wanted to see the lights as you and I did on the night we were there together. People stared at me as I wept silent tears, but I didn't care. The reflection on Lake Watauga looked just as it did when we held hands and strolled along its shore.

Oh, how I wish we'd made a different choice that fateful day.

Do you regret it as much as I?

Peaches

The haunting words held me captive.

Who was Peaches? What choice had she and her unknown lover made?

Without thought to the privacy of the mysterious Peaches—or Miss Nichols, for that matter—I opened the album.

My mouth dropped open.

Bright, colorful memorabilia from bygone days filled page after page. Postcards and pictures from the exposition. Ribbons, dried flowers, buttons, pencil sketches, ticket stubs, and on and on. Each page a lovely, unique piece of artwork.

Had Miss Nichols crafted the beautiful book?

I searched for her name or something to indicate she'd created it, but nothing attributed ownership to the old woman who now lay in a hospital several miles away.

As I carefully turned fragile pages in the waning light, I recalled my mother's scrapbook from her college days. While it held sentimental value, it was nothing like this elaborate, finely crafted memory book.

The elevator chime from down the hall alerted me some minutes later to a returning guest. Exhaustion suddenly washed over me. Time to call it a day.

As I stood and stretched, Mrs. Ruth poked her gray-haired head in the open doorway. "My, you've been hard at work."

"Yes, ma'am." I glanced around. I still had a long way to go to be finished packing up the apartment, but my many hours of work showed. "I'll be back tomorrow. Thank you for staying with Emmett."

When I looked at her, I found her gaze not on the mess of the room, but on the album in my hands.

"What have you got there, dear?"

I held up the leather-bound album. "It's a scrapbook." With a bit of embarrassment, I confessed, "I peeked inside. It's mostly about the Tennessee Centennial Exposition."

Mrs. Ruth nodded. "Priscilla does have a fondness for those long-ago days." Her eyes were drawn to the dozen posters on the wall. "I was a little girl when the expo took place and don't remember the excitement, but from what I gather, Priscilla spent quite a bit of time at the fair as a young woman." She walked over to the bedside table and ran her fingers across the tattered cover of an old Bible I'd neglected to pack, a sadness in her eyes. "It's such a shame to see her things boxed up. I hope your father won't discard them like that attorney suggested."

"I'm sure he won't. At least not until he can speak with Miss Nichols and hopefully find out what she'd like done with it all."

Mrs. Ruth bid me good night and continued to her room down the hall. She'd moved into the hotel years ago after her husband passed away. The weekly rate was cheaper than a small apartment, which was why most of the sixty residents chose to live in a worn-out hotel that had seen better times. But unlike Miss Nichols, Mrs. Ruth had two daughters and grandchildren to look in on her. Still, it must be difficult to watch the life of a friend and neighbor be dismantled with such finality.

I started to put the scrapbook in the box with the other books, but something about the dog-eared cover that hid such exquisite beauty intrigued me.

I bit my inner lip in indecision.

Surely it wouldn't hurt to take the memory book back to our apartment, just for safekeeping. It would be a shame for it to end up in a box for charity or the trash, especially if Miss Nichols was indeed its creator. Maybe the postcards would offer clues about who Peaches and Luca were, which would be especially helpful if they turned out to be Miss Nichols's relatives.

With the album in hand, I stepped into the hallway and closed the door behind me.

Chapter Four

Boisterous male laughter greeted me when I descended the Maxwell's grand marble staircase near the men's salon Friday morning.

Mother remained in our suite of rooms, incapacitated with one of her headaches, no doubt brought on by the full day of travel and excitement from yesterday. Papa had left the hotel to meet with his associates and go over last-minute details regarding their exhibit on the expo grounds as well as their participation in the ambitious opening ceremonies tomorrow morning.

All of which meant I'd been left to my own affairs for the better part of the day.

I smiled and recalled the sweet girl who'd come to my room not long after I'd risen, a breakfast tray in hand and a timid smile on her face. She introduced herself as Gia, my lady's maid for the duration of our stay at the Maxwell. Her accent reminded me of our carriage driver from the previous night, but her demeanor was shy yet eager to please. With her dark hair and eyes, she was an exotic beauty, and I knew many females in my circle would find her threatening no matter her position as maid. We got along famously though. Despite her youth, I was quite pleased with the intricate way she styled my hair. Dressed and ready for a day of exploring, I waved goodbye to Gia and left her and another maid to see to Mother.

At the main floor, I once again stood in awe of the Maxwell's opulence, on full display for the hundreds of guests that occupied every inch of the hotel. A magnificent chandelier, adorned with thousands of crystals that shimmered in the gas lighting, hung overhead like a glorious crown. Beneath, a sea of black-and-white marble, artfully laid out in a diamond pattern, flowed as far as I could see. Rich wood paneling, identical in color and texture to the intricately carved banisters and balusters that circled the mezzanine above, lined the walls, desks, and cabinetry, giving the place warmth despite its vast size and grand columns. Cozy vignettes of settees and chairs upholstered in deep maroon were sprinkled throughout the airy space, offering guests a pleasing place to rest and take in the grandeur.

For a time, I stood and observed men, women, and children as they scurried about. Excitement saturated the air, and I couldn't help but feel it seep into me too. I was in Nashville, staying at the world-famous Maxwell House Hotel, on the eve of Tennessee's centennial celebration. How could I not feel beguiled?

Glancing about, I wondered where to go first. A number of businesses were housed inside the hotel, although those near the men's entrance catered to male patrons, with barbers, tailors, and such. I would need to make my way to the opposite side of the hotel to find shops offering items more to my feminine tastes.

I'd turned in that direction when I heard my name called.

Kenton Thornley and two of his friends waved at me from a doorway where piano music and cigar smoke spilled into the common area.

Fiddlesticks.

I should've pretended I hadn't heard the call. I was looking forward to a bit of freedom the next several hours.

I wound my way through the crowded space to where the three men stood.

"Good morning, Priscilla," Kenton said, smiling. "Don't you look lovely."

"Good morning, gentlemen." I nodded in the direction of the women's entrance on the other side of the hotel lobby. "I'm just on my way to do some shopping."

Eastman Davies, heir to a fortune thanks to his father's railroad investments, snorted. "What a jolly surprise. A woman going shopping."

I let my gaze casually drift over their immaculate jackets, trousers, and ties, all made from the finest materials. "I suppose your clothing simply appears in your wardrobe." I offered a tight smile. "How fortuitous that they're perfectly tailored to fit you."

Kenton and the other man hid snickers behind their hands, but Eastman conceded with a bow. "Touché, Miss Nichols."

"Join us for lunch, Priscilla." Kenton moved next to me

and put his arm around my shoulders. "We need someone to keep us honest."

I shook my head. "I have plans."

"Come now. Don't be coy. We promise to behave, don't we, fellows?"

While the other men chimed in their agreement, I heard someone clear his throat behind us in an obvious attempt to gain our attention.

"Miss Nichols?"

I turned to find the carriage driver from the previous night a few steps away. He gave a polite nod to me; then his dark eyes traveled the circle of men with a boldness few hired men dared.

"I have your carriage ready, *signorina*."

His announcement caught me by surprise. I hadn't ordered a carriage. When I started to alert him to the mistake, he offered a slight grin that could only be described as conspiring.

"Your father has hired me for the duration of your family's stay in the city." He motioned toward the entrance across the sea of marble. "I understand you wish to do some shopping. My services are at your disposal."

How had he known of my plans for the day?

Before I could sort through the odd conversation, Kenton positioned himself between me and the driver.

"The lady has changed her mind, Moretti. You can leave." He turned his back in rude dismissal.

I gave Kenton a look that surely spoke my annoyance at his interference. "I have not changed my mind, Mr. Thornley. In fact," I said, glancing at the driver, who'd moved to where

I could see him again, my thoughts whirling with new possibilities for the next few hours, "I intend to be gone most of the day."

Kenton looked from me to the driver, then back, his unhappiness mounting. "Is your mother accompanying you?"

"She's resting." My chin rose of its own accord. "I'm perfectly able to make my way about the city without her. I do so all the time in Chattanooga."

His frown deepened. "This isn't Chattanooga. Not to mention, there are thousands of visitors here for the celebration. You cannot be alone with this man all day, unchaperoned, in a city as large as Nashville. Your father would never approve and you know it."

I fumed, knowing he was correct about the chaperone and my father but not willing to capitulate.

"Your lady's maid, *signorina*. She is my sister. She would be most happy to attend you."

The driver's voice broke through the tension, the surprise his words carried lifting my spirits. Now I knew why Gia reminded me of him. When I met his gaze, he gave a bow.

"Stay out of this, Moretti." Kenton glared at the driver. "You know nothing of what is expected of a lady like Miss Nichols."

The driver didn't respond and awaited my decision with a calmness I appreciated.

I had a choice: remain at the hotel with the hope of dislodging myself from Kenton and his friends or trust a stranger who seemed oddly like an accomplice.

"Gia will come with me," I announced. "That should satisfy the requirement of a chaperone for my father."

Matching dimples appeared in the driver's cheeks. "As you wish, *signorina*. I will inform my sister of your plans." He departed, his long legs taking the stairs two at a time.

Kenton watched the driver's back before his gaze shifted to me. "Your father's intention in hiring Moretti was to provide passage to and from the exposition, not to flaunt your independence. Eldridge will not be pleased when he hears of this."

"Then I suggest you don't tell him. I'll speak to him myself this evening."

We stared at one another, weighing the repercussions that came with our impasse. We'd never been true friends. Kenton's superior attitude in everything, from a childish game of frog in the middle when we were young to recent discussions about women's suffrage, made it difficult to enjoy his company. While he could be charming and pleasant at times, these attributes were not assigned to him with any sense of regularity. Papa insisted I could grow to love Kenton if I put my mind to it, but I wasn't convinced love came upon one's heart in such a way. Surely the passion between a man and a woman held more mystery, went deeper, than simply forcing it to take root, all for the sake of increasing the family's business empire.

"You're a stubborn woman, Priscilla." He lifted his hands in surrender. "Fine. Go off on your adventure, but don't complain to me if you find yourself stranded in an unsavory area of the city. Moretti's kind are known for being lazy drunkards, you know."

I offered a patient smile. "Perhaps you should take your objections up with Papa, since *he* is the one who hired Mr. Moretti."

I couldn't help but chuckle at his scowl as I walked away, knowing I'd beaten him at his own game.

———————

The morning didn't go as planned.

Emmett woke in a bad mood and refused to cooperate with anything I asked of him. Mama had always been the one to soothe him when he felt out of sorts. She'd sing his favorite songs and rub his back, whispering secrets into his ear that made him giggle. Soon, he would be back to his normal, cheerful self.

But I wasn't Mama, and my patience with my brother evaporated.

"Emmett, stop it," I said through gritted teeth.

He wanted pancakes for breakfast, but I'd made him a bowl of oatmeal instead. We were out of Bisquick and there wasn't time to make a batch from scratch. I planned to meet Jason in Miss Nichols's room at nine o'clock, and I still hadn't figured out what to do with my hair. The popular beehive or even the bombshell would require more time with my Beautymatic electric hair straightener than I had available this morning.

Emmett pushed the bowl across the table again. "Mr. Louis makes good pancakes. You don't make good oatmeal."

I picked up the bowl, resisting the urge to slam it down on the table. "Mr. Louis is busy serving breakfast to the guests. You know Dad doesn't like us to bother the chef when he's busy." I set the now-cold oatmeal in front of him. "If you don't eat this, then you won't have anything until lunch."

A glance at the clock on the wall above the stove told me I had exactly twelve minutes to tame my curls, a feat that normally took at least thirty.

Emmett started to push the bowl away again, but I wouldn't let him.

"Eat it!" I hollered, forcing it back in front of him.

"No!" he screamed, using both hands to keep it from him.

Before I could stop it from happening, the bowl launched out of my grip and flew across our small breakfast table. It crashed to the blue- and white-checkered linoleum floor and shattered into a dozen pieces.

"See what you've done now?" I glared at him, furious. "I'm not cleaning that up. You are."

Angry tears filled my eyes, and I turned my back to him.

I shouldn't have to take care of my brother. That was Mama's job. I'd had a life before she died. A future. It wasn't fair.

"I'm sorry, Audrey." I felt him take my hand in his. "I'll eat your oatmeal."

I looked over my shoulder and found genuine remorse on his face. Emmett didn't know how to fake it.

Resentment seeped out of me until I sagged, drained. It wasn't his fault Mama wasn't here. It wasn't his fault he'd never be able to take care of himself.

"You can't eat it now." I moved to clean up the mess. "When Mrs. Ruth gets here, I'll ask her to take you upstairs to the restaurant and you can have pancakes."

His fleshy face brightened. "I like pancakes."

I nodded. "I know."

Forty-five minutes later, I arrived on the fifth floor. The early upset had stolen the excitement I'd felt ever since Jason Sumner told me he was free today and we made an arrangement to meet in Miss Nichols's room at nine. I'd carefully planned what to wear that was *not* faded jeans and one of Emmett's hand-me-down T-shirts. A favorite pair of navy slim-legged pants with a matching striped top seemed most appropriate yet offered a hint of stylishness. Without time to heat the iron to take some of the frizz from my curls, I wove my hair into a French braid, leaving a few wisps to frame my face.

The door to room 504 stood open. I must have neglected to lock it yesterday. While we seldom had items go missing out of someone's room, I'd make certain to secure the door when I left today.

Morning sunshine and soft music drifted into the hallway.

I found Jason across the small room, his attention fixed on a poster of the giant seesaw from the Tennessee Centennial Exposition.

A sudden, unexpected thought popped into my mind.

How fun would it have been to attend the expo with a sweetheart and ride the seesaw, which surely must have been frightening and thrilling at the same time? That I thought such a thing while getting ready to spend the morning with a handsome young man was a bit startling, but it also sent a delicious kind of shiver through me before I stepped into the room.

"Hi." I shrugged when he turned to me. "Sorry I'm late. Emmett . . . well, we had a few problems we had to work out before I could leave."

He nodded. "It's okay." He shoved his hands into his pant pockets, a habit I'd noticed yesterday. "It must be hard now, without your mom to take care of him."

My face must have revealed my surprise at his knowledge of our family dynamics, because he continued.

"Your dad shared a little with me the other day. He said you had to quit school and come home to help out." He gave a small smile. "I think that's really admirable. Not everyone would do such a selfless thing."

After my angry episode with Emmett this morning over something as simple as pancakes or oatmeal, his words brought a feeling of guilt rather than appreciation.

"Thanks, but trust me, I'm no saint. I don't have Mama's patience. She always knew what to do to help him when he was upset or had one of his headaches." I sighed. "I'm a poor substitute."

He gave me a long look. "You need to give yourself more credit. From what your dad said, you've not only stepped in to help with your brother, but with the hotel as well."

I stood there, stunned. No one had spoken such encouraging words to me in a long time. Not even Dad. He'd been knocked low by Mama's unexpected passing, to the point I feared he wouldn't recover. The doctor called it an emotional breakdown brought on by grief and assured us Dad would heal with time. I didn't care what label they put on it. I just needed my father back. Mama's sister, Aunt Dorothy, came from California and stayed with us for a while, but she eventually had to return to her own family. I found myself alone, taking care of two emotionally needy men, while I struggled through my own heavy fog of shock and grief.

Jason's words seeped into my parched soul the way spring rains soak the landscape.

I smiled for the first time that morning. "Thank you. I appreciate it."

He nodded. An awkward silence followed.

"So," we said at the same time, then laughed.

"I was just looking at these posters." He indicated the framed pictures of the expo. "These are in great condition. I'm not sure of the value, but I think a collector of centennial memorabilia could be interested in them." His gaze returned to me. "That is, if Miss Nichols is interested in selling them."

The idea had merit. "I hadn't thought of that, but you're right." I glanced at the boxes I'd already filled. "I wonder if I should keep a list of the more valuable items she has. That way, if Miss Nichols recovers and wishes to sell some of it, she'll have a record of what she has."

"Good thinking."

We set to work, sorting through the boxes and writing down everything salable. While we worked, we chatted about our childhoods, school, Nashville, and a dozen other topics. I'd never had a male friend, yet it felt so comfortable sharing things with Jason.

By one o'clock, we were tired and hungry.

"You're welcome to come to our apartment for lunch." I felt my face grow pink with my boldness. To make sure he didn't think me too forward, I added, "I found an old scrapbook about the Tennessee Centennial Expo among Miss Nichols's things. I hated the thought of it getting thrown out, so I took it home for safekeeping. It's really quite remarkable. You could look through it while we eat."

A smile brightened his eyes. "I accept the invitation. Both to lunch and to view the scrapbook."

I led the way into the hall and to the elevator.

"Dad and Emmett most likely ate earlier." My words sounded a bit like a confession as we waited for the chime to alert us to the car's arrival. Had he expected the men in my family to be present?

His smile didn't dim. "That's okay. That leaves more for us."

I grinned.

I liked Jason Sumner, I realized. A lot.

And if I wasn't mistaken, he liked me too.

Chapter Five

Dad surprised us and joined us for a late lunch.

"You'll be happy to know I think I've found a replacement for Bea Anderson."

Emmett was in his room, so it was just the three of us seated at our small dining room table. I'd heated up a couple cans of tomato soup and grilled some cheese sandwiches, which Jason declared the best he'd ever eaten.

"That's wonderful." I didn't know whether to ask for details in front of Jason or not, but Dad apparently had no hesitations discussing business with a guest present.

"Betty Ann Williams. She's worked at several well-respected hotels in New Orleans. She's recently relocated to Nashville and seemed rather excited about working at the old Maxwell."

This was good news indeed. "When can she start?"

Dad laughed and shifted a glance to Jason. "My daughter isn't thrilled about working in the hotel. She's ready to make an escape."

I shot Dad a frown. I didn't want Jason to think badly of me, even if Dad's statement was mostly true. "I don't mind helping out." I gave a small shrug, knowing Jason was watching me. I stirred my already-cooled soup, trying to find the right words to explain the situation without sounding like a spoiled child who hadn't gotten her way. "It's just that I miss school and my friends."

After a silent moment, Dad reached over and put his hand on mine. "I know you do, honey. Hopefully it won't be too much longer."

When our eyes met, I saw the sadness that still lingered there. The fact was, I knew he needed me. To help with Emmett. To help with the hotel. And to help him cope when the loss of my mother threatened to engulf him. I suddenly felt selfish for being thrilled he'd found a new employee to take over the front desk duties.

When the meal ended, Jason helped me wash dishes while Dad went back to his office. We were just finishing up in the kitchen when Emmett appeared in the doorway.

"Hi, Jason!"

I turned to see the two shake hands.

"Hey there, Emmett. That's a nice ball cap you've got on. Are you a Cubs fan?"

Emmett shrugged. "Dad watches baseball." He held out a thin book. "Do you want to see my comic book?"

"I sure do." Jason accepted the offering and thumbed through it. "You know, I have quite a few comic books myself."

While Emmett peppered Jason with questions about which ones he owned, I silently watched the exchange. I hadn't realized how familiar my brother had become with Jason or vice versa. Seeing Emmett's eagerness now warmed my heart. He didn't have any friends other than the aging residents of the hotel. The absence of Miss Nichols had left him unsettled and lonely the past few days. I was happy to see him smile now.

When Emmett hurried to his room to retrieve yet another book, I felt the need to make an apology. "I'm sorry if he's a bother. He loves to show his collection to anyone and everyone."

"It's no bother." He grew serious. "I have a cousin who was born with a mental impairment. My uncle and aunt have five other children, and they couldn't cope with Ray's particular needs. He lives in an institution outside of Charlottesville." His face revealed his sorrow. "It's an awful place, Audrey. I know caring for Emmett can't be easy, and it sounds like you had to give up a lot after your mom passed, but I can tell you, it's worth it."

His words drew a memory to the surface.

When I was younger, I'd overheard my parents arguing about whether or not to send Emmett to an institution. He was a child, not more than five years old, but his tantrums and outbursts were frightening. Mama was in tears, refusing to send her son away, while Dad tried to convince her it was for the best.

I'd completely forgotten about that incident. Obviously my mother won, but now I wondered, had Dad really wanted to send Emmett away?

My brother barreled around the corner before I could respond to Jason, waving his newest edition. "Look at this, Jason. It's the *Fantastic Four*."

"Wow, I've heard about this one, but I haven't seen it yet." The two flipped pages excitedly, going on about superheroes and big green creatures.

I stepped back and watched, imagining, not for the first time, Emmett's life had he been like other boys. *Why?* I asked God for what must have been the millionth time. Why had he made my brother this way?

Emmett yawned loudly. "I'm going to my room now." He retrieved his book. As suddenly as he'd appeared, he disappeared down the hall, leaving Jason and me alone.

"He's a good kid."

I nodded. "I appreciate what you said earlier. About it being worth it. Some days are really hard, especially now. Dad is busy with the hotel, plus the new owner is talking about making all kinds of changes next year. Mrs. Ruth is a big help though. I don't know what I'd do without her."

I glanced at the clock. It was already after two. Lunch with Dad and then Emmett's visit took up more time than I'd anticipated. Disappointment washed over me. I'd really wanted to show Jason the scrapbook.

"I suppose we better get back to work. That is, if you have time. I don't want to monopolize your day if you have something you need to do."

"Like I said, I'm free. But—" he hesitated—"you said something about a scrapbook?"

I grinned, pleased to find we were on the same thought wave. "Would you like to see it now?"

"You bet."

We settled on the sofa, sitting close enough that our knees touched as I laid the book across our laps.

"This was on the bookshelf in Miss Nichols's room." I looked at him. "I assure you I only took it for safekeeping." I told him what Miss Nichols's attorney said about getting rid of everything, which still made me angry.

"I'm sure Miss Nichols will appreciate what you're doing. I wouldn't want my things sold or discarded without my permission."

I opened the worn cover. "It seems to mostly be about the Tennessee Centennial Exposition, but there are some other things in the back. Newspaper articles and some odds and ends. There's even a section with pictures from Italy."

Jason's attention fixed on the colorful pages as I turned them slowly.

"Boy, this is well-done." He pointed to a black-and-white picture of the Parthenon. "I haven't been there yet, but I've heard about it."

"I'd be happy to show it to you."

His eyes met mine. "I'd like that."

We continued to study the beautiful pages, commenting on this or that.

When I turned the next page, I gasped. "That's the Maxwell House Hotel." I leaned closer to get a better look at the faded picture.

It had been taken from the corner across Fourth Street, which back then was called Cherry Street. It showed both entrances to the hotel. Pedestrians walked along the sidewalks while horses with carriages lined the streets. Eight tall pillars that no longer existed welcomed visitors to the men's entrance of the hotel.

"My parents stayed at the Maxwell in the thirties when they were newlyweds," Jason said, his eyes on the picture. "They'd saved up money for their honeymoon, which wasn't easy, since that was during the Depression." He glanced up and smiled. "I can't tell you how many stories I've heard about the Maxwell House Hotel. And as you might expect, the only coffee my mother buys is Maxwell House."

We laughed and each told what we knew about the history of the coffee, wondering if Teddy Roosevelt really had declared it "good to the last drop" when he enjoyed a cup on a visit to the Hermitage, Andrew Jackson's estate near Nashville.

"Is that why you wanted to stay here?" I asked, returning my attention to the picture of the hotel. "Because of your parents' connection?"

He nodded. "Plus, I'm a bit of a history buff, so I didn't want to stay in one of the newer hotels."

"And has the old girl lived up to your expectations?"

"She has. And in some ways," he said with a look that sent butterflies racing through my stomach, "she's exceeded my expectations."

We continued to go through the scrapbook, discussing each exquisite page. Every so often, a postcard appeared among ribbons, dried flowers, and other memorabilia. I showed Jason the note on the back of the postcard that had come unglued the previous day.

"I wonder who Peaches is," he said after reading the brief message.

I shrugged. "I've never heard anyone call Miss Nichols by that name."

We found several more postcards in the book. All but one stayed securely pasted to the pages.

Jason picked up the card boasting a picture of a giant statue of a Greek goddess. "This one is signed by Peaches, too. 'No one could accuse Luca Moretti of being a coward,'" he read aloud.

"I wish we could see the backs of the other postcards," I said when he finished reading the message. "But I'm afraid we'll tear the pages if we try to remove them."

He set the two loose postcards on the table, and we continued to look through the book. The edge of a newspaper clipping poked from near the back and caught his interest. He flipped the pages to where several more clippings were loosely tucked.

"'Nashville City Council to Address Dark Problem of Prostitution,'" he read aloud. "That doesn't sound very cheerful."

It certainly didn't. We skimmed the headlines on the other

clippings and found them similar in topic. I couldn't fathom why Miss Nichols kept such depressing things.

Jason closed the book when we came to the end. "I think your Miss Nichols has quite a few secrets. I imagine she has all kinds of interesting tales to tell."

If someone had made that statement only one week ago, I would've laughed. But oddly, in the past two days of working in Miss Nichols's room and looking through the scrapbook, I was starting to realize it was true.

"It would seem so." I reached for the book, thinking of the woman I'd seen most of my life but had never gotten to know. "I've always thought of her as an odd, lonely old woman. I forget she was once young and full of life."

"Are you busy this evening? I'd like to go through the scrapbook again, maybe give it a little more attention this time."

"I'd like that."

It wasn't a date, but it felt close enough to get excited about.

We left the apartment and returned to Miss Nichols's room. As I entered and glanced at the boxes and items still needing to be packed, I had a strange sense that the woman who'd lived here wasn't at all what I'd thought. In fact, I was beginning to believe she might have been a woman I would have liked to know.

Chapter Six

"What a splendid day."

I climbed from the carriage with the assistance of Mr.
Moretti—Luca—whose name had been provided by his sister earlier in the day. Kenton's dire predictions hadn't proved
true—not for the outing in the city nor for Luca's behavior—
and I couldn't remember the last time I'd had so much fun.
The grand Maxwell House loomed above us, a welcome sight
after such an exhilarating exploration of the city's shops and
attractions.

Luca nodded, clearly pleased. "I'm happy you enjoyed
yourself, *signorina*." He let go of my hand and reached to
help his sister exit the conveyance.

Gia looked as fresh and lovely as when we left the hotel
three hours ago. She'd done a marvelous job acting as lady's
maid while I chose two new gowns and a new hat. I normally
dreaded dealing with a dressmaker and milliner I wasn't
familiar with, but Gia's shy suggestions and apparent natural

style turned the situation into a lark. I was more than satisfied with my purchases, thanks to her.

"I'll take your packages to your room, miss. Perhaps you'll want to rest before dinner?"

At my affirmative answer, she bobbed a curtsy and disappeared into the crowd bustling near the women's entrance.

Truly, people jammed every square inch of the city, it seemed. I was certain Nashvillians had never enjoyed—or detested, whichever the case may be—such a vast number of visitors to their fair city. When my shopping was complete, Luca drove us past the mighty Cumberland River as well as the park where the exposition exhibits were under lock and key until tomorrow. I'd overheard someone say four thousand or more men were putting on finishing touches inside the fence, making certain all was in working order for the big day. We'd only been able to see the tip of the giant seesaw through the trees, but Gia and I declared on the spot we would indeed ride it, no matter how thrillingly frightening it might be.

Someone bumped me from behind, jarring me from my musings, and nearly sent me to the pavement. Strong hands steadied me before I toppled.

"You, look where you're going!" Luca's angry voice rang out, but the guilty party continued on his way without a backward glance. Luca muttered something in Italian before releasing me. "Are you injured?"

"No, but thank you, Mr. Moretti." I reached to straighten my hat. "I'm fine."

"May I escort you to your room, *signorina*? The lobby is quite crowded."

I glanced up to a worried expression on his face. For some reason, it pleased me to know he felt concern for my well-being.

"I'm not quite ready to retreat to my room." I remembered seeing an ice cream shop and confectionery near one of the women's salons on the hotel's main floor this morning. Gia and I had enjoyed tea cakes at the milliner's shop, but dinner wouldn't be served for several more hours. "I think I should like something sweet."

With our destination set, Luca led the way into the hotel and wove through the teeming crowd. He kept one hand securely on my left elbow while using his other arm as a barrier should anyone drift into our path. Surprisingly, it was rather delightful to have this tall, strong man act as my protector. Papa very rarely went about town with me, and although Kenton acted as my escort at dinner parties and such, I'd never needed him to play the role of hero.

Delicious aromas came from the sweet shop as we neared. A seat at the counter was conveniently vacant, and Luca steered me into it like a horse to its stall. I almost laughed at the noticeable relief on his face as he stood sentinel once I was settled.

"Mr. Moretti," I said, my voice wobbly with humor, "I do believe you've broken out in a sweat from the excitement."

Surprise at my unladylike statement registered in his dark eyes before a twinkle softened them. "Miss Nichols, I lived in New York City for a number of years, so I am accustomed to crowds. I've no fear for myself, but I believe your father would see me in jail if something happened to you."

I appreciated his honesty. "I must say, the number of

people here to celebrate Tennessee's birthday is shocking. I imagine the crowds at the opening of the exposition tomorrow will be quite unmanageable."

"Which is why I will not leave your side, *signorina*."

The low words of assurance were meant only for my ears. They left a warm trail as their meaning washed over me.

I turned away, remembering he was my carriage driver, not a knight in armor. His job was to take me around the city and keep me safe.

Yet . . . I felt certain he would do just that even without receiving payment.

When it came to choosing which sweet to order, I couldn't decide between peaches and cream or the dozens of fancy candies filling the shelves behind the clerk. I finally settled on the fruit, thinking it a better option for providing sustenance until dinner. As I took the first bite, I closed my eyes and savored the creamy deliciousness.

"Oh, my, this reminds me of summers at my grandparents' home in Georgia." I smiled at Luca. "They have a peach orchard, and I would hide in it when I was little girl, eating peaches off the trees until I was ill."

Luca chuckled. "It sounds like you were a bit willful."

"I was. Still am," I said with a laugh. I took another bite, then looked up. "Would you care for some? I can order a bowl for you."

"No, but thank you, *signorina*. I am content to watch you enjoy the treat."

Self-consciousness washed over me, and I turned away. "What is Gia's favorite sweet? I'd like to take her something in appreciation for her help today."

A glance to him revealed a soft smile on his face.

"That is very kind, Miss Nichols. She would like that."

The desire to pepper him with all sorts of personal questions suddenly assailed me. For instance, how much age difference was there between him and Gia? He appeared quite a bit older, possibly even older than me. He'd mentioned living in New York City, a place I longed to see. When and why had they left, and how had they ended up in Tennessee? Where were their parents? Still in Italy?

At least a dozen more questions rolled through my mind, but of course, I didn't voice any of them. It wouldn't be proper.

A short time later, we left the shop, a sack of peppermint sticks for Gia tucked in my reticule. Luca once again barreled us through the crowds, insisting on seeing me to my room on the third floor.

The hallway was blessedly free of guests when we arrived, and not even our footsteps on the plush carpet disturbed the quiet.

At the door, he bowed. "I bid you a pleasant evening, *signorina*. I hope you rest well. Your father has instructed I drive you to Exposition Park in the morning after I drop him and Mrs. Nichols off, so I will see you downstairs at seven thirty, if that suits. The gates open at eight."

Papa was among the honorary speakers giving speeches at the opening ceremony in the auditorium. Mother planned to arrive early with him, but I preferred to go later. "I don't believe that's necessary. I can take a streetcar. They're scheduled to leave from the hotel every fifteen minutes throughout the day."

A flash of disappointment crossed his face. "The streetcars will be filled to capacity, *signorina*, as you saw today. I'm sure your father only wishes you to be safe, as is my concern for you and my sister."

The memory of the overcrowded streetcars we'd passed today gave truth to his words. Perhaps it would be best to allow him to drive us, as we'd determined earlier that Gia would accompany me. The girl hadn't been able to conceal her pleasure.

"As you wish, but I have no desire to be trampled by anxious fairgoers vying to be first through the gates. Let us meet in the lobby at nine o'clock. Good night, Mr. Moretti." I turned and entered my room.

The door had very nearly closed when I heard his quiet voice from the hallway.

"*Buonanotte, signorina.*"

————————

I sped through the dinner dishes, washing and rinsing so fast I wasn't entirely certain they were clean. No matter. Jason would be here in fifteen minutes, and I still needed to straighten up the living room.

"Emmett is already asleep." Dad came into our cramped kitchen. He picked up a towel and began to dry a plate. "I think Mr. Hanover's little dog, Copper, wore him out. They chased each other around the second-floor gallery for nearly an hour."

I turned to him, shocked. "You never allow anyone to run in the hotel." He put away the plate, and I handed him the pan I'd just washed. "I can't tell you how many times you scolded me for doing so. And you certainly don't allow dogs in the public areas. Are you growing soft in your old age?"

He chuckled. "I wouldn't call forty-eight *old*, although I feel it some days. Mr. Hanover happened to be in the lobby earlier. He lost his grip on Copper's leash, and the dog took off up the stairs. Emmett chased after him." He chuckled again, a sound I'd heard too little of the past year. "They looked so comical and had such a fun time, I hated to spoil it. Mr. Hanover and I sat in the lobby and enjoyed a nice visit as well as a good laugh while we waited for them to tire."

I smiled, imagining my brother and the little dog playing chase. "He'll be sorry he missed seeing Jason."

Dad nodded, then gave me a look of examination. "It was nice of Jason to help you today, but I have to say I was a bit surprised when you said he was coming over tonight. Anything I should know?"

I rolled my eyes and pulled the drain plug, letting sudsy water swirl away. "No, Dad. He likes history. Miss Nichols's scrapbook is full of pictures and interesting things from the exposition. We didn't have enough time today after lunch to really look at it. He just wants to see it again. That's all."

He hung the damp towel on a hook, then gave me a serious look. "I know this past year has been hard. There were days I wasn't sure we'd make it, but we managed." He reached out and stroked my cheek. "I'm glad you've found a new friend. Jason seems like a nice young man." He planted a light kiss on my other cheek and retired to his room.

I'd just finished tidying the small living area when a knock sounded on the door that led into the hotel. I hurried over, took a deep breath, and smoothed the full skirt of my plaid swing dress. I was no Jackie Kennedy when it came to fashion. Should

I have worn a pair of kitten heels instead of saddle shoes and bobby socks?

Too late now.

"Hi." Jason smiled when I opened the door. He'd changed clothes too and looked nice in jeans and a striped pullover shirt.

"Come in." I stepped aside while he crossed the threshold.

We settled on the sofa, with a pitcher of iced tea and some chocolate chip cookies Mrs. Ruth had baked that morning laid out on the coffee table. The scrapbook sat next to the refreshments.

"Where's Emmett and your dad?"

I looked at him, surprised and concerned by the question. Had he hoped my father and brother would be present?

Like a happy balloon caught in a thornbush, my excitement over our evening plans deflated. "Emmett's already asleep for the night, and Dad's down the hall, reading." I bit my lip. "Would you like me to go get him? I don't think he's interested in the scrapbook, but I'm sure he wouldn't mind joining us."

His soft laughter was followed by a firm shake of his head. "There's no need to bother him. I was just curious. I'm glad it's just us."

I smiled.

The balloon bounced to life again.

"I've been thinking about the newspaper articles Miss Nichols saved." He reached for a cookie. "If it's okay with you, I'd like go through them first. Research is one of my favorite things to do."

My shoulders slumped a bit.

Research. Oh, boy.

"Sure." I picked up the scrapbook and flipped it open to the back while the reminder of *This is not a date . . . This is not a*

62

date replayed over in my mind like a record album with a scratch across a favorite song.

Jason popped the last of his cookie into his mouth, then leaned in close to study the clippings.

He smelled nice, I noticed. Like one of the new colognes for men Lucille and I tested at Cain-Sloan department store last week. She'd chosen a different fragrance to give her boyfriend for Christmas, but I'd liked the muskiness of the one I felt sure Jason had on.

"This is interesting," he said, bringing my attention back to the scrapbook.

He pointed to a short article written in crowded, tiny letters. "It's dated May 14, 1897. That's only two weeks after the exposition opened." He scanned the brief notice. "It says a violent prisoner escaped from the hospital, but the police believe he's fled the state."

"That's an odd thing to keep." I pointed to the next one. "What's this one about?" I, too, leaned closer, although I confess my interest was not entirely in the article.

"This one says at least six young women—all of them immigrants—disappeared during the exposition, but no foul play is suspected. The police suggest the women ran away with someone they met. There wasn't an investigation."

I reached for the yellowed paper, dates, non-dates, and manly cologne forgotten. "How could the police assume that? Six or more women gone, just like that? Their families or friends were obviously worried and reported them missing, otherwise the newspaper wouldn't have picked up the story."

"Makes me wonder what would've happened if the missing girls had been Americans. Would the police have made the same assumption?"

My blood boiled just thinking about it.

Injustice was something I could not abide. I'd seen enough of it directed at my brother and our family over the years. Emmett was called horrid names anytime he left the hotel, especially when he attended school for a brief time. It had been a disaster, with Emmett's tantrums and headaches increasing exponentially until my parents withdrew him, much to the principal's gloating. As we walked out the door, the man smugly reminded Dad and Mama that he'd advised them to institutionalize Emmett. Maybe they'd listen to him now, he'd called after us. Mama had shielded my brother from it as best she could, but it opened my young eyes to the sad truth that some people seem to take pleasure in lording over others they find wanting.

Another memory surfaced . . . and my furor vaporized.

I hadn't wanted to be seen with Emmett in public, especially when I reached high school. During my junior year, a popular girl from class saw me with my mother and brother at Harveys department store, waiting in line so Emmett could see Santa Claus. My classmate and I spoke briefly before the girl continued her shopping. The next day at school, she pulled me aside.

"Was that your mom and brother I saw you with?" she asked, clearly appalled at the very thought. "What's wrong with him?"

I'd stood mute for a long moment. Although I knew what I should say, my mouth hadn't cooperated.

"Of course not." My voice echoed her repugnance. "They're guests at the hotel. Dad asked me to take them down to Harveys."

Even recalling it now, several years later, I shrank into my shame. Perhaps I was just as bad as that school principal and my classmate. Being angry about injustice was a good thing, but words without action to back them up are worthless.

"This one is dated April of 1900." Jason picked up another scrap of newspaper. The headline read "Police to Investigate

Prominent Citizen with Ties to Red-Light District." He looked at me, a gleam in his eyes. "Imagine. This newspaper was printed in a brand-new century. People like Miss Nichols had no idea what the new era would bring. Airplane travel. Space travel. Television. They could have never imagined the advances we'd make in the next six decades."

As he bent his head to read the article, I pondered his words.

So many changes had taken place since Miss Nichols was a young woman. Was the ever-changing world frightening or exciting to her? That she'd ended up at the Maxwell House for nearly twenty years, for the most part a recluse, spoke of the former.

What happened? I wondered.

I glanced at the scrapbook.

Would we discover the answer to that question within its brightly colored pages?

Chapter Seven

Following a cold, dreary night, opening day of the Tennessee Centennial Exposition dawned gloomy and gray, with a lingering mist saturating the early morning air. Banners and other decorations lining the streets of downtown Nashville, ready for the much-anticipated parade, drooped from moisture, resembling a bride who'd fallen into a pond on her way to the church. A collective groan from residents and visitors alike surely greeted the first day of May, while the murmur of prayers for sunshine from exposition officials no doubt crossed paths with heavenly waters on the way to the throne room.

Yet despite the unfortunate weather outside, inside our suite of rooms, the air fairly bristled with activity. Maids scurried about with trays of food and steaming cups of the famed Maxwell House coffee. Papa's voice thundered across the hall when his valet couldn't find the cravat Papa declared he'd packed, and again when the poor man misbuttoned Papa's coat.

I glanced to the bed where my outfit lay, ready for the day ahead. Gia had finished with my hair earlier, styling it in an intricate updo I couldn't stop admiring. I'd sent her downstairs to ready herself for our big day and now awaited her return.

I heard a gasp at the door.

"Priscilla, why aren't you dressed?"

Mother swooped into my room, radiant in a gown she'd had made for this very day. The color, a deep midnight blue, was the unofficial color of the expo, said by many Tennesseans to represent their love for their homeland. Mother tried to persuade me to wear blue as well, but my complexion fared better with lighter colors. I'd chosen a mint-green ensemble, with puffed sleeves and a belted waist. Not quite as fine as Mother's costume, but then I wouldn't be seated on the platform with her and Papa.

"Gia will be back in plenty of time to help me dress." I smiled. "You truly look beautiful, Mother. You'll outshine Mrs. Stephens, no doubt."

She sent me a devilish grin. "I couldn't let the wife of the governor of Missouri think she could steal the attention, no matter that she and Governor Stephens are the celebrated guests of former Vice President Stevenson. We Tennesseans must show the world we're not the backwoods farmers they think us."

I chuckled at the description. "I'm sure the world doesn't think that about all of the residents of Tennessee. Isn't Nashville called the 'Athens of the South'? It's a compliment to be compared to Athens, Greece."

"I suppose." She adjusted her ruffled collar in the mirror.

"I do wish you would change your mind and come with us. I don't like the thought of you arriving at the park alone."

"I won't be alone. Gia will accompany me."

She gave me a look I knew all too well. "You know that isn't what I meant. Kenton isn't available to escort you, and it isn't proper for a young unmarried woman to attend an event such as the opening ceremony without a gentleman attendant."

We'd had this same discussion last evening after dinner. Thankfully, Papa saw no reason why I couldn't come later and join them after the ceremony was over.

"I sincerely doubt anyone will notice, Mother. I'm told the auditorium can accommodate six thousand people." I chuckled. "We'll be packed so tightly, no one will know who is with whom."

She scowled. "Yet another reason to join us on the platform. Really, Priscilla, how can you tolerate being in such close proximity to strangers? I daresay it gives me the vapors simply thinking on it."

I went to her and straightened her collar. "I'll be fine. I promise."

When I stepped away, she still wore the scowl. "Your father has arranged for the carriage to take you to the park. The driver—that foreign man who picked us up at the train depot—has assured us he'll see to your safety." Her brows knit. "I don't like leaving you in the care of a hired man, but promise me you'll stay by his side until you're able to join us."

I had to suppress a grin. Was she truly telling me to remain close to Luca?

I hadn't mentioned my excursion with Luca and Gia from

the previous day to either of my parents. Mother's headache kept her abed most of the day, and Papa hadn't returned to the hotel until the dinner hour. When Mother asked how I'd occupied myself, I showed her my purchases. She hadn't inquired how I managed to get to the shops, and I hadn't volunteered the information.

"I promise, but as I've said before, things have changed, Mother. A new century is less than three years away. Women today aren't as dependent on a man as your generation. We're fully capable of attending an event such as the opening ceremony alone."

She didn't appear convinced.

Papa joined us, looking marvelous in his coat and tails.

"It's time we made our way downstairs, my dear." His gaze met mine, a hint of concern in his eyes. "Are you certain you won't join us, Priscilla? I don't know if there's a seat on the platform for you, but you'd be admitted into the auditorium with us rather than waiting with the crowd for the doors to open."

"It's no use, Eldridge," Mother said, her displeasure waning as she donned her wrap. "I've already asked her, but she's set on coming later. We'll look for you when the public is allowed inside, dear." She kissed my cheek and followed Papa into the small parlor that adjoined our rooms.

"I'll see you after the ceremony," I called.

And just like that, I was on my own again.

I was certain if Mother hadn't been so focused on the grand adventure of the exposition and Papa's involvement in the Railway Exhibit, she would have thought through things a bit more thoroughly. Although I was twenty-five years old—well past the age of needing my parents' permission to do anything—I was unmarried. And though societal rules were indeed changing regarding the role of women, there was still work to be done.

Gia arrived to help me dress. I scrutinized myself in the mirror, more than satisfied with the way the skirt made my waist appear smaller. I was no great beauty in my own estimation, but I'd inherited Mother's honey-colored hair and Papa's green eyes, a combination that formed an attractive presentation. I'd had my share of suitors over the years, yet I could never be certain if their interest was truly in me or my father's money.

With my hat pinned in place and an umbrella tucked under my arm, Gia and I made our way downstairs. Before we'd reached the second level, however, the clamor coming from the main floor filled the stairwell.

We stopped at the second-floor mezzanine and gaped at the crowd below. Men in dark coats and women in colorful walking skirts and blouses occupied every inch of the lobby. Shouts came from porters and bellhops trying to steer the crowd into order, but no one appeared to listen. Children zigzagged in and out, squealing and chasing one another, while parents attempted unsuccessfully to corral them. *Electrified chaos* were the only words adequate to describe the scene.

"There is the line for the streetcars." Gia pointed to where dozens of people waited in front of a desk with an already haggard-looking concierge. The line snaked out of sight.

"My, I'm certainly glad your brother will see us to the park."

When we reached the main floor, Gia grasped tightly to

my hand so as not to get separated. I'd just begun to wonder how we would ever find Luca in this mob when suddenly he was there.

"My carriage is not far," he shouted and motioned to the men's entrance.

"But we'll miss the parade," I said over the din.

"I know a place where you can watch it, away from the crowd."

I nodded and we were off.

With his hand at my elbow, he led the way to where the carriage waited with dozens and dozens of others. Several bystanders asked to ride along with us, but Luca refused, much to their displeasure. Once Gia and I were settled, he climbed into the driver's seat. I was surprised when the boy who'd been holding the horse in place climbed up alongside him, but I didn't have time to inquire about him before Luca set the vehicle in motion.

The streets of Nashville were filled with pedestrians, horses, carriages, streetcars, and even motorcars. I was pleased to see the clouds had departed and a northerly breeze was drying out the parade route decorations.

Gia's face flushed with excitement. "I've never seen so many people, miss."

"Nor have I." Truly, it seemed as though the entire country had turned out to celebrate Tennessee's birthday.

True to his word, Luca directed the horse through avenues and back alleys, taking us away from the crowded main streets. When he stopped the carriage near a boardinghouse, we disembarked and walked a short block to West End Avenue, where the parade was underway. Carriages and wagons bedecked with flowers, ribbons, and banners carried pretty ladies and handsome men in top hats. Gia and I gasped when we saw an all-white carriage pulled by four white horses. The occupants wore white costumes, including one dressed as an angel. By the time the last carriage passed, we were giddy with anticipation and eager to make our way to the park.

The drive to Exposition Park took twice as long as it should. Streetcars clanged past, going and coming from terminals set up near the entrances, while we waited in a long line with other horse-drawn conveyances.

When it was finally our turn to disembark, Luca handed the reins to the boy.

He noticed my interest. "Carmelo will take the carriage back to the livery. I've told him to return for us at three o'clock."

His planning sent a shiver of pleasure through me. "My, you've thought of everything, haven't you?"

"I am at your disposal for the day, *signorina*." He gave a gallant bow, knocking his hat off his head in the process.

Gia giggled, and I averted my eyes, not wishing to embarrass him.

We joined the throng of lively visitors being funneled toward the impressive entranceway, a palatial-looking portico complete with more than a dozen columns. A giant statue of Minerva, the goddess of wisdom, stood on its roof, welcoming guests. At the gate, we paid the fifty-cent admission price, with Luca insisting he pay for himself and Gia, and I insisting he not pay for me. We passed through something the attendant called a turnstile and followed the crowd into the park.

Immediately I was struck by how fresh and new everything looked. A lovely, small lake greeted us on the left, surrounded with flowers of every color, shrubs in various sizes, and inviting benches where several people sat and watched the spectacle. An old-fashioned, moss-grown waterwheel turned at the far end of the lake, and a fountain in the center added to the serenity. Someone in the crowd referred to it as Lake Katherine, and I remembered Mother mentioning it was named after "Bonny Kate" Sevier, the second wife of Tennessee's first governor.

Ahead of us, great, off-white buildings came into view. It seemed quite amazing that none of them existed a little more than a year ago. Shortly after plans for the exposition had been announced, Papa explained that the buildings would be temporary. Following the example of previous world's fairs, like the one held in Chicago four years ago, the building materials used were not made to withstand the test of time. The exposition only needed them for a short six months. Most would be torn down when the fair ended in October, which seemed such an odd and wasteful thing in my mind.

We came upon a sizable and handsome structure on our right, where a sign declared it the Minerals and Forestry Building. It had a Roman look to it, with its columns and sculptured gables. The United States Government Building on the left was just as impressive, in a more traditional sort of way, and men in military dress stood at attention on the steps. I hadn't heard Papa mention what type of exhibits were housed inside either of these buildings, but I looked forward to visiting them in the coming days.

"It seems everyone is going toward the building with a tower just ahead."

I glanced at Luca, who was several inches taller than most of the people around us, giving him a nice advantage. "It must be the auditorium, where the opening ceremony is to be held."

Indeed, the massive belfry crowning the auditorium was soon visible to all. Just that morning, Papa gave away the secret that bells would be played after the ceremony ended today, and chills raced up my arms in anticipation.

When we finally arrived on the grounds of the large hall, I glanced at my watch. It had taken far more time to get here than I'd anticipated. If we were to occupy three of the six thousand seats available, we couldn't delay. There would be time enough to see the sights. In fact, now that we were on the exposition grounds, I realized it would take many days to visit the dozens of buildings and exhibits, not to mention the amusements of Vanity Fair. It was simply too vast and far too interesting to rush through.

People pushed and shoved the closer we drew to the doors. Luca took my elbow, and I took Gia's hand as we were swept along in a tidal wave of humanity, with no way to turn back even if we'd desired it. The echo of many voices as well as the sound of musical instruments being tuned grew louder with each step, giving evidence the auditorium was filling despite the start of the ceremony being still thirty minutes away.

My breath caught when we entered the commodious room.

A large stage lay ahead, decorated with banners and flanked by two enormous American flags. Yet it was the impressive pipe organ in the center that commanded one's attention. Music from such a magnificent instrument surely held promise of many enjoyable hours for fairgoers. Chairs were set up to the right and left of the podium, and I tried to find Papa and Mother without success.

"Oh, miss, it's beautiful." Gia's breathless whisper reached me despite the noise around us. I squeezed her hand in agreement.

Seats for the audience filled in quickly, and we were about to take three toward the back of the room ourselves when Kenton Thornley suddenly appeared.

"Priscilla, you've made it. Your mother has been worried." He cast a glare to Luca. "We expected you an hour ago."

"We stayed to watch the parade and then made our way here. You can't imagine how long we had to wait in line before we could disembark from the carriage." I glanced toward the platform. "Where are Papa and Mother?"

"They're in the reception area set up for the dignitaries behind the stage. I'll escort you." He offered his arm.

"Thank you, but I'll watch the ceremony from here and meet them afterward. I told Mother as much."

He frowned. "Why on earth would you do such a thing? We have seats on the front row. Now, come."

"But I don't want to abandon Mr. Moretti and Gia."

"We will be fine, *signorina*," Luca said. "We will meet you outside after the ceremony, if you wish."

I turned to him, frustrated with the situation. I had no desire to join Kenton's party at the front of the hall, yet it wasn't reasonable to sit with Luca and Gia after his invitation. They were hired servants, after all.

Some of the excitement for the event vanished when I acquiesced. "Very well."

Kenton placed my hand in the crook of his arm, but his gaze lingered on Gia as Luca led her away.

"Who is that with Moretti?" he asked after we'd made our way to the front of the auditorium and found our seats near the orchestra pit.

"His sister, Gia, my lady's maid."

Kenton's brow rose. "His sister?" He glanced to where Luca and Gia had found seats many rows behind us. "Well, well. How very interesting."

The Bellstedt-Ballenberg Band began a patriotic tune just then, putting an end to the odd conversation. Why Kenton had an interest in Gia was beyond me. He wasn't one to pay attention to servants and certainly had no need for a lady's maid.

As the crowd began to sing along with the music, a warning sounded in my mind. What it warned against, I hadn't a clue, but I tucked it away for later study just the same.

Chapter Eight

I hadn't seen Jason all day.

The new employee, Betty Ann Williams, arrived this morning, and I'd stayed busy showing her around. Although, as Dad indicated, she had far more hotel experience than I did, so it was more getting her familiar with the Maxwell and how things were run.

I'd been a bit surprised when he introduced her to me. I expected a younger woman, similar in age to Bea Anderson and Lucille, but Betty Ann had to be in her forties. With her blonde hair worn in a curly bob, her big smile, and bright-green eyes peeking out from behind cat-eye glasses, she reminded me of actress Doris Day. Day and her favorite costar, Rock Hudson, had a new movie coming to the Crescent theatre a few days before Christmas. Wouldn't it be a lark to go see it with a Doris Day look-alike?

While we ate lunch in the hotel restaurant—Dad's treat—she told me a little of her life in New Orleans. She'd been married as a young woman, but her husband died in the war. They'd never had children and she'd never remarried. She spent the years caring for her parents, but now with them both gone on to their heavenly home, she'd decided to make a change.

"Tell me a little of the history of the Maxwell," Betty Ann said as we toured the basement after lunch. It was used as storage these days, but in the heyday of the hotel, maids, footmen, waiters, and other staff had rooms down here.

"From what I know, she was the grande dame of Nashville." I chuckled, knowing I sounded just like Dad. He'd drilled the history of the Maxwell into me from the time I could understand the difference between our hotel and the Noel across the street. "When Mr. Overton began building it in 1859, people called it 'Overton's Folly' because it was so enormous. No one believed Nashville needed such a large hotel."

"I must say, it is bigger than I imagined."

"There's a newspaper advertisement from around the time it first opened in Dad's office. It boasts, in bold print, 'Two hundred and forty rooms, elegantly furnished and spacious, with steam heat, gas lighting, and a bath on every floor.' Rooms were four dollars a day, meals included." We made our way to the elevator. "Only a portion of the hotel was finished when the Civil War began. It served as barracks for the Confederates, but after Nashville came under Union control, it was used as a prison and a hospital."

Betty Ann looked astonished by this information. "I would have never guessed. My, the old girl certainly does have a colorful history."

I laughed, enjoying the ease of conversing with her. Since Mama's passing, Mrs. Ruth had done her best to fill the emptiness I hadn't even known was there until recently. Women need women to talk to, she'd say and encourage me to share my mind and feelings. I did a handful of times, but as sweet as Mrs.

Ruth was, I thought of her more as a grandmother than a friend and confidante. Something about Betty Ann, however, gave me the impression we were going to be good friends.

We returned to the front desk. A note with my name on the outside lay beside the telephone.

"Excuse me." With the note in hand, I walked a short distance so I could read it in private.

It was from Jason. He had something he wanted to share with me and invited me to join him for dinner.

I suppressed a squeal of delight, refolded the letter, and tucked it in the pocket of my swing skirt. Dad arrived in the lobby a moment later.

"Well, how have you two been getting along?"

His smile seemed a bit brighter, I noticed. Maybe he'd been more worried about the vacant position than I gave him credit for. The Maxwell might not be a full-functioning hotel as others in the city were, but it still took a great deal of effort and knowledge to run. I hoped the plans the new owner had to breathe life back into the old girl wouldn't put stress on Dad now that he seemed more himself. I knew he worried how the coming changes would affect our long-term residents, but until we knew Mr. Edwin's plans, we had to trust all would be well in the end.

"Wonderfully." I moved to stand next to him while Betty Ann took her place behind the desk. "We've been talking about the history of the hotel."

Dad nodded, pleased. "Guests do ask questions from time to time about things of that nature, so it's always good to brush up on it." He turned to me. "I need to go over the Christmas dinner menu with the chef one last time before he puts in his grocery order. Could you stay with Emmett? I believe we can safely leave the desk duties to Betty Ann."

Music to my ears. "Of course."

"I've heard about the Maxwell's Christmas dinner." Betty Ann settled into the high chair I'd occupied with far too much regularity lately. I was happy to see her in it now. "Didn't they serve leg of Cumberland bear at one time?"

I left Dad and Betty Ann discussing the outlandish delicacy and other holiday traditions at the Maxwell and walked down the hall. I found Emmett in Dad's office, with his face drawn close to the screen of a small television set. It must be time for Tom Tichenor, a local puppeteer, and his cheerful marionettes. Dad recently read an article in *Time* magazine that claimed televisions with colored pictures would soon be in every home. I couldn't help but smile thinking of how much my brother would enjoy watching his favorite shows in living color.

When he saw me, he jumped up and rushed over. "Audrey, can we look at your book?"

My mind blanked. "What book?"

"Miss Priscilla's book."

The scrapbook. I hadn't realized he was interested in it. "Sure."

"Let's go." He took my hand in the same way he used to take hold of Mama's when he wanted her to see something. It brought a bit of moisture to my eyes.

We walked back to our apartment and settled on the couch with the scrapbook across our laps. Upon opening it, I cringed at the crackling sound of old glue giving way. With our recent page-turning, things were beginning to come loose. We'd need to be extra careful so as not to ruin the designs.

I tried to explain to Emmett what the pictures and interesting items were, but I knew he didn't fully understand. Dates and time, old and new. None of these concepts seemed to make a lasting impression on him.

As I turned the pages, another postcard dropped out, but this time a dried flower came with it, falling between us. Emmett retrieved them, handing the card to me but holding the flower up for closer inspection.

My interest landed on the picture of a lake and a vaguely familiar bridge. Large print at the top of the card identified it as the Rialto Bridge crossing Lake Watauga, and I realized why it looked identifiable. It was a smaller yet well-done replica of the real Rialto Bridge in Venice, Italy, which I'd seen in photographs at school. According to the fine print at the bottom of the picture, shops were incorporated into the bridge where one could purchase souvenirs from the expo.

"What's that, Audrey?"

"It's a postcard. A letter without an envelope. You write a note to a friend on the back and then mail it to them."

"Did someone mail it to Miss Priscilla?"

I looked for a postmark but didn't find one. "I don't think so."

I turned it over. The same attractive handwriting as on the other postcards filled the back side. My gaze dropped to the signature. *Peaches.*

A chill of suspense worked its way through me. Was Miss Nichols the author of the postcards? If so, to whom was she writing and why were they never mailed?

"What does it say?"

"It's to someone named Luca."

"Who's Luca?"

I shook my head. "I don't know."

Emmett's attention went back to the flower while I read the note in my hand.

My dearest Luca,

It's late at night and I'm tired, but you are on my mind and in my heart. I spent the entire day at the

83

expo today. I went to every building and exhibit you
and I visited together, remembering our conversations
and how you treated me with such care. I stopped at the
Rialto and bought another figurine of the Parthenon.
The one you bought for me sits on my nightstand,
but I want to give one to you when we see each other
again.

I paused, trying to recall if I'd seen a tiny replica of the Parthenon in Miss Nichols's belongings. I felt certain I hadn't.

I'm saddened each time I pass the lake where we ate
lunch. If only we'd returned to the Maxwell, but it's too
late for regrets. All I can do is pray that you and our girl
are both safe.

Peaches

"I wonder who she means by 'our girl,'" I said. As far as I knew, Miss Nichols didn't have any children, so maybe she and Peaches were not the same person after all.

Emmett stood and handed the flower to me. "I don't want to look at your book anymore," he said and headed for his room.

I couldn't blame my brother for becoming bored, but I, on the other hand, felt drawn to the unfolding mystery. Uncovering the truth was perhaps just the challenge I needed, especially now that Betty Ann would take over most of the desk duties.

So many questions filled my mind. I couldn't wait to share this new discovery with Jason. We planned to come back to the apartment after dinner and continue perusing the scrapbook. When I'd told Dad earlier, he nodded, but I could tell he had something on his mind.

84

"Do you think it's a good idea to become so friendly with a young man who lives in another state? He'll be returning to school after his stay with us."

"I know," I'd said, pretending nonchalance. "We're just friends, Dad." I didn't admit I had the same concerns. The last thing I needed just now was a broken heart. Yet being with Jason was so pleasant, I couldn't help but look forward to our time together, no matter how brief.

I turned the card over and studied the picture once again. The Rialto Bridge crossed over Lake Watauga, where several gondolas, identical to those in Venice, drifted. Women in long dresses and large hats and men in coats and ties sat in the center while a gondolier dressed Italian-style steered the boat. What a romantic setting! I'd never paid much attention to the history of the exposition before, but now I found myself wishing it still existed. To see the places pictured on the postcards and walk where Peaches and Luca walked would certainly make their story come to life.

Reluctantly I put the book away. I needed to check in with Betty Ann and see how she was faring before I began to dress for my date . . . er, dinner with Jason.

I'd just emerged from the hallway that led from our apartment to the interior of the hotel when I spotted Dad. He was casually leaning on the front desk, with Betty Ann seated on the opposite side. Their laughter echoed in the empty lobby. Betty Ann said something to him, and although I couldn't see his face, hers gave evidence she was pleased with his response.

Was our new employee flirting with Dad?

And was he flirting back?

Dad noticed me then. "Audrey, we were just talking about you. I was telling Betty Ann the story of when you were a little girl and how you enjoyed playing hide-and-seek in the lobby."

I joined them, confused by what I'd seen as well as the way it made me feel.

"Mama and Emmett would look for me." I watched to see if mention of Mama brought a hint of guilt to his expression.

It didn't.

Perhaps I was being overly sensitive. Dad was, after all, a widower, and Betty Ann a widow. Yet it hadn't occurred to me until this very moment that he might want to marry again someday. I couldn't imagine such a thing, and selfishly, I hoped it never came to that.

"I saw Miss Nichols today," he said. "She's being moved to a nursing facility tomorrow. Unfortunately, the doctor doesn't expect much, if any, improvement. She isn't able to walk or speak, although we communicated a bit through gestures and such. The doctor said the effects of a stroke are permanent, so a nursing facility is her only option."

After getting a glimpse into Miss Nichols's life by going through her personal belongings, including the scrapbook, I felt a connection to the elderly woman. Of course, that seemed rather odd, even to myself, considering I'd never had much to do with her over the years.

"I'm sorry to hear that," I said with sincerity. "What will we do with her things?"

"I told her we'd store them here at the hotel until she was settled. There's plenty of room in the basement. That way, if there's anything she'd like brought to her, we can access it."

"That's very kind of you, Dan." Betty Ann offered him a sweet smile. "I'm sure she appreciates the care you've shown."

Dan?

Bea Anderson never called my father Dan. In fact, all of the Maxwell's employees called him Mr. Whitfield.

Once again, an unsettled feeling stirred in my belly.

"What time are you meeting Jason?"

Dad's voice drew my attention. "Seven." I glanced at Betty Ann and her pleasant smile. Was I being completely ridiculous about something as silly as calling him by his name?

"I think I'll treat Emmett to a hamburger at Henry's. He loves their french fries."

We said good night to Betty Ann, with Dad going to his office and me returning to the apartment. I set my hair on fat rollers and pressed wrinkles from a rust-colored wool sweater I planned to wear with a matching pleated skirt that reached just below my knees. Dad wasn't keen on the new style of skirts some girls were beginning to wear these days, with the hem just above the knee, and until now I hadn't cared about them either. But if Jason asked me to dinner again, I might sneak down to Harveys department store and try one on, just to see how much shorter they really were.

When I told Emmett about Dad's supper plans for them, he could barely contain his excitement. I couldn't help but smile as he danced a jig around the living room.

They hadn't been gone long when a knock sounded on our door. I took a deep breath before opening it. Jason looked nice. Nothing out of the ordinary—he was always well-dressed and groomed—but something about his appearance tonight said he too had taken care with his attire.

"You look pretty." He smiled.

"Thank you. I don't have too many opportunities to get dressed up these days." As soon as I spoke the words, I realized they made me sound pathetic and lonely. "I mean, since my mom passed away," I added with a shrug.

He nodded and thankfully left that conversation behind us. "I hope you don't mind, but I thought we'd eat at a restaurant a few blocks from here. One of the partners at the law firm where

I've been working recommended it. I can drive us over, if you'd rather not walk."

Deliciously surprised, I grinned. "I don't mind walking. Let me get my coat."

We left the hotel through the Church Street entrance and headed west. The December air felt nippy, but not cold enough to make the walk unpleasant. Quite a lot of people agreed, because the sidewalks and roads were crowded with holiday shoppers, a reminder that I still needed to complete my own shopping list.

Christmas-themed decorations glowed in every store window, and miles of stringed tinsel and multicolored lights criss-crossed the street above us. We passed a couple dressed in Victorian clothes collecting donations for a local charity, and as Jason tossed in some coins, he told them they should be on the cover of the *Saturday Evening Post*. They laughed and thanked him for both the compliment and the donation. A little farther down, the doors to the Presbyterian church stood ajar as we passed by, and the sound of the choir practicing "Silent Night" reminded me of the true meaning of the holiday.

"I love Christmastime in the city." I inhaled the unique aroma of winter. Snow wasn't expected, but the scent of woodsmoke and pine gave evidence of chilly Tennessee nights. "Everything is so cheerful and festive."

"Really? Because I thought . . . well, never mind."

I glanced at him, wondering what he meant. "No, go ahead. What were you going to say?"

He gave a slight shrug. "It's just that there aren't any Christmas decorations in the hotel or in your family's apartment."

He was right. I'd barely noticed, what with all that had been going on the past few weeks. Weddings, new employees, and poor Miss Nichols's stroke had kept my mind whirling.

"Bea Anderson was in charge of the decorations the past

few years, but now that she's married and moved to Texas, Dad will need to find someone else to take charge."

"Why don't you do it?" His question came with a genuine smile. "I could help."

The thought of tackling the task of decorating the hotel felt heavy. "I don't know," I said. Even with the promise of spending more time with Jason, I wasn't sure I was up to it.

"I'm sorry, Audrey." He stopped and faced me. "Of course you wouldn't feel like putting up decorations, with your mom gone and all."

I appreciated his understanding. "You didn't say anything wrong," I said as we continued down the sidewalk. "This will be our second Christmas without Mama. We didn't do much last year. Not even the residents were in the holiday spirit, they loved Mama so much. But you're right. We need to decorate the hotel this year."

"Well, if you decide to do it, I'd be happy to help."

We strolled down another block, and I couldn't have been more pleased when we ended our journey at Corsini's Italian restaurant on Seventh Avenue.

"You can't know how much I've wanted to try Corsini's." Excitement turned my voice into a high-pitched squeal, but judging by the grin on Jason's face, he didn't mind. "Bea and Lucille have raved about it for ages."

Soft violin music greeted us when we entered the small eatery, and I spied an old-fashioned phonograph in one corner. Frescoed walls depicted scenes from Italy, with rolling green hills, vineyards, and an ancient-looking village, while white cloths and a waxy candle stuck in an empty wine bottle graced each small table.

I was utterly charmed.

The maître d' seated us near a window. Across the street,

a mannequin Santa Claus and two elves each wore a pair of the popular cat-eye glasses in an optical store's lit display. A third elf, one without glasses, found himself in a tangle of red ribbon, ostensibly in need of the eyewear. It wasn't the jolliest window display I'd seen this season, but I did appreciate how most businesses downtown embraced the holiday spirit.

The waiter arrived with menus and a glass of water for each of us. I had no idea what to choose; everything offered on the menu sounded scrumptious. When the waiter returned, Jason ordered ravioli while I chose chicken scallopini.

"I've never eaten at an Italian restaurant before." I wondered if my confession made me sound provincial, but it was the truth.

"Then I'm glad we came here." He sat back in his chair, clearly relaxed. "How was your day? Your dad said the new employee started work."

I nodded. "Betty Ann. She seems nice." I didn't want to say more, in case he detected something in my voice that might say otherwise. She *was* nice, but I'd have to keep my eye on things between her and Dad. "What about you?" I said, changing the subject. "What did you do today?"

"I'm still interviewing students who were arrested during the sit-ins last year. Getting their stories down, hearing their firsthand accounts of what happened." A gleam of excitement sparked in his eyes. "I'm meeting with Councilman Looby tomorrow."

My brow rose. "The lawyer whose house was blown up last year?" I remembered Dad telling me about the frightening incident on the telephone while I was still in school in Chattanooga. Sadly, it was only one among many bombings in the South over the past few years.

"I'm honored he's making time for me." He shook his head, growing somber. "It's mind-boggling that someone wanted him dead. One of the attorneys I'm working with said if the dynamite had gone through the window as the bomber most likely intended, the entire house would have been blown to bits. It's a miracle Mr. Looby and his wife weren't injured in the attack."

"Was anyone responsible ever arrested?"

"No, although there are rumors that someone confessed to it, but the police didn't believe him. It'll most likely end up like the bombing of the Hattie Cotton Elementary School the day after black students were allowed to attend. Too many suspects and not enough desire within the system to find the guilty party." He looked at me, and I saw frustration in his eyes. "Mr. Looby was targeted because he's a black man fighting for the rights of other black men and women. Remember when I said civil rights work was almost like going to war?"

I nodded, a shameful awareness sinking in of how little I understood about what the black citizens in my own community endured. Behind the news stories I read were real people—husbands, wives, even children—who simply wanted to enjoy the same freedoms my family and I did. I couldn't imagine the kind of courage it took to keep fighting after something like what Mr. Looby and the others had experienced.

We sat under the weight of his words for several silent moments.

"I don't think I'll ever understand why some people hate others for no reason other than they're different from themselves," I said, thinking of Emmett and how he was often mistreated by strangers.

"That seems to be a question for every generation that has ever existed."

The waiter arrived with our food, and we moved on to lighter topics of conversation.

"Any news on Miss Nichols?" he asked.

I told him what Dad had learned about Miss Nichols moving to the nursing facility and storing her belongings. "It's sad she doesn't have any family to help her through this."

"I talked to one of the partners at the law firm today about her situation. He handles estate planning and the like."

"Oh?"

"Don't worry. I didn't mention her name or any specifics. I said I knew of an elderly woman who'd suffered a stroke and that she didn't have family. I asked him what should be done with her belongings, especially those that could hold some value."

"What did he say?"

"First, if her current will doesn't stipulate what should be done with her belongings, he suggested that if she was still in her right mind, even though debilitated, she should get it changed. He was pretty disgusted when I told him her attorney's plan to dispose of everything." He paused. "If she's been living at the Maxwell for twenty years, she probably doesn't have much in the way of income. Selling some of her exposition memorabilia could generate a tidy little sum for her. Getting her permission to do that would be the next step."

I sat back, amazed. "You've certainly been busy."

He chuckled. "My mom used to say I was like a dog with a bone when I got an idea in my head."

I smiled. "It's really sweet of you to take an interest in Miss Nichols's welfare without even knowing her."

"It's people like Priscilla Nichols who I want to help once I get my law degree. The underrepresented. The forgotten."

An older gentleman who'd been sitting nearby approached our table, a cane helping to keep him upright.

"*Scusami,*" he said, his Italian heritage evident in his voice.

"I could not help but overhear you mention the name of someone I knew long ago. Priscilla Nichols. *Si?*"

Jason stood, casting a look of caution to me. "Yes, sir. You know Priscilla Nichols?"

"Yes, for many years now." He glanced between us. "Tell me, is she well?"

Jason pulled out an empty chair and assisted the man into it. "May I ask how you know her, Mr. . . . ?"

"Corsini. Carmelo Corsini. My cousin owns this restaurant. I worked here for many years until I retired. Now I just come to enjoy the good Italian cooking."

Jason nodded. "I'm afraid Miss Nichols is in the hospital at the moment."

A look of dismay filled the man's weathered face. "I am sorry to hear this. She came here from time to time, but always, she was alone. It made me sad."

"Is that how you met her? Here at the restaurant?" I asked.

"No, no," he said, shaking his balding head. "I met Miss Nichols on opening day of the Tennessee Centennial Exposition in 1897. I worked for the man who drove her carriage."

Chapter Nine

"Imagine," Mother said as we joined the throng exiting the auditorium after the opening exercises ended. "President McKinley pressed a button at the White House in Washington, DC, and machines here at the exposition sparked to life. My, the wonder of all these new inventions is truly magnificent, don't you agree, Priscilla?"

Her use of my name drew my attention. I'd only been half-listening as she expounded upon the splendor of the opening ceremonies while I tried to locate Luca and Gia in the crowd. Kenton remained near the stage chatting with his parents and their friends, but Mother had expressed a need for fresh air.

"Yes, it is truly amazing." I hoped the vague answer would suffice.

"Your father insists we visit the Railway Exhibit first. He's most anxious for us to see the fruits of his hard work these past months."

I offered a smile while suppressing a groan. Although I certainly looked forward to visiting the exhibits in the Railway Building and applauding Papa's accomplishments, there were far more exhilarating offerings I was eager to see, Vanity Fair being one of them.

We'd nearly reached the exit when I spotted Luca, a head above the crowd. His gaze was on me, and I realized he must have seen me long before I saw him. I motioned toward the doors leading outside, and he nodded. I couldn't see Gia, but I assumed she was with him.

"Who is that?" Mother asked, craning her neck in their direction.

"Our carriage driver and my lady's maid. You remember I planned to tour the exposition in their care while you and Papa are occupied."

She frowned. "I'm sure no one would mind if you joined us at the luncheon and reception. Your father is an honored guest."

"Mother, you of all people know I can't. I wasn't included in the invitation."

Clearly my answer displeased her, yet she knew I was right. "Very well. The reception is in the Woman's Building. Why don't we meet there at half past two?"

That only gave me a few hours to explore the fair on my own, but it was better than nothing. "Enjoy the luncheon, Mother. And don't worry about me."

I kissed her cheek and set off before she could change her mind, winding my way through the mass toward the exit. I felt like one of the excited children I'd seen in the Maxwell's lobby earlier, happy to escape the confines of my parents' watchful eyes.

The sun shone brightly as I emerged from the overcrowded building, and I inhaled a deep draught of flower-scented air. Despite a damp start, the day held glorious promise. With most of the mob moving toward the Woman's Building for Governor Taylor's presentation of an immense fountain to Mrs. Kirkman, president of the women's board, I walked to the north side of the large portico.

My reward came in finding Luca and Gia waiting on the stone steps.

"*Signorina.*" He seemed pleased to see me.

Gia scrambled to her feet. "Miss." She bobbed a curtsy.

"Did you enjoy the opening ceremony?"

"We did." Luca smiled down on Gia. "My sister surprised me by knowing all the words to 'The Star Spangled Banner.'"

A faint blush came to her cheeks. "There was a guest at the hotel a few weeks ago who played the piano in the men's salon. That song must be his favorite, because he sang it over and over."

We decided to tour the Minerals and Forestry Building first, it being conveniently across the lawn from the auditorium. We'd barely reached the bottom of the steps, however, when Kenton Thornley reappeared.

"Priscilla, I've been looking everywhere for you." His gaze drifted to Gia before returning to me. "Your mother informed me you weren't attending the luncheon or the reception following it. I volunteered to act as your escort until your parents were free. Besides, I'm rather on my own at the moment as well. We can see the sights together." He extended his arm to me, but his smile was for Gia. "Shall we?"

I glanced to Luca. His expression gave away nothing, but his relaxed demeanor disappeared.

Although I wasn't thrilled at the prospect of being in Kenton's company, I knew it would be rude to refuse. With little enthusiasm, I accepted his arm. "We were just going to the Minerals and Forestry Building."

"Splendid." He led the way, chatting about the opening ceremony, President McKinley's participation, and the band, all the while directing his comments to me but letting his attention drift to Gia behind us.

The strange warning from earlier crept in once again, yet I didn't know what to make of it. I knew I wasn't jealous, although some women would have been threatened by Gia's fresh beauty. The fact that Kenton clearly found her attractive—for there was no other reason for his interest in a maid—mattered not. It was the unease this knowledge brought that disturbed me. Despite her womanly appearance, Gia was young and innocent. I would hate to see her heart broken.

We entered the building, awed by the sheer magnitude of the place. Kenton released me and we drifted along with the crowd, studying and discussing each exhibit. While rock samples and mining techniques weren't as thrilling as some of the other displays promised to be, it was gratifying to see Tennessee's abundant natural wealth presented to the world.

"What do you think, Mr. Moretti?" I asked as we moved through a doorway into a different part of the building. "Can any other place on earth boast of supplying so many useful products? Truly, I had no idea we produced such lovely marble."

"Indeed, *signorina*, the state of Tennessee is much blessed." A lopsided grin brought out a dimple. "But I don't believe it can compare to the abundance of Italy. We export marble as well, but also olive oil, silk, and, of course, excellent wines. Someday you should see the vineyards of Tuscany."

I heard pride for his birth country in his voice.

"See here, Moretti. No one wants to hear about Italy." Kenton's loud rebuke echoed off the high ceilings. "If it was so great, why are you immigrants here in America, taking up jobs that should go to Americans?"

My face flamed with embarrassment for Luca and anger at Kenton. "There's no need for rudeness. We're discussing the riches of both lands. There's no harm in that."

"My point is," he continued, "I should think a foreigner living off the generosity of our glorious country shouldn't sing the praises of a place he clearly has no love for. Otherwise he would be there, not here."

A number of people cast curious glances our way, bringing further discomfiture. "Can we please just continue touring the exhibits? We're drawing a crowd ourselves."

Kenton sent one last glare to Luca, then turned and strode away.

"I'm sorry. Again." I looked up to find Luca's kind eyes on me, with no hint of offense in their dark depths. "I feel I always have to apologize for Kenton's ill manners where you're concerned."

After a moment, he said, "It is not your place to apologize, *signorina*, but I appreciate it. He is correct in some ways. My family did leave Italy, but it was not for lack of love for our homeland."

As we walked, he told me their story. "I was two years old when we came to America. Poor peasants like my parents had no hope in Italy. Much violence and poverty remained after years of unrest in the country. My father's cousin wrote of the new life he'd found across the ocean, and *Papà* could not resist the dream of finding a good life in *L'America*."

We stopped at the next exhibit of hardwoods, but I wanted to hear more of Luca's tale. "How brave they must have been to leave everything they knew and come here."

He nodded, yet there was no smile to accompany it. "Unfortunately, the promise of riches and opportunities was not for everyone. We arrived in New York City with thousands of others from Italy—and Ireland, too—but there weren't enough jobs. Men fought, sometimes to the death, over even the lowliest position. We lived in a crowded tenement with *Papà's* cousin's family, as well as two other families."

He glanced to where Gia stood a short distance away. Kenton had returned and was chatting with her.

"Gia was born two days after my twelfth birthday. *Mamma* worked too hard and had a cough, but she couldn't rest. We needed the income she brought in as a ragpicker." He heaved a sigh and dipped his chin. "God took her home soon after Gia was delivered."

A lump formed in my throat. "I'm so sorry," I whispered. I glanced at the pretty girl. "Do you have other siblings?"

Luca shook his head. "None that survived."

My parents had suffered the loss of my only brother before I was born, so we had that in common.

"And your father? Is he here in Nashville?"

Again, sadness filled his features. "He died of cholera five years after *Mamma*."

"Who raised Gia?" I asked, saddened to learn they were orphaned so young.

A soft smile lifted his lips. "I did."

I stared at him, measuring whether or not to believe him. Even in such a short time of knowing him, I could not be convinced he would jest about something like this.

I wished to tell him of my deep admiration for such a sacrifice, but it wouldn't have been appropriate. "From what I can see, Mr. Moretti, you did a fine job."

Gia and Kenton made their way toward us then. I noticed a high flush on her cheeks, and I wondered what Kenton had said to bring it about.

Again, the feeling of unease stirred in my spirit. I'd known Kenton most of my life. He could be arrogant, rude, and selfish, and I never looked forward to spending time with him and his family. Yet this sense of caution I suddenly felt, this disquiet, was new and rather unsettling.

Was Kenton capable of inappropriate behavior with someone as young as Gia?

That was a question I'd never had to consider until this very moment.

"Shall we make our way to the Woman's Building?" he said, seeming quite pleased with himself. "I daresay the luncheon has ended by now. Your father will be impatient to get to the Railway Exhibit, I'm sure."

Luca cleared his throat. "If you won't be in need of us any longer, *signorina*, Gia and I will take our leave. I asked Carmelo to return with the carriage by midafternoon."

His reminder came with disappointment. I'd enjoyed our time together. "Of course. That does seem the best solution."

Gia couldn't hide her unhappiness with the plan, but I wondered if it had more to do with Kenton than with leaving the exposition early.

Watching them walk away, I couldn't help but wonder how this brother and sister had survived all they'd been through and still come out such seemingly good and decent people.

I glanced at Kenton's smug expression as he too watched them leave. The blessing of wealth and privilege certainly hadn't done him any favors.

As we moved in the opposite direction, a startling question invaded my thoughts.

Was I just as guilty as Kenton?

I'd benefited from my father's wealth and the prestige of his position with the Nashville, Chattanooga, and St. Louis. I'd lived in comfort and luxury my entire life. Had it colored my view of the world around me?

The memory of my haughty words to Luca the day we arrived reverberated in my ears. He'd paid me a compliment and I'd snubbed him.

"My outward appearance should have no bearing on whether you feel honored to assist me or not. It is your job, plain and simple."

As I allowed Kenton to escort me to the Woman's Exhibit, shame kept me silent.

"I still can't believe how lucky we were to meet Mr. Corsini."

Jason and I settled in matching, albeit worn, chairs in the hotel lobby. It was already after nine o'clock at night, and I didn't want to disturb Dad and Emmett by going to the apartment. We'd stayed at the restaurant far longer than we'd intended, but Mr. Corsini had such fascinating stories about the exposition and meeting Miss Nichols that we couldn't pull ourselves away. He promised to come by the hotel tomorrow afternoon and continue the conversation.

"That was a crazy bit of luck." Jason chuckled, then added, "Providence, really. I don't believe in luck."

"Well, whatever you want to call it, it's still amazing that we had an opportunity to talk with him."

"It's a shame he didn't know more about Miss Nichols's life after meeting her, though. It appears she was quite a private person, then and now."

I sank back into the plush cushion, going over the things Mr. Corsini shared. "My greatest disappointment is he didn't remember her ever being called Peaches. Of course, in those days, a hired person would have never dared call her anything other than Miss Nichols. Still, if it had been her nickname, he would have surely heard it. A name like that would be memorable."

My mind flashed to Dad and Betty Ann's interaction earlier when she'd called him Dan. It wasn't quite the same as Mr. Corsini referring to Miss Nichols as Priscilla or Peaches, but there were definitely lines that shouldn't be crossed when one was in service.

"It's great he remembered the opening day of the exposition with such detail. It sure would have been something to see. All those buildings made to look like famous structures. The lakes. Vanity Fair. Crowds of people from all over the world."

I glanced at him. "Have you been to the Parthenon yet?"

He smiled, a twinkle glittering in his eyes. "I hoped you'd go with me."

Warmth swirled in my belly. "Dad's day off is Saturday, so he'll be home with Emmett. We could go then, if you're not busy."

"That sounds perfect."

He stood, then offered me his hand. I placed mine in his, relishing the feel of his warm fingers closing over mine.

"I had fun tonight," I said as we walked to the door of our apartment. I knew he wouldn't kiss me since we hadn't been on a date, but I couldn't keep myself from wishful thinking.

"Me too. I'm meeting with Mr. Looby in the morning, so I should be back in time to meet with you and Mr. Corsini in the afternoon. Have you decided whether or not you'll show him the scrapbook?"

I shrugged. "I think I'll ask Dad his opinion. I don't believe Miss Nichols would mind an old friend seeing it, but I have to remember it isn't mine."

After we said good night—no kiss—I quietly entered the apartment. To my surprise, Dad was still up, watching a movie on television.

"Did you have a good time?" He yawned, stretched, and stood to click off the set.

"I did, but you didn't have to wait up."

He studied me a long moment, his eyes soft with fatherly love. "Yes, I did. Before I know it, you'll be married and move away. If I've learned anything this past year, it's that tomorrow isn't promised to any of us."

He rarely talked about Mama's passing. Sitting up, waiting on me, must have given him time to reminisce.

"Well, don't start planning my wedding just yet. Jason and I haven't even had an official date."

He chuckled. "Duly noted."

"Dad, can I ask you something before you turn in?"

"Sure."

We settled on the couch, the scrapbook on the coffee table in front of us. "We met an old friend of Miss Nichols's tonight at Corsini's. Carmelo Corsini. He knew her when she was a young woman. I think he must be several years younger than her, so he was probably a boy of maybe fourteen or fifteen at the time. He was a carriage driver and took her to the opening day of the exposition."

"My goodness, how did you find him?"

"We didn't. He was at the restaurant and overheard us talking about her. We invited him to come to the hotel tomorrow afternoon and tell us more." I reached for the scrapbook and smoothed its worn cover. "I'd like to show him this, but I'm not sure I should. It isn't mine. Jason has seen it, but he's been helping with Miss Nichols's belongings and all."

Dad nodded with understanding. "I see. I haven't looked through it, so I don't know if there's anything of a personal nature Priscilla wouldn't want people to see."

"I don't believe there is. It's mostly just memorabilia. There are a few postcards to someone named Luca from someone named Peaches, but I'm not even certain they have anything to do with Miss Nichols."

"Then I don't see how it could hurt to show it to him. He might enjoy seeing the reminders of the celebration."

"That's what I thought too."

We turned out the lights and headed down the hall.

"Oh, before I forget," he said when I stopped at my bedroom door. "Betty Ann and I were discussing the Christmas decorations. With Bea Anderson no longer here, Betty Ann has volunteered to take over the responsibility. I told her to get with you tomorrow and have them brought up from the basement."

I knew I should be relieved not to have to worry with the

decorations, but I'd almost looked forward to putting them up with Jason's help. "We can start on it first thing in the morning." I paused. "Dad, what do you think about Betty Ann? Do you think she's going to work out?"

He chuckled. "She's only been on duty one day, honey. It's a little too soon to know, but . . ." He hesitated a long moment. "I like her. So yes, I hope it works out." He leaned in to kiss my cheek. "Good night."

I watched him enter his room across the hallway and softly close the door, an odd protective feeling taking hold inside me. Dad had been through so much the past year. He was only now starting to seem like his old self.

I entered my room and stood in the dark, remembering the terrifying days of his breakdown and how lost he'd been without Mama these many months.

I swallowed tears away and turned on the light, one thing certain in my mind.

I wouldn't let anyone hurt him.

Chapter Ten

Music and conversation filled the magnificent dining room on the second floor of the Maxwell House as we sat down for dinner promptly at seven o'clock on Tuesday night. The frescoed walls. The glittering chandeliers. The polished crystal.

All reminders of the blessed life I lived, especially after hearing the Morettis' story.

A fact I'd thought much about in the past three days while Mother and I toured the exposition together, enjoying one another's company for a change. We'd seen the Woman's Building, the Negro Building, and the art exhibits inside the Parthenon. We'd even gone to the Memphis–Shelby County Building, mainly because it was built in the shape of an Egyptian pyramid rather than having an affinity for the city hosting it. Papa joined us for luncheon each day, including a picnic beside Lake Katherine, although he never tarried long. There seemed to always be something more interesting happening at Centennial Club House, where he and his business associates spent a great portion of their time.

Tonight, Mother had invited the Thornleys and several other railroad executives to dine with us, and she wouldn't hear of allowing me to request a tray brought to my room instead.

Our table sat beneath an enormous chandelier suspended from the recessed ceiling, the gaslights causing a waterfall of rainbows to spill down upon our table. Waiters in smart uniforms scurried about, balancing large trays filled with everything from glasses of champagne to oysters on the half shell to roasted quail, evidence the famous Maxwell House kitchens were living up to their reputation. A band in the corner played "Belle of Nashville," written especially for the centennial celebration, and some people sang along.

"You look quite lovely tonight, Priscilla."

Kenton sat to my right—Mother's doing—and sipped from a small glass of amber liquid. His father occupied the seat on my left, effectively sandwiching me between two men with whom I had little in common. Conversation with the other women at the table would be impossible considering the noise in the room and the distance between us. The evening could not end soon enough.

"Thank you." My gown was new, sewn in the latest style, yet Kenton's approval had never entered my mind at the fittings. More evidence I was not the soon-to-be bride everyone wished me to be.

I glanced at the women seated at tables near ours. All of them wore fine evening gowns and were lavishly adorned with jewels that sparkled nearly as much as the chandelier.

"I wonder if the attire will be this formal throughout the duration of our stay. I fear I haven't brought nearly enough evening wear if it is."

Kenton downed the remainder of his drink. A waiter appeared at his elbow and whisked the empty glass away. "I'm sure you can remedy that. My mother plans to spend an entire day next week making Nashville's shop owners happy. You could join her. It would give the two of you a chance to talk about the wedding."

I would have laughed if he hadn't been quite so serious. "Need I remind you that we are not engaged?" I lowered my voice when Mother cast a curious look my way from across the round table. "I believe I've made my feelings on the subject quite clear. We are on the cusp of a new century. Surely you agree that marriage in this day and age should be more than a business contract."

"I'll agree to no such thing." He waved at the waiter, who immediately disappeared, no doubt to bring Kenton another drink. "I can't tell you how many young women would thrill to become my wife, but I'm vain enough not to want a woman to marry me because I'm rich. Your family has long been acquainted with mine, so there's no mystery in the motives. We are a good match, plain and simple."

Any doubts that might have lingered in my mind on whether I should agree to wed Kenton or not fled with his blasé attitude.

"For once we agree on something, Kenton. I don't want a man to marry me because of the business connection our families enjoy. I want a marriage built on love and mutual respect."

"And you don't believe I love you?"

I studied him, trying to ascertain if the alcohol had loosened his tongue or if he was genuine. "No, I do not."

He leaned closer, his gaze intent. "Perhaps if we could spend time alone, I could show you you're wrong."

I stared at him, certain now he'd had far too much to drink. I turned away, disgusted. "Such a suggestion only confirms my point."

"Oh, Priscilla." He laughed. "As you said, we're on the brink of a new century. Old-fashioned ideas are on their way out. Besides, you're a woman of twenty-five years. Your prospects of marrying diminish with each new day. My friends wonder why I don't pursue one of the younger, more beautiful women vying for my attentions, but I've assured them I'm satisfied with you."

I faced him, not bothering to conceal my anger at the insult. "I'm sure one of the younger, more beautiful women you speak of has a father just as wealthy as mine. Feel free to chase after one of them, Mr. Thornley, for I am not satisfied with you."

Mother stared at us in horror, and even Papa seemed surprised. The others at the table, including Kenton's parents, pretended as though they weren't listening.

I stood, my throat convulsing with indignation and embarrassment. "I'm sorry. I'm not feeling well. Please excuse me."

The men at the table barely had time to rise before I whirled away and wound a hurried path to the exit. I didn't look back, knowing Mother's glare would follow me. No doubt my outburst shamed her in front of her friends, which was something she could not abide.

Crowds of well-dressed people milled outside the dining room doors, waiting for a table to become available. The maître d' cast a curious glance when I rushed past his stand, but a guest occupied his attention before he could follow me to find out what was amiss.

I hurried to the opposite side of the mezzanine and stopped to catch my breath. Below me, people wandered about the marble-floored lobby, the hum of conversation and music vying for prominence. It would be hours before Mother and Papa returned to our suite, but I had no desire to go upstairs. Anger at Kenton's thoughtless, cruel words had me ready to burst, and I needed a distraction. Perhaps a walk around the block would help. I considered going up to retrieve my wrap, but the weather was pleasant enough that I could do without it.

Set on my plan, I followed the polished banister down the staircase to the main floor of the hotel. It wouldn't be proper to exit through the men's side without an escort, so I turned in the direction of the women's entrance. As I passed the sweet shop, however, my empty stomach reminded me I hadn't eaten dinner before my unladylike departure from the dining room. I could order a dinner tray delivered to my room when I returned, but the unpleasantness with Kenton spoiled my appetite. Perhaps just a bite of something delicious would be enough to keep me until morning.

I entered the cheerful shop, noticing the clientele was mainly nannies with their charges. No doubt their parents were upstairs enjoying lobster and French pastries.

I settled at the counter. The attendant, a young woman, smiled. "What can I get you, miss?" Her accent and auburn hair hinted at an Irish heritage.

I faced the same decision I had the first time I came to the shop. Satisfy my sweet tooth or enjoy something a bit more substantial, being that this was most likely my supper.

"Peaches and sweet cream, please."

The attendant nodded and disappeared into a back room.

I felt my body sag, tired from our busy day, but it was Kenton's arrogant words that had caused the tension that now slid from my shoulders. What an insufferable man. Why could Mother and Papa not see how utterly miserable I'd be if they forced me to marry him? Even if I told them of his crude suggestion, they would find a way to champion him. His father was an important man in Tennessee, and Kenton's future looked bright to a potential father-in-law.

The young woman returned with a bowl of sliced peaches covered in thick, sweet cream. My mouth fairly watered as I took the first bite. I closed my eyes, as I'd done the other day, to savor it.

"Are you imagining a Georgia peach orchard, *signorina*?"

Luca's low voice startled me. I whirled to find him a few paces away, a bit of a grin tipping one corner of his mouth.

"Mr. Moretti. What a surprise to find you here."

"I was passing by and saw you." He glanced around the noisy, small space. "Is your family nearby?"

I debated telling him the truth. I felt a bit like one of the children crowding the room. Naughty and in need of a scolding from my nanny. "I've run away from them, if you must know." I shrugged, my only defense. "I simply wanted to be alone."

"I see."

I was sure he did, too. "I thought I'd have a bite, then take a walk. The evening is warm enough."

A frown creased his brow. "If I may say, *signorina*, I would not think it a good idea for a lady to walk alone in the city, especially at night. The streets are still quite crowded."

"Why does no one believe I can take care of myself?" My dissatisfaction spewed unchecked, but it wasn't fair to take out my frustrations on Luca. I heaved a sigh. "I'm sorry, Mr. Moretti. You don't deserve to suffer my ill mood."

"I'm not offended." He chuckled. "In fact, I hear as much from my sister on a daily basis. She says I act like a mother hen."

I smiled. "Gia wishes for more independence, I gather?"

"She does. She wants to travel and see the world. I remind her that holding a job in a respectable hotel like the Maxwell is a blessing, but she doesn't see it that way."

I studied him, wondering about the life he and his sister led. How different it was from the privilege and comfort I enjoyed and, admittedly, took for granted. Papa worked hard for all he'd achieved, but it was a different kind of labor than what Luca and Gia knew. I, on the other hand, had no knowledge of life beyond being the pampered only child of Eldridge and Cora Nichols. And if they had their way, I'd continue that life with a husband of their choosing.

"I hope her dreams come true someday." I motioned for the attendant. "Please bring another bowl of peaches for my friend."

I wasn't sure who looked more surprised at my request, Luca or the young woman, but she hurried away to do my bidding. It was rather brazen, I suppose, for me to order for a man who was an employee. Yet, as I'd said to Kenton, times were changing. If I was to be a spinster the rest of my life, I might as well begin shocking people now with my unconventionality.

"This is not necessary, Miss Nichols. I only stopped to see if I could be of assistance to you this evening."

"I insist. I would enjoy the company, unless you're needed elsewhere."

Indecision rested on his face only a moment before he conceded. "It would be my pleasure." He took the stool next to mine, grinning. "I best not mention this to Gia. She'll be green with envy."

The attendant brought a second dish of dessert and set it in front of Luca. I noticed his helping was larger than my own.

"Thank you, Matilda," he said.

She sent him a shy smile before glancing at me, sobering, and moving away to assist a new customer. I realized in that moment they knew one another and that Matilda possibly had an interest in Luca.

"How long have you and Gia been in Nashville?" I asked after a few awkward moments of silence.

He swirled cream with his spoon, but he hadn't yet taken a bite. "We arrived a year ago. A friend wrote about Nashville's plans for a centennial celebration and said there would be opportunities for us here that weren't available in New York. My friend was in Chicago for the world's fair and did well."

I knew it wasn't polite, but my curiosity drove my next question. "What did you do for a living in New York? Were you a carriage driver there as well?"

He didn't look up from his meal. "No, *signorina*. The only work I could find was shining shoes, like my father had done." After a moment, he faced me, pride rather than shame in his eyes. "But I worked hard and put away money for Gia and me. I purchased train fare to Nashville, and after we arrived, I met a man who wished to sell his horse and carriage. *Signor* Murphy was getting on in years, so he let me take over his business for a percentage of my profits. I thank God every day for seeing to all our needs."

I could only nod. His story, so vastly different from my own, spoke of hard work and heartbreaking challenges, yet this man seemed to have found the peace that felt so elusive to me.

He finally took a bite of the dessert. "Ah, I see now why this is your favorite." He grinned. "I can almost envision you as a little girl, running through your grandfather's orchard. Perhaps your name should be Peaches instead of Priscilla."

I gave a surprised laugh. His comment was highly improper yet incredibly welcome. "Don't look now, Mr. Moretti, but your cheekiness is beginning to show."

We finished our treat and left the shop, with Matilda's bright-green eyes following Luca as he went out the door.

"I'm certain this is as unsuitable to say as my ordering and paying for your meal was, but I believe that young lady is rather fond of you."

A faint blush came to his face. "Matilda is *Signor* Murphy's niece. We are only friends."

I held no doubt Matilda would like to change that, but I'd already said more than I should.

"Do you still wish to go for a walk?" His tone spoke his displeasure at the idea.

I knew he would feel obligated to attend me if I left the hotel, and I didn't want to take up more of his time. When our family was not in need of his services, he was free to take other fares. And after hearing his story, I knew the additional income would be appreciated.

"As a matter of fact, I've changed my mind. I believe I will turn in."

My answer clearly pleased him. "As you wish, *signorina*. May I ask what time you would like me to take you to Exposition Park in the morning?"

"Early." I knew neither Mother nor Kenton would leave the hotel before noon, therefore I'd have several hours to enjoy the fair with Luca and Gia. A prospect that brought a smile.

"Very good." He gave a slight bow. "I bid you good night."

Halfway up the wide staircase, I stopped to glance over my shoulder.

Just as I'd known he would, Luca stood below, his gaze on me. Perhaps to make certain I arrived at my destination safely. Perhaps to see that I didn't trip on my gown and make a fool of myself.

The flutter in my heart, however, told me I hoped it meant so much more.

Chapter Eleven

Mr. Corsini arrived promptly at two o'clock.

I'd baked chocolate chip cookies that morning with Emmett's help—he ate dough while I did everything else—and had a plate of them ready and a pot of coffee warming when the older man knocked on the door. Jason had arrived a few minutes earlier and sat on the sofa chatting with Dad. I saw excitement in his eyes as he mentioned his meeting with Mr. Looby, and I couldn't wait to hear all about it. Surprisingly, Betty Ann volunteered to keep an eye on Emmett while he watched television in Dad's office, allowing Dad to join us. I hoped my brother didn't give her any trouble.

"Thank you for coming, Mr. Corsini." I took his coat and hat and introduced him to Dad.

"I enjoy talking about the old days." He chuckled. "No one in my family wants to hear my stories anymore, so it's nice to have someone new to talk with."

He settled in the armchair. I pulled up a straight-backed chair from the dining table, but Jason stood and insisted I switch with him. We made small talk and enjoyed the refreshments for several minutes. Mr. Corsini asked Dad questions about the hotel, which was always a subject my father enjoyed, and then surprised us by supplying several historical tidbits Dad didn't know but appreciated. When Mr. Corsini mentioned reading about the sale of the hotel last year in the papers and wondered aloud if the new owner planned any changes, Dad provided only vague answers. The truth was, he wasn't sure himself what the future held for the Maxwell. Would Mr. Edwin reinvent the hotel, returning it to its glory days with high-end furnishings and higher rates, thus leaving most of our long-term residents without a place to live? We'd simply have to wait and see.

When the cookies were gone and the coffee was cooling in our cups, I reached for the scrapbook.

"I have something I'd like to show you. It belongs to Miss Nichols, but we think she wouldn't mind if you looked through it."

I handed the book to him. He took a pair of reading spectacles from his breast pocket and examined the worn cover. The puzzled expression on his weathered face told me he didn't know what to make of it.

"She kept a scrapbook of items from the Tennessee Centennial Exposition." I opened the cover to reveal a yellowed flyer glued to the first page that announced the opening of the expo.

Mr. Corsini gasped. "*Che meraviglia!* How wonderful. I remember seeing this very announcement in all the store windows. I was a delivery boy in those days, and I would listen to the store owners talk excitedly to the customers about it. From the moment plans for the exposition were made known, the people of Nashville could speak of little else."

He studied the image of the Parthenon, with cherubs holding the ends of a large banner above it, proclaiming the Tennessee

Centennial and International Exposition was scheduled to open on May 1, 1897, and continue for six months.

"It was an exciting time to be in Nashville. I was only fourteen years old, but I was a hard worker. I got a job as an assistant carriage driver and drove many people to and from the exposition that summer. There were so many, I could not tell you a thing about them." A soft smile parted his lips. "Except for Miss Nichols. I remember her because she was our first customer on opening day. She wanted to see the parade before going to the park to meet her family. I can still see the floats and the bands . . ." He seemed to go back in time in his mind.

"You said last night you also drove Miss Nichols's parents. What were they like?" Jason planted his elbows on his knees, intent on Mr. Corsini's every word. I couldn't help but imagine him as a lawyer, digging into his clients' lives in order to bring about justice.

"As I recall, her father was a railroad man. I think he had something to do with the Railway Exhibit at the exposition, but I never made it to that exhibit." He gave a slight shrug. "You know how boys are. I was far more interested in experiencing the amusements of Vanity Fair than learning how the railroad came to Tennessee."

"I seem to recall Miss Nichols mentioning something about her father's business a few years ago," Dad said, as interested in what Mr. Corsini had to say as Jason and I were. "She didn't talk about her family often, but from time to time she'd let something slip."

"Our carriage was hired out by Mr. Nichols for a month, so I drove him and Mrs. Nichols many times as well, but mostly it was Miss Nichols. I would take her and her maid to Exposition Park in the morning and come back for them in the afternoon."

"Her maid?" I asked. "It seems odd that she would take her maid to the fair."

Mr. Corsini disagreed. "In those days, an unmarried woman wouldn't go out in public without a chaperone. A maid often accompanied the fine ladies around town."

Dad glanced at me. "Times certainly have changed. What would you think about having a chaperone until you're married?"

Heat filled my face. I wouldn't look at Jason. "I'm sure you know the answer."

Mr. Corsini continued turning pages, exclaiming over pictures, pamphlets, and other mementos that brought back a memory.

When he came to a postcard with images of Vanity Fair, however, he grew thoughtful. "I remember the last time I drove Miss Nichols. She and her maid planned to visit Vanity Fair, the amusement area of the park."

"What was it like?" I asked, trying to imagine a fair in the late 1800s. Before Mama died, we'd gone to a few carnivals and county fairs. Dad and I enjoyed the rides while Mama and Emmett watched. Sadly, our excursions usually ended with Emmett having a meltdown, forcing us to leave early. Mama declared the noise and lights too much for him, but shamefully, I hadn't cared. Not back in those days, anyway. In my teenage eyes, my brother spoiled everything.

"Vanity Fair was like nothing I'd ever seen before. In fact, I've never seen anything like it since, either." Mr. Corsini studied the postcard a long moment. "This building—" he pointed to a large circular structure with castle-like turrets—"was quite fascinating. It was called the Cyclorama of the Battle of Gettysburg. Inside, the walls were painted all the way round with scenes from the battle." He continued studying the small images on the card. "This was where the Gorman and Boone animal acts were housed. They had trained lions, tigers, bears, horses, and monkeys. It was quite amazing. Why, they had even performed in Europe before coming to Tennessee.

"Yes, Vanity Fair was an exciting place to be." He rubbed his jaw, slightly stubbled with gray whiskers. "The day Miss Nichols intended to visit the fair, however, was the last time I saw her. It would be many years before I met her again."

Jason glanced at me, curiosity reflected in his eyes. "Did something happen to her?"

Mr. Corsini leaned back in the chair, his eyes squinted in recollection. "The whole thing was an odd business. We were only supposed to drive the carriage, but Mr. Moretti always accompanied Miss Nichols into the exposition."

"Mr. Moretti?" I asked, my spine straightening in attentiveness. The name sounded familiar. "Who was he?"

"Mr. Moretti was my employer. He owned the carriage and horse. He and my father were friends, so when Mr. Moretti mentioned he wanted to hire a boy to help during the exposition, I offered."

"Moretti. I know I've read that name recently, but I can't remember where." I racked my brain, but nothing surfaced.

"Why did Mr. Moretti accompany Miss Nichols into the fairgrounds?" Jason asked.

"I suppose he thought she needed some extra looking after. There were thousands of people about, mind you. Her family never seemed to be nearby. She wasn't married and only had her maid with her."

"So Mr. Moretti *and* her maid accompanied Miss Nichols while she enjoyed the fair. But you said it was an odd business. How so?"

"Well, women of her class didn't associate with men like Mr. Moretti. Not usually, anyway." He gave a shrug. "He was a nice fellow. Handsome, too. Many of the young ladies who worked at the Maxwell were sweet on him." He glanced back to the postcard of Vanity Fair. "But the last time I saw Miss Nichols was also the last time I worked for Mr. Moretti. His horse and carriage sat at the livery for nearly a week afterward before they were sold away. I remember, because I was out of a job. Luckily, another driver needed an assistant, but he worked out of one of the other hotels. I never returned to the Maxwell. Today is the first time I've stepped inside in sixty-four years."

"You never learned what happened to Mr. Moretti?" Dad asked.

Mr. Corsini shook his head and handed the book back to me. "No. There were rumors about him being involved in a crime, but my father didn't believe it. Mr. Moretti was a God-fearing, honest man. He wouldn't've done anything unlawful."

Jason had a few more questions about Vanity Fair for Mr. Corsini, but my mind whirled with the unfolding mystery.

Moretti.

Where had I seen that name?

I tapped the cover of the scrapbook with my fingernail . . . then stilled.

The postcard. The one with the statue of a Greek goddess.

I hurriedly opened the book and flipped pages until I found where I'd anchored the postcard with Scotch tape. Carefully loosening the tape, I turned it over.

No one could accuse Luca Moretti of being a coward.

"Luca Moretti."

The men stopped their conversation and stared at me.

"What did you say, Audrey?" Confusion wrinkled Dad's brow.

"Luca Moretti." I held up the postcard. "I knew I'd seen that name recently. This postcard is written to him." I glanced at Mr. Corsini. His eyes held astonishment.

I handed the postcard to him. After he read the brief message, his wide eyes met mine. *"Mamma mia."*

"Do you think this could be the same Mr. Moretti you knew?" I held my breath, awaiting his answer.

"I cannot say for certain, but his name was indeed Luca," he said, appearing stunned by the discovery. "But the day I took him and Miss Nichols to Vanity Fair was the last time I worked for Luca. He disappeared a week later."

———————————

Brilliant sunshine spilled through the window of my hotel room, heralding what promised to be a glorious day. I sat at the dressing table, wrapped in a warm robe, the scent of rose on my skin after a delicious soak in the bathtub.

"Will you wear the new walking dress today, miss? The seamstress delivered it herself yesterday while you were out."

Gia stood at the wardrobe, looking through my gowns. In the last few days, she'd lost most of her shyness and stepped into the role of lady's maid quite well. We'd had marvelous fun seeing the exposition together, and I looked forward to spending the day with her and Luca at Vanity Fair.

"Yes." I moved to stand beside her. "The blue will work nicely today. The fabric is lighter than my others. Which, as the weather grows warmer, is becoming quite important."

"Very well, miss. Shall I style your hair now?"

I returned to the dressing table and let her brush the tangles from my curls. "Where did you learn to arrange hair?"

Her dark eyes met my gaze in the mirror. "We lived with my mother's cousin in New York before we came here. She taught me and her daughters the latest hairstyles." She looked away. "I think she hoped it would keep me from becoming a ragpicker like my mother."

Shame colored her words.

I had little knowledge of what kind of life her family lived in New York City, but from the few comments she and Luca had made, I guessed it was not pleasant.

"She taught you well. I'm very pleased with your work."

A smile replaced the sadness. "Thank you, miss." She paused. "You may find this silly, but I dream of owning a hair parlor someday, like Mrs. Harper."

Her statement took me completely by surprise. "Who is Mrs. Harper?"

A faint blush filled her cheeks. "Of course, miss, I've never met Mrs. Harper, but my cousin told me about her. She was a servant, like me, and worked for a doctor for many years. Her lovely hair reached all the way to the floor, and he taught her how to care for it with a special tonic he made. When he died, he left her the recipe. She began making the tonic and selling it. Before long, she opened her own hair parlor in Rochester and now has parlors in many cities. They're all owned by women, if you can imagine."

"What an astonishing story." We exchanged smiles. "I will be your first customer when you open your very own hair parlor."

Her smile faded. "I fear it's only a dream, miss. It would take a large sum of money, which I don't have. Luca saved for ages before he was able to purchase his carriage and horse."

While she gathered my hair into an intricate style, I pondered the resourcefulness of these siblings. I could only assume they received such strength from their parents, despite the all-too-brief life they'd enjoyed together. To leave one's homeland in search of a better life in America must have taken great courage. That Luca and sweet Gia were both hard workers with ambition proved the senior Morettis had done their due diligence in raising them well.

A short time later, we descended the marble staircase. The crowd in the lobby wasn't as overwhelming as in the previous days, giving indication the initial excitement of the exposition had settled into a more natural rhythm. People accepted the conclusion it would take many days, if not weeks, to see everything there was to see at the exposition. Pacing oneself, it was decided, was the best course of action.

"There's Luca." Gia waved to her brother, who stood near the bottom of the stairs.

His smile sent an unexpected shiver through me.

"Good morning." He inclined his head. "May I say you both look lovely this morning."

Gia giggled and looped her arm with her brother's. "You may. I was telling Miss Nichols about Mrs. Harper's hair parlor. I fashioned her hair like one of the pictures I saw in a magazine."

Luca pretended to give my hair great study, although my hat concealed most of it.

He patted his sister's hand. "Well done. Soon you will be styling Queen Victoria's hair."

A stranger listening might believe he merely jested, but I heard the pride in his voice.

Gia grimaced. "Oh, she's too old. I doubt she has much hair left these days. I want to fashion for ladies like Miss Nichols. Her hair is thick and lovely."

I felt a flush of heat rise to my cheeks at Luca's returned attention. "We should go." I moved around the pair.

The carriage awaited at the women's entrance. The same boy I'd met the first day Luca drove us to the park sat on the high seat, holding the reins to the lone horse.

"Miss." He tipped his cap in polite fashion as Luca assisted me into the vehicle.

"Carmelo will drive the carriage back to the livery, then return at three o'clock, if that suits, *signorina*." Luca directed his statement to me while helping Gia aboard.

"It does, but . . ." I paused.

"Yes?"

Papa and Mother were invited to a private dinner tonight at the Tulane Hotel. When they mentioned it to me yesterday, inquiring if I would like to join them, I'd begged off. I didn't know the railroad executive hosting the party, nor would I have anything in common with their wives. Mother hadn't made a fuss when I declined, so I took that as a sign I'd made the correct choice.

"I don't need to be back at the hotel to dress for dinner." I glanced between Luca and Gia. "I thought perhaps we might dine at the fair. My treat. Besides, Estella Louise Mann, one of my favorite opera singers, is giving a special concert this afternoon. She was born here in Nashville but lives in New York City now. I would enjoy staying to hear her sing. It's said she will become one of the most accomplished operatic singers of our generation."

"What fun!" Gia clapped like an excited child.

I laughed, then glanced at Luca. His smile was more subdued, but he seemed pleased nonetheless.

"As you wish, *signorina*." He climbed onto the driver's seat. When the boy offered the reins, Luca shook his head. "Drive on, Carmelo. If you would like to earn some extra money today, you may take fares from the hotel to the expo while we're gone. But take care you don't overwork the horse. Give him plenty of water and rest."

The boy grinned. "Yes, sir. I'd like that very much."

The ride to the park went much faster today, with Luca explaining that more people were taking streetcars rather than renting carriages.

"I don't understand the fascination with the contraptions myself." Luca shook his head as though truly baffled. "I much prefer the steady pace of a horse to the clanging noise of an electric trolley that jerks and rattles so much, you must hang on or be thrown to the pavement."

Gia and I exchanged grins. When he turned to glance at us, we both offered serious nods.

"I quite agree." I winked at Gia when Luca faced forward again. "My new outfit would surely be crushed in such a crowd. I would positively weep if someone knocked into my hat and disturbed Gia's wonderful hairstyle."

Gia giggled behind her hand, but Luca's wry glance told me he knew I teased.

The entrance to the park was crowded as ever, yet the lines moved steadily. Some fairgoers had purchased season tickets, complete with their picture printed on the voucher, and merely handed the attendant a coupon and breezed through the turnstile.

While we waited our turn, I noticed several small booths set up along the sidewalk outside the gates. People gathered around them, reading pamphlets offered by the organizations represented. One, identified as the Woman's Christian Temperance Union, had a number of well-dressed ladies milling about, holding animated discussions with expo visitors. Another booth was attended by an older couple, although I couldn't read their signage from where I stood. The woman smiled sweetly as she handed a small book, perhaps a Bible, to a girl who seemed down on her luck by the look of her worn dress and disheveled hair. When the girl hung her head, the woman placed her hand on the girl's trembling shoulder in such a caring manner, I felt the warm acceptance from where I stood watching.

I didn't have a chance to take note of the other booths before it was our turn at the ticket window. Luca offered to pay the fifty-cent admission fee for each of us, but I wouldn't let him. As gentlemanly as it might be, he and Gia were here at my request. I could see he wasn't happy with my decision, but he acquiesced. With that settled, I handed the bored-looking young man in the booth the correct change and we moved under the stately arches of the entrance into what was now being referred to as the "New White City."

With excitement practically tingling in the air, we began our adventure.

Chapter Twelve

Luca, Gia, and I seamlessly joined the river of humanity flowing along the paved avenues of the park. Although the crowds had eased some since opening day, there were still thousands upon thousands of people in attendance, each one intent on visiting as many fascinating exhibits and thrilling amusements as possible. Happily, we were counted among their ranks, making Tennessee history with our presence.

Each time I walked the now-familiar path beside Lake Katherine, with her lilies, ferns, and weeping willows, I marveled at the vast amount of work that had gone into the detailed preparations for the centennial celebration. Papa said over ten thousand men worked twenty-four hours a day for months in order to have the park ready for the opening. Only a few exhibits hadn't been completed by opening day, but they were now finished and ready to welcome visitors who'd come from around the world to enjoy the fair.

Indeed, I'd caught the sound of a variety of languages

over the past few days, most of which I was not acquainted with despite having been tutored in French and German. While most visitors to the park were English-speaking Americans, representatives from other countries were merrily mixed into the pulsating crowds. Vanity Fair itself was a celebration of nationalities, and I looked forward to seeing sights and tasting foods I would never see the likes of in Chattanooga.

"Miss, may we walk under the gourd arbor?" Gia waited for me to catch up to her and Luca, as I'd fallen behind with my daydreaming and contemplations. "One of the maids at the hotel could speak of nothing but its beauty, with its vines and flowers." She gave a dreamy sigh.

"I've heard tell of it myself," I said, my smile not for the arbor, but for the joy of seeing the exposition grounds through Gia's youthful eyes. Even though Mother and I had covered quite a bit of ground the past few days, I consulted the map of the park I kept in my reticule. "We need to go around to the back side of the auditorium. The Children's Building is located at the end of the arbor. Perhaps we should visit it before going on to Vanity Fair. It doesn't look too big, so we shouldn't want for the time it will take to tour."

"That sounds like a fine idea."

Luca's approval showed in his eyes. Oddly, I realized I'd never experienced the kind of respect he constantly demonstrated in my presence. Not by my father nor any man, servant or otherwise. At first, I might have attributed it to his position as a hired driver, but since getting to know a bit about him, I believed it to be genuine. He showed the same respect for Gia, despite her young age and flightiness, as well as for my mother, despite her advanced age and snobbery. Once again, I silently congratulated Mr. and Mrs. Moretti on the fine job they'd done as his parents.

We set off past the Minerals and Forestry Building and rounded the auditorium. Up ahead rose the arched greenery of a long arbor covering the avenue leading to the Children's Building, with people coming and going from the cave-like opening.

Upon entering the shaded tunnel, Gia stopped and inhaled deeply. "Smell the flowers, miss?"

I closed my eyes and imitated her. "Lovely. I wonder what type of vines these are. I'd like to plant some in our garden at home."

The cool air beneath the thick vegetation was a welcome respite from the morning sunshine. The day promised to be a warm one, and I'd already seen several women pop open their umbrellas to create a bit of shade as they strolled along pretty paths. We would do well to retrace our steps later this afternoon and return to the fresh beauty of this place.

The Children's Building was a delight. Built to resemble a genteel Tennessee home, the yard was full of children playing games while mothers rested in wicker chairs on the covered porch. To the right, a fenced enclosure held a variety of deer, all tame enough for children to pet and enjoy.

Gia hurried over to join them without asking permission.

"I must apologize for my sister, *signorina*," Luca said, his eyes on his younger sibling. Her musical laughter rang out when one of the deer tried to lick her face. "She is still a child in so many ways. Her life has not been an easy one. She had to learn to cook and clean almost as soon as she walked.

We had few opportunities for making merry. There certainly weren't any deer in Little Italy."

"There is no need to apologize, Mr. Moretti." His obvious love for his sister moved me. "On the contrary, I hope Gia fully enjoys herself today. She may think of me as an older sister rather than her employer if she wishes."

I thought the offer might amuse him, but instead a frown appeared on his face. Had I offended him? He was, after all, Gia's only close relation. I didn't want him to feel I minimized his importance in her life.

Gia returned before I could retract my comment.

"Aren't they darling? Did you see the one who tried to kiss me?" Her question was directed to her brother.

Luca gave a mock scowl. "Until you are married, no one is allowed to kiss you, not even a deer. *Capisci?*"

I hid a giggle behind my hand when Gia rolled her eyes.

"You're like an old mother hen—overprotective of his little chick. There aren't foxes around every corner, Luca."

Luca chuckled, then grew solemn. He tipped her chin to capture her attention. "Perhaps I do worry about you more than I should, but until the little chick is safe in her own nest, she will have to put up with her big brother. *Sì?*"

Gia's annoyance disappeared, and a look of love passed between the two siblings. "*Sì.*"

I watched the pair walk ahead of me toward the Children's Building, Luca's arm around her shoulders and hers circling his waist. Gia had more growing up to do before she'd be able to truly appreciate how fortunate she was to have Luca. I didn't often think of the older brother I never knew, but I now wondered what it might have been like to have him in my life.

We toured the inside of the Children's Building next. I especially enjoyed peeking into a real classroom, with teacher and students alike, where the new concept of kindergarten was on full display. Having been tutored at home, I marveled seeing children as young as four years of age sitting in a classroom, learning their letters.

Upon leaving the building, I wondered if either Luca or Gia had attended school. The question, however, seemed beyond the scope of our relationship thus far. Despite what felt like a new friendship with the Morettis, I knew they were being paid to accompany me to the fair. Ours was not a true friendship, no matter how enjoyable our time together might be.

We traveled north, past the enormous Commerce Building, the largest building in Centennial Park. The sheer size of the place told me it would take far too many hours to tour than I had time for today. Our mission was to enjoy every amusement Vanity Fair had to offer, which seemed a far more pleasant task than viewing exhibits reflecting the businesses of Tennessee and around the world. We would return to it when being indoors and thoughtful was more the order of the day.

On our right, the Parthenon continued to impress, causing me to feel as though we'd stepped from the streets of Nashville into ancient Athens. An exact reproduction of the real structure at the Acropolis, it looked just like a drawing I'd once seen in a book about Greece. The colossal statue of Pallas Athena, who guarded the front entrance, wasn't visible to us just now, but we'd passed the forty-foot sculpture several times the previous day. That the Kentucky artist, Miss

Enid Yandell, was only two years older than me came as a surprise, and Gia asked several questions about her, her Paris studio, and the Louvre.

"Wouldn't it be wonderful to visit there someday?" she asked, a faraway look in her eyes.

I agreed, but I also reminded her that until we could take a steamship across the Atlantic, we had the opportunity right here in Nashville to view brilliant artwork by artists from around the world, all housed inside the beautiful Grecian-style building.

"Priscilla. Priscilla Nichols."

I turned to see who called out . . . and nearly groaned.

Kenton Thornley waved and hurried down the steps of the Parthenon. We had no choice but to move to the side of the walk and wait for him to reach us. A moment of fear overtook me as we waited. Mother had stayed in her room with another one of her headaches. Papa was already at the park when she decided she would remain at the hotel and rest. I'd halfheartedly offered to keep her company, but she'd declined. The day shouldn't have to be spoiled for both of us.

Now, waiting for Kenton, I worried I'd made the wrong decision. I prayed he didn't have bad news.

When he finally emerged through the crowd, I nearly pounced. "Is Mother all right?"

He looked momentarily confused. "I don't know. Was she ill?"

I breathed a sigh of relief. "No, no. She had a headache and chose to remain at the hotel. I thought perhaps you had news of her condition."

He shook his head. "I haven't the foggiest. I've actually been searching the park for you."

"For me? Why?"

His gaze briefly traveled to Gia. Although his attention didn't linger, a high flush came to the girl's cheeks. "I thought we could spend the day together. I feel badly about our misunderstanding at dinner last night. I want to make amends."

My back stiffened. "We didn't have a misunderstanding, Kenton. We understood one another perfectly well."

His eyes flashed, but surprisingly, he kept himself in check. "Let us call a truce and enjoy the day. I saw your father at the Railway Exhibit and he asked me to keep an eye on you." He raised a hand as I opened my mouth to object. "Not that you need anyone to look out for you." He cast a look of disdain in Luca's direction. "Surely you'd rather see the sights with me than with a hired hackney driver."

I refused to acknowledge his rudeness. "I'm perfectly happy seeing the sights with Mr. Moretti and Gia."

"Perhaps Gia and I should return to the hotel, *signorina*." Although his words were said in a normal tone, the tightness of Luca's jaw gave him away.

"There's no need, Mr. Moretti." I glanced at Kenton. I wouldn't let him spoil our day. "We're on our way to Vanity Fair. You're welcome to join us. If you'd rather not, I'll see you back at the hotel."

I moved around him, hoping he would be too proud to walk about the park with a "hired hackney driver." But alas, he fell into step beside me, with Luca and Gia behind.

"You've always been the independent sort, Priscilla," he said in a low tone so only I could hear. "But lately you seem to have taken it to heart. I don't pretend to approve or understand it, nor do our parents. We only want what is best for you, you know."

His statement rankled. "I only want what is best for me, too. Yet what I want and what others want for me are two different things."

He looked about to speak but then surrendered. "All right. I will say no more. Let us enjoy the day, shall we?"

His smile wasn't quite genuine, but it was better than arguing. "Very well, but I warn you, Gia and I plan to visit every amusement Vanity Fair has to offer." I turned to wink at the girl.

"There's the giant seesaw," she exclaimed, pointing to what looked like an enormous child's toy made from steel. "May we try it, miss?"

"It's quite thrilling." Kenton's words were directed to Gia. "Not only can you see the entire park from the top, but also the State Capitol building, two miles away."

She gave an eager smile in response.

I glanced at Luca to see what he thought about the adventure but found a deep scowl on his face. Thinking him concerned for his sister's safety, I said, "Would you rather we didn't ride it?"

The scowl eased some. "I would never hear the end of it if I didn't allow her to take a ride, *signorina*."

Gia grinned. "He's right."

With that decided, we joined a line of at least one hundred others waiting their turn on the giant contraption. Kenton imparted his knowledge about it as we inched ever closer.

"The seesaw was invented by a local Nashville company.

They hoped to compete with the Ferris wheel that was introduced at the Chicago World's Fair." He smiled at Gia. "I had the privilege of riding the wheel numerous times when my family visited the Illinois exposition."

Gia's eyes shone with interest. "It must have been thrilling."

"Oh, it was. I'm not sure a giant seesaw will have the same effect as the Ferris wheel, but it is quite a building feat nonetheless."

We watched as the enormous steel structure cautiously moved up and down, up and down. On each end was a cage-like box that held a score of people, depending on their sizes. I couldn't believe how high the box went into the air when the seesaw's huge arm lifted it. Watching it dangle so far above the ground made me light-headed.

The line moved along slowly, but we eventually reached the front. Kenton insisted on paying the twenty-five-cent admission for each of us, much to Luca's consternation. He thanked Kenton, but his words were stiff.

The young man attending the ride approached, his denim overalls already covered in dust. "There's only room for two in this car. The other two will have to wait for the next car."

Before I could determine who should ride with whom, Kenton took Gia by the arm. "Miss Moretti and I will go first. I can point out the interesting sights for her."

Luca took a step forward. "I would rather my sister stayed with me."

"And neglect your duties to Miss Nichols?" Kenton asked, challenge in his eyes. "Perhaps her father's trust in you is misplaced."

The two men stood face-to-face for a long moment before Luca conceded. "Very well." He turned to Gia. "Be careful."

She grinned. "I will."

We watched them step into the covered box. After the attendant locked the door, the seesaw set into motion, lifting Kenton, Gia, and the others higher and higher.

I had to smile when Gia happily waved to us. "She's not afraid."

"No." Luca's serious gaze remained on his sister. "But she's also young and naive. She doesn't recognize danger when it's right in front of her."

I glanced at him. Was he talking about the ride or something else?

Soon, it was our turn. My stomach swirled with anxiousness when the attendant locked the door on our car. "Oh, my."

"Ready?" Luca smiled at me.

I nodded and gripped the handrail.

The car moved and suddenly we were rising high into the sky.

"It's wonderful," I said, my fear easing. "I feel like a bird. Look, there's the Maxwell House Hotel."

Luca pointed out several other landmarks, including the State Capitol and the Cumberland River. Green hills surrounded the city, and the detailed gardens and lakes of the exposition were glorious from our vantage point.

I had to admit it was thrilling to be so high, nearly touching the clouds, it seemed. "I could stay up here all day," I said, disappointed when the car began its slow descent.

"Perhaps we should come back at night, when the lights

of the city and the park fill the darkness. I imagine you could reach out and pluck a star from the sky."

"My goodness, Mr. Moretti," I said, pleased by his suggestion. "I believe you are a poet."

"I am inspired by the beauty I see."

For one brief moment, I wondered if he meant me.

When we disembarked, Kenton and Gia waited nearby.

"Wasn't it thrilling?" Gia said, her smile as bright as the sun when we approached. "Mr. Thornley said I could ride the seesaw as often as I wished."

Luca stepped over to his sister, placing himself between her and Kenton. "We don't want to impose on Mr. Thornley. You and I can return to the park on our day off, and you can ride it then."

Her excitement wilted, but she nodded. "Yes, of course."

The pair moved away and spoke in low tones. Kenton started to follow, but I stopped him. "I'm surprised I must be the one to remind you that Gia is my maid. She's also a young, impressionable girl. I wouldn't want her to misunderstand your attentions."

"My attentions? I merely told the child she could ride the seesaw as often as she wished. Are you jealous, Priscilla?"

I held back laughter that bubbled up at his absurd question. "Hardly, Kenton, but I'm fond of Gia. I wouldn't want her hurt."

"You speak as though I'm some roving miscreant looking to harm young women."

His words, meant as a jest, sounded more ominous than humorous. "You know that isn't what I meant. But a fourteen-year-old girl may get the wrong impression when a man such as yourself offers to pay for amusements and the like. Besides, I don't think her brother approves."

"Moretti's approval or disapproval means little to me. I'll not be cowed by an immigrant's whims, especially here. I'm one of Tennessee's sons, with all the rights of citizenship. What is he but a—?"

"Stop this, Kenton." I wouldn't let him continue, guessing at the ugly word he intended to use to describe an Italian immigrant. Why must he act so contrary? "Both Morettis are hardworking and kind. Please show them respect, or I will ask you to leave us."

Kenton's glare narrowed. "Your father wanted to know what was wrong last night after you left the table in such a huff. I answered him honestly. You've become far too outspoken for your own good. You have it in your head that a woman in your position has some say in her future, but the reality is you don't. Your father has agreed to our marriage. It's time you accepted it as well."

I watched him stride toward Gia and Luca. She giggled at something he said as she looked adoringly at him.

With a smirk on his face, he turned, no doubt making certain I noticed.

Chapter Thirteen

Betty Ann, Lucille, and I sat on the black-and-white marble floor of the hotel lobby, surrounded by piles of Christmas decorations, while Ella Fitzgerald's upbeat version of "Let It Snow! Let It Snow! Let It Snow!" played on the radio. I'd forgotten we had so many boxes of holiday decor. After Mr. Hays, the maintenance man, brought them up from the basement, Betty Ann and I had enlisted Lucille's help sorting through them. Thousands of sparkly strands of tinsel; dozens of blown-glass ornaments in various shapes, many with glitter glued in swirly designs; Santa and snowmen figurines; and way too many strings of colorful cone-shaped lights, tangled in a gigantic knot.

Jason arrived in the midst of this. I knew by the look on his face he had news.

"I've just come from the library." Excitement filled his voice and his blue eyes. "You'll never believe what I've discovered about Miss Nichols."

He had my attention.

"Why don't you two go talk?" Betty Ann smiled. "We'll keep sorting and then you can show us where it all goes."

I stood and stretched stiff muscles. "Thanks. I won't be long."

Ignoring Lucille's I-told-you-he-was-interested-in-you look, I followed Jason across the lobby to a grouping of chairs where we would have some privacy.

I had to admit Betty Ann was a genuinely nice person. In the few days she'd been with us, a number of guests had remarked on how helpful and courteous she was. Emmett, too, had taken to her quickly. They'd had a wonderful time together yesterday while Mr. Corsini visited with us.

"I know it's not exactly the same," she'd said later as we hunted among musty-smelling cardboard boxes in the basement storage room, setting aside those marked *Christmas* for Mr. Hays. "But after taking care of my parents until their deaths, I have much more empathy for families like yours. I'm sure it hasn't been easy, yet your parents gave Emmett a wonderful life he wouldn't have had if he'd been institutionalized. There may still come a day, after you have a family of your own and your father isn't able to care for him anymore, when an institution will be the only option. But whether or not that day ever comes, know that you and your father are in my prayers."

Her words stayed with me long after I'd snuggled under the warm covers of my bed. I could hear Emmett in his room next to mine, muttering and moving things around—his nightly routine, Dad called it.

As I lay there thinking about the praise Betty Ann bestowed on Dad, Mama, and me for our sacrifice, shame filled every crevice of my being. I'd resented Emmett for most of my life. Loved him, yes, but resented that he was different from the brothers of my friends. That he took up all our mother's energy and left me with very little time alone with her.

But Betty Ann's comments reminded me that my parents had made a difficult decision all those years ago when Emmett was born. Dad never talked about it, but I remembered the day I found Mama in her room, crying. I must have been about ten years old, making Emmett five. A large manila envelope lay on the bed next to her, its contents sprawled across the flower-print spread.

Mama'd wiped her eyes and sat up. She'd patted the mattress, and I'd crawled up beside her.

"Why are you crying, Mama?" I'd asked, curious but not concerned.

She tucked me against her side, a place I'd rarely occupied since Emmett's birth. "I'm just a little sad, sweetheart. Daddy believes your brother should go live in a place where doctors and nurses would take care of him instead of me."

My ten-year-old heart had leaped with excitement at the prospect of having my mother to myself again. It hadn't happened, of course. I couldn't recall if my parents argued or how the decision was made to keep Emmett at home, but Mama had taken wonderful care of her boy up until the day she died.

"Looks like you ladies are working hard." Jason sank onto the soft velvet upholstery of a chair near the windows.

I fell into a matching one, exhausted from the morning's labor. "Too bad we had to change our plans. Today is supposed to be my day off."

We'd intended to visit the Parthenon today, but the weather turned nasty, with rain and even a bit of sleet mixed in. Jason headed to the library instead while Betty Ann, Lucille, and I tackled the holiday decorations. He hadn't mentioned why he'd gone to the library, but I assumed it had to do with his work. Now he had me curious about the secrets he'd unearthed regarding our resident recluse.

"Let me know if you need help decking the halls, as they say." He grinned.

"I can't believe it's already the middle of December, yet not one Christmas decoration adorns the hotel. Betty Ann is determined to remedy that, pronto. I'm sure your name is on her list of 'nice' helpers." I switched gears. "So what have you discovered about Miss Nichols that I wouldn't believe? Because at this point, I think I'd believe just about anything."

He took out a small notepad from his coat pocket. "In law school, they teach us to search through old newspapers and such for clues to the past. Lucky for us, the Nashville Public Library has hundreds of issues of past newspapers on microfilm." He opened his notepad. "I got curious about Miss Nichols after hearing Mr. Corsini's story. I kept wondering why she disappeared and then reappeared years later here at the Maxwell."

I sat on the edge of my chair, completely enthralled. "Did you discover what happened to her and Luca?"

"Unfortunately, no." He glanced at his notepad. "But I did discover some rather interesting facts about our Miss Nichols."

"Tell me."

"It turns out she was quite an activist in her day."

"An activist? For what?"

"For women's rights, mostly. But she was also involved in . . . well . . ." He paused and looked at me. "Let's just say she was very vocal about the evils of prostitution. I found several articles about her contributions to the Woman's Christian Temperance Union and their efforts to bring change."

"Temperance Union? Wouldn't that have been more about alcohol and Prohibition? What does it have to do with . . . the other?" Heat radiated up my neck. Even though it was 1961,

I felt uncomfortable discussing prostitution with a young man. I couldn't imagine introverted Miss Nichols being involved in such a movement, even as a young woman, in the early 1900s when respectable ladies most definitely did not discuss such things.

He referred to his notebook again. "According to one of the articles, the WCTU was instrumental in raising the age of consent—" He stopped and looked up. "You know what that means, right?"

I nodded, embarrassed and yet intrigued by the whole thing.

"Anyway, Miss Nichols is listed as one of the leaders of the charge, so to speak, here in Tennessee. With a lot of work, they got the legal age of consent raised to eighteen years. That was back in 1920."

I gathered my courage to ask *the* question. "What was the age prior to that?"

A troubled frown creased his brow. "Unbelievably, it was ten years of age. Which, sadly, was quite common throughout the country in those days."

I sat, stunned by this information. "And Miss Nichols helped get the laws changed? Wow."

I heard the incredulity in my own voice, but I had a difficult time picturing old, odd Miss Nichols at the forefront of such a battle, arguing with lawmakers about something so . . . so . . . indelicate. Yet the evidence revealed a woman determined to make a difference, no matter what society or even propriety dictated.

A question popped into my mind.

How had she found the kind of courage it took to get involved in such an unseemly cause? To take the risk, know-ing many people would surely oppose and reject her? Was she simply born brave, or had life and circumstances taught her lessons that molded her into the activist we saw emerging in the news stories?

Life had certainly taught me some hard lessons lately. But what was I supposed to do with them? Would I be willing to get involved in a cause I believed in, the way Miss Nichols had? The way Jason was doing even now with his work for civil rights?

A ready answer didn't come.

"It's pretty impressive," Jason said, tapping his pen on the notebook. "Back then, women didn't have the vote, so male lawmakers often paid no attention to the wants and wishes of the female population."

I scowled. "The jerks."

"Determined women like Miss Nichols, however, found a way around them. According to my research, petitions played a major role in the campaign to change the laws. Many of these petitions were drafted by leaders in the WCTU, and Miss Nichols is cited as helping draft at least one of them." He flipped a couple pages in the notebook, then nodded. "She also helped collect signatures as well as solicited letters of support from prominent citizens."

"I'm shocked." Jason's discoveries were astounding.

His mouth tipped in a lopsided grin when he looked at me. "I think I like your Miss Nichols. I hope I can meet her someday. I'd like to hear her story."

I heaved a sigh. "Unfortunately, she hasn't improved. Dad visited her this morning. She's not able to speak much, but she did try to communicate with him. He reassured her all her belongings were safe, and that seemed to calm her."

"Maybe we can go see her together sometime."

"I'd like to tell her about our conversation with Mr. Corsini. I wonder if she'd remember him."

"I'd like to know more about her activism. What led her to get involved and that sort of thing."

I smiled. "You two do have a few things in common."

He leaned back in his chair, a look of serious contemplation on his face. "Life is funny, isn't it? Miss Nichols was our age when she visited the exposition and met Mr. Corsini. She was planning to spend a fun day at Vanity Fair, but then something happened. Something that, for all intents and purposes, may have altered everything about her life."

"But what? What happened?"

"I don't know," he said, his gaze intense. "But I have a feeling the answer to that question holds the key to why she ended up living alone here at the Maxwell House for more than twenty years."

───────────

Despite the cloud of gloom Kenton brought with him, we set off to enjoy ourselves in Vanity Fair. There were so many fascinating exhibits and amusements, I wondered if we would see them all in one day.

Delicious aromas filled the air when we passed the Old Vienna Restaurant on our way to inspect two log cabins brought down from the mountains of Tennessee, complete with a working moonshine still that fascinated Kenton. Two other famous log cabins were also reconstructed in the park—one the birthplace of President Abraham Lincoln and the other of Jefferson Davis, both Kentuckians. Luca, especially, felt a kinship to the two men whose humble beginnings didn't prevent them from taking their place in history.

Up ahead, a small building that resembled something you'd find in Arabia, decorated with live palm trees in the yard and a rounded dome on its roof, caught our attention.

My map declared it the Thuss Photographic Gallery, where W. G. and A. J. Thuss, the men charged with photographing the exposition, would also take pictures of willing—and paying—fairgoers. Two men in suits and bowler hats stood outside the arched doorway, hawking their trade to everyone who passed by.

Kenton stopped and turned to me, a few steps behind him. "Shall we have our photograph made, Priscilla? To remind us of our courtship days when we're old and gray?" His grin told me he took pleasure in goading me.

I offered a stiff smile. "I think not. We haven't the time." I walked past him, his low chuckle irritating, as he knew it would.

"What about you, Miss Moretti? Would you like your photograph taken? A pretty young woman such as yourself should have your likeness made."

"May I?"

Her eager voice brought me to an abrupt halt, and I nearly collided with Luca, who'd also stopped. I turned to intervene when Luca retraced his steps to where Gia stood near Kenton.

"Come, Gia. We don't have the money for a photograph." He put his hand on her elbow to steer her away.

"I insist on paying for it, Moretti." Kenton removed a fat leather purse from his pocket. It rattled with coins. "I'm quite sure a hackney driver doesn't make enough for such extravagances, so I'm happy to give your sister this pleasure."

Luca's facial expression didn't change, but his shoulders stiffened. "Thank you, *signor*, but my sister is under my care. We cannot accept such a generous offer."

The two men locked eyes. I admired Luca's courage, but I also knew Kenton could make trouble for him if he chose.

"It's nice of you to offer to have our photographs made, Kenton," I said, hoping to soothe male egos before things became ugly, "but we're not dressed for it. Perhaps we can come back another day."

Several seconds passed before Kenton conceded. "Have it your way . . . this time." He returned his purse to his pocket and strode away.

Gia jerked out of her brother's grip. "I wish you would stop treating me like a child. I would have enjoyed having my photograph taken."

At Luca's stern look and slight nod toward me—a reminder, no doubt, that she was still on duty as my maid—her furor faded.

"Forgive me, miss." She hung her head. "I let the excitement get to me." Her dark eyes reflected her sincerity.

"I'm not angry. Perhaps tomorrow we will dress ourselves in our finery and have our picture made so I will always remember sweet Gia who attended me so well." I glanced at Luca, hoping he wouldn't deny her the opportunity.

After a moment, he nodded. "*Grazie, signorina*. For understanding."

We continued along the avenue and found Kenton waiting for us in front of the Chinese Village. Crowds moved up and down wide concrete steps in front of a tall pagoda. Several other similar buildings stood on either side.

"I can't imagine we'd have any interest in this exhibit." His voice dripped with disdain. "It's obvious China isn't up to our modern ways."

"On the contrary." I turned toward the stairs. "Since it's unlikely any of us will ever travel to that part of the world, this will be a fascinating study of their culture. Don't you agree?" I directed my question to Luca and Gia, who both nodded in agreement. Whether they did so because of my position as their employer or because it was their true sentiment didn't concern me. I simply refused to let Kenton's snobbery dictate my day.

He didn't move, a pillar of rigid disapproval. "I'll wait here."

For a brief moment, I felt sorry for him. He'd been raised to think himself better than others less fortunate or different. His father was like-minded, and his grandfather, who'd been in the slave trade business before the war. It was no surprise that Kenton's pretentiousness only grew as he matured.

I retraced my steps and held out my hand to him. Not with friendship or affection, but a peace offering that harkened back to the days of our childhood. He was part of my life, for good or bad. "Come with us, Kenton. It will be exciting to see how people on the opposite side of the world live. Besides—" I grinned—"I've heard there is a real opium den inside. You wouldn't want to miss that, would you?"

His brow rose. "Priscilla Nichols, what would your mother say if she heard you speak of such a thing?" A moment later, he shrugged. "All right. You win. Let us see this Chinese village. But I warn you: If you're jesting about the opium den, I will pay you back tenfold."

Chapter Fourteen

On Sunday, we dined in the hotel restaurant, located in the famous dining room on the second floor. Despite the Maxwell losing her place as the grande dame of Nashville a number of years ago, this room, with its columns, elegant wallpaper, and chandeliers, gave evidence of glorious bygone days when presidents, movie stars, and all manner of famous—and infamous—guests dined on loin of veal with Madeira sauce, prairie grouse with currant jelly, and other chef-prepared delicacies. The annual Christmas Day dinner, especially, drew people from all over the world, celebrating long into the night with English plum pudding, lady cakes, and oranges in sherry wine.

Today, however, we'd enjoyed a simple repast of pot roast and mashed potatoes, a Sunday favorite of the residents. It reminded them of better times, I thought, of when they lived not in an aging hotel with strangers, but in homes filled with loved ones.

"That was a wonderful meal. Thank you, Mr. Whitfield."

Jason laid his linen napkin on the table, exuding perfect Southern manners.

He and Betty Ann had joined us for services this morning at church, a block down the street from the hotel. With the December weather turning mild again, we'd walked there together, enjoying the sunshine and the holiday decorations along the route. Dad, in a burst of unusual cheeriness, extended the invitation to lunch at the hotel, which had been readily accepted by both our guests.

I didn't mind. I'd become quite fond of them both, for different reasons, of course.

Jason was fast becoming someone I wanted to spend time with. We talked about everything, from serious issues like civil rights and the role of US troops in Vietnam, to lighter topics like the latest music on the radio and what went better with hamburgers: french fries or onion rings. We even had a lengthy discussion about the film *Breakfast at Tiffany's*, still showing down the street at the Crescent theatre despite its October release. Jason read that Truman Capote wanted Marilyn Monroe as the star, but we both agreed no one could have played the role of Holly Golightly better than Audrey Hepburn.

Betty Ann, on the other hand, was the friend I hadn't known I needed. Even with our age difference, we had great fun decorating the hotel lobby and other public rooms, preparing for Christmas, just one week away. I always enjoyed time with Lucille, and Bea before she moved to Texas, but conversations with them usually gravitated to boys or the latest hairstyle. Yesterday, while Betty Ann and I decorated the fourteen-foot noble fir tree Dad had delivered for the lobby, she told me she'd dreamed of becoming a teacher when she was a young woman. Marriage and the war ended her hopes, but her admission inspired me to confide that I, too, had considered getting my teacher's certificate. What I didn't say was that after Mama's death and spending more time with Emmett, I'd started to think about the children who were like my brother. They needed someone who understood them.

But that was a secret I hadn't told anyone. The very thought of pursuing it terrified me, yet the idea continued to float through my mind every so often.

Did I possess the kind of courage I would need to take a stand for the Emmetts in this world? Especially when others with far more experience—like the school principal—believed children like Emmett didn't belong in public school? I hadn't come up with an answer to that question yet, but Mama's sudden death taught me that I couldn't let fear rule me and miss an opportunity to do something meaningful.

"Can we get ice cream?" Emmett asked, fidgeting now that he'd finished his meal. Mama used to call his uncontrollable movements "restless energy" and would take him for long walks to help him work it out of his system.

"That sounds like a fine idea," Dad said, more relaxed than I'd seen him in ages. This surprised me, especially with Christmas only one week away. Reservations for Christmas Day dinner were still coming in, and though we didn't host crowds of guests as they'd done in the early 1900s, it promised to be a busy day.

Dad's glance took us all in, but it lingered on Betty Ann. "Would you like to join us? The ice cream parlor has quite a few new flavors for the holidays."

"I want chocolate. With a cherry." Emmett rocked forward and back in his chair.

Jason glanced at me. We'd made plans to scour the newspaper clippings in the back of Miss Nichols's scrapbook to see if we could put some of the puzzle pieces of her life together. "I don't think I could eat another bite, but . . ." His voice trailed, a question in his eyes.

"I don't think I could either." I smiled at Betty Ann. "Why don't you go with Dad and Emmett? Jason and I are anxious to compare some of his library findings to the articles in the scrapbook."

"My, you two are becoming quite the detectives. It's a shame Miss Nichols herself isn't able to answer your questions." Dad's attention returned to Betty Ann. "Emmett and I would be pleased to have you join us."

"Thank you, Dan. I believe I will."

We rose from our seats. Dad greeted several guests on our way to the exit and introduced Betty Ann to a few residents who hadn't met her yet. Mrs. Ruth sat at a table with two other ladies. When Dad and Betty Ann stopped to say hello, Mrs. Ruth grasped Betty Ann's hand.

"I think you're just what we needed around here, dear. Don't you agree, Mr. Whitfield?"

I was certain everyone but Dad guessed the meaning behind Mrs. Ruth's comment. Even though it had been over a year since Mama passed away, I wasn't sure any of us—Dad included—was ready for the kind of changes Mrs. Ruth's words brought to mind.

Our group made our way down the marble stairs to the lobby.

"My, doesn't everything look festive?" Dad said, clearly pleased with our hard work. Wreaths, garland, red ribbons, and colorful lights transformed the cavernous lobby into a holiday wonderland. "You ladies did an excellent job getting the Maxwell ready for Christmas."

"We had fun." I exchanged a smile with Betty Ann. Surprisingly, it was true. I really had enjoyed decorating the hotel with her, a job I'd been dreading.

We parted ways, with Emmett leading Dad and Betty Ann down the corridor to where the small ice cream parlor was located. It had been a sweet shop back in the early years of the hotel's existence and still boasted the original barstools and counter.

"Your dad's right," Jason said as we reached the interior door to our apartment. "I wish we could ask Miss Nichols what happened the day she and Luca went to the park."

"I know, but she's such a private woman." I shrugged before unlocking the door. "I'm not sure what she would think about us digging into her personal life."

Jason followed me into the living room. "I've thought about that. Of course, we aren't doing it for ulterior motives. It would be nice if at the end of our investigation, we found some long-lost family member or someone who would take an interest in her."

I grinned. "You really are on the side of justice, aren't you? You want to help everyone, including old Miss Nichols."

He chuckled. "My mother calls me her Good Samaritan."

We sat on the sofa and rested the scrapbook on our knees.

"Do you mind if we look through the pages again before getting to the newspaper articles?" I asked. "I love looking at the memorabilia."

"We have all afternoon."

I turned the pages slowly, studying each item on each page. We both pointed out things we hadn't noticed before. A ticket stub to the Chinese Village in Vanity Fair. A folded map of the park. Even the placement of dried flowers didn't seem so random anymore. Pink water lilies were glued to the page with a picture of Lake Katherine, while a red rose was pressed into the menu from a place called the Blue Grotto.

When I turned the last page, I realized it was actually two

COUNT THE NIGHTS BY STARS

pages stuck together. "I don't want to tear them," I said after working to no avail to get them apart.

"Maybe if we slid a knife between the pages, they might loosen without tearing."

After I retrieved a thin knife from the kitchen, I attempted to slide the tip between the tops of the two pages with utmost care. It worked. Centimeter by centimeter, the pages began to slowly come apart. "I feel like a surgeon," I joked.

"Or one of the shepherds who discovered the Dead Sea Scrolls."

"Goodness, that's quite the comparison."

He winked. "I told you I was a history nut."

With painstaking effort, I managed to separate the pages without doing much damage to them. Only one corner suffered a slight tear.

Our reward was two full pages of memorabilia, including a postcard. The opposite page, however, held something quite unexpected.

A photograph.

"Is that Miss Nichols?" Jason asked, leaning in to get a good look at the serious-faced woman pictured in the black-and-white photograph. She appeared to be in her twenties and wore a large hat and high-necked blouse with puffed sleeves.

I, too, leaned in to study the picture. "I'm not sure. It's hard to say."

"I wonder if there might be something written on the back that would tell us who she is," Jason suggested.

I bit my lip. "I hate to pry off something Miss Nichols glued to the pages all those years ago."

Jason considered my statement. "True, but if it helps us discover something that might benefit Miss Nichols, wouldn't it be worth it? We can always glue the picture back. No harm done."

His suggestion made sense. "All right."

I took up the knife again. With the same care I'd used prying the pages apart, I carefully slid the knife under the edge of the picture. The glue here wasn't as thick, and the picture was free within moments.

I turned it over, but my shoulders slumped. "All it has is a stamp that says 'Thuss Photography.'"

"Maybe the postcard will give us a hint. The others seemed related to the items glued to the pages where we found them."

I grinned. "Dad's right. You'd make a great police detective if you ever decide to change careers."

The postcard showed several small pictures of structures, titled "The Unique Shapes of the Exposition." There was a replica of the Alamo in Texas, a large beehive with a door and windows, a Native American tepee, and a small building with a dome and palm trees out front.

It came off the page easily. I read the faded handwriting on the back aloud.

"Dearest Luca,

I had my photograph taken at the expo today. I promised Gia we'd have our picture made, and we will once we are all together again. In the meantime, I will keep this one safe for you. Mr. Thuss tried to get me to smile, but I couldn't. Not until I'm in your arms again. Hurry back to me, my darling.

Yours, Peaches"

My gaze returned to the picture of the woman. "This is Peaches."

Jason nodded. "Yes, but is it also Miss Nichols?"

The answer to that question remained a mystery.

Dad and Emmett returned to the apartment a short time later. I couldn't wait to show Dad the picture.

"We found this in the scrapbook." I handed it to him before he'd even had a chance to say hello.

Emmett headed down the hall to his bedroom. His door slammed shut—a bad habit Mama'd never been able to get him to quit.

Jason sent me a concerned look. "Is he all right?"

"Yes. It's perfectly normal." I returned my attention to Dad. "Do you think this is Miss Nichols? Or maybe a friend or a relative?"

Dad took off his dark-rimmed glasses to study the photograph. After a long moment, he handed it back to me. "It's hard to say. There's a bit of resemblance to Priscilla, especially around the eyes, but I couldn't be certain."

I slumped back down on the sofa, disappointed. "The postcard we found with it says Peaches had her photograph taken for Luca. We think this is it."

"That's something, at least. Any luck with the newspaper articles?" He glanced between Jason and me.

"We haven't had a chance to review them yet." Jason shrugged. "I guess we got a bit sidetracked by the photograph."

"Well, I think I'll go read for a while. Have fun digging into the mystery. I believe you're getting close." He headed down the hall, although he stopped at Emmett's room to remind him not to slam the door. I couldn't hear my brother's reply, but I had little confidence this would be the last slamming door we heard.

Jason turned to the back of the scrapbook, where the newspaper clippings were tucked.

"Now that we know Miss Nichols became involved in

women's suffrage and women's rights, it makes more sense why she would have articles about the problem of prostitution." He sorted the clippings by date, if one was available.

"The oldest ones are about the young women who disappeared from the exposition." He paused, a frown deepening with each tick from the clock. "You don't suppose . . ." He shook his head. "No, that couldn't be what happened."

I hated to interrupt his private conversation with himself, but I wanted to know what he was talking about. "I don't suppose what, and what couldn't have happened?"

He riffled through the articles and pulled one out. "This one says an anonymous person came forward with information about the kidnapping and selling of young women." He looked up. "You don't suppose Miss Nichols was one of those women, do you? Mr. Corsini said she disappeared the day he drove her to the park."

My eyes widened. "Surely not."

"Then why did she disappear? Why would she keep articles about all of that unpleasantness?"

I didn't have an answer. "Mr. Corsini said his boss, Luca Moretti, also disappeared. He isn't mentioned in the newspaper article, is he?"

Jason bent his head, muttered under his breath a time or two, before he shook his head. "No mention in this article." He searched through the other clippings, scanning some, reading others. None of them had anything about Luca Moretti.

We sat in silence a long time. My mind whirled with the possibility that Miss Nichols had suffered some great tragedy that left her scarred and afraid of . . . what? People? Love? Why else would she have found her way back to the Maxwell House Hotel, where the story of the scrapbook began, only to live here for twenty years, alone?

"I know this sounds crazy, since the expo took place over sixty years ago, but I wish we could retrace her steps. You know, walk where she walked, see what she saw." Jason tapped out his frustration on his knee.

An idea popped into my head. "Didn't we see a map of Exposition Park here in the scrapbook?"

His face lit up. "Are you thinking what I'm thinking?"

I laughed. "I don't know, but let's find the map and we'll see if we're right . . . assuming we're thinking the same thing."

He chuckled as he flipped pages until he came to the one with the map glued to it. The knife wasn't required this time, as the yellowed paper easily became unattached with a little tug.

With deliberate care, Jason slowly unfolded it and spread it across the scrapbook. The black-and-white map looked hand-drawn before it had no doubt been mass printed, with *Tennessee Centennial and International Exposition* in bold letters off to the left. Small squares, rectangles, and circles had tiny writing inside them, and all were connected by what must be paths or roads.

But what caught my attention—and Jason's too, apparently—were the marks and notations that were added later.

Jason looked at me, his eyes shining.

"You were right," we said at the same time, then laughed at ourselves.

"Do we go now?" he asked.

I didn't hesitate. "Absolutely."

Chapter Fifteen

Like dozens of other fairgoers, we sat on the grass in the cool shade of the trees surrounding Lake Watauga, enjoying delicious pork sandwiches on crusty bread we'd purchased from a vendor in the Cuban Village. I'd never tasted anything like it, with its spices and sauce, and quite honestly wished for another one after finishing the last bite.

"Where should we go next?" I glanced at the pyramid-shaped Shelby County building nearby. There were still so many interesting sights we had yet to explore. I felt relaxed and happy despite Kenton's continued grousing, no matter what exhibit we ventured to see.

He complained about the crowds. He complained about the heat. His rude remarks about the different cultures represented in Vanity Fair grated on me to the point I longed for any excuse to escape his company, perhaps even sneaking away when he wasn't looking. The Cyclorama of the Battle of Gettysburg was the only exhibit he fully embraced, yet he bemoaned the indisputable fact that the victory had gone not to his beloved South but to the North. His statements were overheard by a former Confederate soldier, and the two had an animated conversation for quite some time.

"The Streets of Cairo looks interesting," Luca said from where he reclined nearby, propped up by one elbow.

I envied him, wishing I could stretch out on the soft grass and take a nap instead of remaining in a ladylike position, with my legs folded beneath my skirt. Gia sat next to me in much the same position, gazing out to where ducks and children played near the water's edge. Only Kenton had insisted on renting a folding camp chair for ten cents at one of the stands near the lake, stating he refused to sit on the ground and get grass stains on his trousers.

"I'd very much like to see a show in the Egyptian Theatre." I recalled passing the elaborate entrance to the Cairo exhibit on our way to lunch and looked forward to exploring what lay hidden behind the high walls. "The unusual music can be heard all through Vanity Fair."

"The Streets of Cairo looks dirty and noisy." Kenton tossed his mostly uneaten sandwich to the ground, his facial expression making it obvious he didn't enjoy the spicy meat. "Those nasty camels they're giving rides on are fouling up the place. I heard they're even running donkey races down Cairo Avenue at night. I have no wish to soil my shoes with that mess."

I closed my eyes and inhaled a deep, calming breath. Seeing the exposition with Kenton was like seeing it with an unpleasant child.

When I opened my eyes, I offered him a tight smile. "Why don't you decide what we should see next."

He appeared rather surprised by my suggestion. "If you're sincere, I'd like to be done with Vanity Fair. It's positively suffocating. We could tour the Transportation Building. We haven't seen it yet."

Gia glanced toward the imposing building behind us, and her shoulders wilted a bit. I was sure she felt as disappointed as I with his serious and studious proposal, but I couldn't retract my offer. While I did look forward to seeing the latest in railway travel, from dining cars to comfortable sleeping cars, as well as wagons, carriages from Europe, and even bicycles, today my heart was set on the amusements the park offered.

"Perhaps after we've toured the exhibit, we can ride the carousel. It's located directly behind the Transportation Building."

"Can we, miss?" Gia's face brightened. She truly was still a girl in many ways, despite her womanly figure and grown-up responsibilities.

With our destination decided, we brought our picnic to an end. I gathered the paper wrappings our sandwiches came in while Gia took leftover bread crusts to the ducks gathered on the edge of the lake.

"*Signorina*, may I assist you?"

I looked up to find Luca standing near me, with his hands outstretched to help me rise.

"Thank you." I grasped hold, feeling strength in them. With ease, he had me on my feet. When I looked into his eyes, I nearly got lost in the warmth I found there.

How much time passed, with us standing there holding hands, I knew not, but a shriek from the lake's edge drew us out of the strange yet wonderful spell.

When I turned toward the sound, I gasped. Gia was on the ground, surrounded by squawking ducks as well as an angry-looking swan, its enormous wings spread wide.

Luca dashed to his sister, with Kenton and me on his heels. Luca shouted at the gang of fowl, driving them away.

"Are you hurt?" He knelt beside her, his concern for his sister showing in every movement as he carefully examined her.

"My ankle." She grimaced when he touched it. "I twisted it when I fell. That horrible swan attacked me."

Luca's worried gaze met mine. "I must take her to the infirmary."

"I don't want to be a nuisance." Gia looked from me to Luca. "Help me up, Brother. I'm sure I can walk."

Blessedly, it didn't appear as though her ankle was broken, but it was clear she could not amble about the park.

"I should take her back to the hotel," Luca said, regret mingling with worry in his eyes.

"Maybe we should all return to the hotel," I said, disappointed.

"No, miss." Gia cast a pleading look between me and Luca. "You shouldn't have your day spoiled because I've been foolish and twisted my ankle."

I appreciated her words, but I had no desire to remain at the park with only Kenton for company. "Returning to the hotel is for the best."

With that settled, we slowly made our way to the park entrance, with Luca and me on either side of Gia, assisting her as she limped along. To our surprise, we spotted Luca's rig in line with other carriages waiting for a fare. When Carmelo saw us, he leaped down and came forward.

"I'm glad to see you," Luca said. "Gia has injured her ankle, and we need to return to the Maxwell." He helped his sister into the carriage.

I was about to climb in beside her when Kenton's outstretched arm blocked my path.

"Why don't you remain here, Priscilla? As Miss Moretti said, it seems unnecessary for everyone's day to be ruined. It *was* your idea to visit every attraction in Vanity Fair today, was it not?" He glanced at Gia before returning his attention to me. "Since I'm ready to leave, I can escort Miss Moretti to the Maxwell and see that the doctor examines her. Moretti can escort you safely to your next amusement."

His offer took me by surprise, considering his position only a few days ago about my being alone in Luca's presence. Before I could respond, however, Gia eagerly nodded.

"Yes, miss, that's a wonderful plan. I don't wish to be the cause of you missing the opera singer you spoke of. I will be fine, and my brother will take excellent care of you, won't you, Luca?"

"There," Kenton said, not waiting for Luca's answer as he climbed in to take the seat opposite Gia. He closed the door with finality. "I'll see you back at the hotel later, Priscilla. Perhaps we can have dinner together."

I sought Luca's face. His expression told me he wasn't happy with the plan, but with Kenton ensconced in the carriage, there was little he could do.

"I will check on you when we return. Ask Mrs. Smith to bring you a tray so there's no need to leave your bed."

Gia nodded, then cast a shy look across to Kenton. It

occurred to me that Gia was not disappointed to find herself alone with him. The thought was not a pleasant one.

Carmelo climbed onto the driver's seat, and we watched them set off. Gia waved at us one last time.

When they were out of sight, I turned to Luca, his displeasure obvious in his knit brow. "Mr. Moretti, now that we're alone and can discuss the situation without interference, if you wish to return to the hotel, I'm happy to oblige. I wouldn't want to keep you here if you'd rather be with your sister." I paused. "Besides, it isn't quite proper for the two of us to be here without another person to act as chaperone."

He glanced in the direction the carriage had gone before returning his attention to me. "I believe she will be fine with rest. There isn't anything I could do for her at the hotel, as she lives in the women's dormitory in the basement. So," he said with a slight shrug, "I am at your service, *signorina*. But if you prefer to return to the hotel, we can take the streetcar."

The dilemma we faced—to stay at the fair unchaperoned or leave—might have mattered in a different, more intimate setting, but who could accuse us of anything untoward with thousands of people surrounding us every moment? Besides, the same would have been true had Kenton remained. I knew my father was nearby, either at the Railway Exhibit or the Centennial Club House. I could seek his approval at any time should someone question my being accompanied by an unmarried male.

With a hint of guilt, I couldn't help but see Gia's unfortunate accident as a sort of answer to my earlier wish to be free of Kenton. I would never have wanted her to injure herself, but his departure was like receiving a fresh start on the day.

"If you're certain you don't feel you're needed at the hotel, I would like to stay."

A slow smile spread across his face. "As you wish."

I turned in a circle, feeling like a child who'd slipped away from her overbearing nanny. Happily, we were free to choose where to go and what to see without Kenton's disapproval and grumbling to spoil the fun.

"Where should we go next?" I asked.

When I met his gaze, we both grinned.

"The Streets of Cairo," we said in unison.

Luca winked. "I've always wanted to ride a camel."

Our laughter drew the attention of nearby picnickers, but I didn't care.

Not one bit.

———————————

Centennial Park sat nestled in the heart of Nashville, with Vanderbilt University a stone's throw away. I'd never paid much attention to the area, having little reason to come to this part of town. We'd visited the Parthenon with Mama a number of times and walked around the small lake, but I hadn't thought it any more special than other parks in the city.

Today, however, I felt a strange sense of history come to life as we drove down Church Street in Jason's 1957 sun-gold Ford Thunderbird. This was the same path Miss Nichols would have traveled, going from the Maxwell to the park, riding in a carriage driven by a teenage Mr. Corsini.

I noticed several young men admiring Jason's car as we waited at an intersection. "I think those guys would like Santa Claus to bring them a car like this for Christmas," I joked.

He seemed a bit embarrassed. "Dad bought it for my birthday a few years ago. I told him a civil rights attorney shouldn't show up to his clients' homes in a T-Bird, but he wouldn't listen. I think he hopes I'll give up my dream and join him as a corporate lawyer after I finish school. He's afraid I'll turn into a beatnik or something if I pursue civil rights."

I studied him as we cruised down the wide avenue, past the holiday-themed windows of Cain-Sloan and Harveys department stores. Every year the two stores competed to see who could outdo the other as far as decorations and sales went. I personally preferred Harveys, but that was probably because I had fond memories of riding the carousel on the third floor as a child.

"What inspired you to want to go into that area of law?" I asked, remembering how excited he was when he shared about his meeting with Mr. Looby. The seasoned civil rights leader had left an impression on Jason that was evident.

He grew thoughtful. "I have a friend who's black. Noah and I grew up together, but not in the way that sounds. He's the son of our housekeeper. For a long time, I didn't think there was much difference between us other than the color of our skin. I was wrong. We couldn't attend the same school, eat at the same restaurant, or even sit together in the movie theatre." He glanced at me. "It wasn't right, but there wasn't anything he or I could do about it. I want to join the fight to change all that."

I admired his passion. "For what it's worth, I think what you're doing, and hoping to do in the future, is really great. The world needs more people willing to stand up for what's right and good."

He smiled. "That's exactly what Mr. Looby said to me the other day. I told him that, as a white man, I sometimes felt unworthy of working alongside black people in the fight for civil rights. I mean, what do I know about what they've gone through?"

I nodded when he glanced over at me, perfectly understanding what he meant. I'd felt it too.

"But Mr. Looby said civil rights are important to everyone, no matter the color of their skin. He reminded me about how Hitler targeted people of Jewish descent. His hatred for them didn't have anything to do with skin color."

Once again, the thought of working with children like Emmett circled my mind. Was that my calling, the way civil rights work was Jason's? The way standing up for women's rights and changing unfair laws had been Miss Nichols's? I'd been studying to become an accountant when I had to leave school. After Mama's death and helping Dad with the hotel the past year, the thought of spending my days staring at numbers didn't appeal anymore. The world had plenty of accountants, but Emmett only had one sister.

Yet I wasn't brave or clever like Jason and Miss Nichols. Fear and doubt were my companions. Did I have what it took to help change things for the better for Emmett and others?

A ready answer didn't come.

Jason turned the car into the parking area next to the Parthenon, pulled into a marked spot, and shut off the engine.

"I think that's why I find Miss Nichols's story so intriguing." He picked up the map of the exposition we'd found in the scrapbook and tapped it against the steering wheel. "From the few articles I've read on her activism, I think she was someone who felt the same way we do. She wasn't satisfied to sit on the sidelines. She got out there and did something about the injustices she saw. Seems like the world would be a better place if we all did our part, you know?"

I did.

I had a long way to go and a lot to learn, but something inside me stirred to life at the thought of joining Jason and Miss Nichols. To do something that would help not only my brother, but the brothers and sisters, sons and daughters, of families like mine.

We exited the car a short distance from the life-size Nativity scene erected by Harveys every December, complete with barnyard animals, camels, palm trees, and strings of white lights that came on at dark. The mild weather kept it from feeling much like Christmas, but it was perfect for a day at the park. Quite a few people strolled along the sidewalk that circled the Parthenon, as well as paths around the lake.

"This is amazing." Jason stared up at the replica of the famous Athens, Greece, structure. "The detail is phenomenal. Look at the carvings of the Greek gods above the pillars." He whistled low. "I've read about the Nashville Parthenon and seen pictures of it, but nothing compares to seeing it in real life."

I smiled, pleased with his reaction.

"Can you imagine what people thought of this in 1897?" He shook his head. "The Parthenon, right here in Nashville, Tennessee."

"Dad said all of the buildings were meant to be temporary. That's why they were torn down or moved after the exposition ended."

"Except for the Parthenon."

"Yes, but it had to be rebuilt with permanent materials in the 1920s."

We walked around the entire building, feeling very small compared to the enormous columns that held up the porticos.

"Where was the statue of Pallas Athena?" Jason asked. "I read somewhere it was forty feet tall."

We consulted the map, but it didn't give a location for the

statue. What it did give, however, were clues to the places Miss Nichols visited during the centennial celebration.

"Since the Parthenon and the lake are the only things that remain from the exposition," I said, glancing across a grassy area to the lake, "I think we should start there."

Jason agreed, and we set off.

A small sign gave a brief history of the lake.

"'Lake Watauga is a man-made lake,'" Jason read out loud, "'built for the Tennessee Centennial Exposition of 1897. It is named after the original settlers of Tennessee, who were often referred to as the Watauga or Cumberland settlers.'"

Jason glanced at the map. "It looks like there was a bridge in this area. Someone drew a circle around it on the map."

A hazy memory surfaced. "Do you remember seeing a poster in Miss Nichols's room of the lake with gondolas floating in it? It had a bridge crossing it."

"Wait." He glanced at the map. "I think this bridge was the Rialto Bridge. The one pictured in the postcard that was made to look like the Rialto Bridge in Venice, Italy."

My eyes widened. "Peaches—or Miss Nichols—wrote that she went back to the Rialto to buy a souvenir for Luca to match the one he'd purchased for her. A small replica of the Parthenon."

We both turned to look at the building behind us, resplendent in afternoon sunshine.

"This is where Peaches came," Jason said, a bit of wonder in his voice. "The Rialto Bridge stood right here."

An odd sensation came over me. Not exactly déjà vu, since I'd never spent much time at Centennial Park, but a kind of reverence or respect, perhaps, for the people who'd walked on this very path those many years ago. People who'd lived and loved and dreamed. I'd always considered Miss Nichols an odd bird, but I was fast coming to understand that she'd been far more than the elderly, lonely woman I'd known most of my life.

Or hadn't known, as I was beginning to see.

She'd been a young woman not so unlike myself, possibly in love, if we determined she was indeed Peaches. She'd come to the exposition to enjoy time with family and friends and to make memories that would last a lifetime. Judging by the scrapbook and posters, I had a feeling the exposition had been an important part of her life.

We walked around the lake, discussing what we knew of the exposition, trying to fill in the blanks left on the landscape after the buildings were torn down and most of the parkland was sold to developers. When we came to an empty bench, we sat down, the placid water at our feet.

While Jason studied the map, I tried to imagine Miss Nichols and Luca in this same place sixty-four years earlier. The sights, sounds, and smells would have been worlds different that day. We sat in a quiet park, with birds singing and the occasional voice of a child the only sounds to break the silence. But in 1897, thousands of people would have filled this place. Vendors calling out to passersby, hawking their wares or enticing guests to come see an attraction. Laughter and music from Vanity Fair would have drifted on a summer breeze. Every inch of the two-hundred-acre park would have pulsated with life and excitement in honor of Tennessee's birthday celebration.

Yet I sobered, recalling the newspaper articles in the scrapbook. All was not well. Something evil lurked in the shadow of the Parthenon those many years ago.

Had young women truly disappeared from the exposition, never to be seen again?

If so, had Miss Nichols become entangled in the disturbing story in some way?

These were questions a walk through the park could never answer.

"According to the map, there was a restaurant called the Blue Grotto located on an island," Jason said. He indicated a place on the map with a faded circle of ink around it before pointing to an area across from us. "Somewhere over there."

"Look at this." I showed him where an X had been added near the edge of the lake, not far from where the pyramid-shaped Memphis building had stood. "I wonder what that means."

Jason leaned down to get a closer look. "I don't see any buildings or markings underneath the X. Maybe something is buried there, like on a treasure map."

I chuckled. "I don't believe the people in charge of the park would appreciate it if we dug up the grass, looking for buried treasure."

He laughed. "No, but let's see if we can figure out exactly where this is anyway."

We walked around the lake again, enjoying the antics of ducks that swam about even though winter would officially arrive in a few days. When we reached the area that appeared to be marked with an X on the map, we had a bit of a letdown.

"I don't see anything special about this spot." Jason glanced around as though he expected to see what Miss Nichols would have seen during the exposition.

The grassy area was shaded by a number of trees, but it was hard to know if they'd stood there sixty-four years earlier. A walking path cut through the grass, allowing visitors to stroll the entire circumference of Lake Watauga.

"Where was Vanity Fair located from here?" I asked.

Jason held up the map. "North is that way," he said, adjusting the map to correspond with the correct direction. "It would have been west of here." He looked up. "Over that direction," he said, using his chin to indicate an area that was now occupied by buildings.

"Miss Nichols has a poster of the giant seesaw hanging in her room. And isn't there a postcard in the scrapbook with a picture of it?" I squinted my eyes, trying to envision the gigantic contraption just beyond where we stood. I wasn't fond of heights, but it might have been exciting to ride in one of the cars and see the city spread out below.

"I wonder if there's a note from Peaches to Luca on the back of that postcard, like the others."

Jason continued to survey the area, but his words had my mind racing.

Did the remaining postcards have notes that would give us more clues about the author? Did they have any connection to the newspaper articles about missing women? Would they offer insight into the reason Luca and Miss Nichols seemingly vanished, at least according to Mr. Corsini?

We made our way around the lake one last time before calling it a day. We hadn't learned anything new, but it had been fun to see the park together, imagining what it looked like during the days of the exposition.

When we got back to the hotel, Dad was waiting for me in the apartment. I could tell by his expression he had bad news.

"I received a phone call from the nursing home. Miss Nichols took a turn for the worse. She isn't doing well at all."

For reasons I couldn't explain, tears sprang to my eyes. "Will she . . . ?" I couldn't finish.

Dad shook his head. "I don't know, but I plan to go see her in the morning. Would you like to come with me?"

I nodded, a lump in my throat.

Later, alone in my room, I settled on the bed with the scrapbook. I didn't open it but simply held it on my chest, thinking of Miss Nichols, alone in the nursing home.

"I'm sorry I wasn't kinder to you," I whispered, tears once again springing to my eyes and flowing down my cheeks. Guilt made my chin tremble. "I'm sorry I didn't take the time to get to know you the way Emmett did."

I sniffled and closed my eyes. I hadn't prayed much since Mama died, but now seemed a good time to start.

"God," I whispered as tears dripped off my chin. "Please don't take Miss Nichols. Not yet."

The brief prayer was wholly inadequate and completely ineloquent, but it covered everything I wanted to say.

Chapter Sixteen

The afternoon sun began its slow decent toward the horizon, yet I wasn't ready to return to the hotel. Miss Mann's concert at the gazebo was glorious, with her beautiful voice carrying out over the mesmerized crowd. Luca confessed he'd never heard anything like it, and I was pleased we'd stayed to enjoy the performance.

"They say the park looks magical at night," I said as Luca and I strolled along the path that circled Lake Watauga. In the hours we'd spent alone at the park, he'd been a perfect gentleman, and I'd grown quite comfortable with his company. "There's a fireworks display just as it gets dark. Then afterward, lights on the outside of all the buildings are turned on, and their reflection in the water resembles diamonds."

"I should think you would be tired from our day at Vanity Fair." He grinned. "I believe we visited every exhibit possible."

"Not every exhibit. Remember the Café of Night and Morning?" I shivered despite the warm day.

While standing in line to enter the strange-looking place, a woman who'd already toured it revealed that undertakers and widows in black clothing ushered guests into the building shaped like an aboveground burial vault, where scenes from Dante's *Inferno* came to life. Skeletons with fiery-red eyes lined the walls, and visitors were led to the theatre where ghastly death portrayals were followed by vignettes from hell. When the lady began to tell of refreshments served on tables made from real coffins, by mutual consent, Luca and I hurried away from the dreadful place as fast as we could manage. Later, while chatting with a vendor selling peanuts, we learned that the tour ended in a room with bright lights, white satin drapery, and angelic music, but neither of us felt the need to go back to see it for ourselves.

"Would you like to sit and rest awhile?" he asked when we came upon an empty park bench, a rare find indeed.

I did. I wasn't used to being on my feet all day. "I don't believe the cobbler who sewed my boots intended them for a day at the exposition."

Luca chuckled and settled down on the grass near the bench. It reminded me of our picnic earlier, with Gia and Kenton.

"I hope Gia's ankle is better. We must bring her back to Vanity Fair once she can walk without pain."

Luca nodded. "She would like that, *signorina*. I believe her favorite would be the animal shows."

We remained quiet for several minutes, simply enjoying the moment. Couples strolled past, arm in arm. Children chased one another while their parents sought respite in the shade.

On the water, the faint song of an Italian gondolier reached us as one of the long Venice-inspired boats passed by.

"Have you ever been to Venice?" I asked.

Luca shook his head. "My family came from southern Italy. I was a small boy when we left, and I've never been back."

"I apologize. I shouldn't pry." I felt foolish for asking the question. I remembered now he'd told me he was two years old when he came to America.

"There's no need to apologize." He glanced back as another gondola drifted nearby. A canopy shaded the passengers, comfortably seated in the center of the Venetian boat. "I would like to return someday to see the land of my ancestors, but America is my home."

We watched several more boats drift past when an idea came to me.

"Would you like to take a ride in a gondola?" I grinned when he turned to me, surprise in his eyes. "I think it looks fun. Besides, I'm sure I'll never get to Venice, so this is no doubt my only chance to ride in a real Venetian gondola and pretend I'm there amid the canals and beautiful architecture I've seen in books."

"Very well, *signorina*." He smiled as he stood. "I would not wish to deny you such an opportunity."

We made our way to the dock where the gondolas were launched. While spending time in Vanity Fair, Luca had finally relented—after much insistence on my part—and allowed me to purchase our tickets for the exhibits. I was, after all, the daughter of his employer. It made no sense for him to spend his income on me.

After waiting in line for several minutes, I handed the attendant two dimes and we were off.

The boat was far sturdier than I'd anticipated, and I felt quite safe as we settled into our seats. Luca sat beside me, with the Italian gondolier, in his striped shirt, white pants, and hat, behind us on a small raised platform at the back of the boat. He moved a long oar with seeming ease and set us in motion.

We hadn't been away from the dock long when the gondolier began to sing in Italian. Luca and I exchanged a smile, enjoying the soulful melody.

"What is he singing about?" I whispered, oddly pleased that my companion understood the beautiful words even though I did not.

"He sings of the beauty of Italy. Of her mountains and oceans, of fertile valleys and enchanting villages."

I closed my eyes and tried to imagine I truly was in Venice. With Luca.

My eyes sprang open at the startling thought. Heat rose up my neck, and I hid my face so he couldn't see the stain on my cheeks.

When the song ended, Luca turned and spoke to the gondolier in Italian. They had a lively conversation, with both of them laughing and nodding.

"He is from Venice," Luca said when he faced forward again. "He says he and the other gondoliers were brought over for the exposition and will remain here until it closes in October."

As we floated under the Rialto Bridge, we waved to the people looking down upon us. The coolness beneath the

bridge only lasted a few moments before we emerge[d]
late-afternoon sunshine once again.

The gondolier began another song, and this tim[e]
joined in on the chorus. His voice, a rich baritone, bl[ended]
perfectly with the gondolier's. Passengers in another g[ondola]
applauded as they passed by.

"What were you two singing about?" I asked whe[n the]
song came to an end.

He seemed hesitant to answer. "It is . . . an Italia[n love]
song, *signorina*, but sad. They are like Romeo and J[uliet.]
Ill-fated."

I couldn't look away when his gaze met mine, his
eyes gently caressing my face. I'd never felt such a pow[erful]
attraction to a man before. The gondolier, the crowd[,]
exposition seemed to fade as we drifted across Lake Wat[auga.]

When the gondolier announced we'd arrived at our d[esti-]
nation, however, reality returned. Like for the couple i[n the]
song, nothing but trouble would come if I allowed myse[lf to]
fall in love with Luca Moretti. The same was true for [him.]
We were from two different worlds.

I tore my gaze from him to find we'd arrived at the is[land]
we'd seen from the shore. Moss-covered cliffs, palm t[rees,]
willows, and pink water lilies greeted us as we disembar[ked.]
Above us, an ancient-looking medieval castle, complete w[ith]
a tower, rose from the rocks.

"Come," beckoned a guide.

He led us to the mouth of a dark cave, with a sign ab[ove]
that read *Entrance to Theatre*.

I held back. "I'm not certain I want to go in there."

Luca grinned. "It is not like the Café of Night a[nd]

Morning. In Italy, on the island of Capri, there is a sea cave. Sunlight comes through the cave's entrance and makes the water appear a deep blue. They call it the Blue Grotto. Emperor Tiberius is said to have used it as his personal swimming hole in ancient times."

"How do you know all this?" I asked, impressed.

He gave a nonchalant shrug. "My father was a master storyteller. Everything I know of Italy, I learned from him."

Convinced we would not be attacked by ghouls, we entered the cave. The cool, dark tunnel felt very much like we were deep inside a mountain. The sound of water grew louder as we slowly wound our way through the rock passageway.

When we reached the end of the cave, we found ourselves transported to the Bay of Naples. I had no knowledge of how the architect and designers of the exhibit accomplished such a feat, but they'd managed to re-create nature's glorious beauty at sunset, making me believe I was truly looking at a golden Italian sky. The blue water around us grew dark as the sunlight faded, but a moon suddenly appeared, casting its white light into the depths until a rich azure colored the lake.

In the distance, a sweet voice began singing, accompanied by what sounded like a mandolin. A moment later, a boat drifted into view, with a lovely woman on the stern, dressed in an elaborate costume. Her voice floated around us, echoing inside the cave.

I stood in awe, not wanting to move. Luca, too, seemed captivated by the beauty around us. I couldn't help but be disappointed when the attendant reappeared, bringing the magic to an end.

"Would you care to dine in the castle?" he asked.

My gaze met Luca's. With Papa and Mother dining elsewhere, I'd thought it would be nice to dine at the park. But after Gia's accident and departure for the hotel, I wasn't certain it would be appropriate. Yet I had no desire to return to the Maxwell and join Kenton. In the dusky light of the fading day, with delicious aromas drifting down from the café above, the moment seemed too enchanting to pass up.

"Yes," I said, feeling bold and liking it. "I believe we would."

A slow smile filled Luca's eyes. "But only if you allow me to pay."

I laughed, not willing to spoil the moment with an argument. "You win, Mr. Moretti."

We followed the attendant up a winding staircase to the castle above, where music and a cool breeze greeted us. The maître d' seated us in the open-air pavilion, with a magnificent view of the "White City" spread out below.

Luca ordered two glasses of Chianti, "to celebrate Italy," he said, along with two plates of spaghetti and a loaf of crusty Italian bread. We talked and laughed and thoroughly enjoyed the simple yet delicious meal, while the sun sank behind the hills without us even being aware.

Suddenly the sky filled with brilliant, colorful fireworks. The pop and sizzle caused onlookers to gasp and cheer, and children squealed out their delight. When the display ended, we joined the thunderous applause coming from groups all around the lake. True to my prediction, electric lights from the Parthenon, the Shelby County building, the Commerce Building, and more illuminated the entire park.

"I'm glad we stayed."

I found Luca's gaze on me. My heart pounded in my chest. "So am I."

I had no idea what was happening between us, but when he reached for my hand across the table, I entwined my fingers with his.

We left the Blue Grotto the same way we'd arrived. A different gondolier slowly steered us back to the dock, singing in such a way I felt certain the song was meant for lovers. Luca's arm touched mine when the boat rocked, but neither of us moved.

All too soon, we were back on land. Despite nightfall, the crowds in the park were still thick.

"I suppose we should return to the hotel," I said, reluctant to bring our enjoyable time to an end, yet knowing we must. "I wouldn't want Papa and Mother to arrive back at the suite and find I'm still away."

"No, *signorina*. We would not want that."

Lights from the Rialto Bridge cast a golden glow as we passed by on our way to the Terminal Building. We would take a streetcar back to the Maxwell House rather than hiring a hackney. Carmelo would have long ago returned Luca's carriage and horse to the livery.

"Wait here." Luca suddenly dashed up the steps to the bridge and disappeared into one of the tiny gift shops. I couldn't imagine what he was up to, but I waited as he'd instructed. A few minutes later he emerged, a grin on his face. I could detect nothing in his hands.

"Are you going to tell me what that was about?" I asked.

"Close your eyes." He smiled and nodded when I didn't immediately obey. "Please. Close your eyes."

I did.

"Now hold out your hands."

I laughed. "Are you going to put a frog or something equally slimy in them?"

"Perhaps. Perhaps not."

I shrugged and did as he asked.

A moment later he placed something cool in my palms. "You may open your eyes."

I looked down to find a small, white replica of the Parthenon. We'd seen them throughout the park, being sold by vendors and shop owners, along with dozens of other inexpensive souvenirs. I recalled mentioning how darling they were. He must have been paying attention.

My eyes found him.

A faint smile rested on his lips. "So you will remember this moment." His soft voice barely reached me.

I clutched the keepsake to my chest, my heart full of happiness. "I will treasure it."

The hotel was bustling with activity when we arrived, allowing us to blend into the crowd unnoticed.

At the foot of the staircase, I turned to Luca. "Thank you for a wonderful day. I enjoyed every minute of it."

"As did I, *signorina*."

"Mr. Moretti, after spending the entire day together, I believe we can dispense with *signorina*. At least when no one else is around."

My daring statement should have shocked him, but he only grinned. "Perhaps I will call you by the name I've given you in my mind."

I couldn't look away from him. "And what name might that be?"

"*Pesche.*" His voice was soft, meant only for my ears.

"What does that mean?"

He winked and backed away, blending into a large group of people moving toward the exit. "Peaches," he called with a wave.

I watched until he disappeared into the night. A warm tingle moved through my body as I slowly mounted the stairs, oblivious to the noise from the lobby or the people observing the activity from their place at the banister of the mezzanine. All I could think of was Luca Moretti. His smile. His touch.

Pesche.

Peaches.

I knew nothing would ever be the same again.

Chapter Seventeen

Dad and I arrived at the nursing home at ten o'clock Monday morning. The nurse at the front desk didn't crack a smile when we asked to see Miss Nichols. She simply pointed down a hallway, then ignored us.

I'd never been to a place like this before and wasn't sure what to expect. Walking down the corridor to Miss Nichols's room, I decided I didn't much care for it. It looked like a hospital, with bare walls and tile floors, but an odd, unpleasant odor reminded me it wasn't a place of healing. Patients who came here usually didn't return home.

The door to room 12 stood slightly ajar. Dad knocked, but no one answered. I felt awkward standing in the hallway and wondered if it had been a mistake to accompany him.

"Miss Nichols?" He slowly pushed open the door and stepped into the room. I glanced around to see if anyone would stop us, but the hallway was empty.

With hesitant steps, I followed him inside.

Two hospital-type beds, two bedside tables, and one

vinyl-covered chair with a tear on the seat were all that filled the space. Miss Nichols occupied one bed; the other was empty. A stained porcelain bedpan sat on the floor between them.

Dad moved to her side, but she appeared to be sleeping. It brought back the memory of the day Jason and I found her in her room at the Maxwell. I'd thought the worst, but thankfully Jason had been there and knew what to do.

I hovered near the door. If she was asleep, we shouldn't wake her, should we?

Dad, however, didn't agree. "Miss Nichols?" He laid his hand on her exposed arm. "It's Dan Whitfield, from the Maxwell. I've come to see how you're doing."

A few moments passed before translucent eyelids fluttered, then opened. She blinked several times and looked confused when her gaze landed on Dad.

"Hello, Miss Nichols. It's good to see you again."

She stared at him a long moment before a sense of recognition came to her eyes. She tried to speak, but it sounded more like a garbled moan than words.

I couldn't believe the change in Miss Nichols's appearance. If Dad hadn't been here, I would've believed I'd come into the wrong room. She'd always seemed old to me, but on the occasions when she ventured down to the lobby or the dining room, she was neatly dressed, with her gray hair wound in a bun on top of her head. She wasn't warm and friendly, like Mrs. Ruth, but she was polite and asked about Emmett whenever we crossed paths. Since Mama's passing, I'd noticed a softening in her during our brief exchanges. She didn't offer words of wisdom about how to deal with loss, but I got the impression she knew how I felt.

The frail woman lying in this depressing place seemed a different person altogether.

Her long hair hung loose and limp on the pillow, appearing

as if it hadn't been washed in ages. An unhealthy yellowish hue colored her skin, the likes of which I'd never seen before. Food stains dotted the chest of her dull-white nightgown, evidence that whoever was charged with feeding her hadn't bothered to wipe away the spills.

"I've brought Audrey with me." Dad motioned me over.

I moved into the room, noticing how chilly the air felt in here compared to the hallway. The window nearby obviously let in a draft.

I stopped beside Dad. When her eyes met mine, I pushed a smile forward. "Hello, Miss Nichols. It's nice to see you."

Her gaze traveled over my face, but I couldn't determine if she knew me or not. Just when I felt I should offer an explanation, a lopsided smile tipped her mouth. "Arrry."

Dad and I exchanged a look of surprise before he nodded. "Yes, Audrey. She wanted to visit you too."

While Dad launched into a one-sided conversation about the weather, the Christmas decorations at the hotel, Mr. Hanover's dog, and anything else he could think of, Miss Nichols's gaze stayed on me. Her mouth had settled into a peaceful smile, and I kept one on my face too.

A nurse appeared in the doorway a short time later and beckoned to Dad.

"I'll be right back," he said to both Miss Nichols and me.

Left alone with her, I didn't know what to say or do.

Again, I felt chilled air come from the window.

"Are you cold, Miss Nichols?" I asked. "Would you like your blanket pulled up?"

She nodded.

With care, I tucked the blanket under her chin. Her eyes never left me.

I felt I knew her much better now than I had in all the years she'd lived at the Maxwell. Going through her belongings, studying the scrapbook, reading about her in the newspaper articles, all helped me see her with new eyes. She wasn't the strange reclusive woman she appeared to be on the outside. She'd been a young woman, with hopes and dreams, not so different from me or any other young person. I realized I'd judged her in ignorance, and I felt disappointed for the wasted time. I could have learned directly from her about the exposition and Luca and what happened that caused them to disappear, as Mr. Corsini had described.

The awkwardness of being in this place with her vanished.

I pulled the chair next to her bed. "Dad asked me to put your things in boxes until you need them again."

She nodded, a hint of sadness clouding her eyes.

"I found your scrapbook. The one you kept about the Tennessee Centennial Exposition. Do you remember it?"

She blinked several times before she nodded. "Yesssss."

"I hope you don't mind, but I've been looking through it. It's so beautiful. I didn't know a lot about the exposition, so it's been fun learning about Vanity Fair and the Parthenon."

I thought reminding her about the scrapbook would cheer her, but tears suddenly filled her eyes.

"Miss Nichols," I said, alarmed. "Is something wrong?"

She sniffled and wiped the tears with her left hand. "Th'ow book away."

I didn't understand. The right side of her mouth drooped, so the words came out slow and slurred.

"Do you mean you want me to throw the scrapbook away?"

She nodded. "Th'ow away."

"Oh, Miss Nichols." I stared at her, wondering if she were in her right mind. "It's so beautiful. There's so much history on the pages. It would be a shame to dispose of it."

I wished she could communicate better so we could discuss the situation. I'd tell her about Jason and how the scrapbook led us to read about her activism and how her work for women's rights inspired both of us. I might even confess the idea that had been floating around in my head about helping children like Emmett. I believed she loved Emmett, so I was sure she'd encourage me to pursue it.

Before my thoughts were complete, she reached for my hand. Ice-cold, bony fingers wrapped around mine. "You keep book. Arrry hold on to my mem'ries."

I gasped. "I can't, Miss Nichols. It's yours."

She tugged my hand. "You keep. I don't need anymo'."

She seemed sincere, so I clasped her hand in both of mine. "Thank you, Miss Nichols. I'd be honored to have such a beautiful memory book."

Dad returned then. We stayed another half hour before bidding the elderly woman goodbye. When I promised to come back to see her, a lopsided smile was my reward. On the way home, Dad revealed what the nurse told him.

"They don't expect her to live long." He heaved a sigh. "The nurse wondered who they should contact when the time comes. Her attorney hasn't returned any of their phone calls. I gave them my name and number."

His news left my heart heavy. "It's so sad, Dad. She shouldn't have to just lie in that place, waiting to die. Isn't there anything we can do? Maybe bring her back to the hotel?"

"I'm afraid not, honey. She needs around-the-clock nursing. I know that facility isn't great, but it's the best place for her."

I didn't agree, but there also didn't appear to be anything we could do about it.

Betty Ann and Emmett were playing cards in the lobby when we returned to the hotel. They both smiled when we approached.

"We're playing Go Fish. I'm winning." Emmett held up his cards.

"Good for you." Dad smoothed Emmett's cowlick, then turned to Betty Ann. "Any phone calls while we were out?"

"No calls, but the chef has some questions about the refreshments for the dance Friday night. Also, one of the maids is sick, so I reassigned the others to make sure all the rooms are cleaned."

Dad smiled. "Thank you, Betty Ann. I appreciate you handling things." He grew thoughtful. "Maybe you and Audrey can finish boxing up Miss Nichols's belongings. Visiting with her today reminded me that we should have it completed, just in case." He glanced at Emmett, careful not to say anything that might upset him. "I know her attorney isn't interested in keeping the items, but I'd like to have it organized should her will include any specifics about keepsakes or jewelry."

"I'd be happy to help." Betty Ann laid her cards down and stood. "We'll have to finish our game later, Emmett. Maybe I'll actually win a hand next time."

"I always win," Emmett said, continuing to play without her.

"Thank you for watching him this morning," I said as we walked to the elevator. "Mrs. Ruth wasn't feeling well."

"You're welcome. I enjoyed it."

I filled her in on Miss Nichols's condition, leaving out the part about the scrapbook. I wanted to tell Jason my good news first. I hadn't even mentioned it to Dad yet.

When we reached Miss Nichols's old room, a pang of grief washed over me. "It was so sad seeing her lying there. You should see the nursing home. It's cold and ugly and depressing."

"I'm sorry she had to be placed there." Betty Ann surveyed the room. "After my mother died, it became difficult for me to care for my father without help. I looked into several nursing homes, but God took him home before I had to make that decision."

I thought about her words. "I'm glad you didn't have to go through that with your dad, but it doesn't seem very fair. Why didn't God keep Miss Nichols from having a stroke? She doesn't have any family or anyone to take care of her."

"God's ways are a mystery sometimes." She went to the bedside table where Miss Nichols's Bible sat. "This looks well-read," she said, thumbing the pages. "It reminds me of my mother's Bible."

"And my mother's," I said softly, thinking of the Bible tucked in the drawer of my bureau, where it had been since Dad gave it to me on the day of her funeral. I couldn't bear to look at it, let alone read it. My pain had been too raw.

She offered a sad smile. "The truth is, Audrey, death and sorrow are part of this world. I don't know why Miss Nichols couldn't have been spared her suffering or why my husband was killed in the war or why your mother died when she was still needed by her family." She walked over and handed the Bible to me. "But what I am certain of is if we believe what this book says about God and accept Jesus Christ as our Lord, then death isn't the end. It's only the beginning of something so wonderful we can't fully understand it."

I knew she was right, but the fragility of life was difficult to accept sometimes.

"I think I'll take this to Miss Nichols," I said, laying the Bible on the bed. "She might not be able to read it, but maybe it will give her some comfort just to hold it."

We spent the next two hours packing the last of Miss Nichols's belongings. Boxes stored beneath the bed held paperwork as well as a dozen or so bundles of letters. A quick glance revealed they were all written to Miss Nichols from different women over the course of many years. The address on the envelopes, however, wasn't for the Maxwell House but was somewhere on Tenth Street. I marked the boxes with the letters *VIP* so we'd be sure to store them in the basement where they could easily be accessed.

Jason arrived in time to help take down the framed posters, expressing a desire to purchase them from Miss Nichols if she was willing to sell. I was anxious to tell him about the scrapbook, but I didn't want to say anything in front of Betty Ann.

"Well, I think that's everything." I surveyed the room one last time. It looked barren and sad rather than homey and eccentric.

"What's that?" Betty Ann rose up on tippy-toes, trying to see the top of a tall bookcase. "I can't make it out, but it looks like there's something up there."

Jason pulled over the desk chair and stood on it.

"Do you see anything?" I asked.

When he looked down at me, he wore an odd smile. "You're not going to believe this."

"What? What is it?"

He retrieved something small and handed it to me.

My breath caught. "The Parthenon." The small replica of the famous building bore the yellowing of age and was covered in dust, but I cradled it in my hands like a priceless jewel.

Betty Ann came over to see it. "That looks quite old."

Jason climbed off the chair, excitement in his eyes. "If it's what we think it is, it came from the exposition. And if this is the Parthenon souvenir that Luca gave to Peaches, then that means—"

I finished his sentence.

"Miss Nichols *is* Peaches."

Chapter Eighteen

I lay in bed long past nine o'clock. Morning light filtered through the curtains, but I snuggled beneath the covers, my mind and heart full.

Had my time with Luca only been a dream? If so, I wanted to stay abed forever and relive it over and over. The way his dark eyes caressed my face. How his strong fingers closed over mine.

"Miss?"

I turned to find Fanny, Mother's maid, peeking into the room. "Good morning, Fanny. I'm not quite ready to greet the day. I'll let you know when I need your assistance."

"Very good, miss." She bobbed a curtsy and closed the door behind her.

The appearance of the red-haired maid, whose roots were most certainly Irish, reminded me I must check on Gia as soon as I dressed and went downstairs. The poor dear.

Perhaps I should stop by the sweet shop and take her something special to cheer her in her recovery.

Stretching, I rose with reluctance and padded to the window. Nashville's streets bustled with activity below, with carriages, riders on horses, and pedestrians hurrying about. By now, Luca would have already driven Papa to Exposition Park, as was their usual custom. Papa liked to take breakfast with his business associates at the club, while Mother and I preferred a tray in our rooms, allowing us to leisurely prepare for the day ahead.

When I turned from the window, my gaze fell on the small replica of the Parthenon resting on the vanity table.

My heart skipped.

It hadn't been a dream.

I picked up the small keepsake and emitted what a romance novelist would surely deem a dreamy sigh.

I couldn't wait to see Luca today. I'd never been in love before, but if this was how one felt—alive and blissfully happy—I hoped it would last forever. I knew we must be careful, but our relationship had changed in the delightful hours we spent together at the exposition. I didn't know what would happen between us, but I refused to allow anyone, even my parents, to stand in the way of such an unforeseen yet wonderfully welcome discovery.

I'd just completed my toilette when Fanny arrived. "There's a message for you, miss." She handed me a note, folded with tight creases.

I glanced at the handwriting. It wasn't from Papa or Mother. I didn't think Kenton had reason to send a note, but I wouldn't put anything past him. I laid it aside to read later.

Once I'd dressed in a patterned navy skirt and my favorite coral blouse, Fanny set out to fix my hair, weaving a matching blue ribbon through the curls. While she did a fine job, she didn't have the skills Gia possessed.

An idea began to form in my mind.

What if I hired Gia to be my lady's maid full-time? When we returned to Chattanooga at the end of the month, she could come with me. She was young, but working in a home rather than a hotel might appeal to her.

A sly smile filled my reflection in the mirror.

Her brother would certainly need to come visit her.

After Fanny left the room, I opened the note with little enthusiasm. My eyes fell to the signature, expecting to see Kenton's name scrawled in ink.

Luca.

With a gasp, I read the one-line message.

Meet me at the ice cream parlor.

My gaze flew to the clock on the table beside the bed. Nearly an hour had passed since Fanny brought the message. He must think I wasn't coming.

I hurried from the room, using the door that led into the hallway rather than going through our suite. I couldn't risk encountering Mother.

I was out of breath by the time I reached the mezzanine, but I didn't stop until I neared the sweet shop on the ground floor.

He leaned against the wall, his arms folded across his chest. A look of worry creased his brow as he watched people come and go.

Relief swept over me at seeing him there. "Luca." I hurried to him.

He straightened. "I thought you were not coming." He didn't smile. Was he angry?

"I must apologize. I slept later than I usually do."

He glanced about, then bent his head toward me. "I must speak with you. It's urgent. But not here."

Fear circled my belly.

Did he regret the evening we'd spent together? Was he sorry we'd held hands under the twinkling lights of the Blue Grotto? Would he tell me we couldn't see each other again?

We made our way through a door and down a corridor I'd never seen, apprehension twisting a terrible path through my heart. We stopped at the top of a set of stairs leading to what must be the basement of the hotel.

Several silent seconds ticked by before he met my gaze. "Gia is missing."

I blinked. The shocking statement was not at all what I expected him to say. "What do you mean, *missing*?"

"She never returned to the hotel yesterday." He ran a hand through his hair, worry in his eyes. "Mrs. Smith, the woman in charge of the maids, found me this morning, full of anger that Gia was not in her bed last night."

I stared at him, confused. "But she did return to the hotel. Kenton said he would have the doctor look in on her."

"I checked with the doctor who services the hotel." His tone hardened. "He never spoke to Mr. Thornley, and he never examined my sister."

My mind raced, trying to come up with a logical reason

why Gia wouldn't be in her room. "Could a different doctor have examined her? Maybe taken her to the hospital?"

"Dr. Bergson has an agreement with the Maxwell. He would be the one to tend Gia, had a doctor been summoned."

"Is there any place else she may have gone? To the home of a friend, perhaps? Maybe Carmelo would know."

He shook his head, his jaw set. "Carmelo said he dropped them off in front of the hotel. Thornley has done something with her, and I intend to find out what."

"What are you insinuating, Luca?" The fierce look in his eyes sent a tremor of alarm through me.

"He is the last person seen with her. If Thornley escorted her to the hotel, where is she?"

I had no answers. "We'll find Kenton. He can tell us where he took her and we'll go get her."

He stared at me, regret in his eyes. "She's all I have. If something has happened to her, I will never forgive myself."

His unspoken words hung in the air between us.

He would never forgive me either.

We returned to the lobby and searched for Kenton to no avail. When I sent a message upstairs with a bellboy, he came back with my unopened note. Mr. Thornley was not in his room.

"What do we do now?" Luca paced the lobby like one of the wild tigers we'd seen at the animal show in Vanity Fair.

"We keep looking. He's bound to be here somewhere." I felt certain Kenton hadn't gone to the exposition today. Not after having such an unpleasant time yesterday. When we located him, he'd tell us where to find Gia and all would be well.

We searched in the dining room, the men's salons, the tailor's shop, and the cigar shop next to it, but Kenton was nowhere to be seen. I asked the porter if he knew Mr. Thornley's whereabouts, but he didn't recall Kenton hiring a cab or leaving the hotel that morning. I thanked him and we continued on our way.

We'd already looked in the billiards room, where a blue cloud of cigar smoke hung near the recessed ceiling, but Luca insisted on checking again. I stayed outside the entrance, a feeling of hopelessness fast taking hold in my heart. We couldn't give up though. Kenton was the only one who could tell us where to find Gia.

"Thornley, what have you done with my sister? Don't ignore me. I demand an answer."

Luca's angry voice echoed from within the room.

Alarmed, I hurried forward amid glares from the male patrons, clearly unhappy that I dared to intrude inside their private domain.

I found Luca and Kenton near the back of the room, with a billiard table mercifully between them as they faced each other.

Kenton's frown deepened when he saw me.

"Priscilla, what are you doing in here? It isn't proper." His glare returned to Luca. "Moretti, you have no business in here either. This room is for gentlemen."

I came to a stop beside Luca, noting his clenched jaw and rigid stance. He was like a keg of gunpowder, ready to explode at the slightest spark.

"Kenton," I said, hoping to reason with him and defuse the tense situation. "We're concerned about Gia. She didn't return to her room last night. Do you know where we can find her?"

The man playing against Kenton missed his shot. "It's your turn, Thornley."

I sent the stranger a look of annoyance. Couldn't he see we were engaged in conversation?

Kenton walked around to the end of the table and eyed the colored balls on the green cloth-covered field. "I have no idea where she is. She's your maid." He lined up a shot and hit a white ball with the end of his cue stick. A red ball in its path dropped into the net without a sound.

"You were the last one to see her," Luca growled, his patience on the brink of running out. His fists tightened, as though he was preparing for a physical fight.

"Kenton, please help us," I said. "We're worried about her. Just tell us what happened when you returned to the hotel yesterday. Did you call a doctor?"

After a long moment, he huffed, indicated to the other man the game was over, and set his cue stick on the table. With arms crossed, he faced us. "When we got back to the hotel, she said she could manage on her own. I offered to alert the doctor, but she refused. She said she'd been enough trouble as it was and didn't want to cause any more inconvenience." He shrugged. "That's the last I saw of her."

This information was not what either Luca or I wanted to hear.

"That's a lie," Luca said. "No one has seen her. She never returned to her room."

Kenton's mouth curled in an ugly smirk. "Maybe your sister has a few secrets, Moretti. She *is* quite pretty."

Luca lunged, but Kenton sidestepped fast enough to avoid him.

"Stop this," I said, trying to get between them.

"Do not speak of my sister in such a way, or I will insist we step outside," Luca said, his rage barely contained.

I couldn't blame him. Why would Kenton say such a repulsive thing about sweet Gia?

"What's going on here?" The burly attendant we'd passed on our way into the room arrived. "Mr. Thornley, is everything all right?"

Kenton sneered. "It is not. This man has insulted and attacked me. I want him removed at once."

The attendant turned to Luca. They were nearly the same height. "You need to leave, Moretti. You don't want trouble."

"I will not leave until he tells me where my sister is."

The man looked confused. "Gia? What's she to do with this?"

"She has nothing to do with this," Kenton roared, gaining the attention of the other men in the room. "Either remove this man or I will call the manager. You'll both be out of a job by the end of this."

"Luca, let's leave." I placed my hand on his arm. "We'll keep searching."

"Luca?" Kenton's ugliness landed on me. "Well, now I see why you sent me back to the hotel with the girl. Perhaps she wasn't even injured and was part of your plan to be alone with this man."

I felt Luca tense, but I held his arm firmly. "You volunteered to return to the hotel, Kenton." I refused to be baited by his crude insinuation. "You know as well as I do that Gia couldn't walk on her own. Don't add lies to this serious situation. Something is wrong. Very wrong. Gia is missing. Our efforts need to be focused on finding her."

I turned to move toward the door, but Luca didn't budge.

"If you've done something to hurt her," he said, his voice low, deadly seriousness in each word, "you will be sorry."

Fury colored Kenton's face. "Get him out of here."

The attendant grabbed Luca by the arm and hauled him away. I hurried to follow them, ignoring the murmurs and stares from the men we passed.

In the lobby, the man released Luca. "You can't go back in there, Moretti."

Luca blew out his frustration. "I'm sorry you had to become involved, Walsh."

"It's my job. Now, what's this about Gia?" The man's concern seemed genuine despite the rough way he'd escorted Luca moments before. Obviously he was acquainted with both Morettis.

"Gia is Miss Nichols's maid," he said, indicating me. "My sister and I attended the exposition with her yesterday. Mr. Thornley joined us after we arrived at the park. Gia injured her ankle and Mr. Thornley offered to return with her to the hotel. He didn't wish to remain at the fair any longer and promised to have a doctor examine her." He shook his head, anger in his eyes. "I shouldn't have let her out of my sight."

His words filled me with guilt.

"Now she's missing?" A deep frown settled on Mr. Walsh's brow.

"Mrs. Smith said Gia was not in her bed last night. No one has seen her."

The other man nodded gravely. "Let me ask around. Maybe someone saw something."

"Thank you, Walsh. I appreciate it."

He left us then.

Luca ran a hand through his hair. "I cannot stay here," he said, his voice hard. "I must go search for her."

I didn't ask where he would look because I felt the same sense of urgency. We would search the entire city of Nashville if needed. "I'll inquire of anyone—maids, butlers, bellboys—until we find her."

He grew still and looked at me with an intensity that took my breath. "I do not blame you."

My throat tightened and tears blurred my vision. "We should have returned with her. It was selfish of me to ask you to stay."

"You did not ask. I wanted to be with you."

Our gazes held, regret and fear filling the space between us, crushing the blossom of love I'd known only an hour before.

Then he turned and walked away.

———

I lay awake in the stillness of night.

Dad and Emmett had gone to bed hours ago, but I'd tossed and turned since climbing beneath the covers. Sleep refused to come despite my exhaustion after carrying boxes of Miss Nichols's belongings to the basement. The image of the elderly woman lying in that cold, sterile room, all alone, filled my memory. Even if she wasn't long for this world, as the nurse told Dad, she deserved to spend her remaining days someplace friendlier and more peaceful.

With a groan, I turned on the lamp next to my bed. The small replica of the Parthenon sat beside the scrapbook on my desk across the room. Now that we knew Miss Nichols was most likely Peaches, I felt curious about the remaining postcards in the book. Would they offer more clues to what happened the day Mr. Corsini drove her and Luca to the exposition?

I tugged on my robe and padded to the desk. A chill hung in the air, so I snatched up the book and returned to the warmth of my bed. With as many times as I'd perused the beautiful pages, they were becoming quite familiar. I knew just where to go to find the postcards I sought.

The picture of a castle-like building atop a hill caught my eye. Below the structure, two long boats floated in a lake, with one boasting several women in elaborate costumes. Behind them, tucked into the side of the hill, a sign over what looked like a cave opening read *Entrance to Theatre*. Unless I freed the postcard from the page, I couldn't be sure what I was looking at.

I bit my lip.

Since I discovered the book, I'd had the uncomfortable feeling of invading Miss Nichols's privacy by reading the notes on the postcards. Even though her name wasn't on them, nor did I know Luca's identity, it still didn't seem quite right. They were personal, private notes from a woman who'd loved a man.

But now that she'd given the book to me, I wondered if it might not be an issue anymore. Perhaps all these years later, the messages on the postcards were simply bittersweet memories, one couple's love story among thousands from the Tennessee Centennial Exposition.

I tapped my fingernail on the card.

A glance at the page revealed several dried flowers, with a blue ribbon, faded with age, woven throughout. A page torn from a music book also filled the space, but the words were in Italian. Were these items related to the picture on the postcard?

I thought back to our visit to the nursing home. Miss Nichols seemed pleased to give the book to me after I spoke of its beauty. I felt certain if she truly wanted it disposed of, she wouldn't have offered it to me. What was it she'd said? That I would be the keeper of her memories now?

The thought made me smile.

With care, I gently tugged the postcard free of the page. Hardened spots of glue dotted each corner, but otherwise it was intact.

The same handwriting from the other postcards filled the back. My eyes traveled to the printed words across the bottom.

The Blue Grotto restaurant. Beautiful Italian butterfly dancers perform on a decorated barge on Lake Watauga.

My curiosity piqued, I read the message written on the back of the card.

My darling,

I thought to take lunch at the Blue Grotto today, but I found I couldn't. It reminds me too much of you. I can't help but feel guilty when I remember our evening together there. The music. The lights. It was the most romantic night of my life. But then the nightmare began. And continues still. I'm sorry for everything, my love. I'm sorry for my selfishness then and now. I want to treasure the memory of our time together, yet how

wicked I am to want you here with me. I know you
must search for Gia until she is found and is safe.

Are my prayers reaching heaven?
I think not.

Peaches

My heart raced.

Nightmares? Selfishness? And who was Gia?

I had to find the answers to my questions.

I quickly turned pages until I came to another postcard, this one boasting a photograph of the giant seesaw in Vanity Fair. In my haste to remove it from the scrapbook, I created a slight tear in the yellowed page. I'd need to be more careful.

I flipped it over and scanned the brief note. Peaches reminded Luca of the view from the top of the seesaw—did he remember seeing the Maxwell House Hotel?—but there was nothing about Gia or nightmares. Only wistfulness in the memory of the amusement ride.

A yawn escaped as I searched for the next postcard. I'd be worthless if I didn't get some sleep soon. With the annual Christmas dance on Friday and Christmas Day dinner the following Monday, we had some busy days ahead of us. The staff knew their jobs and did them well, but Dad would require my help to make sure everything was ready for both events.

I came to a postcard with the images of several buildings, including one shaped like a pyramid, with Lake Watauga in the foreground. I recognized it as the Memphis building, patterned after an Egyptian pyramid. Miss Nichols had a poster of it in her room. Or she had, until we'd carried them all to the basement. I needed to remember to tell Dad about Jason's interest in the posters.

With more care than I'd used on the previous postcard, I worked to remove this one from the page. I felt victorious when I didn't tear the yellowed paper.

> *My dearest Luca,*
>
> *President McKinley arrived at the fair today, Ohio Day, with crowds and tumultuous applause as he waved from the steps of the Cincinnati Building. Yet the honor and excitement I should have felt as a daughter of Tennessee was lost upon me. The two people I desperately long to see are not here.*
>
> *I've determined I cannot come to Exposition Park again. The memories are sweet yet too painful.*
>
> *Return to me, my darling. I will be waiting.*
>
> *Peaches*

I looked for more postcards, but this was the last of them. My shoulders slumped with disappointment. I'd hoped to discover answers to the questions I had about Peaches and Luca, and now Gia, but the short missive offered nothing but more mystery.

Why was it painful to remember her time at the park? And if Luca and Gia were the ones missing, why had Mr. Corsini not seen Miss Nichols for so many years?

I yawned again.

The answers to those questions wouldn't make themselves known tonight.

I laid the book aside and turned out the light. Rolling over onto my side, I spoke into the darkness as my eyes drifted closed.

"I won't give up, Peaches."

Chapter Nineteen

Two days.

Two full days and Gia still had not been found.

I hadn't seen Luca since he left the hotel in search of her, and I desperately wished to see him, to speak to him, to comfort him. Between crying, praying, and questioning anyone who might have seen her, I was beyond exhaustion. Yet I couldn't rest. Two people I loved—yes, loved—were in trouble.

"Priscilla?"

Mother poked her head into my room, dressed for dinner in a new teal-blue ensemble. "We're leaving. I do wish you'd join us in the dining room." A frown creased her brow. "You look positively ill, child. I know you're concerned for your maid, but you mustn't let it affect your health." She glanced into the receiving area of our suite, then stepped inside my room and closed the door. "Kenton told your father the girl was quite forward when they were alone. He didn't come right out and say it, but he suspects she may be the sort to take payment for certain . . . favors."

Her insinuation repulsed me. "Mother." I rose from where I'd been resting on my bed. "Gia is a sweet, innocent child. Barely fourteen years old. How can you say such a thing when you yourself remarked on her skills as a lady's maid?"

"I am simply telling you what Kenton said." She scowled. "Really, Priscilla, do we know anything about Gia other than she works at this hotel? I confess I'm rather put out that the girl was assigned to us. I'm sure none of the other women in our group has been exposed to such lurid business."

I wanted to scream. Gia was missing and could be in danger this very moment. Her brother was distraught, combing the city for his only family member. Yet all my mother could think to be concerned over was the fact that her friends might gossip about the whole affair.

"Go to dinner, Mother. I'll see you in the morning."

My curt tone didn't go unnoticed. "Have a care you don't become too involved in this situation. It wouldn't look well for your father. Word travels fast through our set, as you know. If Kenton has told your father such tales about the girl, you can be assured he's told others."

"Kenton can say what he pleases, but it's a lie." I turned my back on her. "Good night, Mother."

After a moment, she harrumphed. "Heed my warning, Priscilla. If this situation becomes public, your father will have much to say about it."

She left my room and closed the door with a bang.

I squeezed my eyes shut, angry tears escaping the corners. How dare Kenton spread such appalling lies about Gia. I refused to believe any of it. She'd been flattered by his attention, as any young and inexperienced girl might be, but Kenton was mature enough to distinguish harmless flirting from an improper proposition. I could not bring myself to believe Gia was capable of doing the things he and Mother insinuated.

But what was the truth?

Kenton claimed he left Gia at the front desk of the Maxwell and never saw her again. Although I wasn't fond of Kenton, I had never thought him a liar. Yet why would he feel the need to spread such a foul story about Gia? Had something far more sinister than I was willing to imagine taken place? Something that would cause Kenton to lie?

A soft rap on the door interrupted my thoughts. "Yes?"

Fanny entered at my call. "Miss." She wore an uncharacteristic frown. "There is a man here to see you. It's the driver, Mr. Moretti. I wasn't sure I should admit him without your parents here."

I sprang to my feet. "It's fine, Fanny. I'll meet him in the parlor." I gave her a reassuring smile in the hopes she wouldn't tell Mother about my visitor. "Papa's birthday is coming up. I thought Mr. Moretti might know where to find a particular gift."

She bobbed a curtsy, but I couldn't tell if my story convinced her or not. When I'd questioned her yesterday about Gia's disappearance, she hadn't known anything beyond the common gossip circulating among the staff: Gia hadn't been in her bed all night, and no one knew where to find her. Whether Fanny had heard that Luca and I were together when the girl went missing was unknown.

I followed Fanny into the outer room. My breath caught at the sight of him standing just inside the door, his hat in his hands. His clothes looked as though he'd slept in them, and his hair hadn't been combed in days, but it was his eyes, full of despair, that stilled my heart.

Did he have news concerning Gia?

I waited until Fanny closed the door behind her.

"I've been so worried." My whisper sounded loud in the silence. "Have you found her?"

He didn't move toward me. "No." His jaw clenched. "But I have found someone who saw her with Thornley that day, and they were not at the Maxwell."

"I don't understand. Carmelo brought them to the hotel, and Kenton said he didn't see her again."

"Carmelo did bring them here, but they didn't stay."

Confusion swirled. "Where did this person see them?"

He looked away and shook his head. "I shouldn't be here. You don't need to know all of this."

Fear took hold of me. What had he learned? "Tell me, Luca."

His eyes met mine, with unmistakable sorrow shining out. "A man I know saw them together in a rented carriage in an area of the city where young girls like Gia should not be. He recognized her, so he followed them." His throat convulsed. "It did not appear that she was there against her will."

I clutched my chest. The rumors . . . they were true?

"Oh, Luca."

"I must see Thornley. I have to know."

"Of course."

What Kenton's role in this darkening tale was, I couldn't

fathom, but we wouldn't know until we found him. He was most likely dining with his parents and mine, but a confrontation between the two men in the grand dining room wouldn't do. He and some of the other men in our group usually went downstairs to one of the salons for a brandy after dinner. If we caught him before he'd had too much to drink, we might be able to reason with him.

Luca agreed with my idea. "I'm sorry to involve you, *signorina*."

It hurt to hear him address me so formally again, but I understood.

We made our way to the lobby. I took a seat in one of the many maroon upholstered chairs sprinkled throughout the area, where I had a view of the grand staircase. Luca stood a short distance away, his face a mask of grief. I couldn't take my eyes from him. I prayed Kenton would provide a reasonable explanation for taking Gia into a disreputable part of town, but I couldn't comprehend his involvement in her disappearance nor why he hadn't confessed to the truth from the beginning.

More than an hour later, I spotted Kenton descending the stairs.

"Kenton." I stood to get his attention.

He seemed surprised to see me. "Priscilla, what are you doing here? Your mother said you've been unwell the last few days."

Leave it to Mother to make up an excuse for my absence. "I'm fine, but we need to speak with you. It's important."

"We?"

Luca moved into his line of vision. "I want to know the

truth about where you took Gia. You were seen together—" he glanced at me, then back to Kenton—"in a part of town where she shouldn't go. Why would you take her there?"

Kenton's demeanor changed in an instant. "How dare you, Moretti. Don't drag me into your sordid family affair. The truth is, your sister is a trollop. She made it very clear to me that she was willing to do anything for money."

"She's a child!" Luca shouted. "Innocent of the vileness you claim. There has never been a moment . . . never a reason to think . . ." His words faltered.

My heart broke for him. Gia was his little sister. Of course, he couldn't think she was capable of all that Kenton's hateful words insinuated. I couldn't bring myself to believe it either.

"Whether or not you accept the truth, Moretti, isn't my problem."

Kenton started to move away, but Luca grabbed his arm. "Tell me why you took her to a house on Eighth Street."

Kenton wrenched free. "I didn't take her there. It was her idea." He sneered. "If I were the kind of man who enjoyed that sort of thing, I might have been tempted. Your sister is quite good at what she does."

Before I could stop it from happening, Luca's fist slammed into Kenton's jaw. A woman nearby screamed as Kenton stumbled backward, knocking over a small table.

"You'll pay for that." Blood oozed from a cut in his lip as he lunged for Luca.

The brawl I feared commenced there in the lobby. There was nothing I could do to stop it, and none of the men gathered to watch seemed inclined to get involved.

Fists flew. A lamp fell to the marble floor and shattered.

Suddenly the shrill whistle of a police officer echoed in the hall. Two uniformed men broke through the onlookers and jerked Luca and Kenton apart. Both had blood on their faces and fists.

"Unhand me." Kenton tried to yank his arm from the officer's grasp, unsuccessfully. "I'm Kenton Thornley. My father is Ambrose Thornley."

The men must have recognized the name. They exchanged a look I couldn't discern, and the officer immediately released Kenton's arm. The other man indicated Luca. "And you? What's your name?"

"Luca Moretti."

"This man attacked me for no reason. He's been harassing me for days. I want him arrested. Now." Kenton used the back of his hand to wipe at blood dripping from his nose.

The officer nearest Luca jerked his arm behind his back, causing Luca to grimace. "Come on, you."

"We'll need you to come down to the station to give your statement, Mr. Thornley," the other man said. "But you might want to see a doctor first."

The crowd parted as the officers hauled Luca away. He didn't look back at me.

"What has gotten into you, Priscilla?"

I turned to find Kenton beside me. He dabbed at a cut on his cheek with a handkerchief. The crowd slowly dispersed, although several people hung back, whispering behind their hands as they gawked at Kenton and me.

"How can you ask such a thing? My maid is missing and you're spreading hateful rumors about her. Now Luca's been arrested, and I have no idea what will happen to him."

Kenton's upper lip curled. "So you've fallen in love with the immigrant hackney driver. What do you suppose your father will say when he learns you refused marriage to me, a respectable gentleman, and instead chased after the likes of Moretti, the brother of a trollop?"

I stared at him, disgusted. "There was a time I thought we could be friends in spite of our differences of opinion regarding marriage, but I see now that is not to be. You treat people as though they don't matter. As if you are somehow better than them because of your family name and position. But you're not, Kenton. In truth, you're a pathetic, selfish bully, and I have no desire to ever speak to you again."

I turned and strode away. I cared not that people stared at me as I passed.

I had but one thought, one mission.

I must get to Luca.

He needed me, whether he wanted to admit it or not.

Despite Papa's threats and Mother's tears, I left the hotel and took a streetcar to the jailhouse on Second Avenue for the third day in a row. From the moment Luca was arrested, he'd been allowed no visitors, yet I refused to give up. I'd sat in the outer office of the jail for hours, with all manner of reprobates passing by on their way to incarceration. Drunken men offered lurid comments, while women dressed improperly looked on me with contempt. But still I sat and waited. And waited.

Today I came with a new plan.

Wearing one of my finest gowns, I entered the dank building. A young man I'd never seen before sat at the front desk.

Fortuitous, indeed.

When he looked up, I bestowed my brightest smile on him. "Hello, sir. I hope you can help me."

A look of interest filled his eyes. "Yes, ma'am."

I fluttered my lashes. "My papa, Mr. Eldridge Nichols, is concerned for one of our employees who, unfortunately, got into some mischief and landed himself here in your fine jailhouse. We have yet to hear the charges or anything regarding his release." I feigned distress. "Poor Papa. He isn't able to come himself, so I'm here on his behalf."

The young man's brow creased. "I'm sorry to hear this, ma'am. If you'll tell me the prisoner's name, I'll check for you."

"Moretti. Mr. Luca Moretti."

He ran his finger down a ledger. "Yes, he's still in holding." He glanced at me. "It's not very pleasant down there, ma'am. Are you certain you wouldn't rather wait for your father to feel well enough to come himself?"

"Papa is beside himself with worry over Mr. Moretti. He's a fine employee and has never caused us a moment's worry. But—" I shook my head in despair—"with all the celebrating going on, you know how one drink can lead to another, followed by trouble."

He nodded sympathetically. "We've had quite a lot of that since the exposition opened."

"Papa gave me strict instructions not to return until I'd seen Mr. Moretti for myself." I batted my eyelashes again. "You are such a dear man to help a lady in this way."

Within minutes, I stood in front of Luca's cell. Despite bright sunshine outside, the small space held such a gloom, it took a moment for my eyes to adjust. When they did, I gasped.

"Luca."

He lay on a barren cot, his face grotesquely swollen. Dried blood covered his shirt and trousers, and I could detect no breath in his body.

"Open this cell at once," I ordered. Gone was the genteel belle who'd flirted her way into this dungeon.

The startled young man sprang forward to obey.

I flew to Luca's side as soon as the door creaked open. "Oh, Luca. What have they done to you?"

His injuries were far worse than what he'd received in his brawl with Kenton. Clearly someone had beaten him after he left the hotel. I leaned closer, fearful of the worst. Thankfully, breath, although shallow, was there.

"Has a doctor seen him?" I asked the young man.

"I . . . I don't know, ma'am."

"He needs to be in the hospital." I stood, ready to fight whomever I needed to in order to get Luca out of this place. "I demand to speak with the man in charge. Go."

The young officer hurried from the cell. If my presence here earned him a reprimand from his superiors, so be it. Luca was barely alive. I would not allow him to die in this filthy place.

A burly man in uniform soon arrived, with several others behind him. "What's this? Who are you and what are you doing in this cell?"

I gathered every ounce of courage I possessed and faced the men. "I am Miss Priscilla Nichols. My father is Mr. Eldridge Nichols of the Nashville, Chattanooga, and St. Louis. This man—" I indicated Luca—"is our trusted employee. I came here to discover what the delay is with his release, only to find him barely alive. I demand he be removed to a hospital this instant or there will be consequences. My father is a good friend of Governor Taylor, and I'm sure he will have much to say on this matter when I inform him of our employee's deplorable condition while he was in your jailhouse."

The men stared at me, whether in awe of my bravery or with concern for my sanity, I didn't know, but I continued the farce. "Hurry, gentlemen. This man's life—and your jobs—hang in the balance while you stand here gawking at me."

The burly fellow's gaze shifted from me to Luca. His frown deepened. "What is this man in for?" he asked no one in particular.

"Instigating a fight at the Maxwell, sir," said one of the men behind him. The young officer I'd met upon my arrival was no longer present.

"He did not instigate the altercation. I was there." I rested my fists on my hips. "His injuries were minor when he was arrested. This—" I waved my hand toward Luca—"was done after he arrived here, at *your* jailhouse. I doubt the governor will be pleased when he learns of this."

The man eyed me before moving to Luca's bedside to get a closer look.

He studied Luca a long moment, although I could detect no concern in his perusal. Finally he looked at me. "I've no knowledge of when or where this fellow received his injuries, Miss Nichols, but I agree he needs to be transferred to the hospital." His gaze narrowed on me then. "But don't think your threats and mention of the governor swayed my decision. I've been a police officer longer than you've been alive. I know a bluff when I hear one."

I dropped my haughty persona, a bundle of gratitude and humility. "Thank you, sir."

Things happened quickly. Two men loaded Luca onto a stretcher and carried him from the jailhouse. Someone informed me which hospital he would be taken to, then left me forgotten on the sidewalk as the ambulance wagon carried him away. I'd wanted to touch him, to reassure myself he still clung to life, but I couldn't so much as brush a hand across his cheek. I was the daughter of his employer, simply come to inquire after his well-being. To act on impulse would reveal my heart to these strangers.

Everything in me wanted to wave down a cab and follow, but I feared someone would recognize me and guess the truth. I must wait and inquire at the hospital tomorrow, as a good employer would. Until then, my prayers on Luca's behalf would not cease.

When I returned to the hotel, Mother sat in the small receiving room of our suite. Her unhappy glance told me her anger had not cooled.

"I thought you would be at the park by now." I removed my shawl and hat. "Isn't there a luncheon at the Woman's Building you planned to attend?"

"How can I show my face when my daughter is traipsing off to the jailhouse to see her Italian lover? Oh, the shame of it. How could you do this to me, Priscilla?"

I forced myself to remain calm despite her hysterics. "Luca is not my lover, Mother. He's become a friend. As has Gia." I knew that wasn't entirely truthful, but she need not know how my heart had opened to Luca in a way I'd never experienced before. "I'm concerned for them both. Kenton's involvement in this situation is my fault. I introduced them to him."

Her eyes flashed. "Kenton is an innocent party to this sordid business with the Morettis. I can't imagine that you've become so enamored with a hackney driver that you would risk your reputation, and ours, by going to a jailhouse to see him. What did you think you could accomplish?"

"You'll be surprised to hear that I may have saved his life today."

She scowled. "How on earth?"

"He'd been beaten again, most likely after he was arrested. His injuries were far worse than the few bruises he received from Kenton." My throat tightened with the memory of Luca lying unconscious in the dank cell. "No one thought to call a doctor or see to his wounds. He was barely breathing when I arrived."

A spark of curiosity intruded on her scowl. "What did you do?"

"I convinced the jailer to remove him to the hospital."

A silent moment passed before she offered a small concession. "Well, I hope he recovers." Her compassion evaporated. "Still, your behavior is scandalous. Surely you see that. The Thornleys are outraged that not only have you refused their son in marriage, but now it appears you're throwing him over for a . . . a . . ." She closed her eyes. "I can't utter it. It's simply too awful to say aloud."

Her dramatics I could tolerate, but I would not allow her to denigrate Luca. "Mr. Moretti is as fine a gentleman as you will ever find, Mother." She turned away to stare out the window, pretending not to listen. "I daresay he's treated me with more respect since we arrived in Nashville than Kenton ever has."

She whirled on me. "Of course he has, Priscilla. You're the only daughter of a very wealthy man. Someone like Mr. Moretti could easily take advantage of a woman like you."

"A woman like me? And what kind of woman is that?"

Her lips pinched. "Unmarried at twenty-five years of age, that's what. The daughters of all our friends are safely married with children, but here you are, chasing after a hackney driver who isn't even an American. He no doubt saw an opportunity to seduce a woman who, in all likelihood, is destined to be a spinster."

I stared at her. Although I'd suspected her feelings for some time now, it stung to hear them said aloud. "Is that all I am to you, Mother? A disappointment?"

Her heavy sigh echoed in the stillness of the room. "Don't become melodramatic, Priscilla."

"Why shouldn't I? I learned from the best example." I ignored her outraged expression and retrieved my shawl. "I'm going to the park. I don't know when I'll be back."

"You're going alone?" She looked aghast.

"Yes, Mother. Alone. My maid is missing and my driver is in the hospital. It's high time I began to act like the eccentric old spinster you have proclaimed me to be."

I strode out of the suite without a backward glance.

Chapter Twenty

Jason found me in the dining room, where I balanced atop a ladder, hanging holly branches above the arched windows. The lunch crowd had dispersed, so the big, elegant room was quiet.

"Can you get away for an hour or so?" He seemed excited about something.

I climbed down from the ladder, glad for the interruption. My hands stung from handling the prickly greenery. "Sure. What's up?"

He grinned. "I contacted the newspaper office to see if they had anyone who could help track down information from the old clippings we found in the scrapbook."

"And?"

"A reporter named Curtis Brown called me back. He said we could come down to the office and he'd see what he can dig up. He'd also like to see the scrapbook, if you don't mind showing it to him."

I wasn't sure how I felt about that. "You told him about the scrapbook?"

He shrugged. "Yeah. His dad collects memorabilia from the expo. I thought he'd enjoy looking at it."

"I guess that's okay," I said. "Miss Nichols did give it to me."

We drove to the newspaper office and met Mr. Brown, a fellow not much older than Jason. After Jason made our introductions, we settled in chairs across from Curtis's desk in the noisy newsroom, surrounded by other reporters clacking away on typewriters or talking on the telephone.

"I'm a bit of a history buff when it comes to the Tennessee Centennial Expo." He smiled. "May I see the scrapbook?" he asked, eyeing where it sat in my lap.

For some odd reason, I suddenly felt protective of it. Now that we knew Miss Nichols was indeed Peaches and that she'd written the notes on the postcards, I didn't want to betray her trust in giving the book to me. Her privacy was something I intended to guard.

"Yes, but we haven't much time. I need to get back to the hotel soon."

I stood and laid the book on the desk. The three of us discussed the items found on each page, with Curtis genuinely intrigued by them all. Even though I'd returned the postcards to their original locations using small stickers made to hold the corners of pictures in albums instead of glue, I purposefully didn't remove them.

"Boy, my dad would love to see this," he said when I closed the book. "He has quite a collection himself."

"Has he ever heard about young women being stolen from the exposition and sold into prostitution?" Jason asked, getting right to the unpleasant point of why we were there.

Curtis sobered. "After we spoke on the telephone, I called Dad and asked him, but he couldn't recall ever hearing anything like that. Can you show me the articles you found about the investigation? That might help me know where to look for others."

I took the articles out of the scrapbook and handed them to him. He read each one, jotting down notes on a pad of paper. I glanced at the clock. We'd been here nearly an hour. I needed to get back to the hotel and finish decorating before the dinner crowd arrived.

"Hmm. This is interesting. An anonymous source came forward and accused Kenton Thornley of being involved in the kidnapping of a young immigrant woman and forcing her into prostitution." He tapped his finger on the book. "The Thornley family is still pretty prominent in these parts. That one of their ancestors might have been involved in something sinister is worth looking into." He returned the papers to me. "I'll see if I can dig up anything else, but it'll take some time. Everything is on microfilm nowadays."

We thanked him for his time and left the office.

"Well, that wasn't as helpful as I'd hoped." Jason opened the passenger door of his car for me and I climbed in.

When he was behind the wheel, I said, "I thought he might ask to keep the scrapbook to show his father. I'm glad he didn't, because I would have told him no."

He grinned. "It's become important to you, hasn't it?"

I thought about my answer before speaking. "I can't exactly explain it, but this book has made me realize I never really knew Miss Nichols. I was a little girl when Dad took the job as manager of the hotel. She was already living there, so I grew up seeing her from time to time. I always thought of her as a strange old woman, but this book . . ." I looked down to the album in my lap. "It's made me see her in a different way."

"I think I understand. Young people like us forget older people were young once, too." He smiled at me. "This whole experience has made me want to spend more time with my grandparents. I think I'd like to record their life stories. Who knows what family secrets I might uncover."

Back at the hotel, we parted ways. Jason went upstairs to his room to do some studying while I finished my decorating project. I was putting the ladder away in the utility closet down the hall from Dad's office when I heard him talking. A woman laughed.

I froze and listened.

Betty Ann was in his office with him. Should I alert them to my presence? It wasn't unusual for an employee to be in Dad's office, I reminded myself. It wasn't unusual for Betty Ann to be in Dad's office. Yet even though the door stood open, something about finding them here made me uncomfortable.

I decided to make some noise so they'd know I was nearby. I let the ladder crash against the wall, making a loud bang.

Dad immediately appeared in his doorway. "Audrey, are you okay?"

"I was just putting away the ladder." I felt deceitful, even though it was entirely true.

Betty Ann came up behind him. "Well, I best get back to work. Thank you, Dan. I just might take your advice."

She smiled as she passed by on her way back to the lobby.

"Mr. Corsini called while you were out," Dad said once we were alone. "He said he remembered something and wanted you to know. I wrote it down."

I followed him into his office, where he picked up a note from his messy desk. "It's about the day Priscilla and Luca disappeared. He recalled her maid spraining her ankle while they were all at the expo. Luca asked Mr. Corsini to drive her and Mr. Thornley back to the Maxwell while Luca and Priscilla stayed at the expo."

I gasped. "Kenton Thornley? The guy mentioned in the newspaper article?"

Dad shrugged. "He left a number if you want to call him back."

I tucked the paper in my pocket. I'd call Mr. Corsini after I talked to Jason about it.

I headed to the apartment to start dinner. Dad arrived in time to help Emmett set the table, and we sat down to a simple meal of macaroni and cheese with salads.

Emmett chattered about the *Make Room for Daddy* episode he'd watched on television, but I was only half-listening. My thoughts bounced from the newspaper guy to the scrapbook to Mr. Corsini to Dad and Betty Ann, landing there with an unpleasant thud.

"Audrey?"

I looked up from my half-eaten dinner to find Dad's attention on me. "Yes?"

"Your brother asked you a question, but you seem miles away from us."

"Oh, sorry. Emmett, what did you say?"

He repeated the question and I made an effort to show some interest in the conversation, but I was glad when the meal came to an end. Emmett went to his room while Dad and I cleaned up the kitchen.

"Is something troubling you, Audrey?" he asked, toweling off the pot I'd just washed.

I shrugged. "No."

He chuckled. "When a woman says no like that, it clearly means yes. Do you want to talk about it?"

Yes.

No.

I wasn't even sure myself why I was so bugged about Betty

Ann's friendship with Dad. It was nice to see him smile and hear him laugh, but Mama had only been gone a little over a year. Was it too soon for him to have a special female friend?

"What do you think about Betty Ann?" I blurted.

He looked surprised by my question. "Has she done something you're not pleased about?"

I plunged my hands into the soapy water and pulled out the rubber drain stopper. "No. Not exactly."

Dad hung the towel on a hook. "Let's go into the living room and talk."

Great. Now I'd done it. What was I supposed to say? "I think she's flirting with you and I don't like it"?

We settled on the sofa. I grabbed a throw pillow and clutched it against my chest.

"Now, what's going on between you and Betty Ann?" he asked, concern on his face.

"I was going to ask you the same question."

His brow rose. "What do you mean?"

"Well, she's always hanging around you. She's in your office a lot. It just feels . . . weird." I felt like a petulant child, not wishing to share my toys, but I couldn't help it. He'd asked what was wrong.

"She's a new employee," he said, his tone that of the hotel manager, not of my father. "Even though she has prior hotel experience, there are things she has to learn and ask questions about. I don't feel I've spent more time with her than any other new employee."

I felt ridiculous. His answer made sense. "I guess I'm being overly sensitive or something. It just seems like she's very *friendly* with you. Calling you Dan and all." I shrugged, the young person's way of communicating a plethora of feelings, words, and emotions.

He didn't laugh or scold. Instead, he seemed thoughtful for a long moment. "I see your point of view. I do like Betty Ann. It's nice to have someone closer to my age on staff. I suppose that's why it seemed natural for her to call me by my given name rather than Mr. Whitfield."

His eyes sought mine. "I miss your mother every day," he said softly. "She's never far from my thoughts."

"Me too." I hugged the pillow. "I'd like to tell her about Miss Nichols and the scrapbook. She always spoke well of Miss Nichols."

He nodded. "Your mother was a kind and generous woman. She saw people as they were—unique creations made in God's image. That's a rare gift in a world that says you need to look or act a certain way to be considered cool or smart."

"Emmett was lucky to have her," I said, wishing I was more like her. Was that where the idea of working with children like my brother came from? Because I wanted to be like Mama?

"He was." He blew out a heavy breath. "I, on the other hand, didn't see things as she did. Not at first, anyway. I had so much to learn, but she was a patient teacher."

"What do you mean?"

He glanced down the hall to Emmett's room. We could hear him muttering to himself, beginning his bedtime routine. All his comic books had to be lined up just so. He did the same thing with his shoes, his pencils, and anything else left out where he could see them.

"I was in Europe when your brother was born."

"You were fighting in the war."

"Yes. I couldn't get leave to come home for his birth, so I relied on the letters your mother sent. I was so proud to have a son and a daughter. What man could ask for more?" He looked at the black-and-white picture of Mama on the end table. It had been taken before she and Dad married. "The thing is, Irene didn't tell me he was . . . different. It came as a shock when the war ended and I returned home. I tried to love him. He's my son, after all. But I couldn't get over the disappointment."

I sat silent, stunned by Dad's admission. "But you love him now, don't you?"

He smiled. "Yes, sweetheart. I love him. I love you both, with every fiber of my soul. But . . ." He grew serious again. "I'm ashamed to admit it took several years for me to see Emmett the way your mother did."

I recalled my own shameful feelings about my brother I'd experienced growing up. I couldn't imagine my father—Emmett's father—having similar feelings.

"You wanted to send him away," I said, the memory I'd recently had of Mama reading the papers from the institution resurfacing.

"I did, I'm sorry to say. When your mother refused, as she had a right to, I gave her an ultimatum. She could keep Emmett, but I would leave and take you with me. If she wanted to keep you, then Emmett had to be sent to an institution."

I gasped. "You were going to make her choose between us?"

He nodded. "I was. I did, in fact. When she said she couldn't send him to an institution, I took that as her answer. I packed your things, put you in the car, and drove to Louisville. You and I stayed with my parents for a week. I thought I was teaching your mother a lesson, but I'm the one who had things to learn."

"I don't remember any of this."

"No, you wouldn't. You were just a little girl going to visit your grandparents."

"What happened?" I asked, shocked by the whole thing.

"Well, your mother and your grandmother started praying

for me. Harder than they'd prayed when I was in the war, I think. But God used you, my little girl, to open my eyes."

"Me?"

He reached to touch my cheek. "'And a little child shall lead them.' That's a verse about the coming Messiah found in the book of Isaiah, but I think of it when I think of the day you taught me how to love my son." A tear slipped down his cheek. "I'd argued with your mother on the telephone, angry she continued to fight me on sending Emmett away. I'd had enough and told her I would file for divorce the next day. What an ignorant, arrogant fool I was in those days." He shook his head. "You and Grandma had been working a puzzle that day, but when you got to the end, you discovered one piece was missing. The puzzle couldn't be completed. As I tucked you into bed later, you started to cry, saying you missed Mama and Emmett. I tried to convince you we were on an adventure, but you weren't having it. You took my face in your hands and said, just as serious as can be, 'Daddy, let's go home. We're not complete without Mama and Emmett.'"

He took a handkerchief from his pocket and wiped his nose. "You were right, of course. We were a family. The four of us. We drove back to Nashville the next day. When we walked through the door, Emmett's face lit up. 'Daddy,' he hollered and came running to me. I scooped him up and his little arms went around my neck. I held him and wept like a baby."

"And Mama? Did she forgive you?"

He nodded. "She did. We never spoke of it again."

After Dad and I said good night, I went to my room, my mind full of my parents' story. I still couldn't image that Dad, my loving, patient father, had once been so selfish he was willing to tear apart our family. What if he'd made a different choice that long-ago day?

"And a little child shall lead them."

I turned out the light, a sense of awe covering me even as I climbed under the blankets.

Had God really used me to save my Dad? To save our family?

Mama's words came back to me as I lay in the darkness.

"God has a wonderful plan for you, Audrey," she'd said the last time I saw her. We stood at the bus station, with noise and people and distractions all around. I was headed back to school after summer break, anxious to be away from her and Emmett and the hotel. Carving out a life far from Nashville was my only desire.

Now here I was, home, but she was gone. Oh, what I wouldn't give to go back in time. Maybe not to the beginning of my life, but to that day. Had I known it was the last time I would see her alive, I would have told her how much I loved her, how grateful I was to be her daughter.

I closed my eyes, thinking of the story Dad told. I realized he and I were not so different. He'd been selfish and hadn't appreciated all God had given him. Wasn't I guilty of the same thing?

But Mama and Emmett were our teachers. Teaching us still.

"Thank you for not giving up on us, Mama," I whispered into the darkness.

———————

The hospital buzzed with activity when I arrived the following afternoon. It seemed the flood of visitors to Nashville for the centennial celebration had spilled over into a need for medical services for many of them. With the halls and waiting areas filled with patients and their family members, I found it quite easy to slip past the busy nurse in charge and search for Luca.

I located him in a large room with a dozen beds, all occupied by men of varying ages. A uniformed police officer sat in the hallway outside the door reading a newspaper, but he didn't look up when I passed.

I entered the room with an air of confidence lest anyone question my presence there. A few men had visitors, and I nodded politely to a woman across the aisle who sat next to a man with a broken leg.

Luca rested in a bed near one of three windows in the room, each partially open to let in fresh air, a welcome respite from the sour smell of illness and unwashed bodies that lingered in the hallways.

His eyes were closed, but thankfully the terrible swelling in his face had gone down. Bruises colored his skin and bandages circled his head like a crown, but he was alive.

I glanced out the door. The officer continued his study of the paper.

"Luca," I called softly, bending near his ear. "Can you hear me? Luca?"

He must not have been sleeping, because his eyes immediately opened. A look of confusion clouded his face. "Priscilla, you should not be here."

I found it encouraging he didn't call me *signorina*. "I had to come see how our favorite employee is doing." While I wasn't speaking overly loud, we were afforded no privacy. If someone overheard our conversation, I wanted them to hear only what I intended them to hear.

"But your parents—"

"Are concerned as well." I gave him a pointed look, hoping

he would not say something to give me away. "Now, tell me, what did the doctor say? Have you any broken bones?"

He shook his head, then grimaced. "Only a concussion."

"And you will recover quickly?"

"I should be improved in a few days."

I peeked at the men in the beds on either side of Luca, but they appeared to be asleep. I hoped so, anyway. "What happened at the jail? Who beat you?" I whispered.

"I cannot say. They wore hoods."

I frowned. "Hoods?" An image surfaced in my memory. Several years ago, I'd seen a drawing in an issue of *Harper's Weekly* of two men in robes and white hoods covering their faces. I'd asked Mother about them, but she'd given a vague answer. It had been our housekeeper, Gloria, who told me the terrible truth. "Do you mean the kind worn by the Ku Klux Klan?"

He nodded. "I heard Thornley's voice. He was there."

I reeled back. "Are you certain?"

"I am."

As much as I didn't want to believe my childhood playmate would participate in the hateful organization, I had no reason to think Luca would make up such a tale. Besides, Kenton's recent words and actions revealed a deeper level of vileness in him than I could have imagined only a week prior. An association with hooded men who threatened and beat those they found inferior would not surprise me.

He slowly moved his head to glance toward the door. I forced myself not to turn in the same direction. If the officer was still at his post, he might become suspicious if we both looked his way.

He motioned me closer and lowered his voice. "They mean to take me back to jail in the morning."

Alarm swept through me. Returning Luca to the jailhouse meant they had no intention of releasing him anytime soon. Kenton's idea, no doubt. If Kenton was able to get himself and his hooded cohorts inside the jail to beat Luca, he surely had connections that allowed him to dictate what became of Luca.

Panic surged through me.

I couldn't let them take him back, yet I hadn't a clue what could be done. Papa might hold some influence, but it was doubtful he would use it to free Luca, especially considering it was Kenton who had Luca arrested.

"We must get you out of here before then," I whispered, shocked yet emboldened by my brazen declaration.

"How, *signorina*? There is a guard all day and all night." He blew out a breath that revealed his frustration. "It is *impossibile*."

He was right, of course. How could we manage to get him past the guard, past the other patients, and out the front door without being noticed? Then there were his injuries to consider. Would he even be able to walk on his own if we somehow managed to exit the building?

A shaft of afternoon sunshine landed on Luca's blanket. I glanced out the window, but all I could see was the solid brick wall of another building, separated from the hospital by a narrow alley.

If only there was a way to—

An idea suddenly spilled into my mind.

Utterly ridiculous. Completely insane. Impossible, as Luca said.

And yet . . .

"Luca, where is your horse and carriage?"

He gave me a curious look. "At the livery near the docks. Why?"

I leaned close, gazing into his eyes. "Do you trust me?" I whispered.

A silent moment passed before his body relaxed and a faint smile creased his bruised face.

"With my life."

Chapter Twenty-One

Our plan nearly failed before it began.

The livery owner refused to release Luca's horse and carriage to me despite my insistence that I had his permission. When he asked after Luca's whereabouts, I told him the truth. Mostly. I said Luca was in the hospital and needed me to fetch the carriage to transport him home. I left out the part about him being a prisoner with the intent of escaping. When the man volunteered to drive the carriage himself, I thanked him profusely but insisted I could manage. The generous tip I offered finally appeased him, and he set about harnessing the horse, with only a few sideways glances at me during the process.

The rig was larger than I remembered. Climbing up to the driver's seat, I realized it was one thing to be a pampered lady, driven about town by a handsome man, and quite another to do the driving oneself. Luckily, Luca's horse was a mild-mannered Tennessee walker and gave me no trouble as

I maneuvered down unfamiliar streets, trying to retrace the route I'd taken to the livery.

With only one wrong turn on our journey, we arrived at the alley behind the hospital. I waited to see if anyone would object to my presence, but after many long minutes of solitude, I set the brake and climbed down.

Sunset was only a half hour or so away, so I needed to get my bearings before the alley was plunged into darkness. Before leaving Luca's room, I'd torn a piece of lace from my handkerchief and anchored it on a loose nail on the windowsill while pretending to spy an unusual bird, should anyone be watching.

Relief washed over me when I spotted the lace, flapping in the light, southerly breeze. The feeling evaporated, however, when I realized the drop from the window ledge to the ground was much farther than it appeared from the inside. I could only assume a basement beneath the hospital was the cause, but now I wondered if the drop would be too much for Luca's injured body. After studying the situation, I determined that if I could manage to pull the carriage up to the window, Luca should be able to lower himself onto the driver's seat.

I didn't linger at the window for fear someone inside would see me. Luca's horse bobbed his head in greeting when I returned to the carriage.

"Not too much longer, sweet boy." I rubbed his powerful neck. "We'll have your owner safely away."

Or so I prayed.

Helping a prisoner escape wasn't something a good Christian woman would normally do, yet hadn't angels helped Peter escape when he was wrongly imprisoned? Surely God could see the injustice of Luca's incarceration and would grant us success.

After petitioning the Almighty on Luca's behalf, my prayers turned to Gia. Where was she? Had she willingly left the hotel with Kenton the day she hurt her ankle? And if so, why?

"Keep her safe," I breathed.

Darkness soon blanketed the alley, with only a sliver of moon that posed no threat of exposure. All was quiet in this part of town, with the exposition fairgrounds, hotels, and restaurants many blocks away. An occasional wagon or carriage passed the opening to the alley, but no one stopped to investigate why a lone woman waited outside a hospital window.

When the lights in Luca's room went out, my heart began to race. Luca was to decide when to make his escape, as he would be the only one able to determine if the other men were asleep and if the police officer in the hallway had dozed off.

Over an hour passed before I spotted movement at the window. I hurried to climb onto the driver's seat, loosened the brake, and flicked the reins, trusting that Luca's horse could see in the dark. I tugged him to a stop beneath the window.

Out of the shadows, Luca's legs swung through the opening. A moment later he was sitting on the ledge, breathing heavily.

"Can you get onto the seat?" I whispered, trying to keep the horse steady.

He put his finger to his lips, with a glance behind to be certain no one stirred.

In the next instant, he launched himself from the window and landed on the seat next to me with a great thud. The horse whinnied, startled by the movement.

"Who's there?" came a voice from inside the room.

"Go," Luca said, bent over and gasping beside me.

I slapped the reins, sending the frightened horse into a gallop. We flew from the alley into the street, where thankfully few vehicles or pedestrians were about. I didn't know where to go and simply let the horse run.

"Let me take over." Luca took the reins from me and soon had the beast under control with some soothing Italian words. We drew to a stop on a dark street.

"I can't believe the plan worked." He clutched his ribs.

"Are you hurt? I mean, more than you were before?"

He shook his head. "Just bruised. I'll be fine in a few days." His eyes met mine. "You've risked everything to help me. How can I ever thank you, *signorina*?"

I grinned. "You can stop calling me *signorina*."

But he didn't smile at my joke. In fact, he grew even more serious. "We must get you back to the hotel before your family misses you."

"No." I placed my hand on his. "I want to help you find Gia."

"I am an escaped prisoner, *sig*—Priscilla. You cannot be seen with me."

Fear took hold in my heart then. I knew what we'd done tonight was unlawful, but I hadn't thought ahead to how it would affect us. "What are you saying? That I won't ever see you again?"

A distant shout reached us. Whether it had anything to do with his escape, we couldn't be certain.

"I must get you back to the hotel." He gave the horse a command in Italian and flicked the reins.

My question hung heavy in the silence as we drove toward the Maxwell. Even as my heart ached to stay with him, I knew I couldn't. It was too dangerous for both of us.

"Stop here." We were still several blocks away. "Someone from the hotel might recognize you if you take me all the way back."

"I cannot let you walk from here. It isn't safe."

"You must." I reached to tug on the reins. "I'll be fine." When the carriage came to a stop, I turned to him. "I wish there was more I could do to help. Maybe Papa could speak with Kenton and have the charges against you dropped."

"Don't you see? If you become any more involved, they will guess at who helped me." His eyes implored me to listen. "You must act normal. Go to the park. Eat dinner with your family. Don't give them a reason to suspect anything is amiss."

"Where will you go?"

"I have a friend I can trust. He'll give me a place to sleep. I'm no good to Gia in this condition."

I couldn't let this be the end. "In a few days, when things have settled, send me a message and let me know where I can find you. Please."

I thought he would refuse, but finally he nodded.

"In a few days."

I climbed from the seat and watched him drive away. A lone tear slid down my cheek. I didn't know if I would ever see him or Gia again.

Exhausted, I started down Second Avenue in the direction of the Maxwell. I'd never walked through the streets of Nashville before and found I was more than a little apprehensive. Gas streetlights cast eerie shadows, and only a few pedestrians were about this close to the river.

When I came to the public square, I noticed several young women loitering in the glow of a streetlamp in front of a store that sold liquor. I couldn't imagine why they'd be out so late, but then the centennial celebration had altered normal hours to be out in the city. Men came and went from the business, some stopping to chat with the women while others continued on their way, carrying their purchases in paper bags.

I quickly crossed the street, intent on getting to the Maxwell, but I kept glancing back at the odd scene, as though I needed to understand what I was seeing. The women were not customers at the store as far as I could tell. They simply milled about, laughing and flirting with the men.

Just before I turned down Charlotte Avenue, I glanced back one last time.

My breath caught.

A man who looked very much like Kenton climbed from a hackney. The four girls moved toward him, their excited chatter reaching me, although I couldn't make out the words. Whether the man was indeed Kenton, I couldn't be positive, but a moment later, he climbed back into the hackney and was joined by two of the women.

I slipped into the shadows as the vehicle passed. It was

too dark to make out their features, but a chill of foreboding swept over me as I watched it head into the dark night.

I had no knowledge of what I'd just witnessed, but my instincts told me all was not well.

I glanced back to the two remaining women, their youth reminding me of Gia.

Did their families know where they were tonight? Was someone worried because they weren't home, safe in their beds?

The answers haunted me as I made my way back to the Maxwell House Hotel.

———————————

Wednesday morning found me behind the guest services desk. Betty Ann was occupied with preparations for the annual Alpha Chi fraternity dance at the hotel on Friday, so I'd volunteered to watch the desk.

The elevator chimed.

A few moments later, old Mr. Hanover and his dachshund, Copper, exited into the lobby. The *click, click, click* of the little dog's nails and the *tap, tap, tap* of Mr. Hanover's cane on the checkered marble floor made me smile as the two approached the desk.

"Good morning, Mr. Hanover. How is Copper today?"

The gray-haired gentleman grinned. "Fit as a fiddle and ready to take me on my walk." He winked.

I expected him to continue on his way, but he set a newspaper on the counter in front of me. He tapped a place on the open page. "That's an interesting article about you and that scrapbook of Priscilla's."

I blinked. "Excuse me?"

He thumped the paper again. "Right here. Says you found

an old scrapbook about the Tennessee Centennial Exposition in her room. Talks about how she was a collector of centennial memorabilia and such. Made me wish I'd visited the exposition when I was young, but back then I was living in Lexington."

He launched into a story of his boyhood in Kentucky, but my attention raced to the newspaper. Small yet bold print proclaimed, "Old Scrapbook Offers New Leads into Dark Thornley Past."

Copper whined, out of sight from where I sat with my mouth gaping in shock.

"I better get this fellow outside before we have a puddle to clean." The pair headed across the lobby to the exit.

I snatched up the newspaper and read, with horror, every detail Jason and I had shared with Curtis Brown the previous day about the scrapbook. Although he didn't mention Miss Nichols by name, he referenced her as an elderly longtime resident of the Maxwell who'd recently suffered a stroke. He went on to detail how I'd discovered the scrapbook and that evidence found within its pages alluded to a link between Kenton Thornley and the unsavory topic of kidnapping and forced prostitution.

I held my breath as I read the last paragraph.

Thornley and his father were suspected members of the Ku Klux Klan, although this reporter could not verify the information. It is known, however, that the senior Thornley's father owned several ships that transported slaves in the 1800s.

My heart hammered, and a sick feeling overcame me. What had we done? Why had Curtis Brown published the article? We hadn't gone to him with a story. We'd simply asked for help researching the link between Miss Nichols and the clippings in her scrapbook. Never did I dream Curtis would print any of it.

And the references to the Thornleys' questionable past? I hadn't had a chance to call Mr. Corsini back and ask about Kenton Thornley. Now it was too late. The whole city knew about him.

I groaned and closed my eyes.

What would Dad say when he found out? He loathed bad publicity about the Maxwell.

I had to find Jason.

Without giving any details about the mess I was in, I called Lucille and asked her to keep an eye on the front desk while I ran an errand. Thankfully, Mrs. Ruth was with Emmett in our apartment baking Christmas cookies for the hotel residents, so he would be occupied for some time.

I took the elevator to the third floor. Jason had planned to stay in and study today and quickly answered the door when I knocked.

"Hey." He greeted me with a smile and a bundle of towels. "Sorry; I thought you were the maid." He chuckled but sobered when he saw my face. "What's wrong? Has something happened to Miss Nichols?"

I pushed the newspaper into the towels. "I could wring Curtis Brown's neck."

Surprise lifted his brow. "Why? What's he done?"

I pointed to the paper. "Read it."

He dropped the towels and read. When he finished, he gave a low whistle, then looked up at me. "Oh, boy."

"'Oh, boy' is right." My angry voice echoed in the hallway. "How could he do this? We didn't give our permission for any of this to be printed in the newspaper."

Two doors down, Mr. Carlson, another resident, stepped into the hallway and looked over his thick-rimmed glasses at us. "Oh, it's you, Audrey. Everything all right?"

I offered a false smile. "Yes, Mr. Carlson, it is. I'm sorry we disturbed you."

"No bother." He turned back to his room, then stopped. "By the way, that article in today's paper is a doozy. Never thought of Priscilla as the sort to get involved in something like that."

When he closed his door behind him, I moaned. "This is bad, Jason. This is really bad."

He handed the paper back to me. "Hold on. Let me get my coat and we'll go someplace to talk."

We made our way downstairs. Lucille gave me a sly look when I told her we'd be back in a bit. I didn't have time to set her straight. This was no date.

We walked around the corner to the Copper Kettle restaurant. Luckily, the lunch crowd hadn't arrived yet, and we found a quiet booth in the corner. The waitress took our order for cheeseburgers and fries, although with my stomach in knots, I wasn't the least bit hungry.

"I feel responsible for this, since it was my idea to contact the newspaper." Jason blew out a breath. "Some law student I am, huh? I should have made sure he understood everything we talked about was confidential."

"Mama always said blame wasn't useful. This isn't your fault. Curtis Brown took advantage of us. Isn't there anything we can do? Sue him or the newspaper?"

Despite the seriousness of the situation, Jason's mouth tipped in a slight grin. "These aren't national secrets. The best we can do is try to get a retraction from him, but—" he sobered—"the damage has already been done."

I knew he was right. "It just makes me so angry. Poor Miss

Nichols. If she knew what I'd done with her personal belongings . . ." Tears stung my eyes.

He reached across the table and put his hand over mine. "You haven't done anything wrong. The articles in the scrapbook are available for the public to read at the library, and Brown found the information about the Thornleys on his own. We had no knowledge of their connection to the Klan or slavery."

"But we're the ones who opened this can of worms with our snooping into Miss Nichols's private life."

He removed his hand and leaned back against the red vinyl bench. "That's true, but there isn't anything we can do about it now."

"I hate to think what Dad will say when he learns about all this. He's very protective of the Maxwell and the residents."

Our food came, but both of us picked at it until we finally gave up. Jason paid the bill, and we walked back to the hotel. Lucille waved me down when we entered.

"You had a call while you were out, Audrey."

I waited for her to hand me a message, but instead she wore an odd expression. "The woman wouldn't give her name. She asked when you'd be back and said she'd call again."

"That's strange." I had no choice but to wait until the mystery woman called back.

Jason returned to his room, and I returned to my post at the desk.

I dreaded telling Dad about the article, but I'd rather he heard about it from me than one of the residents. Mr. Carlson's remarks told me the wheels of the gossip mill were already turning. Dad would need to do something fast to squelch it. Miss Nichols didn't deserve to have her good name sullied because of Jason's and my stupidity.

The phone on the desk rang a short time later.

I glanced up to see Lucille wave at me from the door to her small office. "It's that woman," she hollered across the lobby, something Dad would scold her for if he knew.

I grabbed the receiver. "Hello, this is Audrey Whitfield. How may I help you?"

The other end of the line was silent for a long moment before the woman spoke. "You can stop spreading lies about the Thornley family," she said, a thick Southern drawl drawing out her words. "Then you can destroy that scrapbook, if you know what's good for you. Or I may have to do it myself."

With a click, the line went dead.

Chapter Twenty-Two

The calendar said it had been three days since Luca escaped from the hospital, but it felt like an eternity.

Despite my determination to act normal, Mother questioned me multiple times about Luca after news of his escape appeared in the newspaper the previous day. I'd feigned shock when she read it to me, with her filling in details given to Kenton by the police about their suspicions that someone had aided Luca. A witness saw a carriage in the alley, but he couldn't say who was driving it. After I'd returned to the hotel that night, Mama found me sitting in one of the women's salons, listening to a poetry reading. We'd gone upstairs together, unexpectedly providing an alibi should it come to that. According to Kenton, the police believed Luca and his accomplice had long fled the city and posed no threat to the Thornleys or the public. I couldn't help but feel on edge, however, knowing I was the person the police sought.

The subject regrettably resurfaced today after lunch when

Mother asked if I'd like to tour the Children's Building. Without thought, I said I'd seen it with Luca and Gia.

"Good riddance to the both of them." She dusted a crumb from the lace-covered table in the open-air restaurant on top of the Woman's Building. We'd spent the morning with Papa touring the Commerce Building, but he'd declined our invitation to dine on shrimp and crab salad, promising to return to escort us back to the hotel at three o'clock.

"It's quite appalling those Morettis were allowed employment in a fine establishment like the Maxwell House," she continued, much to my dismay. "I suppose the manager can't be completely to blame, as they certainly hid their bent toward crime well. Why, the girl even lied about her age in order to secure a job. I daresay he'll be more careful about who he hires in the future."

I bit my tongue to keep from defending Luca's and Gia's reputations. In the short time I'd known them, I could safely say I'd never met a more loving and hardworking set of siblings. Yet it would do no good to say such to Mother. I only hoped Luca would contact me soon to let me know how he fared and if he'd located Gia. That was all that mattered.

"Your father is pleased with the turn in your behavior the past few days." She eyed me over the rim of a china teacup, took a dainty sip, then set it down without clinking the plate. "He's hopeful this means you will reconsider Kenton's offer. Despite the unpleasant business of the past few days, Kenton is still willing to see things through."

A warm breeze carrying the perfume of the flower garden below wafted over us.

I inhaled the calming scent. "Mother, the day is much too lovely to argue. Can't we talk about something else?"

She looked offended. "I have no intention of arguing. I'm simply reminded, today of all days, that life is short."

The wistful comment puzzled me. Then I remembered the date. My older brother would have turned thirty years of age today, had he survived infancy. All these years later, Mother still grieved the loss of her only son. Papa never mentioned it, but I suspected he did as well.

"I want grandchildren, Priscilla." She glanced to where a young mother bounced a baby in a frilly white gown. "Several, in fact." Her attention returned to me. "My only desire is for your happiness. You understand that, don't you?"

Her sincerity touched me. "I do, Mother, but marrying Kenton Thornley would not make me happy. I see things in him that . . . disturb me." My mind raced back to the night of the escape, when I'd seen a man who resembled Kenton in the public square, soliciting women I believed to be harlots. I'd come to the conclusion there could be no other explanation for the scene I'd witnessed, no matter if the man was Kenton or not. Then there was Luca's belief that Kenton had been among the hooded assailants who beat him in the jailhouse.

Disappointment shaded her face. "It pains me to say this, Priscilla, but if you do not accept Kenton, another offer may not come. Aside from the fact you would never have children, have you considered the great burden that would be thrust upon you when your father leaves this world? Without a male heir, the responsibility for his wealth and his business interests would fall to you." She shook her head, as though the mere thought of a woman handling financial affairs would be her demise.

Had she learned nothing while touring the Woman's Building? Why, the place was full, from one end to the other, with inventions, patents, books, artwork, and a host of items, all created by women. Even the building itself had been designed by Mrs. Sara Ward-Conley to resemble the Hermitage, the home of President Andrew Jackson.

Yet there was truth in her words. I hadn't considered what would happen should I never marry. Taking over Papa's business affairs wasn't something I had an interest in doing, but without my brother or a husband, there was no one else. Mother's unhappy confidence that spinsterhood loomed in my future was worrisome, but not to the point of being willing to sacrifice my happiness by marrying someone completely unsuitable.

Seeing as she would not leave the subject, I turned the tables on her. "Why do you wish me to marry Kenton? What is it about him—not his family—that makes you believe he would make a good husband?"

She seemed taken aback by my question. "Why, we've known him since he was a boy. You grew up together."

"Yes, and if I recall correctly, you thought him a spoiled, churlish child."

A moment passed before she chuckled. "I suppose I did."

"And you believe he has outgrown these characteristics?" I continued, knowing she could not avoid the truth.

"What is your point, Priscilla? No one is perfect. Your father has his faults, as do I, but we've had a good life together.

That's all I want for you. And yes, I believe you can have that with Kenton."

"That is where we differ, Mother. I don't believe Kenton could ever be the man I'd wish to spend my entire life with, let alone be the father of my children." I thought of Luca. His smile, his eyes. His love for Gia. His respect toward me. "I believe there is someone out there for me, but if not, I'll carve out a life for myself." I grasped her hands. "There are worse things than being a spinster, you know."

She scowled. "Name one."

I laughed and stood, putting an end to the conversation. "Let's wait for Papa outside. I hear the gardens are glorious, and you know how you love a good rosebush."

We returned to the Maxwell shortly after three o'clock. Mother and Papa had tickets for the theatre tonight, so she went upstairs to rest while Papa headed to the men's salon to enjoy a cigar. I wandered the lobby, my thoughts on Gia and Luca. Perhaps I would seek out Mrs. Smith once again to see if she remembered anything more about the day Gia disappeared. I'd questioned the older woman after Luca was arrested, but she clearly hadn't appreciated my involvement. She'd wrongly believed I thought her responsible in some way, but even after I explained I merely wanted to help find the girl, she'd pinched her lips and walked away.

Feeling rather useless, I decided to go upstairs after all. I'd just arrived at the bottom of the staircase when an older man, vaguely familiar, approached.

"Miss Nichols, may I speak with you?" His eyes darted about, and he appeared quite nervous.

I suddenly recognized him as the livery owner. Did he have news of Luca?

"Of course." I motioned him over to a set of empty chairs off the main lobby. No one lingered nearby to overhear our conversation.

I sat down, but when it became obvious he had no intention of doing so, I stood again.

"I have a message for you, miss." Once again, he glanced around before handing me a folded square of paper.

Elated, I accepted it and slipped it into my reticule. "Have you seen our friend?" I whispered.

He hesitated before nodding. "I purchased something from him."

Did he mean Luca's horse and carriage?

"I best be on my way, miss. Wouldn't want anyone getting suspicious."

I watched him leave. I wanted to chase after him and ask a hundred questions, but I remained where I was, clutching my reticule to my heart.

I raced upstairs. Thankfully, Mother's door was closed and Fanny was not in the suite. I hurried to my room, turning the key in the lock to ensure my privacy.

My heart pounded as I took out the note. No handwriting marked the outside, but what mattered was what was written inside.

Need your help. Meet at Rialto at sunset.

The brief message wasn't what I'd hoped for, yet a surge of elation went through me. Luca was safe and he needed me.

I glanced out the window. It was still several hours until the sun set. I wasn't certain I could sit still and wait, worrying about what was happening and why Luca needed help. Besides, what would I say to Mother when I prepared to leave the suite? I'd already informed her I would have a tray brought up for my dinner and spend the evening reading while she and Papa enjoyed dinner at the Tulane Hotel with friends, followed by a play at the theatre.

I moved to the desk. To leave a note indicating I'd gone shopping seemed the best solution. To make certain it wasn't a lie, I would indeed purchase something, perhaps a gift for Mother, at one of the shops lining Church Street on my way to catch the streetcar to the fairgrounds.

After two attempts at wording the message just so, I hurried to tidy my hair, grabbed my shawl and hat, and exited the suite before Mother woke from her nap and Papa returned to ready for the evening.

I slowed as I came to the marble stairs, not wishing to draw unneeded attention. I prayed I wouldn't encounter Papa or Kenton and quickly turned toward the women's entrance once I reached the lobby. Outside in the late-afternoon sunshine, I inhaled deeply to quiet my racing heart.

With a casualness that belied the anxiety swirling through me, I strolled down Church Street, glancing in windows and nodding politely to women or children I passed on the sidewalk. I stopped and studied a lovely gown, a book, a hat. Anything that might catch the eye of someone out for an afternoon of shopping. I didn't believe anyone was following me, but the knowledge that I planned to meet Luca, an escaped prisoner, wouldn't allow me to relax.

After purchasing a hair comb decorated with red glass beads in the shape of a flower, I proceeded to the streetcar stop. With so many people going and coming from the exposition, trolleys ran nearly nonstop.

I boarded and found a seat. Pleasant conversation took place around me, with fairgoers chattering about the exhibits, Vanity Fair, and the delicious food they planned to enjoy. A wistfulness engulfed me, remembering the happy day I'd spent with Luca at the park.

Yet the memories were bittersweet. Dear Gia was whisked away from us, a grin on her face, never to be seen again. And Luca was now a wanted man.

At the park, I paid the fee and entered, unsure where to go. I still had two hours or more before the sun set. I had no interest in touring the exhibits I still hadn't seen and instead found a bench in the shade of a tree near the gourd arbor, not far from the Children's Building.

The warm breeze nearly lulled me to sleep as I watched little boys and girls run and play. They reminded me of Mother's desire for grandchildren. I, too, hoped one day I would be blessed with a son or daughter, but the fact remained that I would not marry Kenton. I hadn't wanted to share my true misgivings about him with Mother, mainly because I had no proof of his involvement in Luca's beating or Gia's disappearance, but they were enough for me to feel confident in my decision to refuse his offer.

My thoughts shifted to Luca.

I knew my heart belonged to him. I think it had from the moment I saw him in the lobby of the Maxwell, refusing to allow Kenton to belittle him. Yet I also knew our situation was impossible. What future was there for us with Gia missing and him an escaped prisoner? The evening we spent together at the park, drifting along in the gondola, with Luca singing softly, I'd let myself imagine a life with him. Dream of a small, comfortable house with flowers in the yard and the happy voices of children drifting from the open windows. Ours would be a simple life without gowns, balls, and amusements, but at that moment, it sounded heavenly.

Mother's unkind words about Luca's interest in the money I stood to inherit blotted out the pleasant image. Perhaps I was naive about many worldly issues, but I wasn't so silly that I couldn't tell if a man's interest was genuine or not. I'd had plenty of experience fending off would-be suitors in Chattanooga, each hoping to attain the status of Eldridge Nichols's son-in-law. Their contrived affections were the only reason I'd briefly considered Kenton's offer, revealing, at least to me, my desperation to avoid becoming the wife of a man who didn't love me.

With the sun hanging low on the horizon, I stayed where I was, even as the crowds began to thin. The dinner hour fast approached, and families with young children headed toward the exits while couples strolled in the direction of the Blue Grotto or the Old Vienna Restaurant. I'd wait another half hour before making my way to the Rialto Bridge. I couldn't see it from my location, with the gourd arbor obstructing my view, but it would only take a few minutes to reach it.

I was just turning away when someone at the far end of the arbor caught my attention. Long dark hair hung down her back and she wore no hat, but something about her seemed familiar. She appeared to be waiting for someone, looking back and forth as people passed by.

I stood and started toward her, still some distance away, my curiosity piqued.

When she turned my direction, I gasped.

Gia.

I didn't know if I spoke her name aloud, but the young woman's gaze met mine. Her eyes widened.

"Gia," I shouted and waved, too surprised to know what to do.

I thought she would immediately come toward me, but instead she bolted in the opposite direction.

"Gia!"

I lifted the hem of my skirt and ran after her, ignoring the strange looks of bystanders. When I reached the arbor, I was out of breath, and Gia was nowhere to be seen. I stood there, panting, tears stinging my eyes as I searched to no avail.

Why had she run away? Where had she been all this time?

My mind couldn't formulate a logical reason for what had just happened, but I knew I needed to tell Luca I'd seen Gia. That she was here, at the park. Perhaps we could find her together.

I hurried to the Rialto. Sunset was still several minutes away, but I prayed Luca was early.

I nearly wilted with relief when I saw him sitting near the water's edge, partially hidden beneath the bridge. He wore a dark hat pulled down over his ears and a long coat I didn't recognize, but I knew it was him.

He stood when he saw me.

Several people hung over the bridge above him, watching

a gondola drift by, so I motioned for him to follow me. We walked toward the Parthenon, stopping in the shadow of the enormous Pallas Athena statue.

"Luca, I've seen Gia," I blurted before he had an opportunity to speak.

His brow tugged in confusion. "What do you mean? Where?"

"Here. Over by the arbor. Just a few minutes ago." I took his hand. "Come, we must look for her."

But he didn't move. "I don't understand. Why would she be here and not let me know she is safe?" His eyes bored into mine. "Are you certain it was her?"

I let go of his hand. "Yes. She looked right at me but then ran away. I tried to follow her, but she vanished into the crowd."

A pained expression came over his face. "Did she seem well?"

I realized then that Gia's presence at the fair was not good news to Luca. His sister was here, but she continued to stay hidden from him.

"She looked different, with her hair loose. I've never seen her in anything other than her maid uniform, but today she wore a bright-red dress."

His frown deepened. "She doesn't own a red dress."

I didn't know what to say. I was as confused as he about what I'd seen. "Should we search for her?" I asked, knowing it would be next to impossible to find her in the park, but surely we needed to do something.

A tired sigh passed over his lips, and he shook his head. Fading bruises still marred his face, and he looked exhausted.

I couldn't let him lose hope. "Gia wouldn't have run away from me unless she'd been told to stay away from anyone who knew her. I refuse to believe she's acting in this alone."

"But if she was in danger, why wouldn't she come to you? She knows she can trust you."

I put my hand on his arm. "I don't have the answers, Luca, but we mustn't give up. She needs us."

After a long moment, he nodded. "I asked you to meet me because I've learned something about Thornley." The ominous tone in his lowered voice sent a chill through me despite the warm evening. "It is not something I would ever discuss with a lady—you, especially—but I find I have no alternative. You are the only one who can help me."

I swallowed, dreading what he had to tell me.

He glanced around to make certain no one could hear us. "The friend I've been staying with knows a man who is a frequent customer of . . . houses of ill repute." His discomfort in relaying such information to me was evident, and I loved him all the more for it. "He is certain a man named Thornley is in partnership with the madam of one of these houses."

My mouth gaped. "Surely not."

"He mentioned it to my friend after reading about my escape in the newspaper. The article said I'd been arrested for attacking Kenton Thornley. This man recognized the name."

I knew I shouldn't be surprised to discover yet another disturbing revelation about Kenton, but I was. How could the boy I'd grown up with be involved in something like this? Yet the evidence revealed it must be true.

"Did your friend ask about Gia? Maybe the man saw her there."

Luca shook his head. "My friend asked, but no, this fellow has not seen her."

"What do we do now? If we go to the police and tell them what's happened, they'd have to search the house for Gia."

Luca gave a humorless laugh. "Before or after they lock me up?"

"I'm sorry," I said, feeling the fool. "I wasn't thinking."

He offered a sad smile. "I'm the one who should apologize for involving you in this mess, *signorina*."

"You didn't involve me. I involved myself. What do we do now if we can't go to the police?"

Darkness descended on the park, and lights on the buildings were beginning to come on. Music from a band playing in the gazebo across the lake danced on the night breeze.

"We need proof that Thornley is in business with the madam." His voice turned hopeful. "Would your father help us if we had solid evidence?"

I hadn't considered going to Papa. "He is a fair man, but it would have to be very convincing evidence. He's been friends with Kenton's father as long as I can remember. But where will find the proof we need?"

"At the Maxwell," he said, hard resolve in his voice. "In Thornley's room."

Chapter Twenty-Three

"That's all she said. Destroy the scrapbook or she'd do it herself."

I stood with Jason in the police station, giving a statement to the uniformed officer behind the front desk. More officers sat at smaller desks behind him, some speaking into telephone receivers, some doing paperwork.

I'd never been inside the police station before, but the threatening phone call from the unknown woman had me shaken. I hadn't known what to do, other than call Jason down to the lobby and tell him about it. Lucille joined us as we discussed the situation and suggested going to the police.

"Making a threat like that over the telephone is illegal," she said, clearly offended that a stranger would abuse the Maxwell House telephone lines in such a way.

Jason agreed. "Not much can be done about it, since the woman didn't give her name, but they'll at least have it on record if it continues."

The thought of receiving another call from the woman sent my stomach into knots.

What had she meant by "I'll do it myself"? Was she related to the Thornley family? Even if she was, it seemed a bit extreme to make threats against someone you didn't know, all because of an article in the paper. Who really cared about such things anyway?

The officer jotted down everything I said and asked a few questions of his own. "I doubt the woman calls back," he said, bringing our conversation to an end. "But let us know if she does."

We walked out of the police station, a chill in the early evening air. Snow was predicted overnight, but it probably wouldn't amount to much. We didn't usually get a decent snowfall until January.

"I need to tell Dad about this," I said, sliding into the passenger seat of Jason's T-Bird while he held the door open. "He won't like it."

Jason climbed behind the wheel and headed the car toward the Maxwell. "I should come with you when you tell him." He sent me a sideways glance. "This isn't your fault, you know. I called the newspaper, and the woman called you. You're innocent."

I grinned despite the seriousness of the situation. "Thank you, Your Honor. You'll make a great judge someday."

He chuckled. "I hadn't thought that far ahead in my career. If I pass the bar next year, I'll be happy."

We walked through the lobby to the apartment. Dad and Emmett sat at the table eating grilled cheese sandwiches when we arrived.

"Where have you two been?" he asked, rising. "Jason, would you like to join us? I make a mean grilled cheese."

"Dad puts lots of cheese." Emmett held up his half-eaten sandwich, where a gooey string of yellow cheese oozed from between the slices of toasted bread.

Jason smiled. "That sounds good, buddy." He glanced at me as though checking to see if I would tell Dad about the phone call now or wait until later.

It seemed best to get it over with and face the consequences. "I have something to tell you, Dad."

He studied me. "By the look on your face, it isn't good."

I heaved a sigh. "Yesterday Jason and I went to the newspaper office and spoke with a reporter named Curtis Brown about the articles we found in Miss Nichols's scrapbook. We hoped to find out more about them and maybe find others. We weren't there to give him a story," I said, glancing at Jason for support. He sent me a small nod of encouragement. "But Mr. Brown published an article about it anyway in today's paper. It doesn't mention Miss Nichols by name, but it does mention the Thornleys and a possible link to the KKK and slave trade. I don't know where Mr. Brown came up with that information."

Dad's shoulders fell. "Oh, dear. I haven't had a chance to read today's paper. Did the article mention the Maxwell?"

I hated to answer. "It says I work at the hotel and that's where I found the scrapbook. Thankfully, I didn't tell Mr. Brown I was your daughter."

Dad's expression grew grim. "It doesn't matter. Mr. Edwin, the new owner, knows who you are. He plans to revitalize the Maxwell. This type of publicity isn't good for business, to say the least."

I finished the tale. "This afternoon, a woman called the hotel. When I asked how I could help her, she said, 'You can stop spreading lies about the Thornley family and you can destroy the scrapbook, or I'll do it for you.' She hung up after that."

"She threatened you?" Dad sank into his chair, his sandwich forgotten.

I nodded. "We thought it best to report this to the police."

"What did they have to say about it? I don't suppose there's anything to be done if the woman didn't give her name."

"The officer took a statement and it's on record if the woman calls again."

A look of guilt spread over Jason's face. "This is my fault, sir. I contacted Curtis Brown and convinced Audrey to talk to him. I'm sorry I got her and you into this mess."

"I appreciate that, son, but it doesn't sound like you did anything wrong by talking with the reporter. If you didn't give him permission to print the article, he's in the wrong. And the woman, of course." He stood up again. "Well, we'll just hope this all blows over. Christmas is five days away. We sure don't need anything spoiling the day. But I'll need to call Mr. Edwin after dinner and let him know what's going on."

Dad made sandwiches for us, with Emmett requesting a second one. We didn't mention the newspaper article or the phone call again, but I could see concern on Dad's face throughout the simple meal. I hated that it might bring him trouble with the new owner, but there wasn't anything I could do now.

After dinner, Jason said good night and went upstairs. I cleaned the kitchen while Dad helped Emmett bathe, their laughter bringing a smile to me after a trying day. I shut off the light and carried the scrapbook to my room. Sitting in the middle of the bed, I took my time turning pages, once again transported to the exposition through the colorful memorabilia.

Who was the woman who'd called today and warned me to destroy the scrapbook? It seemed odd that someone could become upset about such a small, unimportant article in the newspaper. Even if she had ties to the Thornley family, the people in question were long gone.

Unless . . .

I knew the KKK still existed in parts of the country. Every so often we'd read about their opposition to equal rights and desegregation. Maybe the woman who'd called didn't want anyone to connect the current Thornleys to the hate group.

A chilling thought assailed me once I'd turned out the light.

If the woman was bold enough to call and make threats, was she bold enough to carry them out?

I pulled the covers over my head.

Nearly every window of the Maxwell House Hotel glowed with golden lamplight in the dark night.

Luca and I stood at the southeast corner of Church Street, across from the hotel, watching as well-dressed guests came and went from both the men's and the women's entrances. Dinner was still being served in the grand dining room, but I knew Mother and Papa were down the street, dining with friends at the Tulane Hotel before heading to the theatre. It would be hours before they returned.

My main concern was Kenton. Where was he? If we were to search his room, we must be certain he wouldn't return and find us there.

"I don't think you should do this, *signorina*," Luca said for the third time. From the moment we arrived across from the hotel, he'd had second thoughts about involving me. I'd assured him each time that he needed my help, but he wasn't having it. "You should wait for me downstairs."

I crossed my arms. "The plan only works if we both play our part. Besides, there isn't anything dangerous about what we're doing. We'll be in and out of Kenton's room before anyone knows we were there."

He scowled. "If we're caught, they'll know it was you who helped me escape from the hospital. You could be arrested. Have you considered that?"

Little did he know I'd thought of nothing else for days. That I'd become an accomplice in helping a prisoner escape, and now planned to break into someone else's hotel room, should have worried me. But the injustice of Luca's imprisonment, and the fear in my heart for Gia's safety, revealed I cared more about them than I did for propriety. Mother would not approve, which was why I trusted it.

"I know what could happen, but I choose to believe it won't." I placed a hand on his arm. "I want to do this for Gia. She deserves our help. If Kenton had anything to do with her disappearance, we need to prove it."

Our gazes held; then he nodded. "For Gia."

"Then we'll stick to the plan?"

"Yes." He glanced at the hotel. "I'll go through the back service entrance and take the baggage elevator to the fourth floor. You'll enter through the women's side and tell the desk clerk that Thornley lost his key and sent you to fetch another."

"If I'm given any trouble, I'll resort to tears."

A slight grin lifted the corner of his mouth. "Mr. Bowles is no match for a woman's tears."

The plan appeared flawless. "Even if Kenton is dining at the hotel, he'll go to the men's salon afterward for a brandy and cards. It will be late before he retires and we'll be long gone, with proof of his involvement with the brothel, I hope."

He stared at me, his expression unreadable. "How can I thank you, *signorina*? You've risked much to help me and Gia."

I wanted to tell him I loved him and his sister, but now was not the time for such declarations. "It's the right thing to do."

We parted ways. Luca disappeared into the dark alley behind the hotel, and I made my way to the women's entrance. True to form, Mr. Bowles stood behind the long, polished guest services desk, his pleasant smile more practiced than genuine.

"Miss Nichols, how may I help you?"

"Good evening, Mr. Bowles. Mr. Thornley—the younger—has unfortunately misplaced the key to his room. I was coming downstairs and volunteered to bring a replacement up to him." I offered my brightest smile.

The man, however, frowned. "Oh, dear. I'm afraid it's against our policy to give a key to anyone other than the guest occupying the room in question, Miss Nichols. I do apologize, but Mr. Thornley will need to retrieve the key himself."

Luca had warned me this would happen, so I was prepared.

I worked up what I hoped was a distraught expression. "Please, Mr. Bowles." I glanced to either side of me, pretending to check if anyone was nearby. I leaned closer, as did he. "Mr. Thornley isn't well, if you understand my meaning, sir. A bit too much time in the saloon, I'm afraid. It would shame him and his father, *the senior Mr. Thornley*, if he should be forced to come to the lobby in such a state."

The man's eyes widened before he gave a slow nod. "I see, Miss Nichols." He tapped the desk with his finger. "I wouldn't want the senior Mr. Thornley to become dissatisfied with our service." Several more taps sounded before he reached into his pocket and withdrew a small key. Using it, he unlocked a large wooden case behind the desk, removed a brass key, and handed it to me. "Please don't mention this to anyone, Miss Nichols. The manager would not be pleased."

I took the key and tucked it into my reticule. "You can rest assured, Mr. Bowles, I will not tell a soul. Your discretion is greatly appreciated as well."

We exchanged polite smiles and bid each other good night.

Heartened by my success, I made my way to the mezzanine on the second floor. A peek into the spacious dining room revealed nothing. I could only hope Kenton was downstairs, fulfilling his part of the story I'd told to Mr. Bowles.

When I reached the fourth floor, relief swept over me at finding the hallway empty. I made my way to the baggage elevator at the end of the corridor and softly rapped on the door three times.

Luca opened it immediately. His eyes asked the question.

I held up the key in answer.

He chuckled. "I don't know if this is a compliment or not, *signorina*, but you are quite resourceful when you want to be."

We found the door to Kenton's room. I slipped the key into the lock and we were inside in a moment. A lamp on the bedside table provided enough light to see throughout the single room. Thankfully, Kenton had not wanted to share a suite with his parents.

"What are we looking for?" I asked, unsure where to begin.

"I don't know exactly. A note or a name. Anything that might connect him to Gia or the woman who runs the house."

While Luca searched the wardrobe, checking the pockets of Kenton's coats, I went to the small writing desk near the window. Nothing out of the ordinary caught my attention, so I opened one of the two drawers. It held the usual writing items, although they looked unused.

I reached to open the second drawer, gasped, and quickly turned away.

"What is it?" Luca moved to my side.

My face flamed. "I've heard of those types of playing cards, but I've never seen one."

I kept my back to the skimpily clad women, disgusted that Kenton would have such things in his possession.

To my surprise, Luca picked one up. He turned it over. "It says 'Madame LeBlanc, Nashville, Tennessee.'"

"Is that the woman in the picture?" I continued to avert my eyes from the inappropriate photograph.

"No." He picked up another. "They all have it written on the back."

"Could that be the name of the madam your friend mentioned?"

"Perhaps. I'll ask him." He returned the cards to the drawer and closed it with a firm hand.

"I don't think we're going to find anything," I said, disappointed.

At the same moment, a familiar voice echoed in the hallway, alerting us to Kenton's arrival at his door.

"Into the water closet; hurry," Luca whispered, pushing me toward the tiny room attached to the bedchamber. It wasn't big enough for both of us.

I hadn't been inside but a moment when the door to the room opened.

"Let's have some fun." Kenton's words slurred.

A female giggled before she screamed.

"What . . . what are you doing here, Moretti?" Kenton's angry voice sounded before something crashed to the floor.

"Tell me where to find my sister, and I'll leave." Luca's voice was dangerously calm.

"How dare you come into my room," Kenton said, clearly inebriated. "The police will be hap . . . happy to know you're still in town. I was furious when I heard they let you escape."

I heard a click. Was that a gun cocking?

"You won't get away this time." Kenton cackled. "In fact, I think I'll do them a favor and get rid of you now."

"Mr. Thornley, should I call the police?" the woman asked, her wobbly voice revealing her fear.

I couldn't stand there another moment and listen as Kenton threatened to murder Luca. I opened the door to the water closet, barely missing the woman—a girl, really—who screamed again.

Kenton turned toward the commotion, but his reflexes were slowed by drink. Luca lunged and had him on the floor in an instant. The two rolled across the carpet, with Luca trying to pry a small gun from Kenton's hand.

I took the girl by the arm and tugged her out of the room.

"Listen to me. Mr. Thornley isn't the man he appears to be. I have reason to believe he's involved in the disappearance of a young woman, about your age." I motioned into the room where the two men continued the brawl. "That man is her brother. We need to find out where Mr. Thornley took her."

The girl stared at me with wide, frightened eyes. I thought her convinced and willing to listen, but in a flash, she turned and bolted down the hallway.

"Help! Someone, help us," she yelled as she fled down the stairs.

I knew we didn't have long. I had to get Luca out of here.

I'd just reached the door to Kenton's room when I heard the gun go off.

Chapter Twenty-Four

No!

I flew into the room, expecting to find Luca dead, but it was Kenton who lay on the floor, blood dripping from the corner of his mouth.

Luca rolled off of him, breathing heavily. A small derringer lay on the carpet.

"Luca," I whispered, grateful he was safe. My gaze went to Kenton's still form. "Is he . . . ?" I couldn't finish the awful question.

Luca stood and shook his head, his own lip bleeding. "No. The bullet missed us both, but he hit his head on the table. Either that or he passed out."

Excited voices from the stairwell reached us.

"We must leave," I said. "The girl went for help."

Luca took my hand. We sprinted down the hall in the opposite direction of the stairs and around the corner to the baggage elevator. He'd just closed the door when we heard footsteps charge toward Kenton's room.

My heart pounded as the slow-moving carriage took us to the basement. I feared someone would be waiting for us when Luca opened the door, but the hallway was empty.

"This way." He pulled me along with him as we turned down another corridor to a door that opened into the alley.

We didn't stop but kept running in the dark, through the alley and away from the main entrances of the hotel. Down one street, up another, until I could go no further.

"I must stop," I said, breathless.

Luca, too, panted, but his eyes stayed alert. "You should go back," he said between gulps of air. "Get to your room so they won't suspect."

"No." I shook my head when he started to say more. "Not yet. I won't be missed for some time."

"It's too dangerous. They will be looking for me."

I'd come too far to give up now. "We must speak with Madame LeBlanc before Kenton warns her about you. He knows you won't give up until you find Gia. If Gia is there, we can get her tonight."

Indecision swept across his face. "I can't let you go with me."

"You don't have a choice, Luca. If you refuse to take me with you, I'll just follow on my own. We must go—now."

Finally he nodded.

We caught a streetcar and rode it for several blocks. When we disembarked, I felt a chill go up my spine despite the warm night air. The neighborhood looked ominous in the dark, with only a few gas lamps lighting the sidewalk.

"My friend said the house is on Jackson Street." He reached for my hand and wrapped his fingers around mine. "Stay close."

His warning wasn't necessary.

It wasn't difficult to locate the house we sought. Light, music, and laughter spilled from the windows and open doorway of a two-story dwelling. Several carriages as well as horses with saddles waited at a hitching post, and on the porch, two scantily dressed women smoked cigarettes, chatting with one another.

Luca and I kept to the shadows across the street, out of sight.

"Should I go speak to them?" I whispered. "They may talk to me since I'm a woman."

But Luca shook his head. "You can't be seen in this place. Stay here while I go."

He didn't wait for me to argue with him, just crossed the street.

"Good evening, ladies."

The two women immediately showed interest. I couldn't hear their words as he walked up the steps to the porch, but each of them took one of his arms and escorted him inside.

I stayed close to the trunk of a tree, hoping I blended with the shadows. My body trembled with fear, but I refused to give in to it. If Gia was inside that house, she was no doubt far more frightened than I was.

A hackney pulled up, and for one terrible moment I thought Kenton had arrived. Thankfully, it was a man I didn't know. I averted my eyes when a skimpily clad woman came out the front door to greet him in much the same way the other women had greeted Luca. I didn't want to imagine what they said to Luca, thinking him a handsome customer.

After a long time, movement at the door had me alert. Before I could blink, a huge hulk of a man stormed from the house, dragging someone with him. I covered my gasp when I recognized Luca as the one being hauled down the steps without care.

"Don't ever show your face here again, or you'll be sorry." The hulk spit on Luca and marched back into the house.

I dashed across the street as he struggled to stand. "Luca." I reached him as he got to his feet, shaking his head as though clearing cobwebs.

I led him into the shadows at the side of the house, out of sight from the front porch. "What happened?"

He rubbed the back of his head. "They don't appreciate anyone asking questions."

"Were you able to speak to Madame LeBlanc?"

"I saw her, but that beast of a man wouldn't let me near her."

I didn't ask if he'd seen Gia. The answer was obvious.

"What should we do? You can't go back inside."

Time was not our friend. The police would be searching the city for Luca. He needed to go into hiding again.

"I can't leave until I know if Gia is here or not." He glanced to the upper windows of the house, as though he planned to scale the porch.

Just then, a door banged on the back side. A young woman with golden hair stepped into the light of a window, her filmy dress revealing far too much. She stared up to the stars for a long moment before she lifted her hand to her cheek.

Was she crying?

Luca and I glanced at one another. He tilted his head toward the girl.

I nodded.

With quiet steps, I moved into the light. "Miss?"

She startled and looked at me with a wary expression. "Who are you, and what do you want?"

Her Irish accent reminded me of Fanny back at the hotel. "My name is Priscilla." I smiled, praying she wouldn't rush back inside. "I'm looking for a friend of mine and hope you can help me."

Her gaze traveled my length, a sneer on her lips. "You ain't got a friend here, lady."

"But I do. Her name is Gia. Dark hair, pretty. She hasn't been here very long. Do you know her?"

Recognition flitted across the girl's face before she looked away. "I don't know anyone by that name." She turned to go inside.

"Please. I have money." I reached for my reticule. "I just want to speak to her. I won't cause any trouble for you."

She looked at my purse with interest. "How much?"

"Five dollars." It was all I had with me, but I'd get more if necessary.

Her eyes widened, then squinted in suspicion. "Let me see it."

I took the bills from my purse. She reached for them, but I held back. "Tell me about Gia."

She glanced to the door, then took a step closer to me. "A girl like the one you described was here. We don't go by our real names. Madame called her Rosa."

"What do you mean she *was* here? Is she not here now?"

She shook her head. "The mister took her away yesterday. She won't come back. They never do."

"The mister?" I asked, a sick feeling in my gut. "Do you mean Mr. Thornley?"

At the mention of Kenton's name, fear rolled onto the girl's face. "How do you know about him?"

The brush rattled behind me. She looked like a scared rabbit when Luca appeared.

"Miss, Gia is my sister," he said, his voice low, pleading. "Please, help me find her."

Her gaze darted between Luca and me. "You promised me the money," she hissed, growing agitated.

"Can't you tell us anything? Where would he take her? Someplace here, in Nashville? Another city perhaps?"

"I don't know. I can't help you. You promised the money." She put out her hand. There were bruises on her arm.

"Come with us," I said, surprising not only the girl but myself. Yet didn't she need rescuing as much as Gia? "We'll take you someplace safe. My family can help you."

She stilled and stared at me. Was that hope in her eyes?

A shout came from inside the house.

The mask of fear returned. "Give me the money."

When I reluctantly handed her the bills, she snatched them and disappeared inside.

Luca started to follow, but I held him back. "You can't, Luca. That man will kill you if you go back in there."

He stood there, staring, before despair washed over his face.

"She was here," he said, his voice full of anguish. "Now

she's gone. How will I find her? Oh, my Gianetta. I have failed you."

I'd never seen a man weep before, and it broke my heart to witness Luca's pain. Without thought to propriety, I wrapped my arms around him, and we wept together.

A carriage drove past, and I knew we had to leave.

We walked the dark streets, each lost in our sorrow, wandering a city that had become a prison. Eventually we found ourselves not far from the north entrance to the fairgrounds. The hour was late and the park was closing. It seemed the perfect place to sort out what we'd learned tonight and make plans for tomorrow. I couldn't return to the hotel and leave Luca in this state of grief. He needed me, and I him. If my absence at the hotel was noticed, I would deal with the consequences later.

With the mass of visitors and employees heading to the station to catch the last streetcars, we easily slipped through the gate. I thought it best to avoid the large buildings, with their bright lights illuminating the night, so we stayed to the edges and made our way across the park to the arbor, the last place I'd seen Gia.

Inside the dark tunnel, we collapsed on a bench. Exhaustion fell over me, yet my mind was alive with regret. "We mustn't give up," I said, my voice sounding loud in the stillness of night. "We must keep searching."

Luca didn't respond.

I could only see his profile in the darkness, with muted light from the auditorium filtering through the vines. He stared straight ahead, unmoving.

"You mustn't lose hope, Luca. We'll find her."

"She's gone." His voice sounded hollow. Dead.

"No, Luca." I grasped his hand and found his fingers cold despite the warm night air. "She's still out there. She needs us to continue searching."

He snatched his hand away and shot to his feet. "I wish I had killed him. I wish I had picked up his gun and killed him."

The vehemence in his words frightened me. I didn't think him capable of what he declared, but I couldn't let him go back to the hotel to find Kenton. He'd be arrested again, or worse.

"Killing Kenton and getting yourself arrested wouldn't help Gia. It would only make you a murderer." I went to him, imploring him to listen. "Kenton is an evil man, doing evil things, but you're not like him. You're a kind, wonderful man, and . . . and I love you."

The words sprang from my heart on their own, but I needed him to know. Wanted him to know my true feelings.

He gazed down at me. "Ah, *mie Pesche*." His cool hand touched my cheek, and I leaned into it. "You shouldn't love me. I'm not worthy of a woman like you."

"You are everything a man should be," I whispered, placing my hand on his.

He took me in his arms then, where I'd ached to be since first meeting him. I couldn't say how long we stood with our hearts pressed against each other's. An eternity, perhaps.

We returned to the bench, our hands clasped and our shoulders touching.

"What will happen now, Luca?" I rested my head on his shoulder, weary from the long, emotional day.

He didn't answer immediately but tightened his grip on my fingers. "I must go away," he finally said.

His soft words pierced my heart, and I lifted my head to look at him. "Take me with you."

My brazen offer should have shocked him, but he only gave a sad smile.

"I cannot, *Pesche*. You must forget me."

"Never." I clasped his hand to my lips. "We can be married. We'll go to another city and find a minister. We can change our names and start a new life together."

I knew I sounded foolish, but desperation drove me on.

"I love you, Luca Moretti." Tears flowed from my eyes. "I love you as I've never loved another—or will ever. I can't let you walk out of my life."

He wrapped his arm around me then and pulled me tight against his side while I wept. He murmured words I didn't understand into my hair, every so often dropping a kiss on top of my head. I closed my eyes, determined to hold on to this moment, sealing it deep within my heart.

We didn't argue again. We stayed in the arbor until the stars disappeared, spending the hours holding hands and speaking in low tones of things that didn't matter. The flowers on the arbor. The sound of soldiers walking past, keeping watch over the exposition buildings. We laughed quietly when they didn't bother to peek into the darkness of the arbor.

The gates to the exposition would open soon, and Luca wanted to be away before then. We walked hand in hand across the park beneath a purple-streaked sky, stopping one last time beside Lake Watauga, with the Blue Grotto behind us. Sweet memories of our time there flooded my soul, but I refused to weep.

I wouldn't beg him to take me with him. I knew he couldn't. "You'll send me word as soon as you find Gia?"

"I will."

"Send it to the Maxwell."

He nodded.

"You won't let me give you any money?"

He shook his head and offered the same answer he'd given each time I'd asked. "I have the money from the sale of my horse and carriage. Mr. Anderson at the livery was fair."

Our gazes held. I tried to think of something—anything—to say, just to keep him here a moment longer, but time moved too quickly. Workers would arrive to open the park soon.

"I love you, Priscilla Nichols." He captured my face between his hands, his eyes locked on my own. "I've tried to fight it, knowing it would only lead to pain. But I want you to know, if things were different, I would be honored to have you as my wife."

His lips, warm and gentle, found mine. The kiss was not full of passion, as one of young lovers, but rich in the sweet promise of *if only*.

When he stepped away, his eyes glistened. "Count your nights by stars, not shadows. Count your life with smiles, not tears. *Arrivederci, mie Pesche.*"

He turned and crossed the bridge that separated Lake Watauga from the smaller Lily Lake. I shielded my eyes from bright morning sunshine and watched until he was out of sight.

Would I ever see him again?

The answer I feared most threatened to crush me.

Chapter Twenty-Five

Sunday afternoons were normally reserved for reading and naps, but today, Christmas Eve, there was no rest for the weary, as they say. Jason had once again joined us at church this morning, then volunteered to hang out with Emmett while Dad, Betty Ann, and I ran around the hotel like busy elves, seeing to last-minute details for the big day tomorrow.

"The new parking attendant is sick." Dad came into the dining room, where I was adding water to the two dozen table arrangements of red roses, white carnations, and holly. "Probably just a cold, he says, but I can't have him coughing all over the guests tomorrow night. That leaves Robert as our only valet, but he said his brother is home from college for the holidays and might be willing to help."

"Let's hope no one else calls in sick." I thought of the million little details that still needed attention before the hotel was full of guests, dressed in their Christmas finery, ready to dine on delicacies the Maxwell House had been known for since the 1800s. Even though the hotel no longer catered to wealthy overnight guests, this one tradition—the annual Christmas Day dinner—was still a well-attended event, enjoyed by people from all walks of life.

"I have more bad news." Dad's grave expression commanded my attention. He held up today's edition of the newspaper. "There's a second article about the scrapbook. Unfortunately, this one names Priscilla as the owner of it."

My heart sank. "It can't be worse than the first article, can it?"

"I'm afraid so. See for yourself." He handed the paper to me.

I sat at the table where I'd been working and read the article, smack-dab in the center of page two. The first paragraph was a repeat of how I found the scrapbook and what it contained, but then Brown outlined Miss Nichols's connection to the book.

Priscilla Nichols, daughter of Eldridge and Cora Nichols of Chattanooga, was said to be engaged to Kenton Thornley, who called off the engagement for unknown reasons. He later wed Carol Ransling, a wealthy railroad heiress. Miss Nichols, in an apparent fit of jealousy, made false accusations against Thornley regarding his involvement in the disappearance of a young Italian immigrant. By all accounts, Kenton Thornley was an upstanding citizen, donating large sums of money to various charities throughout Tennessee. The Thornley family has long been one of our state's finest. This reporter regrets the misleading information published in a previous article.

I looked up, fuming. "So he prints a retraction but retracts the wrong thing."

Dad nodded. "I can't image why he'd do such a thing, unless his editor had second thoughts about printing the original article."

"Or he too received a threatening phone call."

Jason stood in the arched doorway and joined the conversation. He planned to leave late this afternoon, driving home to spend the holidays with his family. My brain told me we were just friends and his leaving didn't matter, but my heart refused to agree.

"Have you heard the news?" Dad asked.

Jason came over to us. "I just got off the phone with Curtis. He apologized for printing the first article without asking our permission, then said he was forced to write the second after receiving an anonymous phone call."

"Was it the same woman who contacted me?" A chill raced up my spine, recalling the thick Southern drawl.

"It seems so. He said he was at home Saturday night when he received the call. The woman didn't give her name, but she told him if he didn't withdraw the allegation against Kenton Thornley, she would see that he never worked for another newspaper again."

"I would think it's unusual for a reporter to kowtow to an anonymous call like that." Dad frowned. "With everything they print in the papers these days, some of it's bound to be misleading or downright deceptive. They'd have to print retractions every day."

Jason nodded. "I thought of that as well, so I asked Curtis why he took this call seriously." The concern on his face deepened. "He sounded pretty nervous when he told me the woman knew things, personal things, about him, his family, his previous work. She made it clear she had the power to make things very difficult for him here in Nashville if he didn't do as she asked. I didn't mention the phone call you received," he said to me. "After his bad decision to use information we shared with him in confidence, I didn't trust him to keep it to himself."

We stood in the big dining room, dumbfounded by this new turn of events. "Who *is* this woman?" I asked, knowing neither Dad nor Jason could give me an answer.

"She sounds like someone we don't want to become involved with." Dad's frown intensified. "Mr. Edwin was understanding when I explained the situation, but the last thing he wants is negative publicity for the Maxwell. I think the best thing we can do is let this blow over. Tomorrow is Christmas Day. We have the big dinner to prepare for, food to see to, and guests to welcome into the Maxwell. By Tuesday, this will be old news."

I hoped he was right.

Dad left us, and Jason joined me at the table. "After I talked to Curtis, I called one of the attorneys I've been working with the last couple weeks. Without giving too many details, I asked him if he knew the Thornley family."

"Does he?"

"He's had a few dealings with their attorneys, mostly cases involving the various businesses they own, but he did tell me something interesting."

"Don't keep me in suspense," I said when he paused.

"The daughter of Kenton Thornley is the current matriarch of the family. Gladys Thornley Houghton."

I stared at him. Was she the woman who'd threatened me?

"Apparently she's quite a formidable woman," he continued. "Her husband was much older, and when he died twenty or so years ago, between his fortune and hers, she became one of the wealthiest women in the country."

I groaned. "No wonder she's upset about the newspaper articles."

"If she's the one who made the phone calls, yes. But there's bound to be other people associated with the Thornley family who would be disturbed by the things Curtis Brown alluded to."

I thought of the overconfident reporter. "I don't wish ill on him, but I hope he's learned his lesson. Using information without permission has consequences."

Mr. Hanover passed by the open doorway and waved on his way downstairs with Copper. "I sure am looking forward to the dinner tomorrow," he hollered, as though Jason and I were as hard of hearing as himself.

I smiled and returned the wave as he continued on his way.

"I have something else to tell you." Jason shifted in his seat, then fiddled with the place setting. If I didn't know better, I would think him nervous. "I've . . . I've decided to stay in Nashville for Christmas."

My heart skipped. His words were completely unexpected. "Really? Won't your family miss you?"

"Mom wasn't too keen on the idea," he said, his eyes never leaving me, "but I told her I'd met someone. Since I haven't dated much, that made her happy."

I pressed my lips together in an attempt to contain my squeal of delight, but I was certain the rest of my face gave me away.

"I hope it's okay with you."

I couldn't keep from smiling. "It is."

He reached for my hand and intertwined his fingers with mine. "Good."

Betty Ann and Emmett entered the room then. We unwound our hands and stood, but the grin on Jason's face matched my own.

"Audrey, look what Betty Ann gave me." Emmett hurried forward and held up a new comic book. "She let me open it even though it isn't Christmas yet."

I laughed. "You've been asking to open presents since breakfast." I winked at Betty Ann. "I hope you told her thank you."

"Thank you." He thumbed through the pages without looking up.

"Maybe we can read it together tonight after dinner," I said.

Emmett nodded. "The lady wanted to see your book, but I didn't know where it was."

When I glanced at Betty Ann, she indicated she didn't know what he was talking about.

"What lady, Emmett?" I asked, reaching to lift his chin so he would look at me, the way I'd often seen Mama do. She said it helped him focus on the other person.

"The lady that came to the apartment."

I glanced at Jason for help. "Do you know who he's talking about?"

He shook his head. "No one came by while I was there."

Emmett's attention was once again on the comic book.

"When did the lady ask to see the book, Emmett?"

He squinted. "Two yesterdays."

Today was Sunday. "Do you mean Friday?"

He nodded. "She looked sparkly. She went to the dance."

I thought back to Friday night. Dad and I took turns checking on Emmett throughout the busy evening while we greeted guests, checked in coats, and lent a helping hand wherever we could. Jason and Betty Ann had also helped, but we hadn't wanted to bother Mrs. Ruth so late, which meant there were times when Emmett was alone in the apartment, watching television.

"What book did she want to see?"

"Miss Priscilla's book."

My gaze met Jason's. "You don't think . . ."

"Did she say anything else, Emmett?" Jason asked.

"No. She wanted to see the book. Then she left." He grinned at Betty Ann. "Can we get ice cream?"

Betty Ann took his hand. "Let's see what your father says first."

As soon as the pair left the room, Jason turned to me. "I think we should tell the police about this. Who else would want to see the scrapbook other than the woman who made the threats?"

A wave of fear rolled through me. "It frightens me that a stranger came to our apartment while Emmett was alone."

"We better find your dad and let him know before we go to the police station."

I dreaded telling Dad, but I knew we didn't have a choice. We found him, Emmett, and Betty Ann having ice cream at Simmons Sweet Shop, next to the hotel.

Upon hearing the tale, Dad grew somber. "From now on, we can't leave Emmett alone." He looked at my brother, worry in his eyes. "If something happened to him . . ."

Jason drove us to the police station, where we told our story to the officer working the front desk. He didn't seem impressed.

"I'm sure it was a guest who read about the scrapbook in the newspaper. I wouldn't be concerned."

His lack of interest annoyed me. Thankfully, Jason agreed.

"Sir, we realize there are many more important things going on in the city that require police attention, but if you'll just add this information to the report we made a few days ago, I would appreciate it."

The officer huffed. "Fine."

We left, unconvinced he'd taken us seriously, and returned to the hotel.

Bing Crosby's "White Christmas" echoed in the lobby when we entered. Dad, Emmett, Betty Ann, and Mrs. Ruth were setting up a table for the small party we held each year for the residents on Christmas Eve. Many of them lived far from family, so Mama'd started the tradition some years ago.

Dad came over when we arrived. "How did it go?"

"The police officer we spoke with doesn't seem concerned," I said, my annoyance evident in my voice. "He says it was probably just a guest here for the dance who read about the scrapbook in the newspaper."

"I thought of that myself," Dad said, "but I don't like that she came to the apartment instead of asking one of the employees to get me."

I agreed. I'd never felt unsafe in the years we'd lived in the manager's apartment, but after the phone call and the mysterious woman, my nerves were on edge.

After telling Dad that Jason wasn't leaving town after all—to which Dad gave a sly grin—Jason and I helped bring in the trays of cookies Mrs. Ruth and Emmett had baked, as well as a large bowl of fruit punch. The reception was a come-and-go affair, although most of the guests came and stayed down in the lobby, chatting with each other, for several hours. Jolly Christmas music played in the background while Emmett greeted each guest with a smile. Some had gifts for him, which thrilled him to no end.

A memory surfaced from last year's party. Mama had only been gone a few months, so Mrs. Ruth and some of the other ladies took over the responsibility of putting it together. Miss Nichols, I remembered, came up to me and offered her sincere condolences for our loss.

"Your mother was a lovely woman, inside and out. She will be missed."

When the evening ended, we cleaned things up. Jason walked me back to the apartment but declined my invitation to come inside for a cup of hot chocolate.

"Mrs. Ruth had me try every flavor of cookie," he said with a laugh. "I don't have room for anything else."

I could hear Dad and Emmett inside, with Emmett too excited to go to bed.

I looked back to Jason, happier than I'd been in a long time. "I'm glad you stayed."

"Me too."

I thought he might kiss me, but he took a few steps backward instead. "I guess I'll see you in the morning," he said, smiling. "I hope you've been a good girl all year so Santa Claus brings you something."

I laughed. "It depends on his definition of *good*."

"I'll say good night now." His eyes held mine for a long moment. "Merry Christmas, Audrey."

The soft words washed over me like warm honey. "Merry Christmas."

I floated to my room, certain my dreams would be filled with sugarplums and dancing elves.

I couldn't wait for Christmas Day to arrive.

Chapter Twenty-Six

I stayed in bed for three days after Luca walked out of my life. Not even Mother's hysterics could drive me from the covers.

"People are beginning to talk, Priscilla." She hovered near the window on the morning of the fourth day, a tight frown on her face as she watched shoppers and fairgoers bustle through the streets below. "There are rumors that your *association* with those horrid Morettis went beyond the bounds of propriety. Thankfully, members of our group are rising to your defense, but it would be in your best interest if you came downstairs for dinner tonight." A shudder swept through her when she turned from the window. "I have a mind to bring charges against the Maxwell House for inflicting those Italian siblings upon us. Why, that man might have killed poor Kenton had a chambermaid not been passing by and witnessed the altercation."

I gave a humorless laugh. "Yes, lucky for Kenton she just happened to be there."

Mother scowled. "I don't understand your attitude about this entire affair. From the moment we learned of the terrible attack on Kenton, you've shown no trace of compassion."

When I didn't respond, she glanced at the closed door, then moved closer to my bed. "I'm no fool, Priscilla."

I shot her a wary look. "Meaning?"

"Meaning, I know you had a *fondness* for Mr. Moretti. He was handsome and had pretty words for a pretty lady."

I felt my blood begin to boil but forced myself to remain silent.

"It wouldn't be the first time a woman of our set succumbed to the attentions of a working-class man." She sat on the edge of the bed, commanding my attention. "But I refuse to believe that my daughter is capable of doing anything illegal, all for the sake of some silly romantic feelings for a man who is completely unsuitable. A man who is, at this very moment, a fugitive of the law."

That Mother suspected my feelings for Luca surprised me. I'd thought them well hidden in the depths of my heart. "I assure you, Mother, I would not do anything for the sake of *silly romantic feelings*. I simply haven't felt well the past few days."

Her gaze narrowed on me. "I was young once too, Priscilla. Remember that." After several ticks from the clock on the dresser, she stood and smoothed her skirt. "Shall we expect you to join us for dinner?"

A refusal would only feed the fires of gossip and Mother's suspicions. "Fine. I'll see you at dinner."

A satisfied smile inched up her face before she left me alone.

Fanny appeared in my room a few minutes later with instructions from Mother to draw a bath and help me dress for the day. Although I would have preferred to stay in bed, I didn't want to bring trouble to the girl by not complying.

I soaked in rose-scented water until it was cold, all the while thinking of Luca.

Where was he? Was he still in Nashville? How would he find Gia?

After I climbed from the tub, Fanny dried my hair and worked a comb through it. I watched her in the mirror, curious whether she'd known Gia and Luca well.

"How long have you been at the Maxwell House?" I asked, pretending it was simply conversation to fill the silence and not an attempt to gain information.

"Two years, miss. Me mum works here as well, in the kitchens."

"That's nice for the two of you. Have you any other family?"

She shook her head. "Me da passed some years ago when I was a wee girl. I have no brothers or sisters."

I nodded, wondering how to broach the subject without causing suspicion. "It's a shame about Gia, isn't it?"

Green eyes met mine in the reflection of the mirror, yet they held no scorn or hostility. "Has there been word about her, miss?"

"No." With all my heart, I wished it weren't so. "I thought she was a very sweet girl. To go missing as she has . . . well, it's a shame."

Fanny nodded. "I liked her, too, miss. We got along well." She continued to brush out my hair, shaping curls as she went. Several moments passed before a troubled look came over her face. "There have been others, miss." The soft words were barely audible.

"What do you mean, *others*?"

She met my gaze in the mirror again. "Some girls leave service and become fancy girls."

I'd never heard the term before. "Fancy girls?"

A deep blush colored her face, hiding her freckles. "The kind of girls that . . . men visit."

Only one week ago, I would have considered our conversation scandalous. To discuss such things, even in the privacy of my own bedchamber, simply wasn't done. Yet, after all that had transpired over the past few days, with Gia missing and Kenton's involvement with a brothel owner, I didn't think anything could ever shock me again.

"Have some of the maids here at the Maxwell become 'fancy girls'?"

She nodded, sadness in her eyes. "A friend. She said she can earn far more money doing that than she would as a maid."

I thought of the young woman Luca and I met behind the brothel. She'd reminded me of Fanny, with her Irish lilt. We'd offered her a chance to leave, but she hadn't taken it.

"I'm sorry."

"Me mum heard that a maid from one of the other hotels went missing, same as Gia."

I stared at her. "When was this?"

"A few days ago, miss. Me mum is scared. She won't let me leave the hotel, even on me day off. Says I must either be in our room or here, with you and Mrs. Nichols."

My stomach swirled with a horrific possibility.

Had Kenton been involved in that young woman's disappearance, too? The night Luca and I went to his room, a maid was with him. What had he intended to do with her?

The disturbing thoughts plagued me the rest of the day. I didn't leave the hotel but wandered about, watching the female employees with new eyes. Most were young, like Gia. Quite a few were obviously immigrants from Ireland or Italy, come to America for a better life after the Irish potato blight and unrest in Italy made it difficult for the poorer classes.

I felt ashamed I'd never considered these young women before. I had no knowledge of how much a hotel maid could earn, but I found it difficult to believe the life of a "fancy girl" could tempt someone away from a respectable job. Yet didn't Fanny's story of her friend prove me wrong?

I went through the motions of preparing for dinner with little enthusiasm. Papa escorted Mother and me into the brightly lit dining room, already alive with conversation, music, and waiters bustling hither and yon.

I was relieved to learn the Thornleys were dining away this evening. I couldn't bear to sit next to Kenton, knowing his dark secrets. In their place was an older couple, both with genuine smiles I found refreshing. The woman especially seemed familiar, although I didn't believe we'd ever met.

"Reverend and Mrs. Meyer, may I present our daughter, Priscilla." Papa made the introductions. It was quite surprising to find a reverend at our table, a place usually occupied by wealthy railroad executives or businessmen and their jewel-adorned wives.

"It's a pleasure to meet you, Miss Nichols." Reverend Meyer's eyes were kind when he greeted me.

"Mrs. Meyer is Cornelius Vanderbilt's cousin," Mother said, clearly pleased to have a member of the esteemed family at our table.

Now I understood why they'd been invited to join us.

We sat down to a fine meal, but my appetite had not returned since Luca's departure. How could I enjoy beef Wellington and potato croquettes when I was sick with worry about him and Gia? When young women were being lured away from their decent lives to enter into a life of ill repute?

"Miss Nichols, have you enjoyed the exposition thus far?"

Mrs. Meyer's query brought me back to the table. "I have, ma'am. It's been an eye-opening experience."

Mother's own eyes narrowed from across the table, as she surely wondered at my odd answer.

"Indeed," Mrs. Meyer continued. "I most heartily agree. The reverend and I have been kept busy with the needs of so many, we haven't yet had the opportunity to explore the fair to any great length. But from what I have seen, it's a marvelous bringing together of nations and people from all walks of life."

Her comment captivated me. "What a lovely way to describe it. May I ask what you meant when you said you and the reverend were busy meeting the needs of others?"

"The reverend and I have the privilege of helping the less fortunate of our fair city. We have a soup kitchen and dormitory in the basement of the church where Reverend Meyer is pastor. With so many visitors coming to the exposition, we felt compelled to offer our services to the broader public. Our booth at the entrance to the fairgrounds has allowed us to do just that." Her smile included everyone at our table before she returned her attention to me. "To see a hungry child fed or a young woman who's lost her way given another chance at life are the greatest rewards of our work."

I remembered now seeing the older couple in their booth the first day Luca, Gia, and I attended the fair. A young woman much like the one Mrs. Meyer described had been there, and Mrs. Meyer had given her what I'd thought to be a Bible. I suspected I was correct in that assumption now that I'd met the couple.

Someone asked a question of the reverend, leaving me to ponder the work they did. What did she mean when she mentioned giving young women another chance?

Glancing about the table, I knew the question wasn't appropriate for dinner conversation. The startling revelations about "fancy girls" Fanny provided earlier convinced me of my ignorance of the world outside my sheltered window. I hoped for an opportunity after the meal to discuss the topic further with the woman.

"Your work sounds intriguing," Papa said to Reverend Meyer, although I detected a falseness in his tone. "I can't imagine it being very lucrative, but intriguing, nonetheless." He laughed at his little joke, as did his friends.

Only the older couple and I didn't join in.

"I want to make a contribution to your efforts with the downtrodden, Reverend," Papa continued. He took out his wallet. "It must be a constant thorn in your side, finding enough funds to care for those wretches."

"Thank you, Mr. Nichols." Reverend Meyer offered a

patient smile. "But you must allow me to decline. We've all the funds we require, thanks to my dear wife's inheritance and various charities that provide food and clothes."

"Indeed, Mr. Nichols," Mrs. Meyer joined in. "We've been wonderfully blessed in the area of finances, but what we need are workers. Volunteers to help cook and serve in the soup kitchen. To help care for the widows and orphans who find themselves homeless. To be the hands and feet of our most dear Savior."

An uncomfortable silence fell over the table. Papa cleared his throat and put his wallet away. Mother adjusted the cutlery on the table.

"Well, now," the reverend said, lifting his glass of water. "Let us drink to our health and enjoy a fine meal."

Conversation resumed, although the topic of the Meyers' work was never mentioned again. When the evening drew to an end, Papa and the other men at the table went downstairs for cigars and brandy. Reverend Meyer didn't join them.

"It's been a lovely evening, Mrs. Nichols," he said to Mother as the other women exited the dining room. "We'll look forward to seeing your family at services on Sunday."

"Of course, Reverend. Good night." Mother smiled, then moved away to join her friends where they peered over the banister into the lobby.

I accompanied the older couple down the marble stairs. "I hope you don't think this prying, but when you mentioned helping young women, I wondered what exactly it is you do for them."

Reverend Meyer led us over to an unoccupied sitting area of the lobby, then motioned for his wife to explain.

"Our church," she said, her words meant only for our ears, "has become a safe haven for women who find themselves with no alternative but to sell their bodies to survive. They arrive desperate and broken, poor things. We do our best to find them shelter and jobs, if possible. If they have family, we try to reunite them, but in some cases the families won't or can't receive them."

"May I ask why you're interested, Miss Nichols?" Reverend Meyer's kind eyes met mine.

Although they were very nearly strangers, I believed their compassion for others was real. I needed to trust someone. "I have a friend—well, not exactly a friend . . . she was my lady's maid here at the hotel. Gia. Gia Moretti. She's disappeared. Her brother, Luca Moretti, was our driver, and we have reason to believe she's been lured into the kind of life you spoke of."

"Oh, my dear," Mrs. Meyer said, her voice full of concern. "How very tragic."

"Do you ever search for the girls? I mean, at the . . . brothels?" I whispered, glancing about to see if anyone could overhear the scandalous topic of our conversation.

"Unfortunately, rescuing a young woman from a house of ill repute is far more difficult than it might seem." Reverend Meyer sighed. "Believe me when I say we've tried. The women who come to us for help are ready to leave that life behind. A few return to it, sadly, but most don't."

I thought of the Irish girl at the brothel. "Why do they do it? Go back, I mean."

"The reasons are as different as the women themselves. Fear. Loneliness. Doubt in themselves. Doubt in God."

Reverend Meyer shrugged. "We're all sinners in need of a Savior. Our job is to simply love them."

"How do you do it, day after day? I think I'd grow discouraged."

A look of peace settled over Mrs. Meyer's face. "Are you familiar with the Bible story about Hagar? She'd been Sarah's servant, but when Sarah couldn't conceive a child, she gave Hagar to her husband, Abraham, in the hopes of building a family." She shook her head and sighed. "Poor Hagar. As soon as she became pregnant, Sarah grew jealous and treated her with contempt, to the point Hagar ran away. As Hagar sat alone and weeping, the angel of the Lord saw her and spoke into her pain. 'You are the God who sees me,' she said of him."

Mrs. Meyer reached out and gently laid her hand on my arm. "That is our mission, dear. To *see* people for who they are beneath the pain. Beneath the sin. To see them as God sees them: a beautiful creation, with plans and purposes only he knows."

I nodded, touched by the truth of her words.

Wasn't that what we all longed for? To be seen? Truly seen?

"If we learn any information about your Gia, may we contact you here at the Maxwell?"

Mrs. Meyer's offer felt like the first ray of light in a very dark situation. "Yes, please. I'd greatly appreciate it. And . . ." I paused. "If you would keep our conversation confidential, I would be grateful. Mother and Papa don't approve of my getting involved."

Reverend Meyer placed a comforting hand on my shoulder. "The Lord bless you, Miss Nichols."

I watched the couple walk toward the main entrance to the hotel, my soul filled with unexpected hope. Gia was still missing and Luca in hiding, but the Meyers' story of sacrifice and love for humanity reminded me there are good, caring people in this world. Men and women who use the gifts God gave them for more than selfish purposes.

I didn't know how I would apply their example to my own life, but with more surety than I had ever felt about anything before, I knew I would.

Chapter Twenty-Seven

Christmas Day dawned sunny and cold.

Emmett's excited voice broke into my dream, a strange vision of the postcards from Miss Nichols's scrapbook frolicking with Mrs. Ruth's cookies. "Audrey, come see. Come see."

I cracked open my eyes to find my brother's smiling face looming over me. "Merry Christmas to you too."

He nodded. "Come see," he shouted and flew from my room.

I yawned, tugged on my robe, and padded down the hall to the living room. We hadn't put up a tree in our apartment again this year, mainly because neither Dad nor I remembered to buy one. Before turning in last night, I'd added my wrapped gifts to Dad's neat stack on the kitchen table.

So when I saw the glow of lights at the end of the hallway, my eyes grew misty at the sight of a small tree, fully decorated with tinsel and our family ornaments.

"When did you do this?" I asked Dad, knowing he'd gone to bed at the same time I did, or so I'd believed.

He grinned. "I had a little help from an elf. When Betty Ann found out we didn't have a tree, she went down to the lot and bought one. I told her where to find the box of Christmas ornaments in the basement, and she decorated it in my office. I had quite a time dragging it through the lobby last night after you kids went to bed."

Emmett sat next to the tree, picking up wrapped packages and shaking them. "Christmas came, Audrey."

I nodded and hugged Dad's neck. "It sure did."

"I invited Jason to join us for breakfast." He chuckled when my hand went to my messy hair. "Don't worry. You have time to get dressed. I told him we'd eat at eight."

I hurried to my room to change clothes. I'd just finished applying bright-red lipstick that matched my sweater when I heard a knock on the apartment door and Dad's greeting.

Butterflies floated through my belly when I saw Jason's smile. "Merry Christmas."

"Merry Christmas." His eyes revealed his appreciation for my efforts on my appearance. "You look really nice."

Despite Emmett's pleas, Dad insisted we eat his famous chocolate chip pancakes before opening gifts. As we sat around our small table, laughing and chatting, I couldn't help but recall the sadness of last year. Mama's unexpected death stole the joy of the holiday. Aside from a few presents for Emmett and me, we'd let the day go by unnoticed for the most part.

After breakfast, we settled in the living room, with Emmett on the couch between Jason and me. Dad sat in the armchair with Mama's Bible in his lap. He'd come to my room last night and asked if he could read the Christmas story from it today. I'd taken it from its hiding place, the pain that usually came with seeing it absent. I'd smoothed its worn cover before handing it to him.

"Mama would be pleased we're moving on, wouldn't she?"

Dad nodded, a bit of sadness in his eyes. "She would, honey. She wouldn't want us to grieve forever."

Now he opened the book to the second chapter of Luke and read the beautiful story of Christ's birth. After Dad thanked God for seeing us through a tough year, we opened our gifts. More comic books for Emmett, plus a ball cap from Jason and a magnifying glass from me. Dad was thrilled with the mystery novel I gave him, as well as a book on Nashville history from Jason, both from Stockell Books. We laughed when we realized we'd shopped at the same store, right around the corner from the hotel. Unbeknownst to me, Dad had a gift for Jason—a framed photograph of the Maxwell House Hotel taken in the late 1800s.

When it was my turn to open my gifts, I nearly wept. Each one had been chosen with thoughtfulness. From Dad, there was a pearl necklace that had been Mama's. From Emmett, one of his treasured, dog-eared comic books. And from Jason, a surprise—a brand-new scrapbook.

While Dad read one of Emmett's new comic books to him, Jason and I moved to the table.

"Thank you for my gift," I said, a warm, fuzzy feeling settling deep inside me. "I'm sorry I didn't get you anything."

He grinned. "You can make it up to me next year."

"I'm not sure what I'll put in my scrapbook." I turned blank pages, envisioning them full of . . . something.

"Maybe we can collect things from the places where we go, like Peaches did."

I gazed into his blue eyes, amazed this was really happening to me. "I'm glad you came to stay at the Maxwell House."

He glanced at Dad, whose attention was on Emmett and the book, then reached under the table to take my hand in his. Our fingers intertwined. "Me too." A playful grin tipped his mouth.

"Being able to enjoy a cup of the famous Maxwell House coffee every morning has definitely been the highlight of my trip."

I released his hand and pretended to slug him, laughing when he ducked.

The remainder of the day was full of activity, preparing for the big Christmas Day dinner. Betty Ann arrived after lunch and pitched right in. By five o'clock, the lobby began filling with beautifully dressed ladies wearing jewels and gloves and men in tuxedos and bow ties.

I changed into an emerald-green sleeveless party dress, with Mama's pearls nestled around my neck. Jason came downstairs after changing his clothes, too, and looked handsome in a dark suit. Lucille and her boyfriend, Earl, joined us for the meal at our table near the front, along with Betty Ann and Mrs. Ruth. A band played Christmas music while tuxedo-clad waiters brought in plates loaded with turkey and stuffing, ham, leg of lamb, roasted duck, and all manner of delicious delicacies from the famous Maxwell House kitchens.

I couldn't imagine a more perfect evening.

By eight o'clock, Emmett was worn-out and becoming grumpy. Many of the guests had headed home, and things were winding down.

"We'll take Emmett back to the apartment," I said to Dad.

I'd been watching him enjoy Betty Ann's company throughout the evening, chatting and singing along with the music. Oddly, I found I didn't mind. Our brief conversation about Mama last night reassured me life did continue, even after suffering loss. Dad had loved my mother—there was no doubt in my mind about that. But she was gone now, enjoying her second Christmas in the presence of Jesus.

I smiled.

Mama would have liked Betty Ann.

"Thanks, honey. I'll be there soon." Dad kissed Emmett and me good night.

At the apartment, Jason helped Emmett into his pajamas and into bed. My brother was asleep almost as soon as his head hit the pillow. He'd been so exhausted he hadn't even put his comic books away and left them scattered across the floor.

We settled on the couch, with the lights from the Christmas tree giving off a warm, colorful glow.

"This has been a fun day." Jason put his arm around my shoulders.

I leaned into him, relishing the feel of being cuddled on the couch with him. "We usually have some catastrophe—the chef burned the turkey or a waiter dropped a crate of champagne— but today was perfect."

"I wonder if Miss Nichols had a nice day," he said, his eyes on the scrapbook on the coffee table.

"I was thinking about her, too. We should go see her tomorrow."

He smiled. "I'd like that."

I asked about his family's holiday traditions and his favorite Christmas memories. He'd just begun to tell a funny story about trying to catch Santa Claus in the act when we heard loud footfalls of someone running down the hall toward the apartment. A moment later, Dad burst through the door.

"There's a fire," he said, breathing heavily. "Get Emmett and go to the Noel across the street. I've asked Lucille to call the residents and tell them to evacuate the hotel."

Jason and I rose to our feet simultaneously. "It's that bad?"

Dad was already headed for the door again. "I don't know. There's a lot of smoke coming from the fourth floor. The fire department is on the way." He turned before leaving. "Audrey, stay with Emmett. He'll need you."

"I will, Dad." Fear rolled through me. I ran to him and felt his arms go around me. "Be careful."

He nodded; then he was gone.

"I'll get Emmett," Jason said. "You grab a few things. Coats, mementos. Stuff like that. But we don't have a lot of time."

I stood, frozen. "Do you think the fire will reach our apartment?" I asked as the muffled sound of sirens came from the open door.

"There's no way to know. Let's hope the firemen have it contained quickly."

We sprang into action. I grabbed some shopping bags and began stuffing our belongings into them. Mama's Bible, photographs, some clothes for each of us. I heard Jason tell Emmett we were going to have ice cream at the Noel restaurant and needed to hurry. A sleepy-eyed Emmett emerged from his room, still in his pajamas but bundled in a warm coat and hat. Jason carried a pillowcase full of Emmett's things.

As I surveyed the living room, searching for items that couldn't be replaced should the worst scenario happen, my eyes fell on the scrapbook. I didn't know why, but I couldn't leave it behind. I stuffed it into the bag, along with the photograph of Mama, and followed Emmett and Jason out the back door that opened into the alley.

We stepped into chaos.

Fire trucks filled the streets, with firemen in suits tugging long hoses here and there. A blue haze filled the alley, and the acrid smell of smoke hung in the air. A fire engine honked; men yelled. The scene was loud and frightening.

Emmett wouldn't budge. "I want to go home," he said, fear and flashing red lights reflected in his wide eyes as he stared at the pandemonium.

"We can't go back to the apartment right now." I took his

hand, his fingers already cold in the night air. "Dad is going to meet us at the Noel Hotel. Remember the Noel? You like to look at the electric trains in the window."

He nodded.

With Jason's help, we got him moving. I deemed it impossible to get through the commotion on Church Street, so we headed north through the alley where we'd pass through the arcade to Fourth Avenue. The sound of more sirens echoed against the tall buildings as we hurried along. When we reached Fourth, we crossed the street and wove our way through crowds of bystanders, all staring up at the Maxwell.

My gaze followed theirs.

I gasped.

Thick, black smoke billowed from arched windows on the fourth and fifth floors. Firefighters sprayed rivers of water from swollen hoses, all aimed at the top of the building.

Raw fear took hold.

"Have all the guests been evacuated?" I looked around, but I didn't recognize anyone in the crowd. "Where's Dad?"

Panic sent a tremor through my soul.

I couldn't lose Dad.

"You and Emmett go inside the Noel." Jason handed the stuffed pillowcase to Emmett. "I'll find your dad."

He was gone before I blinked.

I held tight to Emmett's hand and we worked our way through the groups of bystanders gawking at the Maxwell, transformed from a stately old hotel into a pathetic smoke-belching spectacle. I led him into the lobby of the Noel, filled with worried guests, onlookers, and thankfully, some of the Maxwell's residents.

Mrs. Ruth hurried over. "Thank goodness you're safe." She took Emmett in her frail arms. Like him, she wore her night-clothes beneath her coat.

"Have you seen my father? Do you know if all the guests were evacuated?"

"We're gathered over here." She led us to the cluster of residents, many in their pajamas as well.

I took note of those congregated, including Mr. Hanover and Copper. At Mrs. Ruth's feet sat a cage with her two mynah birds. Other residents sat huddled in winter coats, worry and fear in their eyes. I counted forty-two out of the sixty full-time residents we currently had. Where were the others?

"Mrs. Ruth, would you keep Emmett here with you? I need to find Dad."

"Of course, dear. We'll make sure he's safe, won't we?" she said, receiving affirmative answers from other residents nearby.

I left our belongings with her and rushed outside into the increasingly terrifying night. Trucks, firemen, and police were everywhere I looked, shouting, running, desperate to save the hotel. Long, fat hoses lined the street, appearing like gigantic slithering snakes in the darkness. The entire area teemed with activity, and I couldn't get to the entrance to the hotel for it all. I'd been visiting my grandparents in Kentucky when the hotel caught fire in the summer of '58, so the scene before me was new and frightening. There was some damage during that fire, but the hotel made it through.

"Get more lines! Get more lines in there!" a fireman yelled from nearby.

I searched for Dad, Jason, and anyone from the hotel but could see nothing beyond the fire trucks and smoke drifting down from the upper stories. I kept going toward Church Street, offering up frantic, disjointed prayers that everyone was safe.

I didn't know how much time passed—a moment, an eternity—while I searched faces. More and more bystanders congregated on the sidewalks, staring up at the smoking hotel in disbelief. How could such a tragedy happen? The Maxwell couldn't burn. It just couldn't.

"Audrey!"

Dad's voice reached me. I spun in a circle, desperate to see him. He waved at me from the corner of Church and Fourth, and like a lost little girl, I ran to him and fell into his arms, tears running down my face.

"It's okay, sweetheart. Shhh." When he loosened his grip, he asked, "Is Emmett safe?"

I sniffled. "He's with Mrs. Ruth and some of the others in the Noel." I glanced behind him to where a band of residents, along with Betty Ann, Lucille, and her boyfriend, stood in front of the Third National Bank building looking as helpless as I felt. Jason wasn't among them.

Fear gripped me once again. "Have you seen Jason? He went to look for you."

"Yes. I sent him to get a head count of the residents at the Noel for the fire marshal. You must have just missed him."

My body sagged with relief.

We were all safe.

Dad led our group into the Noel through the Church Street entrance, avoiding the commotion on Fourth Street. When we made it to the lobby, Maxwell residents greeted each other with hugs and tears, as though it had been days, not merely an hour or two, since they'd seen one another at the Christmas dinner.

Jason found me. Soot rimmed his eyes and smudged his face. "Are you okay?" I asked, my eyes traveling the length of him.

"I'm fine."

"He went back into the hotel to help some of us get out." Mr. Goad, standing nearby, patted Jason on the back. "Brave young man you've got here."

Jason gave a sheepish shrug as the older man walked away.

"Did everyone get out?" I asked. I hadn't done a head count myself, yet it appeared that everyone was here.

But Jason didn't offer an affirmative nod. Instead, he leaned close to my ear. "According to Mrs. Ruth, one resident is unaccounted for." He whispered the man's name. "Your dad doesn't want everyone to know just yet. We're hoping he'll turn up once things calm down."

I silently said a prayer for that very thing.

We left Dad and the others and went back outside. It had been over an hour since the fire was first discovered, yet it didn't seem as though the firemen were making any progress. Every fire truck in the city was here, it seemed. There were even some from neighboring counties.

I shivered, and Jason wrapped me in his arms as we stood with dozens of others, watching the beautiful old hotel burn.

Tears rolled down my face, unchecked. The Maxwell had been my home since I was a child. Except for the few items I'd grabbed, as well as Mama's pearls around my neck, everything we owned was inside our apartment. I felt grateful we were all safe, but I knew I would deeply grieve the memories going up in flames as we stood powerless to do anything about it.

Dad joined us sometime later. We watched in silence as firemen fought valiantly to save the hotel, but when an explosion of flames shot fifty feet into the air from the roof, we knew the historic building was doomed.

Not long after, the drillmaster for the fire department approached Dad.

"It looks like it's gone, sir." Regret filled his eyes. "We have orders to pull back. We're going to have to let her go."

Dad solemnly thanked the man, agreeing that the safety of the firemen was what mattered most. The drillmaster thought the Maxwell's fire walls would hold, preventing the fire from spreading to other buildings, but they'd stay through the night to be certain. The fire marshal would evaluate what was left of the building in the morning, but in his opinion, it looked like a total loss.

After the man walked away, Dad stood there, staring at the hotel, tears wetting his cheeks.

I moved out of Jason's arms and into his.

Sorrow had found us once again.

Chapter Twenty-Eight

The bold headline on the front page of the newspaper the following morning said it all: "Maxwell House Burns."

A picture of the burning building filled the page, along with a smaller picture of Mrs. Ruth and Mrs. Garrison coming down the stairs in their nightgowns and coats. The women had declined to give the reporter their names, but their picture was printed nonetheless.

"It says here the fire started at eight forty-five on the fourth floor."

I glanced at Jason, seated on the opposite side of the table from me in the Noel restaurant, where he read the article. "Dad is with the fire marshal now, but because there's so much damage, he's already warned Dad it will be difficult to find the cause of the fire."

I looked out the window again to the smoldering shell of the once-magnificent hotel. The sun had just come up, and early morning light revealed what had been hidden in the darkness. Blue sky could be seen through the glassless windows on the fifth floor, giving evidence that the roof had completely collapsed. Firemen with powerful hoses continued to shoot water high into the air, aimed at the top of the hotel, where it would flow down into the depths of the building, where fires still burned.

Jason folded the paper and set it aside. He took a sip of his coffee and grimaced. "This isn't Maxwell House coffee, that's for sure."

I gave a halfhearted smile at his attempt at humor. "Just one of the hundreds of things we're going to miss."

I refused to cry again. Besides, I didn't think I had any tears left inside me.

At midnight, after watching the hotel burn for hours, Dad had made us go to bed in borrowed rooms graciously offered by the manager of the Noel. Many of our sixty displaced residents who had nowhere else to go were also given rooms. Some had family who came to get them, while others stayed with friends. The loss of belongings wasn't important when compared to the loss of the kind, older gentleman from room 508 who'd perished in the disaster. Things could be replaced; life could not.

The crowd of spectators thinned overnight. Still, people occasionally walked past the restaurant window, staring up at the smoldering, burned-out shell of the once-proud Maxwell House. A young man stood in the blocked-off street, an 8mm movie camera in his hands.

"It's strange how people are drawn to things like this," I said. I didn't blame them for their gawking. It was a sight the likes of which Nashville residents had never seen. The Maxwell House had always existed in our lifetimes. Many of the older people I'd seen in the crowd last night stood with tears in their eyes as flames shot from windows. So much history—the hotel's and that of the citizens who'd loved it—was forever lost. All we had now were our memories.

Dad and Emmett joined us a short time later. Emmett wanted a chocolate shake even though he'd eaten breakfast earlier. We put in an order, knowing the confusion and displacement were hard on my brother. Anything that might help him stay calm was welcome.

"What did the fire marshal say?" I asked once the waitress walked away.

"The same thing he said before his inspection." He sighed. "The chief city building inspector is here too. It's his opinion Mr. Edwin will have to tear down the hotel and rebuild from the ground up."

The news was sobering.

We talked in low tones, about the hotel, the fire, the future. A friend of Dad's owned a small rental house that was currently vacant, and he'd generously offered it to us, rent free, for a year.

"The ladies from church are collecting clothes and other items for us and the residents," I said. "Mrs. Ruth told me they're also offering hot meals to anyone displaced by the fire."

Dad nodded. "It's nice to see that in difficult times like this, people really do care about one another."

Emmett's shake arrived. While he enjoyed it, Dad said, "I'm glad you were able to save his comic books."

"Thanks to Jason's quick thinking," I said. "I didn't know what to grab. I'm not even sure why I chose to save Miss Nichols's scrapbook instead of something of ours."

"I'm glad you did, honey," Dad said. "All of her belongings are gone too."

I hadn't thought of that.

"Maybe the lady can see the book now."

We all turned to Emmett. Chocolate ice cream rimmed his mouth.

"What do you mean, Son?" Dad asked.

Emmett spooned another bite into his mouth. "The lady in the fuzzy coat."

"Did the lady come to the apartment again?" I asked, alarmed.

Emmett shook his head. "She ate at the party."

"Which party, Emmett?"

"The Christmas party. With the music and cake."

Dad, Jason, and I exchanged worried glances.

"Emmett." I lifted his chin so he would look me in the eyes. "Was the same woman who came to the apartment also at the Christmas dinner last night?"

He nodded.

My stunned gaze met Dad's across the table. "You don't think . . ."

The thought was too frightening to say aloud.

"I better share this information with the police and the fire marshal. They may want to question some of the guests who were at the dinner." Dad stood and left the restaurant.

Emmett finished his shake. His eyes went to the scene out the window. "I want to go home now, Audrey."

I scooted my chair over so I could put my arm around his thick shoulders. "I do too, Emmett, but we can't just now. But you and me and Dad are all together, and that's what matters."

He leaned his head on my shoulder for a moment but popped back up. "And Jason."

Jason and I grinned at each other.

"Yes, buddy. And Jason."

Later that afternoon, when the excitement was over and most of the fire trucks were gone, Jason and I found a quiet sitting area in the lobby of the Noel and fell into comfortable chairs.

"You should go upstairs and rest," he said, his tired eyes full of concern.

"So should you."

We chuckled when we both stayed where we were.

"I called my parents." He glanced across the polished marble to the windows. The bottom floors of the Maxwell could be seen, appearing almost normal, as though the three floors above were not completely destroyed.

"Had they heard about the fire?"

"They had, but they couldn't get a call through. Mom was disappointed when I told her I wasn't coming home just yet, but she understands that I want to be here with you and your family. At least for a few more days."

I didn't know what I'd done to deserve this guy, but I was grateful he'd come into my world.

We were talking about the Maxwell's history when a lovely older woman came toward us. Many people from area businesses had stopped in to offer their sympathies and help, so I thought she was yet another kind neighbor.

She wore a hesitant smile. "Pardon me. Are you Audrey Whitfield?" A light accent clung to her words.

I stood. "I am," I said, trying to place her in my mind.

"I'm sorry to bother you," she said sincerely. "I know this is a difficult time."

I nodded.

"I'm looking for one of the residents of the Maxwell, and they said you could help me."

"Of course," I said. "Who is it you're looking for?"

"Priscilla Nichols."

Surprised, I glanced at Jason, who also stood.

"Are you a friend of Miss Nichols's?" he asked.

"I'm Grace Moore." She extended her hand. "Priscilla's daughter."

Papa made arrangements for us to leave Nashville on Sunday afternoon's train.

"It's time to go home and get back to life," he announced at dinner.

Several of his business associates agreed, stating they too would depart the city soon. Others spoke of returning in October when the weather was cooler. A grand celebration was to take place on the thirtieth of that month, bringing the exposition to an end in glorious fashion.

I kept my thoughts to myself as Papa, Mother, and their friends discussed travel plans. The flicker of an idea had come to life after speaking with the Meyers last week, but I had yet to convince myself I was capable of putting it into action.

What if I stayed in Nashville?

The question swirled through my mind.

I held no desire to go back to my life in Chattanooga. There would be no wedding preparations to keep Mother busy. No grandchildren to hope for. She'd finally accepted, with many tears, my refusal of Kenton. Thankfully, the Thornleys had already vacated Nashville, more than ready to be away from the gossip and rumors circulating after Kenton was found drunk and beaten in his room.

"He isn't the man you think him to be, Mother," I'd declared after listening to her sing his praises one too many times. "I can't tell you how I know, but you need to trust me when I say I will never marry that man."

Later, I apologized for raising my voice to her, but the truth of my statement held. After she relayed the information to Papa, he acquiesced. "We shall never speak of it again."

My fate as a spinster was sealed.

The meal came to an end. Mother retired to her room while Papa joined the men for a game of billiards. Left on my own, I wandered the lobby for a time, then decided a breath of fresh air would be nice. With the days getting warmer, the evenings were wonderfully pleasant.

Outside, the sidewalks weren't as crowded as they'd been in the early days of the exposition. Many families had returned home, although I'd overheard the desk clerk say the hotel was still filled nearly to capacity, with most of the 240 rooms in service.

I headed up Cherry Street, looking in shopwindows, closed for the night but lit to reveal lovely displays of gowns, books, watches. Whatever the shop might carry.

I continued up the avenue, with no particular destination in mind. Yet when I arrived at the public square, I knew why I'd come this way.

Across from me, the liquor store looked as it had the night I helped Luca escape from the hospital. The glow from a gas streetlamp spilled a yellow circle on the sidewalk—an empty sidewalk.

My shoulders fell with what could only be disappointment.

I didn't know what I'd expected to find or what I'd do if I found it. I only knew my heart had led me this way for a reason.

COUNT THE NIGHTS BY STARS

The memory of the young women gathered on the corner filled my mind's eye. Were they involved in the soul-stealing business of prostitution? I'd only seen them from a distance, but from my vantage point, they'd appeared youthful, like Gia. Where were they now?

The hour was late, and I knew I should return to the hotel. Walking alone at night wasn't the wisest thing to do, but I also accepted that I might have to become used to it, given my choice to remain unmarried.

I turned and started down the street toward the Maxwell, two blocks away. The clip-clop of a horse, however, drew my attention. I watched as a carriage came from the direction of the river and stopped in front of the shop. I knew it couldn't be Kenton, him having returned to Chattanooga in disgrace.

A young woman climbed from the vehicle. When she turned to speak to the driver, he tossed something at her before slapping the reins and driving off. He didn't pass by me, so there was no reason to move out of sight.

The woman bent to retrieve what I suspected were coins. When she'd collected them all, she glanced in both directions, but I could see no other carriages in the vicinity. With what appeared to be weary steps, she walked to the corner and leaned against the light post.

My heart thudded.

Could I do this?

I'd already offered one girl a way to break free from the dark world she'd become involved in, but she'd taken my money and walked back into the shadows.

Would this girl do the same, should I gather enough courage to approach her?

I blew out a breath.

If I was going to do this, it needed to be now, before another carriage arrived and whisked her away.

I stepped into the street and walked toward her. I knew the moment she spotted me. She pushed off the post and watched me through narrowed eyes.

"Good evening." I took care not to approach too quickly. I didn't want to frighten her before I'd even had an opportunity to speak. When I reached the outer edge of the circle of light, I saw that the woman—a girl, really—couldn't be more than fifteen or sixteen years of age.

"I wonder if you can help me." I offered what I hoped she saw as a friendly smile. "Can you tell me how to get to the Maxwell House Hotel?"

Her gaze took in my dress and hat before returning to my face. After a moment, she pointed in the direction I'd been headed. "Down that street until you come to Church Street. It'll be one block over."

Her voice was soft, almost childish, and my heart went out to her.

"My name is Priscilla. What's yours?"

She frowned and hesitated to answer. "They call me Claudia," she finally said.

I remembered the young woman at the brothel told us the owner called Gia by another name. The way this girl worded her answer, I suspected the same was true for her as well.

"Thank you for helping me, Claudia." I chuckled. "I can get lost in a paper sack."

A tiny smile touched her lips.

"May I walk you home? A young woman shouldn't be out alone at night."

The smile disappeared. "No. I'm fine."

A man inside the liquor store looked out the smudge-covered window. His frown at seeing me gave the impression he wasn't happy with my presence on his corner. I must hurry if I held any hope of taking Claudia with me.

"May I ask you something?"

Wary eyes met mine.

"I know of a place where you can be safe and cared for by good people. I'd like to take you to them. Will you come with me?"

Claudia glanced behind her to the store, but the man from the window was gone.

"You need to leave, miss," she hissed. "If Frank hears you, he won't like it."

I'd come too far to stop now. "Is Frank the man who sells you to men?"

She shrank into herself, wrapping thin arms around her waist. Shame colored her face.

"You can trust me, Claudia. I'm only here to help you." I took another step closer and lowered my voice. "Come with me, now. You'll be safe. You'll never have to see Frank, or anyone else who's hurt you, again."

Her chest heaved, like a child frightened by a nightmare that wouldn't go away. "I can't, miss." Tears sprang to her eyes. "I owe the madam money. For the dress and food. She says I can't leave until I've paid it all back."

"Madame LeBlanc?"

Her eyes widened before she nodded.

Fury took hold inside me, but I kept my outward demeanor calm. "If you come with me, Madame LeBlanc can never touch you again. I promise."

I spoke the words with unexpected confidence. Beyond any doubt, I would do everything in my power to see that Claudia was safely delivered into the loving care of the Meyers.

Claudia swallowed, then bit her bottom lip in indecision. "Frank will tell her I've gone. That's his job. To keep watch on us."

The sound of a carriage approaching echoed in the street.

"We need to go, Claudia." I reached a hand to her. "Now."

When she didn't immediately take hold, I thought she would turn and run into the liquor store. But in the next breath, I held her small, trembling hand in mine.

"We must hurry," I whispered.

We took off running, headed for the Maxwell House. I wouldn't take her inside for fear Papa or someone who knew me might see us together, but I could hire a cab there to take us to the Meyers' church.

Someone hollered as we turned the corner, but we didn't stop.

Within the hour, we stood on the stoop of a small house, next to a white-steepled church. I knocked softly, praying the couple hadn't retired for the night.

When Reverend Meyer opened the door, he didn't seem surprised to see us.

"Come in," he said before I could explain the situation.

We stepped into a cozy living room, with the smell of freshly baked bread filling the small space. Mrs. Meyer came from a back room, her hair in a nightcap and a robe cinched at her waist.

"This is Claudia," I said, my arm around the girl's trembling shoulders. "She needs our help."

Mrs. Meyer offered a smile and her hand to Claudia. "Welcome, child. We're very glad you're here."

As Reverend Meyer spoke to Claudia in a fatherly voice, Mrs. Meyer's gaze found me.

"I knew you'd come," she whispered, her eyes glistening. "'Here is our new worker,' I said to the reverend when we left the Maxwell that night after meeting you. 'The harvest truly is plenteous, but the labourers are few.'"

She touched my cheek and smiled. "Welcome to the Lord's harvest, Priscilla."

Chapter Twenty-Nine

Grace Moore sat next to me on a small sofa in the lobby of the Noel Hotel. Dad and Jason sat in chairs flanking us. I couldn't stop staring at her, dumbfounded that Miss Nichols had a daughter we hadn't known about.

"I apologize for not contacting you about the fire, Ms. Moore. I was unaware Priscilla had a daughter." Dad looked as shocked as I felt at learning the news. "She's never mentioned you, I'm afraid."

This revelation didn't seem to bother Grace. "She's a very private person, as am I. I grew concerned because I didn't hear from her on Christmas Day. I tried calling last night, but the line wouldn't connect. This morning, my son saw a story in our local newspaper about the fire, and we jumped in the car and drove up here. He's a fireman in Atlanta, so you can imagine his alarm."

She glanced toward the front of the lobby, where the view out the windows showed what was left of the Maxwell across the street. "It's just awful." She turned away, almost as though she couldn't bear to see the Maxwell's burned-out shell.

"Yes, we're all still in a bit of shock," Dad said.

While he gave her the details about Miss Nichols's stroke, her move to the nursing home, and the fire, I tried to study the woman without staring. Well-dressed and stylish, she didn't resemble Miss Nichols at all. Their coloring couldn't be more different, and though I knew children often took after one parent and not the other, something just didn't fit. She seemed too old to be Priscilla's daughter, but then I had to confess I had no idea the ages of either woman. If Miss Nichols had a baby out of wedlock when she was a teenager, that could account for the secrecy as well as the age difference.

"The law firm handling my mother's affairs has recently gone through some changes," Ms. Moore said. The scowl on her brow revealed her feelings about it. "They should have contacted me when she was admitted to the hospital. You can be certain I'll make my displeasure known about how they've handled this situation."

As Dad explained the loss of Miss Nichols's belongings and how to file an insurance claim, I picked up the scrapbook I'd asked Dad to bring downstairs when I called to tell him about Grace.

"This is all that's left." I held it out to her. "She gave it to me, but you're welcome to keep it."

She took it, surprise in her eyes. "How wonderful that you were able to save it."

"It's a scrapbook of the Tennessee Centennial Exposition," I added.

In an instant, her body tensed. "The expo?" She let go of the book, as though it had grown scorching hot. It dropped onto the couch between us.

I glanced at Dad, who indicated he didn't understand what just happened either.

I picked up the book again, and although her eyes remained on it, she didn't reach for it.

"You must be anxious to see your mother," Dad said, changing the subject, but his voice trailed when Grace continued to stare at the scrapbook.

"I'm surprised she kept it," she said, more to herself than to us.

After a long moment, she cautiously reached for the scrapbook again. She took a deep breath as though preparing for something—what, I couldn't guess—and opened the cover to the first page.

The familiar flyer, yellowed with age, bearing a picture of the Parthenon and cherubs holding up a banner, announced the opening of the exposition sixty-four years ago.

Grace clutched her throat. "Extraordinary," she exclaimed under her breath. "I haven't seen this advertisement since I was a young woman, working at the Maxwell House Hotel."

Dad, Jason, and I exchanged confused looks.

"You worked at the Maxwell?" I asked, hoping to prompt more information from her.

She nodded and closed her eyes. When she opened them again, she offered a wobbly smile. "I'm sorry. I knew coming back to Nashville would stir up memories I'd rather not think about, but I hadn't expected this." She indicated the scrapbook in her lap.

"Ms. Moore, I think you better tell us what's going on," Dad said kindly, yet with a firmness that told me he had suspicions of his own about Grace Moore's story.

A lone tear slipped down her cheek, but she didn't brush it away. She turned to me. "Yes, I worked at the Maxwell House Hotel. I was a maid, but when the exposition opened, I was elevated to a lady's maid in order to serve the fine ladies who would stay at the hotel."

She touched the flyer, running her finger across the words *Tennessee Centennial Exposition*. "Two days before the exposition opened, the Nichols family arrived at the Maxwell. I was given the duty of acting as lady's maid for Priscilla."

I gasped.

"Are you saying you're not her daughter?" Dad asked, his face revealing his confusion. Jason, too, looked puzzled.

Grace's lips formed a sad smile. "Not by birth, no. But she took me in when I had no one else."

My mind whirled with the mystery. If Grace wasn't Priscilla's daughter, then who was she?

The message from one of Miss Nichols's postcards floated through my mind. Something about a missing girl and Peaches's fear for the girl's safety.

"Are you . . . Gia?"

Surprise shone in her dark eyes. "How do you know my name?"

I grinned, almost laughing at Dad and Jason's shocked expressions.

I pointed to the book. "The scrapbook told me."

Grace—Gia—thumbed through the pages of the scrapbook, exclaiming over this item or that. When she came to the page with the postcard of the Parthenon, she carefully removed it and read the message Peaches wrote sixty-four years ago.

"My Luca," she whispered. "How I miss you."

I knew Dad would prefer I treat Grace like a guest, which meant not prying into her personal life, but a tidal wave of questions flashed through my mind. I couldn't hold them back. "Who was Luca?"

She lifted a tear-filled smile to me. "My brother. Tall, handsome, kind Luca Moretti. He was twelve years older than me. When our parents died, he took care of me." She sighed. "We were living in New York City when he learned about Nashville's plans for an exposition. A cousin convinced him he could make a fortune driving fairgoers throughout the six months the expo was open. He spent everything he had on train fare and purchasing a horse and carriage."

"How old were you?"

Her gaze drifted across the lobby to the Maxwell. "I was barely fourteen when I hired on as a hotel maid. I'd lied, of course, and told the manager I was seventeen. It was hard work, so I was quite pleased when the manager told me I would be a lady's maid." She gave a small laugh. "I'd dreamed of operating my own hair salon someday, like a woman in New York had done.

"I liked Priscilla the moment I met her. She was different, kinder than her mother and some of the female guests. She treated me and the other maids with respect instead of bossing us as though fine clothes and rich husbands made them better."

I glanced at Jason, knowing he would appreciate hearing this about Priscilla. He'd felt a kinship with her after reading about her activism in the articles. I made a mental note to show them to Grace.

"One of the postcards mentions you needing to be found, as though you were lost and in danger," I said, trying to remember which card it was.

A shadow came over her face. "May I see it?"

We searched until I stopped at the postcard of the Blue Grotto. Grace lifted it free and read the brief note.

"Poor Peaches," she said, sadness in the nickname. "She must have written this, collected all of this—" she indicated the scrapbook—"while Luca was still searching for me." She breathed out a sigh. "Priscilla carried such guilt over that day, but it was my fault. I knew what I was doing when I left with Kenton Thornley, or so I'd thought. He'd flirted with me for days, whispering exciting things in my ear. Things my brother would not have approved of, so I kept them secret.

"I truly did hurt my ankle that day, but not so badly as I let on. When Kenton volunteered to escort me back to the hotel and leave Luca and Priscilla at the fair, I played along with the plan. I'd suspected my brother was in love with her and vice versa. Being a silly, starry-eyed teenager, I imagined leaving them alone together would help them see how well they were matched."

Her smile faded. "But if I'd known how fast my life would spin out of control, I would have never left the park with Kenton Thornley."

Dad shook his head at me, indicating I shouldn't ask any more questions. And I had to admit he was right. I shouldn't pry into memories that were obviously painful.

"Why does Priscilla sign her name as Peaches?" Jason asked.

Grace smiled. "Luca gave her that nickname. She loved to eat peaches and cream in the sweet shop in the lobby of the Maxwell House. She once told him they reminded her of being a child and visiting her grandparents' peach orchard in Georgia." She chuckled. "I remember the first time I went to that same orchard after I moved to Atlanta. Like Priscilla did before me, I ate peaches until I became ill."

"Ms. Moore," Dad said, a serious expression on his face, "if you don't mind my asking, why did you introduce yourself to us as Priscilla's daughter instead of as her friend?"

"Because I am her *legal* daughter." Her face softened with memories. "When I was sixteen, Priscilla adopted me. She wanted me to live with her here, in Nashville, where her work was, but I couldn't come back to this city. It held too many dark memories. I needed a fresh start, so she sent me to live with one of her cousins in Atlanta."

"Is that when you changed your name?" I asked.

"Yes. My name was . . . is Gianetta Moretti. Gianetta means 'God is gracious.' Priscilla suggested Grace, and Moore is close to Moretti. The name Grace Moore helped me feel as though I was still me on the inside, even as I began a new life as someone else. When I married, I was Grace Moore Chamberlain for a time, but my husband passed away soon after our son was born." She shrugged. "I wanted to be Grace Moore again."

She paused, frowning. "I realize, though, that no matter what name I'm called by—Gia or Grace—I owe my life to Priscilla." She smoothed a hand over the scrapbook in her lap. "Many other women would say the same thing. In fact, dozens of them wrote letters of thanks to her after they settled into their new lives. Priscilla Nichols saved hundreds of us. Did you know she owns the Peach House for Women on Tenth Street?" At our dumbfounded looks, she nodded. "There's a small peach orchard in the backyard. She was matron of the house for many years, before her health began to fail. Women still come from all over Tennessee to find help within those walls. Desperate, broken women, very much like the young woman I was once."

Her gaze traveled to Dad, Jason, and me, each of us hanging on her every word.

"I'm seventy-eight years old, and I've lived most of those years in fear. Fearful that someone would discover my past. Fearful that if I spoke out against those who'd wronged me, I'd face repercussions. Fearful that my husband or son would be ashamed of me."

Once again, she glanced at the burned-out shell of the Maxwell House Hotel, a faraway look in her eyes. "Peaches often said life is too short for regrets. Forgive others, then forgive yourself, she'd say. It may sound strange, but I could easier forgive the people who'd hurt me than I could forgive myself.

"You see, my foolishness," she said with a shaky voice, "cost me—cost us—everything."

Chapter Thirty

"Welcome to the Lord's harvest."

The words Mrs. Meyer spoke over me the night I helped Claudia to freedom became an anthem in my heart. Witnessing a life go from darkness to light was something I would never forget, and I knew I'd found my calling. Convincing Papa and Mother of it, however, would take every ounce of courage I had within me.

Memories of Reverend Meyer's sermon from this morning brought a smile as I packed the toiletries on the vanity table near the window. Unbeknownst to my parents, I'd taken a single room for myself here at the Maxwell. The suite was far too large and costly for one person. They assumed I would board the train for Chattanooga with them later this afternoon, so the time of my confession fast approached.

The sermon on the Good Samaritan, however, bolstered my confidence. Hearing the familiar story reminded me that what I was doing was right and good, even when others might not understand. I dreaded Mother's reaction the most. All her hopes and dreams of grandchildren and a happy future were tied up in me, her only living child.

Guilt washed over me, yet in my heart of hearts, I was certain that what I was doing was exactly what I was meant to do. Perhaps God never intended for me to marry and bear children. I couldn't say what the future might hold, but for now, anyway, this was the path I'd chosen.

As they often did, my thoughts drifted to Luca.

Would I ever see him again?

I stopped myself from letting my mind go beyond that. Simply knowing he and Gia were safe would be a gift.

Fanny bustled about the suite, getting Papa's and Mother's things packed. Trunks, cases, and bags were loaded onto a wheeled cart and taken to the end of the hallway to the baggage elevator. When a porter came for my things, I discreetly gave him my new room number as well as an extra tip to keep this information to himself.

When we three were alone, checking the room for anything we might have overlooked, I took a deep breath. The time had come to share my heart with my parents.

"Papa, Mother, I need to speak with you before we go downstairs."

Mother pulled open a drawer on the small writing desk, rifling through the odds and ends that were not going to Chattanooga with her. "Can't it wait, Priscilla? We'll be late for the train as it is."

Papa's gaze narrowed on me from across the room. He'd always been better at sensing my moods than Mother. "The train won't leave without us, Cora. Come, let's hear what our daughter has to say."

I sent Papa a look of appreciation, although I knew neither of them would be pleased after I gave the speech I'd rehearsed in my mind.

Mother moved to the velvet-covered settee, where Papa joined her. I remained standing, too nervous to sit in the matching chair. "You know I love you both very much," I began, my voice wobbly with emotion. I'd never lived apart from them, and the consequences of my decision suddenly seemed very real.

"We love you, too, Priscilla, but tell us what this is about." Papa's demeanor grew serious.

I gulped a lungful of air. "I'm not returning to Chattanooga with you."

Mother scowled. "Whatever do you mean, not returning with us? We're leaving today. Your things are being loaded onto the train as we speak."

"No, Mother, they aren't." I sank onto the edge of the chair, feeling deceitful yet convinced of my decision. "I'm staying in Nashville. I've taken a room here at the Maxwell, so you mustn't worry about my safety." I swallowed, preparing for the final blow. "Reverend and Mrs. Meyer have invited me to join them in their work here in the city . . . and I've accepted the offer."

Mother's confused stare shifted from me to Papa. "Eldridge, what is she talking about? Did you know of this?"

Papa shook his head, but he didn't seem surprised by my announcement. "I knew nothing until this very moment, but—"

"But what?" Mother's shrill voice echoed in the room.

"But I knew a day would soon come when our daughter would spread her wings and fly away from us."

Papa's poetic words filled me with gratefulness, but Mother appeared horror-struck. "Spread her wings? Fly away? Why, this is preposterous." Her angry gaze returned to me. "I don't know what you're trying to prove, Priscilla, but you will not work with the Meyers in . . . whatever it is they do. It's unseemly. They deal with the lowest of the low. The dregs of the city. I will not have my daughter involved in such business. Not even Mrs. Meyer's Vanderbilt cousins could change my mind."

"I already have, Mother," I said softly. I didn't want to argue or be difficult, but she had to understand—as Papa surprisingly already did—that my decision was made. "I helped a young woman a few nights ago. She'd been desperate and alone when an unscrupulous woman found her and convinced her to come work for her . . . in a brothel."

Mother gasped and covered her mouth with her handkerchief.

"Where did you find this girl?" Papa asked. "Here, at the Maxwell?"

"No. I went for a walk one evening and happened upon her." While that limited version of the story was true, I didn't see the need to tell them about the liquor store or how I'd seen young women there on the night I helped Luca escape from the hospital.

"This is ridiculous." Mother rose to her feet. Eyes full of fire landed first on Papa, then on me. "I won't listen to another word. You will come home with us today, young lady, and never speak of this nonsense again. Why, if anyone found out that you'd become involved with women who . . ." She shuddered and shook her head. "No. We will not speak of this again. Now—" she moved to the door—"let us go home."

My gaze sought Papa. "You understand, don't you, Papa? I don't want to disappoint you, either of you, but I have to do what my heart tells me is right. Reverend Meyer's sermon this morning reminded me that God has a purpose for each of us. I believe this is mine."

"I blame the Meyers for this." Mother marched over, hands on hips. "I watched you the night they joined us for dinner, whispering and conspiring with them."

She must have seen me from the mezzanine when I shared Gia's story with the compassionate couple after we left the dining room. Yet there was no shame in wanting to help others.

"They're good people, Mother. Kind and caring. When I brought Claudia to them, they took her into their home without blinking."

"What will happen to the girl now?" Papa asked.

That he would inquire about Claudia's fate filled me with love for him. We weren't as close as I would have liked, mainly because I wasn't the son he'd always wanted, but I knew he loved me.

"They've already found her a position as nanny with a family in Memphis."

"Does the family know she's a soiled dove?" Mother's harsh tone saddened me.

"Claudia is fifteen years old. Her mother abandoned

her and she's never known her father. Doesn't she deserve a chance at a good life?"

Her tight lips didn't move, but the hardness in her eyes lessened.

"And yes, the family knows about Claudia's past. The Meyers are always honest with the employers they work with."

We sat in silence for a long minute before Papa stood. "Well, I believe that's all that need be said."

Mother opened her mouth to respond, but he held up his hand to prevent her from speaking. "Our daughter is a twenty-five-year-old woman, Cora. It's high time we stopped treating her like a child."

He turned to me. "I won't pretend I'm happy about the choice you've made, Priscilla. I believe you will suffer many rejections and closed doors in the future because of it. But I can see your heart is in this, and that is something I greatly admire. We will miss you, our only child, but you will be in our prayers."

I fell into his arms, with tears escaping down my cheeks. "Thank you, Papa," I whispered.

He nodded. "I'll see that your account at the bank has adequate funds for your needs. My solicitor, Henry Green, has an office here in Nashville. Contact him should you run into any trouble or need help in any way."

"I will, Papa." I turned to Mother, her face stony. "I'm sorry, Mama," I said, using the name I hadn't called her since I was a small girl. "I know I've disappointed you again."

I expected her to turn and storm out of the room, but she didn't. After several silent moments, she came to me, eyes sparkling with tears.

"You've always had a mind of your own," she whispered, placing her hand on my cheek.

My chin trembled, and I smiled. "I learned from the best."

She chuckled, then nodded. "I suppose you did." Her heavy sigh told me how difficult this was for her. "I don't understand any of this, but I want you to know you're not a disappointment, Priscilla. You're beautiful and strong, and you will always be our cherished daughter."

Her arms went around me then. I couldn't remember the last time Mother hugged me, and I relished the feeling. "I love you, Mother."

"I love you, too."

When we parted, I knew something had changed in our relationship. Something for the better, I believed.

We made our way downstairs. Mother kissed me goodbye and climbed into the carriage, tears wetting her cheeks. Papa took me in his arms once again before joining Mother. I waved until their carriage was out of sight. I thought loneliness and regret would engulf me as the realities of my decision sank in, but they never came. Instead, budding possibilities for my future filled me with an excitement I'd never experienced before.

I stood on the sidewalk for a long moment, gazing around me. People hurried past. Carriages came and went. The Maxwell gleamed in glorious sunshine, and the lifeblood of Nashville pulsated around me.

I grinned as a new truth settled within me.

I was home.

———————

Grace Moore and her son, Adam, joined us for dinner in the restaurant in the Noel Hotel. They'd taken rooms there for the night, and we planned to visit Miss Nichols in the morning.

I couldn't help feeling disappointed after we said good night to them. I'd hoped Grace would fill in the missing details about Priscilla, Luca, and what happened to her—Gia—but she hadn't. She'd become emotional talking about the past, and her son suggested she call it a night.

"I'll be up soon," I said to Dad as we waited for an elevator to take us upstairs to our rooms. Emmett yawned, and even Jason looked beat. I, however, felt too keyed up. "I'm not quite ready to turn in. I think I'll have some hot chocolate in the café."

The elevator doors opened. Emmett stepped inside and started pushing buttons.

"Don't stay up too late," Dad said and joined Emmett.

Jason held the doors open with one hand. "Do you want me to stay with you?"

"No, I'll be fine." I smiled, appreciative of his concern. "I'll see you in the morning."

He nodded and let the doors close.

A small café was located just off the lobby of the hotel. It was strange being here. The Noel had been the Maxwell's rival for years. That was, until the Maxwell turned into a residential hotel. Still, I couldn't remember the last time I'd eaten at the Noel's restaurant or spent any time in the lobby.

I watched as people continued to walk and drive past the burned hotel, gawking at the terrible spectacle. The big electric red-and-white sign attached to the hotel—with *Maxwell* in bold, white vertical letters and *House* in smaller, horizontal lettering—was eerily dark after illuminating the corner of Church and Fourth for decades.

I settled at a small table and ordered a hot chocolate. We'd been in shock since the fire roared to life, but now it was beginning to sink in that the hotel was a total loss. Everything we owned had gone up in flames or been ruined by water and smoke. The fire marshal told Dad we could poke through the debris in a few days, but I didn't hold any hope we'd be able to salvage much.

The waitress brought my drink and left me to my thoughts.

I'd just taken the first sip of piping hot deliciousness when Grace walked in, carrying the scrapbook. When she saw me, she indicated the cup of chocolate.

"You won't believe this, but that's exactly what I came downstairs for."

I smiled and motioned to the empty seat across from me. "You're welcome to join me."

She did, placing the scrapbook on the table. The waitress brought another cup of cocoa.

"I'm sorry for earlier." She slowly stirred the hot liquid. "Adam is a bit protective of me, especially now that I'm old." She chuckled. "He's been the man of the house since he was a boy, but I'm grateful I have him."

I nodded in understanding.

Her eyes fell on the scrapbook. "It's funny," she said, deep in thought. "I tried for so many years to forget the exposition and the memories of that summer, but Peaches did everything she could to preserve it."

"Didn't she ever show you the scrapbook when you visited her?"

"That's just it." She took a small sip of her drink before setting the mug down again. "I never came to visit her."

At my look of surprise, she nodded. "It's true. I'm not proud to admit this, but I never wanted to see Nashville again. After I moved to Atlanta, she'd visit several times a year. She was at my wedding and Adam's christening. She came for Thanksgiving and Christmas, but I refused to come here."

Now I knew why Miss Nichols never had visitors.

She squinted her eyes as though remembering something. "My brother had a favorite saying. I think it's an old Italian proverb or some such. It goes something like 'Count your nights by stars, not shadows; count your life with smiles, not tears.'" She grinned. "He was quite the romantic. But the meaning of the proverb is live life without looking back with regret. *If only* are two of the saddest words one can say."

"What happened to Luca?" I asked softly.

"Dear, dear Luca." She sighed, her eyes on the scrapbook. "The day I left the exposition with Kenton Thornley, I thought him in love with me. He said he wanted me with him, that we would see the world together. I was young, with a head full of silly ideas, and I foolishly believed him." She stirred her chocolate and shook her head. "He had a friend, a woman, who would help us be together. Madame LeBlanc."

She closed her eyes as though the name brought back bitter memories.

I chewed my lip. Maybe Adam was right. I shouldn't ask questions about things better left in the past.

When she looked up again, she shrugged. "I should have known what kind of woman she was, but I only had eyes for Kenton. Madame gave us a room in her house—a boarding-house, she called it—and I gave Kenton my innocence. I felt as though we were on our honeymoon. We went to the exposition; we ate at restaurants; he bought me presents."

Her expression grew troubled. "But Luca knew something terrible had happened to me, even before I realized it myself. He suspected Kenton's involvement, and when he accused Kenton, they fought, with Luca ending up in jail. I didn't know any of this at the time, but Kenton had Luca severely beaten while he sat in jail. Our dear Peaches saved his life, too."

"How?" I asked, captivated by the tale.

"She forced her way into the jailhouse. When she saw he'd been beaten, she demanded they move him to the hospital . . . then she helped him escape."

My mouth dropped open. "Miss Nichols?"

"Yes." She chuckled, but soon her smile faded. "Kenton's attitude toward me changed after that. He grew mean and said cruel things about my Italian heritage. When I demanded to be taken back to the Maxwell, he said he'd tell my brother and Priscilla what I'd done. He even threatened to expose me publicly if I didn't do as he wished." She laid a hand on the scrapbook. "I saw Priscilla at the exposition one day, but I ran away. I realize now she would have helped me escape, too, had I trusted her the way Luca did.

"When Kenton's interest in me ended, Madame LeBlanc declared I owed her money for room and board, and the only way to earn it was to become what I knew I already was—a prostitute."

Grace grew quiet for a long moment before continuing. "Luca was determined to find me, but I didn't want to be found. I was ashamed of what I'd become. When the exposition ended, Madame moved her business to New York City, and I went with her. My brother searched brothels from Tennessee to New York before he tracked me down a year later. Unfortunately, brothels are breeding grounds for all kinds of disease, including tuberculosis."

A tear slid down her cheek. "When Luca found me, he was very ill. I didn't know what to do, where to go for help. The brother of an Italian whore wasn't important to anyone in my world."

"What did you do?" I asked, heartbroken for the young, frightened woman she'd been.

A soft smile parted her lips when she met my gaze. "I did the only thing that made sense. I sent a telegram to the Maxwell House and prayed it would find its way to Priscilla."

Chapter Thirty-One

"Good day, Miss Nichols."

Mr. Bowles stood behind the front desk of the Maxwell House, peering at me over the rim of his wire-framed spectacles as I walked past.

The greeting came as a surprise. In the past year, the man hadn't said more than a few stiff words to me, those being *thank you* and *you're welcome* when I paid my bill each month. I assumed my deceiving him into giving me Kenton's room key was the cause, but Fanny informed me shortly after I'd taken a room of my own that Mr. Bowles was quite scandalized that I, an unmarried woman, would dare to stay in *his* hotel without a proper chaperone.

"Good day to you as well, Mr. Bowles," I said and continued past the desk.

He, however, walked parallel along the opposite side. "May I have a word, Miss Nichols?"

The unusual request brought me to a stop. "Of course."

He returned to his place at the exact center of the long desk, clearly expecting me to retrace my steps as well. When I was in front of him, he reached under the desk and retrieved a folded paper.

"This arrived for you earlier." He cleared his throat and looked down his thin nose at me. "You weren't in your room when the bellboy tried to deliver it. Out on one of your *missions*, I presume."

Although I'd tried to be discreet about the reason I'd chosen to remain in Nashville without my parents, word soon traveled through the staff and guests alike that I was working with the Meyers. Fanny herself accidentally perpetuated the gossip when she told her mum that I'd helped rescue Claudia. Her mum, shocked that a lady like me would do such a thing, told someone, who told someone, until most everyone eventually knew.

I hid a smile beneath my hand and cleared my throat. "As a matter of fact, Mr. Bowles, I was helping Mrs. Meyer—you recall Mrs. Meyer, the cousin of Cornelius Vanderbilt? Yes, of course you do. Anyway, I was helping Mrs. Meyer serve soup to a family who lost their home in a fire. We're collecting clothing and furniture for them. Perhaps you'd like to make a donation? The father is about your size."

His lips pinched. "I haven't time for dillydallying, Miss Nichols." He handed the paper to me. "Good day."

I chuckled as he stormed to the far end of the desk, feigning busyness with the big guest ledger. I resumed my journey toward the grand staircase, intent on changing clothes before joining the Meyers and some of the other volunteers for dinner.

A glance at the paper, however, brought me to a stop.

It was a telegram.

I ducked into a quiet area of the lobby. Since the exposition closed last October, the hotel wasn't nearly as crowded, and one could enjoy a quiet moment in the lobby if one chose.

The brief message nearly brought me to my knees.

Luca ill. Come at once. Gia.

My hands trembled, and tears clouded my vision.

Could it be true?

Praise be to God!

Luca found Gia. He'd promised he would. But now he was ill and needed me. The address at the end of the message was in New York City.

I realized I was crying when a woman passing by offered her handkerchief.

My mind whirled with all that needed to be done. I couldn't travel to New York City alone. There was only one person I could ask to go with me.

"Of course," Mrs. Meyer said the moment I collapsed in her arms and sobbed out my story. Reverend Meyer made our travel arrangements while I hurried back to the hotel to throw items into a carpetbag.

"Gia's been found," I told Fanny, with tears of joy streaming down both our faces as we danced and hugged. Fanny and her mum had become volunteers at the Meyers' soup kitchen, so she knew Gia's being found was nothing short of a miracle.

Mrs. Meyer and I traveled by train to New York City that very night. The journey took three days, with many hours wasted in train depots along the route, and we were exhausted when we arrived. We hired a hackney to take us directly to the address Gia provided, without thought of stopping at a hotel first, but I wasn't prepared for the squalor and chaos of the crowded neighborhood.

"Little Italy," the driver said with disdain. "Don't know why ladies like you would want to dirty the soles of your shoes down here."

He left us in the middle of a busy street, full of carts, wagons, and vendors selling everything imaginable, from fruit and bread to whole dead chickens, the feathers intact. Buildings taller than the Maxwell were stacked next to each other, with laundry hanging on lines stretched across alley- ways, going from windows on one building to the next. Amid the squeals of children and the barks of several roaming dogs, words were shouted and spoken in a language I could not understand.

Thankfully, the bedlam didn't deter Mrs. Meyer. In her usual no-nonsense fashion, she collared a young boy speed- ing past and asked where to find the address. He pointed to a gray building down the street before she set him on his way again.

The stench once we entered the building nearly made me gag. I couldn't imagine what it was, nor did I wish to.

"We've made a mistake," I whispered to Mrs. Meyer as she searched the filth-covered doors for a number that matched the address on the telegram. "Luca and Gia couldn't possibly be in this place."

She gave me a patient smile. The kind I'd earned repeatedly over the past year whenever I revealed how little I understood about the world outside the safety and luxury of my parents' home.

When we finally found the correct door, the cry of a baby came from the opposite side. I knocked, but the baby's cry drowned it out. I tried again. This time, someone called out in Italian.

At my questioning glance, Mrs. Meyer shrugged and reached for the handle.

The dimly lit room wasn't even as big as my single room at the Maxwell. Blankets, clothes, and dishes with dried food filled the space. I could find no real furniture of any sort, although a chair or stool might have been hiding beneath the mess.

The smell of urine overwhelmed me.

A baby wailed from the adjoining room.

"This can't be right." I backed into the hallway, my heart thundering. "We're in the wrong place, Mrs. Meyer. Let us be gone from here."

I'd turned to leave when a familiar voice stilled me.

"Miss Nichols?"

I glanced over my shoulder to see a woman emerge from the other room—far too thin, with stringy hair and pale skin, a baby in her arms. I couldn't believe what my eyes beheld.

"Gia?"

Bony shoulders shook, and her face crumpled. "You came."

Before I could take a breath, she was in my arms, baby and all. Her wails matched those of the child, and my tears joined theirs. Somehow, Mrs. Meyer managed to take the baby from Gia's arms, and we held each other for long, wonderful minutes.

When we finally parted, I pushed her disheveled hair from her face. Large, luminous eyes met mine. "Gia, it really is you."

She nodded. "Thank you for coming. I didn't know what else to do."

"Luca?"

Her face told me the news even before she spoke. "He's dying, Miss Nichols." Her agony-filled whisper pierced my heart.

I inhaled, then exhaled just as quickly. "Where is he?"

She led the way to the adjoining room. Unlike the first, this tiny room held a bed and not much else. Luca lay sleeping, with a blanket pulled nearly to his whiskered chin. My eyes took in his hollowed cheeks and skin the color of death. A rattle in his chest came with every shallow breath.

I moved to his side, gazing at the man I loved. "Luca."

Eyelids fluttered before opening. He seemed confused when he saw me.

"I never thought I'd see you again," I breathed, reaching for his hand, his fingers cold to the touch.

"Pesche?"

I smiled through my tears. "Yes, Luca. It's me. Your *Pesche*."

"How did you know where to find us?"

I glanced at Gia. "Your sister sent me a telegram, and I came right away."

His gaze drifted to Gia, and a look of peace came over him. "I found her. I found my Gianetta."

"You did." I squeezed his hand.

A bout of coughing overtook him then, and he freed his hand from mine. Gia moved around me, picked up a cloth, and held it to his mouth. I gasped when she pulled it away, spotted with blood.

When the episode was over, his eyes closed, and he sank into the dingy pillow.

"He doesn't stay awake for long," Gia said, her voice low and sad. She dropped the cloth into a bucket with other similarly soiled rags. "It'll be time to feed him some broth soon. You can stay and help, if you'd like."

My mind swam with questions. "Gia, what are you doing here, in New York City? When did Luca find you?"

The baby cried from the other room, and I remembered Mrs. Meyer had taken it from Gia. "Is that your child?"

"No." She led me back into the other room. Mrs. Meyer had laid the baby on one of the blankets, while she worked on tidying the messy room.

"Gia, this is Mrs. Meyer. She traveled with me from Nashville."

The two women greeted each other; then Gia turned to me. "Six other people live in this apartment with us." She indicated the bedding and food. "Evelina is the daughter of one of them."

After working with the Meyers for over a year, I thought I'd seen every form of poverty and desperation humanity could suffer. Yet this filthy, tiny hovel in the bowels of a run-down tenement in Little Italy revealed a level of despair I couldn't fathom.

"Gia," I said, focusing on the most important issue. "We must get Luca to a hospital."

She began to weep. "I don't have any money. I had to give it all to the landlord so Luca could have the bed."

I reached to wipe her tears. "You did well, sweet girl. Now let me help."

She nodded. "I knew sending the telegram was the right thing to do."

We flew into action.

Gia took the baby to a neighbor while I packed a bag of Luca's meager belongings. I didn't know how she managed it, but Mrs. Meyer left the apartment and returned with an ambulance wagon. The attendants put Luca on a stretcher and carried him out of the squalid dwelling and into warm sunshine. A soft smile touched his lips before they whisked him away.

At the hospital, Mrs. Meyer once again came to the rescue. When the nurse in charge heard Luca's last name, her pleasant demeanor disappeared. A bed that had been available minutes before suddenly was not. Mrs. Meyer did something I'd never seen her do in all the time I'd spent with her and the reverend.

She looked down her nose at the nurse. "My cousin, Cornelius Vanderbilt, will be most interested when I tell him a hospital that he's donated large sums of money to is denying medical care to a gravely ill patient. What is your name, dear, so I may be certain to give you credit?"

The nurse's eyes widened before she scrambled to find a bed for Luca.

As we followed behind the gurney, I leaned over and whispered, "Has your cousin truly given money to this hospital?"

Mrs. Meyer winked. "I'm sure there is a hospital somewhere in this city that Cornelius has donated money to that has denied medical care to a patient at some point. Whether or not it is *this* hospital, I couldn't say."

They took Luca to a ward specifically for patients with consumption. We were warned that entering the ward would put us at risk of contracting the highly contagious illness, but I knew I couldn't leave Luca. Gia felt the same.

"You should return to Nashville." I stood with Mrs. Meyer outside the ward while the nurses settled Luca in a bed with Gia's help. "I don't know how long I'll be here, but I'll be here as long as he has breath in his lungs."

Sympathy shone in her eyes. "I'm so very sorry, Priscilla. I know this isn't how you hoped your and Luca's story would end."

Tears blurred my vision. "No, but at least I have him in my life again. Even for a brief time."

She gave Gia and me each a motherly hug. "You will all be in my prayers."

Gia and I sat with Luca until the nurses made us leave. Visiting hours were from ten o'clock in the morning until five o'clock in the evening, no exceptions. Luca offered a weak smile when we told him good night.

"My Gianetta and my *Pesche*. I am a blessed man, indeed."

I took Gia to a hotel not far from the hospital where we rented a suite of rooms. "You're not going back to that apartment." I ordered baths for both of us as well as two trays of food. "Tomorrow we'll do some shopping."

When we were clean and fed, exhaustion set in. "Good night, Gia." I turned to my room.

"Miss Nichols?"

"Yes?"

Tears welled in her dark eyes. "I'm sorry for the trouble I caused you and Luca. If I hadn't—"

"No, Gia." I stopped her. "This is not your fault. Someday you can tell me what happened when you left with Kenton, but no matter what you may or may not have done, this is not your fault. You were an innocent girl. People with evil intentions took advantage of that innocence." I took her hand in mine and squeezed. "The past is just that. The past. Tomorrow is a new day."

She sniffled, then nodded. "Good night, Miss Nichols."

I chuckled. "If your brother can call me *Pesche*, I think it's appropriate for you to call me Priscilla."

She smiled through her tears. "Good night, Priscilla."

Our days settled into a familiar yet agonizingly painful routine. Hope was not something doled out in the tuberculosis ward. That every patient was slowly dying was the accepted understanding.

Gia and I arrived at the hospital promptly at ten o'clock each morning and stayed until the nurses shooed us away. Several times throughout the day, however, we allowed each other privacy with Luca, knowing there were things that needed to be said without anyone else listening.

Luca and I were alone on one of these occasions. Gia had announced her need to stretch her legs and hurried out the door, promising to keep to the small private park adjacent to the hospital. Wearing one of the new outfits we'd purchased for her, with her thick hair clean and styled in a simple fashion, one would never suspect the ordeal she'd been through the past year. Only Luca and I detected the changes in her, with a shadow of sorrow and regret ever in her eyes.

"She looks good. Healthy. Not like when I found her." His distressed gaze returned to me. "I barely recognized her."

He'd given me the details of how he searched brothel after brothel, refusing to quit despite the seeming impossibility of finding her. At one point, he feared she'd gone west to San Francisco, but then someone told him Madame LeBlanc was in New York City. His hard work ended in success, but it now appeared it would also cost him his life.

"God answered my prayers," he continued, the worry on his face easing. "She is safe."

While I was grateful he found peace in knowing his sister was no longer in danger, I struggled to understand why God allowed it to happen in the first place.

"What is it, *Pesche*? I see you are troubled by something."

I met his gaze. Should I be honest? "Wouldn't it have been better had God prevented Kenton from harming her? You wouldn't be lying here with a devastating disease if he'd kept her safe back in Nashville."

He squeezed his eyes closed, and I feared I'd said too much. But when he looked at me again, his face softened. "Who are we to tell God what he should or shouldn't do? I, too, wish things had turned out differently, but we cannot live in the regrets. Choices were made that cannot be unmade. You must help Gia. I fear she will never forgive herself, no matter how many times I tell her I love her."

I reached to brush a lock of hair from his feverish fore-head. "You sacrificed everything for love of your sister."

"Promise me," he began, but a bout of coughing inter-rupted. Gratefully, it wasn't a bad episode—the kind that sounded as though his ravaged lungs were being expelled from his body—and he continued. "Promise me you'll take care of her. Take her back to Chattanooga or Nashville or wherever you settle. I want her to marry and have a good life, but I fear she won't let herself be happy. She feels such guilt."

"I promise, Luca. I'll take her home with me." I smiled. It was time to share my surprise. "What would you think if I adopted Gia?"

His brow knit. "Why would you do such a thing?"

I leaned close so others in the room wouldn't overhear. Although the patients and their visitors paid little atten-tion to anyone else. We knew time with our loved ones was precious.

"I know I shall never marry," I stated, only to have him scowl and shake his head.

"Do not say such things."

"Listen to me, my darling." I smoothed his brow until the frown eased. "I know in my heart I will never love anyone as I love you. I could never settle for less. My work with the Meyers is fulfilling, and I've found a measure of happiness. But Gia . . ." I paused. "She will need a new start in life. I want to give that to her. I am my father's only heir, Luca. If I adopt Gia, she will become my heir."

He stared at me, astonishment in his eyes. "*Pesche*, you would do that for my Gianetta?"

"Yes, my love. I would do that for *our* Gianetta."

"But . . . how?"

I took an envelope from my pocket. "I sent a telegram to my solicitor in Nashville the day after I arrived in New York and asked him about the legalities of my adopting a child. I didn't give any specifics but wanted to know if there were any restrictions."

"And?"

"There aren't. Because both of Gia's parents are deceased, she is the only one who has to give consent to the adoption."

Tears rolled down onto his pillow. He reached for my hand. "I know it was foolish, but while I searched for Gia, I dreamed that after I found her, you and I would marry." He smiled. "I wanted to take you to Italy and show you my homeland."

"I would have loved it, my darling." We'd been told not to have physical contact with the patients, for fear of transmitting the disease, but I couldn't stop myself from placing a gentle kiss on his lips. "Perhaps Gia and I will go someday."

When Gia returned, we chatted for several minutes before I cleared my throat. "I have something to ask you, Gia."

I glanced at Luca for his permission. He nodded, with peace shining in his dark eyes.

"What is this about?" Gia asked, looking between us.

"It's about family." I took Luca's hand in one of mine, then reached across him with the other. She grasped hold, curiosity shining out from eyes that were so like Luca's.

"We are a family." I gazed down on Luca. "It wasn't God's plan for us to be united through marriage," I said softly, then turned to Gia. "But we can be united through adoption."

She looked confused. "I don't understand."

"Gianetta Moretti, would you do me the honor of becoming my daughter?"

I knew the moment she grasped my meaning. Her face crumpled, and she covered it with both hands. I stood and took her in my arms, this motherless girl who was losing the one person in the world who'd been her rock, her protector, her hero. I knew I could never be a replacement in her life for Luca, but I would do my best to be a sister, a mother, a friend.

She clung to me and sobbed, declaring herself unclean, unworthy of being loved. *"You don't know what I've done,"* she said over and over, as though that knowledge would make a difference. As though I would turn my back on her, as many people already had, no doubt. My heart broke seeing her like this, yet I knew only time and a gracious God could truly heal her.

When she finally quieted, I took her face in my hands and kissed each tearstained cheek.

"God forgives our sins when we ask him, Gia. Your brother and I forgive you, too. Now, dear girl," I said, my heart bursting open with the love of a mother for her child, "it's time to forgive yourself."

Chapter Thirty-Two

Miss Nichols gave a lopsided smile when Grace walked into the small room in the nursing home. "Gia . . . my girl."

"I've missed you." Grace leaned down to plant a kiss on Miss Nichols's wrinkled cheek.

Adam, Dad, and I hesitated at the door, not wanting to intrude on the reunion. Jason had volunteered to stay with Emmett, and the two had plans to visit the lunch counter at Harveys and enjoy one of their famous chocolate chip cookies and hot cocoa.

Adam joined his mother, bending down to kiss his grandmother.

Miss Nichols waved us in when she spotted us. "How did you find my girl?"

I smiled, thinking it sweet to hear a seventy-eight-year-old woman referred to as a *girl*.

"I grew worried when I didn't hear from you on Christmas Day." Grace pulled a chair up next to the bed and settled in it. "I had to make sure my *mamma* was behaving." Her strong Italian accent, usually not very noticeable when she spoke, brought a grin to Miss Nichols's face.

It was good to see Miss Nichols improving. Her speech still slurred, but I thought she sounded much clearer than when we were here last.

"I'm afraid I have some bad news," Dad said. He'd talked it over with Grace, and they both felt Miss Nichols needed to know about the Maxwell.

As Dad told her about the fire, Miss Nichols's expression went from astonishment to sorrow.

"I'm afraid it's a total loss." Dad's voice wobbled. The shock of the fire had worn off and left us all with a deep sadness. "We'd moved your belongings to the basement, so there's a chance some of it survived."

"So many memories." A faraway look came to her eyes.

"I saved your scrapbook, though," I said. "I offered it to Grace, but she said I should keep it."

Miss Nichols's gaze rested on me. "Yes, you keep my memories now."

Grace leaned forward and took Miss Nichols's hand. "How would you like to come live with me in Atlanta, Peaches? Your old room is just waiting for you."

"Atlanta?" Miss Nichols's eyes widened.

Grace kissed her fingers. "Say yes. Just like I did all those years ago when you asked permission to adopt me. It's my turn now, Peaches. It's my turn to take care of you."

Tears formed in Miss Nichols's eyes. "My family."

"We are," Grace said.

"Luca, too." She sighed and closed her eyes. "I see him . . . in my dreams. He didn't let us stay, Gia. Why not?"

She grew quiet, her even breath indicating she'd fallen asleep.

"She had her first stroke twenty years ago," Grace said softly, settling back into the chair. "She'd been so busy with her mission work and fighting for her causes that she neglected herself. The doctor said if she didn't slow down, it was guaranteed she'd have another stroke, one that she might not recover from."

My eyes drifted to Miss Nichols. "Is that when she moved to the Maxwell House?"

"She loved that old hotel," Grace said, a wistful smile on her lips. "While it brought painful memories to me, it was home to her. It's where she and Luca fell in love."

"What did she mean by 'He didn't let us stay'?" Dad asked. When I shot him a look of surprise, he gave a sheepish shrug. He must have gotten caught up in Miss Nichols's life story, too.

A shadow came over Grace's face. "When Luca found me in New York City, he was already gravely ill. Tuberculosis had found him. In those days, there wasn't a cure. More people died from consumption than anything else until a treatment was discovered. Unfortunately, it was much too late for my brother.

"I felt such guilt. We can't be certain, but he'd most likely contracted the disease while searching brothels for me. When I saw him, my big, strong brother, looking so pale and sick, I was crushed. Peaches came as soon as I telegrammed. She had him moved to a hospital, and we visited him every day. I watched her care for him with such love. When the nurses were busy, she bathed his face and arms, cleaned him when his stomach was sick, read to him from a Bible she purchased. Even though they hadn't married, she was his wife in those final days, loving him until the cruel hand of death parted them."

Her gaze went to Miss Nichols's face, peaceful in slumber. "The day came when we knew it was his last on earth."

She grew quiet, the pain of that long-ago day in her eyes.

"Luca's journey was coming to an end, but hers was just beginning."

"Good morning."

I offered my usual greeting to the nurse behind the desk as Gia and I arrived to spend the day with Luca. The woman, the same one who'd initially denied Luca a bed two months ago, still wasn't a well of friendliness, but she treated us with reserved respect.

We passed through the familiar corridors, nodding to doctors, nurses, and patients we'd come to know. Word had traveled quickly that Cornelius Vanderbilt was a friend of ours, and though the story wasn't true, I didn't correct it. If Luca received better care because of it, so be it.

"Good morning, Miss Nichols, Gia." The young nurse on duty in Luca's ward didn't greet us with her usual smile. Something in her eyes made me pause.

My gaze flew to Luca's bed, and I was relieved to find him in it.

Yet . . . all was not well.

I knew it in my mind before my heart would accept it.

"He took a turn for the worse during the night," she said, sincere sympathy in every dreadful word. There was no need to say more.

We made our way to his bedside. Gia clung to my hand and I to hers as we looked down upon our Luca.

We'd seen this happen in the ward three times since Luca was admitted. The signs were always the same. His skin bore a terrible shade of gray, and a horrific sound came from his chest, his lungs brutally ravaged by the disease.

Gia's shoulders trembled with silent sobs. I cradled her in my arms, shushing her.

"We must be strong for him." I fought tears that threatened to fill my own eyes. "He needs to know we will be all right, so his passing from this life to the next will be joyous and not sad."

"I can't be joyous." She cried all the more. "He's my brother, and I did this to him."

I tightened my embrace. "You didn't do this, Gia. Each of us has a time when our lives on earth will end. Today is Luca's. But even though his body will be no more, his spirit will live on in the presence of our Lord. That is where our joy is found."

We stood in each other's arms for long minutes before we felt ready to face what was ahead. When Luca awoke for a brief time, his eyes sought out Gia.

"I love you, my Gianetta," he rasped, too weak to rise up when the coughing came.

Blood trickled from the corner of his mouth, and I gently wiped it away. The end was not far.

When his gaze found me, I forced a smile. "I will count my nights by stars, not shadows. And I will count my life with smiles, not tears."

Gia's sobs filled the room. She fell to her knees beside his bed, her face buried in her hands.

"Take her and go." Luca's eyes pleaded with me. "Do not let her see this."

I knew what he meant. The final hours as death's grip

took hold were frightening. He didn't want those images to be the last his sister remembered of him.

Yet how could I leave him?

"I'm at peace, *Pesche*. The angels are near."

With slow movements, he dug something from beneath his covers. It was the tiny replica of the Parthenon I'd given him the day we moved him to the hospital. The one I'd purchased when I had no hope of ever seeing him again.

"Arrivederci, mie Pesche," he whispered and placed the small souvenir in my hands. "My heart will stay here with you."

The flood of tears I'd held back poured down my face then, and I kissed him with all the love I would never give another.

I gathered Gia in my arms, and after we each placed a kiss on Luca's forehead, with whispers of meeting again someday, we turned and walked out of the ward for the last time.

When we returned to the hotel, I gave Gia some sleeping powders and tucked her into bed, despite its not even being noon. I, however, felt like a caged animal. Anger, sorrow, regret. I wouldn't let my mind wander to the hospital, but my body would not be still, knowing what was taking place.

I made sure Gia was fast asleep before I slipped from our room, leaving a note on the desk should she awaken. The city was bustling with activity when I walked out into sunshine. I glanced up to the cloudless blue sky and imagined I saw angels escorting Luca home.

I'd left instructions with the hospital for his burial, but he hadn't wanted a service of any kind.

"I won't be there, *Pesche*," he'd said two days ago, a look of wonderment in his dull eyes. "I will be in paradise, waiting for you."

A hackney driver approached me, his accent reminding me of my beloved.

"A ride, *signorina*?"

I shook my head. "No thank you. I'll walk."

He tipped his hat and moved on.

My feet carried me along sidewalks and streets, yet I had no knowledge of what I passed or where I went. Only Luca's face filled my mind's eye. Happy, smiling, beautiful Luca.

This city had once been Luca's home, and I found comfort in walking the streets he might have traveled. Over the last two months, we'd talked often about my work with the Meyers. He smiled when I told him about Claudia, his eyes drifting to Gia where she'd stood at the window.

"There are so many of them." He grew somber. "All so young. They need you. They need someone who cares if they live or die."

When Gia wasn't in the room, he told me about the brothels he'd gone to in search of her. Some were horrid and filthy while others were palaces of debauchery. All filled with young women like Gia.

"I'm proud of you, *mie Pesche*."

The sweet memory of his words echoed in my heart as I turned down yet another crowded street. I didn't know where I was or how far I'd gone, but my head felt clearer from the exercise. Strangers brushed past. No one knew or cared that

I'd lost the person dearest to my heart. There was nothing more for us here.

It was time to go home to Nashville.

I searched for a cab to take me back to the hotel, but none were in sight. Without knowing which way to go, I looked around to see who might give me directions.

That's when my eyes fell on a young woman across the street.

Her plunging neckline and painted face told her story. Yet even from my vantage point, I saw she was barely more than a child.

I watched for several minutes as she approached men walking past, smiling and taking hold of their arms. Most shook free and continued on their way, but one or two acted interested for a time before moving on. That this scene played out in broad daylight wasn't unusual in this city, I'd learned.

I had a decision to make.

I could turn away and pretend I hadn't seen her, as the majority of people passing did. I'd just lost the love of my life, and I had Gia to consider. Today of all days, no one would blame me if I had nothing left to give.

Luca's words returned to me.

"They need someone who cares if they live or die."

My mind made up, I stepped off the sidewalk and crossed the street. When she saw me coming, her posture grew tense and her eyes narrowed, no doubt prepared to hear a lecture or worse. In the past year, I'd witnessed well-meaning people— and others not so well-meaning—bring down cruel and vile judgments on young women like Gia. This girl's posture told me she'd heard her share, too.

"Hello." I smiled and stopped several steps away. "My name is Priscilla Nichols. I wonder if you'd allow me to buy you a cold drink. The weather has certainly turned warm."

She stared at me as though I'd taken leave of my senses. "Are you jesting? Why would you do such a thing?"

"I'll tell you about it if you'll join me at the café." I indicated a restaurant down the street.

The girl clearly thought me a lunatic. "No thanks." She turned to walk away.

"Please," I said, drawing her attention again. "I promise you have nothing to fear from me."

Her wary gaze drifted over me, from head to toe and back again, before she finally shrugged thin shoulders. "Fine. I could use something to drink."

I held back a grin. "What's your name?" I asked as we made our way to the café.

She hesitated before answering. "Rosemary."

"It's very nice to meet you, Rosemary," I said, feeling Luca's smile of approval deep in my soul. "Very nice indeed."

Chapter Thirty-Three

New Year's Day brought a sense of fresh beginnings unlike anything I'd experienced in my twenty-two years.

I stood on the porch of our small borrowed house, bundled in my coat, and watched the sunrise, despite having stayed up long past midnight with Jason. He rang in the New Year with Dad, Emmett, and me, although Dad and Emmett were asleep on pallets on the floor long before the New Year arrived. The four of us spent the last day of 1961 unpacking and sorting through boxes of donated dishes, pots, pans, and clothes, trying to turn this unfamiliar house into a home. There were still plenty of items we needed—beds, for one—but I felt confident this place would soon be warm and inviting.

"Happy New Year."

I turned to find Dad in the doorway, holding a cup of steaming coffee. The Maxwell House Coffee company donated a year's supply to us, assuring that each morning we could close our eyes and pretend we were still in the hotel's restaurant, enjoying a cup to the very last drop.

"Happy New Year to you too."

Back inside, we settled on the sofa, the only piece of furniture in the living room so far.

"What do you suppose 1962 will bring?" he mused, glancing at the mess surrounding us.

"I'm almost afraid to guess." Our family had suffered two major losses in the past two years. Surely good things were ahead for us.

"One thing we can be certain of," Dad said with confidence. "God has a plan for this new year."

I thought about this for a time. "But why would he let Mama die and the hotel burn? Were those part of his plan?"

"After I returned from the war, I asked that question. I'd seen terrible things. Millions of innocent people were killed, in the camps, in their homes, on the battlefields. Then I came home and discovered that the son I'd hung many of my hopes for the future on would always be a child, unable to ever care for himself." He nodded, deep in thought. "Yes, I asked that question a lot."

"Is there an answer?"

Dad turned to me, a soft smile on his lips. "Not one that we humans want to hear. The book of Isaiah says God's ways are not our ways, that his ways are higher. I think what that means is we aren't meant to understand the whys of everything. We're simply asked to trust in the One who does."

We sat in the stillness of the morning, pondering what trust would look like in the New Year.

"I've been thinking," Dad said, his expression serious. "You need to go back to school."

His words surprised me. "But you'll need help with Emmett when you find a new job."

"That's just it. I don't think I'll look for a new job. Not yet, anyway." He glanced down the hall to the room he shared with Emmett. There were only two bedrooms in the house, and he'd jokingly named their room the boys' room. "Mr. Edwin has been very generous to me. I also have some savings tucked away. I think I'd like to just be Dad for a few years. Losing your mother and now the Maxwell has forced me to reevaluate my priorities."

Dad's unexpected announcement fit perfectly in the mood of this new day in a new year. "I've been thinking too," I said, a feeling of excitement taking hold. I shared with him the idea I'd been mulling over for weeks about working with children like Emmett.

"Your mother would be so proud to hear you say that, Audrey." Moisture wet his cheeks. "She dreamed of a day when Emmett could go to school and learn like other children, but the system wasn't ready for him yet. Maybe you can be the next generation of teachers that will welcome the Emmetts of the world through the doors of public schools."

Jason and Betty Ann arrived at noon, bearing baskets of fried chicken, canned food, baked goodies, and a new comic book for Emmett.

"Happy New Year." Jason's voice was low while the others were in the kitchen, unloading groceries.

A chill went up my spine at the look of love in his eyes. He'd kissed me at midnight, our first of many, I hoped. I hated that he had to return to Charleston tomorrow, but he promised to write and call as often as I'd let him.

When Jason asked about the investigation into the fire, Dad had disappointing news. "It's still unclear how the fire got started. And the police don't believe the woman Emmett saw had anything to do with it. As far as they're concerned, she was a guest and the fire was an accident." He glanced at the scrapbook lying on the floor. "To be safe, though, I don't think we should let it be known that the scrapbook survived the fire."

I couldn't agree more.

We'd just finished lunch when Grace arrived with a large potted plant, a bow around the container.

"I wanted to come by and thank you for taking such good care of Priscilla all these years."

Dad invited her to join us. Jason, Emmett, and I sat on the floor while Grace joined Betty Ann on the sofa. Dad sat on the arm of the couch close to Betty Ann and smiled at her when she offered one of her own.

"I wish I'd known Miss Nichols better," I said, sad that I hadn't taken time to get to know the older woman when she lived at the Maxwell. The stories Grace shared about her showed Miss Nichols to be a remarkable woman. After settling Grace with her cousin in Atlanta, Miss Nichols had wanted to bring charges against Kenton Thornley, but Grace wouldn't let her. It was the only time they argued, Grace said. She was too frightened of what he might do, and she couldn't face the public shame that would come when the story broke. Miss Nichols finally acquiesced, but she often let Kenton know she was watching him. He died of a massive heart attack some years later.

"You have the scrapbook now," Grace said, then winked. "And the legends that go with it. I'm sure I can speak for Priscilla when I say we'd love to have you all come visit us in Atlanta once she's settled." She'd already told Dad an ambulance would drive Miss Nichols to Georgia the following day and that the older woman looked forward to the ride.

The afternoon went quickly, filled with laughter, conversation, and some of the goodies Betty Ann had baked. It also brought an unexpected surprise when Mr. Corsini arrived.

"I was worried about my new friends," he said when Dad

answered the knock on the door. "The manager of the Noel told me where to find you."

Jason and I exchanged a look of concern before our gazes settled on Grace. She and Betty Ann were chatting about recipes when Dad invited Mr. Corsini inside.

When I glanced at Dad, he too wore an expression that told me he wasn't sure how to handle this unexpected meeting.

"Ladies, this is our friend Carmelo Corsini," he said, including both women.

They each nodded politely, but when Mr. Corsini issued a greeting in Italian, Grace looked surprised.

"You speak Italian?" she asked, then proceeded to say something in that language.

Mr. Corsini beamed and responded likewise.

They went on for several moments, back and forth, before Grace glanced around the room. "Where are my manners? I'm sorry. It's just so wonderful to chat with someone in our native tongue."

"No apologies necessary," Dad said.

Mr. Corsini's attention landed on the scrapbook next to Grace. "And how is Priscilla? I'm sure she was saddened to hear about the hotel. It held many memories for her."

Grace's brow shot up. "You know Priscilla?"

It was Mr. Corsini's turn to look surprised. "Yes, I've known her since the days of the exposition. I was her carriage driver."

I held my breath as Grace's eyes widened in recognition.

"Carmelo?"

Mr. Corsini squinted behind thick-rimmed glasses, examining Grace, before he exclaimed, "*Mamma mia!* You are Luca's sister, *sì?*"

"*Sì.* Gia Moretti."

They stared at one another in stunned silence for only a

moment before a flood of Italian filled our tiny house. Betty Ann offered her seat to Mr. Corsini so he could sit next to Grace on the sofa, and we watched with dumbfounded grins as the two elderly people talked and talked and then looked through the scrapbook, exclaiming over this or that. I couldn't understand their words, but the laughter and smiles on their faces were enough to tell me the scrapbook had once again proved itself a priceless treasure.

"You must come see Priscilla," Grace said as Mr. Corsini helped her with her coat an hour later. "She would enjoy visiting with you, her friend."

Mr. Corsini reached for Grace's hand and held it between both of his. "I will indeed."

After they and Betty Ann left, Dad, Jason, and I burst into joyful laughter, amazed at what had just happened.

"Isn't God good?" Dad said, wiping the moisture at the corner of his eye. "Even the smallest details of our lives are important to him. Mr. Corsini's visit, I think, was just what Grace needed."

The thought made me happy.

She and Miss Nichols had become dear to me. I looked forward to seeing them again when we drove down to Atlanta in the spring to celebrate Miss Nichols's birthday. Jason promised to do his best to come too, and I planned to hold him to it.

When it came time for him to leave, Dad and Emmett said goodbye and went to their room, giving us some privacy.

"I have something for you." He reached for a large shopping bag he must have tucked behind some boxes when he first arrived. It had *Stockell Books* printed on the side.

"What's this?" I couldn't hide my surprise.

"You'll see."

I reached into the bag and took out a new scrapbook, just

like the one he'd given me for Christmas. Like everything else, it had been destroyed in the fire.

"Thank you." I clasped it to my chest, my heart spilling over with real, pure joy.

"I want to start making memories with you, Audrey Whitfield." He tucked a strand of hair behind my ear, causing a delicious shiver to race up my spine. "Memories that will last a lifetime."

"You already have," I whispered just before he kissed me.

I knew I would hold on to this moment forever.

The old diary lay open to the page I'd never finished.

No one came to my sixteenth birthday party.
It's a selfish thing to be concerned with,
considering all that is happening to so many people,
my family included. Yet I can't help but wonder
if my very existence became invalidated when the
world shifted that day. As though my presence on
the planet no longer matters in light of such terrific
loss and misery. To know that money, status, and
privilege supplanted the place I'd held in my family
for sixteen years set an ache in me I fear will never
heal. How could it, when the evidence faces me
every waking moment?

"Are you going to see Mr. Armistead today?"

Mama's voice startled me. From my place on the back porch steps, I turned and found her inside the house, speaking through the screen door. The frown on her thin face made me wonder how long she'd been there, watching me. I could hide the diary I held, but what would be the point? She'd already seen it.

I shrugged. "I suppose, but I know what his answer will be."

George Armistead, editor of the *Nashville Banner*. Six months ago I called him boss. I still didn't understand why I'd been fired—"let go," as Mr. Armistead liked to put it. Despite being a faithful employee since graduating high school, starting in the mail room and ending in the news office as a city reporter, I was fired on a Monday. So every Monday for the last six months, I'd made my way to his smoke-filled office to beg him to rehire me. And every Monday he'd said no.

"I don't know why you put yourself through that humiliation each week. If the man hasn't rehired you by now, he isn't going to. Something else will come along. Something that better suits you."

Her words, meant to encourage, only grated. I wished Mama would, just once, kick and scream and complain with the rest of us. I wasn't sure which was worse: my mother's continued pretense that everything was fine or my father's wallowing in a whiskey bottle.

I tucked the book under my arm and stood. "Mrs. Davis asked me to help her hang wallpaper next week. She said she'd pay me ten dollars."

Mama's eyes widened. "Sissy Davis? Oh, Rena, I hope you told her you didn't need the money."

"Why would I tell her that? I do need the money. *We* need the money. Lots of people are out of work, Mama. There's no shame in accepting help when help is offered."

My tone was far from respectful, considering to whom I was speaking, but I wouldn't amend it. I was sick of ignoring the fact that our family was broke and broken. Mama thought asking Mr. Armistead for a job was humiliating. Had she forgotten the humiliation of learning my own father severely mismanaged thousands of dollars belonging to his customers? When he didn't come home at his usual time the day of the stock market crash, we'd feared the worst. It was the only time I could recall Mama letting herself sink down into the pit of despair. He eventually banged on the front door at three o'clock in the morning. Mama, Mary, and I silently watched him stumble inside without a word of explanation about the crash, the bank's fate, or his whereabouts all evening—although the smell of alcohol and cigarette smoke gave us the answer to that question. He locked himself in the study with a bottle of bourbon, and that's where he'd spent most of the past seven years.

"Sissy Davis is one of my dearest friends. I won't have my daughter performing manual labor for her."

So many words flew to my lips. I stopped them all from escaping. I'd come to the recent conclusion that Mama's sanity was tied to her determination to act as though all was well in the Leland household. Of course, most of Nashville knew it wasn't. People who'd once been considered friends turned away and whispered when we ventured beyond the house.

To make ends meet, Mama took a job at a sewing shop in a neighborhood where she was certain her friends wouldn't see her. That was, if one could still call the women she used to associate with friends. Most of their husbands had lost money in my father's bank failure, and although they didn't blame Mama, they weren't completely forgiving either.

"Mrs. Davis simply needs help, Mama. She enjoys decorating her home herself." I stomped up the steps and faced her through the screen. "I'm not too keen on manual labor myself, but I don't have much choice, do I?"

After a moment, she conceded. "I suppose it wouldn't hurt for you to help a friend with her decorating. Sissy does have excellent taste. You can learn about the latest trends in decorating while you're there."

Leave it to Mama to put a positive turn on hanging wallpaper.

I joined her inside. A glance toward the study revealed a closed door. I hadn't seen Dad in three days. Mama took food to him when she got home from work in the evenings, but despite being home nearly all day together, he and I rarely spoke. Not because I didn't have plenty to say to him, but because I realized shortly after my sixteenth birthday that he somehow linked me to the stock market crash. As though the date on my birth certificate served as a painful reminder of the day he lost everything. He retreated from my world and barred me from his, with a whiskey bottle between us.

"I'll stop at the library after I see Mr. Armistead. Some new job listings might've been posted over the weekend." Odds were there weren't any, but I enjoyed going to the cool, quiet building to think without the scrutiny of my mother or the indifference of my father looming over me.

Mama opened a high cabinet and took down a soup can. She turned it over and removed the false bottom. A wadded-up handkerchief was stuffed inside, and she unwrapped it to reveal dozens of coins and some dollar bills. I'd seen her do this a hundred times or more in the past seven years, yet it still struck me as one of the saddest things I'd ever witnessed. A banker's wife hiding money from her husband in a soup can.

She handed me two nickels for the streetcar. "I won't be home until late. Mrs. Watkins needs me to help with inventory."

I nodded, if only to cover the awkwardness that always stood between us when she mentioned her job. I still found it difficult to accept my mother working in a sewing shop. Before the crash—that was how I measured time: before and after the crash—I'd never seen Mama sew anything, not even a loose button. How she'd managed to find this job, I didn't know, but she'd been there over four years now. Her meager wages kept food on the table, although she had to hide the money so Dad wouldn't take it and buy liquor. Somehow, he managed to get his hands on alcohol anyway. Even during Prohibition, he was rarely without bootleg bottles.

The morning was sunshiny and cool, which made the three-block walk to catch the streetcar pleasant. Gone were the days when my parents drove the latest cars. An old 1925 Ford sat in the garage behind the house, covered with dust, its tires flat. Fuel cost too much, as did repairs and upkeep. I wasn't certain the thing even ran anymore. Grandma Lorena owned a car and used it from time to time, but I didn't like to trouble her if I could take the streetcar.

The *Banner*'s offices were located in Printers Alley, a street teeming with publishers and the city's two largest newspapers. I missed coming downtown each day, feeling a part of the city's lifeblood and flow. Nashville's business district hummed with activity, although I noticed men's suits were more threadbare and fewer vehicles clogged streets in desperate need of repair. Our city, like the rest of the country, was feeling the effects of the depressed economy, yet folks valiantly met each day head-on with the determination to *get back to normal.*

Every time I heard that phrase, I silently asked myself if we'd ever see normal again. What was normal anyway? It had only been seven years since the crash, but the life I'd lived then seemed to belong to someone else.

Mr. Armistead's office sat at the back of a noisy room filled with desks. Several reporters looked up from their typewriters as I entered, nodded at me, and went back to work. No doubt they'd guessed long ago what my weekly visits were about, but I trusted Mr. A. not to divulge the details of my begging sessions, which was what I'd dubbed them. He might not be the most compassionate person in town, but he was no gossip.

He saw me coming through the glass window that separated his office from the larger newsroom. His thick graying brows folded over the black rim of his glasses. "Leland." His gruff greeting never changed. Smoke swirled from an ashtray on his messy desk where a stub of cigar rested.

"Good morning, Mr. Armistead. How are you today?"

I put on my brightest smile even though I knew he wasn't fooled. He might be as old as most grandfathers, but he was no pushover.

"Same as I am every Monday. Behind schedule and in need of a front-page story." He continued to shuffle papers and act busy.

I stepped into the room. "You know I'd love to help with that."

He nodded without looking up. "And you know why you can't."

My smile drooped. Yes, I knew. The crash. The failing economy. Money. Money. Money. The failures of other people had dictated my future for too long, yet what choice did I have?

After a long moment, the question I'd avoided the past six months resurfaced in my mind. I feared his answer, which was why I had yet to verbalize it, but perhaps it was time to know the truth and move on.

With a deep breath, I plunged forward. "Mr. A., if things were different and you were able to hire staff again, would you rehire me?"

His hands paused over the mess that was his desk.

My stomach clenched. Now I'd gone and done it. I'd handed him the perfect opportunity to get rid of me once and for all.

Yet when he finally looked up, it was with an expression I'd never seen on his face before. Sympathetic, I suppose, which seemed out of place on the hard-nosed news-paperman.

"I would, kid."

Three simple words, but oh, how they lightened the heaviness in my heart.

I smiled again, satisfied. "Thanks, Mr. A." I turned to leave.

"Kid, wait."

My heart skipped with hope. Had my boldness changed his mind?

He dug through piles of paper until he found the one he sought and handed it to me. "This came in the other day. Maybe you should take a look into it."

A quick glance revealed it was typed on letterhead from a government agency called the Works Progress Administration. I looked back to Mr. A. "What is it?"

He jabbed a fat finger at the paper in my hand. "Read it, Leland. It's a job. A writing job."

A writing job? My interest piqued. However, the more I read, the more confused I grew. When I reached the end of the brief missive, I met his gaze. "I don't understand."

He huffed. "The WPA is Roosevelt's baby. It's his idea of providing jobs for folks out of work. Writers, as you are well aware, are among the unemployed. Under the umbrella of the WPA, they've created something called the Federal Writers' Project. That letter states they need writers here in Nashville to do interviews. You're a reporter with experience. No reason you shouldn't get the job."

I glanced back to the typewritten words. "But it says something about former slaves."

"Yeah, that's who's being interviewed. To preserve their stories or something of that nature."

I was sure my expression revealed too much because Mr.

Armistead sat back in his chair and narrowed his gaze on me. "I never thought of you as the type to care about the color of a person's skin, Leland."

"I don't." Dovie had been one of the dearest people in my world before it all fell apart.

"So why not do this?" He indicated the letter again. "They'll pay twenty dollars a week. All you have to do is spend an hour or two with each interviewee, type up your notes, and turn them in to the WPA office. Sounds like easy money to me."

It did sound like easy money, and yet . . .

"I'll think about it," I finally said.

Mr. A. shrugged and returned his attention to the chaos on his desk. "Suit yourself, but this opportunity won't last long. Plenty of writers are willing to do the job if you aren't."

I left his office with the letter tucked in my purse and frustration rooted in my mind. I needed the job, but to interview former slaves? My ancestors had owned slaves. Shouldn't that disqualify me from the position?

The job posting board at the library held a small number of new handwritten cards, but they required experience I didn't possess. As restless as I felt, sitting in the quiet solitude of the big building didn't appeal today. I needed to walk. And think. I left the building and headed in the direction of home.

Questions poured from my brain. Why would the government care about preserving the stories of former slaves? Wasn't it the government who created the very laws that had kept people in bondage for over two centuries? Surely there were more important issues to write about. With so many people suffering these days, no one even thought about slavery anymore. The War between the States happened when Grandma Lorena was a small child, over seventy years ago.

But twenty dollars a week was more money than I'd made at any of the odd jobs I'd taken over the past six months. Even with occasional help from Grandma Lorena, who survived the stock market crash surprisingly well, I knew we were in terrible financial shape. Mama never verbalized how destitute we actually were, but I'd seen the bankruptcy papers she'd hidden in her bedroom bureau shortly after the crash. I hadn't meant to see them, but I was putting away laundry and there they were, plain as day.

My feet grew weary in my heeled shoes, so I sat on a bench at the next streetcar stop and waited. A minute passed before an older black man, neatly dressed, walked up. When our eyes met, he nodded politely but remained standing as he too waited for the streetcar. Although we were the only people at the stop and there was plenty of room on the bench, I knew the unspoken rule as well as he did.

A colored man could not sit next to a white woman.

An odd thought struck me as we waited for the streetcar. What would this man think about the Federal Writers' Project and its proposed interviews? Did the stories of former slaves interest him? I couldn't imagine they would, since they would bring up an unpleasant time in the history of our country. People had moved on from the issues of slavery, leaving the ugliness in the past.

The image of nine black teenage boys on the front page of a newspaper flashed across my mind.

The Scottsboro boys. Convicted of raping two white

women in Alabama despite overwhelming evidence of their innocence.

When the trolley arrived, I boarded in the front of the vehicle while the man boarded in the rear. I sat beside a young white woman with a small child on her lap. The pair was too engrossed in their babbled conversation to acknowledge me.

As the streetcar jerked forward, I peeked behind me.

From his place at the back of the vehicle, the older man I'd boarded with looked right at me.

A Note from the Author

Human trafficking is a global crime that is committed every day, in every region of the world, according to data collected by the United Nations Office on Drugs and Crime. It's probably happening where you live, whether you dwell in a big city or a small, peaceful community. It's as old as the ages, and sadly an end is nowhere in sight. More awareness of this vile crime, however, has brought recent hope to thousands of victims. Private agencies, governments, and citizens alike are becoming involved in rescuing vulnerable people caught in the perilous snare of human trafficking, but more action is needed. More laws, more donations, and more people speaking out and lending a hand. With each of us doing our part, we can make a difference in someone's life. Thanks to you, dear reader, a portion of the proceeds from *Count the Nights by Stars* will go directly to a Christian organization that helps reach, rescue, and restore victims of human trafficking.

For this novel, I focused on the subject of forced prostitution in the late 1890s. During my research, I was disheartened to learn how little was done in those days to prevent and discourage the practice. Laws were lacking and some even regulated prostitution. Women involved were treated with contempt by police and often forced to submit to humiliating medical examinations in order to protect their male customers from disease. Immigrants especially were targets of unscrupulous people, and the term *white slavery* was used to describe human trafficking victims from China and Europe.

Yet in the midst of this darkness, light came in the form of women like Josephine Butler, Rose Livingston, and Harriet Burton Laidlaw, to name a few, who dedicated their lives to helping victims around the world. Josephine especially served to inspire the character of Priscilla Nichols. Both came from upstanding families, were well-educated, and never intended to become involved in activism. But like Josephine, Priscilla could not walk away after learning the terrible truth of what was taking place in the shadows.

Three simple words illuminate the theme at the heart of *Count the Nights by Stars:* **I see you.** Each of the main characters—Priscilla, Audrey, and Jason—saw people who were marginalized and ignored by society and, in their own small way, took action. For Priscilla, it was offering women like Gia a way out. For Audrey, the seed to becoming involved in helping those with special needs was planted by her devoted mother. And Jason's desire to join the civil rights movement is something many people recognized— and recognize still today—as being vital to making the future a better place for everyone. Much work toward that goal was needed in 1961, and much work is still needed today.

The other main "character" in the story is the Maxwell House Hotel. The first time I read about it, I knew I had to set a novel there. Colonel John Overton Jr. began construction on it in 1859 and named it after his wife, Harriet Maxwell Overton. The hotel was so enormous, it was dubbed "Overton's Folly" by the citizens of Nashville. But despite the unflattering nickname, the hotel soon became *the* place to stay, with Christmas Day dinner a highlight of the year.

Unfortunately, by 1961 the hotel was old and run-down. It had lost its place as the grande dame of Nashville and was now a residential hotel, housing approximately sixty long-term residents. Although there was an acting manager of the hotel at the time of the fire, I placed the Whitfield family—fictional characters born in my imagination—in the manager's apartment. Edwin B. Raskin was the owner of the Maxwell House at the time of the fire, having purchased it the year before, but I've tweaked his name for this story.

The sad events of Christmas night 1961 are as I've portrayed them in the book. Smoke was seen coming from the fourth floor at 8:45 p.m. The source of the fire was never discovered, and the hotel was a total loss. Tragically, one guest perished, but out of respect for him and his family, I did not include his name in the book.

Last but not least, I hope you enjoyed visiting the Tennessee Centennial Exposition as much as I did. Like the characters in the book, I sometimes stroll through Centennial Park, imagining what it looked like during the exciting days of the exposition. My research led me to the book *Tennessee Centennial: Nashville 1897* by Bobby Lawrence, and I highly recommend it if you're interested in learning more. Should your travels bring you to Nashville, do visit the Parthenon. It is magnificent.

Thank you for taking this journey with me. Sharing my passion for history and storytelling with you is truly an honor.

Acknowledgments

The husband of a novelist on deadline deserves a solid gold crown. My sweetheart of thirty-seven years made sure I ate, slept, and had clean clothes during the writing, rewriting, and editing of this book. Brian, you are my treasure, my best friend, my biggest fan, and the hero of every novel I write. Thank you for loving me and putting up with all my crazy ideas. God willing, we have many more adventures awaiting us in the days ahead.

Heartfelt appreciation to my cherished family and friends for your continued love, prayers, and support. You may not realize it, but there's a little bit of each of you tucked in the pages of my novels.

I cannot say enough good things about the team at Tyndale House Publishers. What a blessing to partner with delightful, Jesus-loving people. Jan Stob, Karen Watson, Erin Smith, and everyone who had a hand in getting this book to publication, as well as those who work tirelessly after the book is in print: thank you, from the depths of my heart. Working with you is a gift from above.

Many thanks to my agent, Bob Hostetler. I'm grateful to

be represented by an agent committed to serving God with your wisdom and talents.

Thank *you*, dear readers, for recommending my books to friends, for suggesting them to book clubs, and for taking time to leave reviews, ratings, and comments online. Your thoughtful emails and kind words never cease to put a smile on my face and in my heart. I hope we'll continue this journey together for years to come.

Psalm 139:15-16 reveals that God knows us long before we're born and has all our days recorded in his book before we take our first breath. He knows the plans and purposes he has for each of us, and I'm incredibly humbled that mine include writing books for him. My sincere hope and prayer is that our perfect God will be exalted in and through the imperfect work of my hands. *Soli Deo gloria.*

Discussion Questions

1. As *Count the Nights by Stars* begins with a potential tragedy, Audrey Whitfield finds herself in a position of needing to give comfort and assurance to her younger brother. What gives her the courage to be the strong one in that moment? What's behind the fear she's hiding? When you have been in a situation where life seems uncertain, where have you turned?

2. In an age when women have few rights, outspoken Priscilla Nichols has strong opinions about the way things should be. What surprised you the most about life for women and children in 1897? Are there aspects of today's society that would have Priscilla speaking up now?

3. Audrey is surprised when Jason points out how much she's been a help to her family since her mother died. What does it mean to Audrey to have someone see her? Later, Mrs. Meyer uses the story of Hagar in the Bible to remind Priscilla of one of God's names: "You are the

God who sees me." What does this verse, this attribute of God mean to you?

4. Injustice is a major theme in the story. Where are injustices at play in Priscilla's scenes? In Audrey's scenes? Today? What do Priscilla, Audrey, Jason, and others do to combat injustice? What can you do to bring more justice into the world?

5. Passion is another theme in *Count the Nights by Stars*. Audrey can see Jason's passion for his civil rights work. What calling does Priscilla find? What events inspire Audrey to find her passion? What cause makes you excited?

6. Priscilla is convicted when she realizes her upbringing affords her wealth and privilege others don't have. In what ways does this change her interactions with those of a "lesser status"? Have you ever had an experience that opened your eyes in a new way to those around you? What happened as a result?

7. Audrey has a lot of doubt about what she can do to make a difference. Do you believe one voice is all it takes to enact change? What advice would you give her?

8. Priscilla creates a scrapbook full of details about the centennial exposition. In what ways do you preserve memories of happy times? Why might it be important to remember sad times or moments that carry mixed emotions? Why do you think Miss Nichols insists on giving Audrey her scrapbook from the exposition?

9. Audrey's father tells her a story about how she impacted his life, and their whole family, when she was just a little girl. What does that moment say about the way God uses the people around us? Have you ever been convicted by the honesty or simple faith of a child?

10. Priscilla notes that helping a prisoner escape from custody might not be something a good Christian woman would consider. How does she justify her actions? Is she right to take such desperate measures? Why or why not?

11. Priscilla's mother, especially, is interested in seeing her marry Kenton. What reasons does she give Priscilla in favor of this union? What reasons does Priscilla have for avoiding it? What does it cost Priscilla to defy her mother's wishes? Is it fair to say Priscilla is a disappointment to her parents?

12. When Gia first has an opportunity to find safety with Priscilla, she doesn't take it. Why? What reasons does Reverend Meyer give for why someone might return to a "life of ill repute"? Is there anything you would add to his list? What advice does he offer in response? How are he and his wife living that out?

13. The title of the book, *Count the Nights by Stars*, is part of a sentiment about living life without looking back with regret. Which characters carry the weight of regret longer than they should? Which are able to let go of it? Is there anything in your life you regret? How do you move past it?

14. When difficulties come to the characters in this story—whether it's the loss of Audrey's mother or Gia's disappearance—it's tempting to ask why God allows bad things to happen. What does Audrey's father say in response to her questions? What is your answer to the "why" question?

About the Author

Michelle Shocklee is the author of several historical novels, including *Under the Tulip Tree*, a Selah Awards finalist. Her work has been featured in numerous Chicken Soup for the Soul books, magazines, and blogs. Married to her college sweetheart and the mother of two grown sons, she makes her home in Tennessee, not far from the historical sites she writes about. Visit her online at michelleshocklee.com.

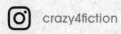
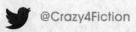

By purchasing this book from Tyndale, you have

helped us meet the spiritual and physical needs of

people all around the world.

Tyndale | Trusted. For Life.